THE CROWDED GRAVE

Also by Martin Walker

Bruno, Chief of Police
Dark Vineyard
Black Diamond

THE CROWDED GRAVE

An Investigation by Bruno, Chief of Police

Martin Walker

Quercus

First published in Great Britain in 2011 by

Quercus
55 Baker Street
7th Floor, South Block
London
W1U 8EW

A CIP catalogue reference for this book is available
from the British Library

ISBN 978 1 84916 321 7 (HB)
ISBN 978 1 84916 322 4 (TPB)

10 9 8 7 6 5 4 3 2 1

Typeset in Swift by Ellipsis Digital Limited, Glasgow

Printed and bound in Great Britain by
Clays Ltd, St Ives plc

To Hannes and Tine

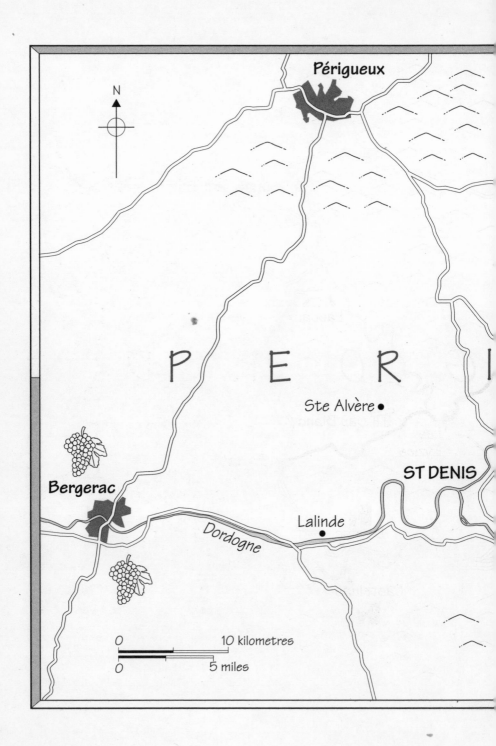

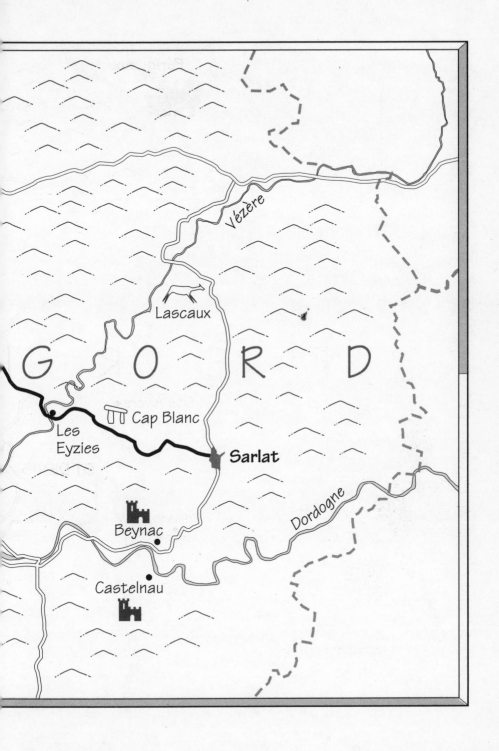

For once, the Chef de Police of the small French town of St Denis was carrying a gun. That morning Benoît Courrèges, known to everyone as Bruno, had taken his official weapon from the office safe in the Mairie where it stayed throughout the year, except for his annual firearms refresher course at the Police HQ range in Périgueux. He had cleaned and oiled it carefully, and the elderly MAB 9mm was now tucked into the leather holster that he had polished just after dawn, along with the belt and the shoulder strap he hardly ever wore. His full-dress uniform smelled faintly of the dry cleaner's where he had picked it up on the way to the Mairie that morning. His hair was newly cut, his morning shave had been unusually close and his boots were polished to the kind of brilliant shine that only a former soldier can achieve.

Beside him, Sergeant Jules and the rest of the small team that staffed the Gendarmerie of St Denis stood in formal ranks in front of their modest, stucco-fronted building. The Gendarmes also wore full-dress uniform, and it would have taken a careful observer to note any difference between their dress as functionaries of the French state and Bruno's as

an employee of the town of St Denis. On the flat roof of
the Gendarmerie, beside the radio antenna, the tricolour
flew at half-mast, and above the door was a plaque of the
flaming grenade that has been the symbol of the Gendarmes
since their founding in 1791. Of Capitaine Duroc, the
nominal head of the post, there was no sign. He had called
in sick, in order to avoid rather than disobey the official
order that the police and Gendarmes of France should not
formally commemorate the death of Brigadier Nerin. But
here in St Denis, as in police stations and Gendarmeries
across France, the rank and file and many of the officers
had chosen to mark his killing with a parade of honour.
Over a glass of wine the previous evening, Bruno had
arranged with Jules that he would read out the brief statement and take the parade. Employed by the Mairie, Bruno
was less at risk than the Sergeant of an official reprimand
or even demotion. Jules had his pension to consider.

Now Bruno checked his watch for the precise time. He
came to attention, marched forward and turned to address
the Gendarmes. He noted that each of them, men and
women alike, was wearing the same black armband of
mourning that he had attached to his own right sleeve. A
small knot of townsfolk stood in silence, watching. Bruno
nodded at the young boy who stood to one side, dressed in
a grey shirt and black tie and carrying a bugle.

'Respected colleagues,' Bruno began. 'We are here to mark
the death on active duty of Brigadier of Gendarmes Jean-
Serge Nerin. He was murdered at Dammarie-sur-Lys in the
Department of Seine et Marne while hunting down the

terrorist cell that killed him. This is the first killing of a French policeman by the *Euskadi Ta Askatasuna*, or ETA, the Basque terrorists who have already killed over eight hundred people in Spain. Death on active service has always been a risk in our profession, but murder by terrorists is a special event. Our colleagues across France have agreed, despite official discouragement, that we shall all observe a minute of silence in honour of our fallen comrade, Brigadier Nerin.'

He paused, and then in his best parade ground voice, called out, '*A mon commandement.*'

The line of Gendarmes braced, ready for his next command.

'*Escadron, garde à vous.*'

They came to attention and Bruno raised his right arm to the brim of his hat in salute, the signal he had prepared with young Jean-Michel. The boy raised the bugle to his lips and blew the first haunting note of the *Sonnerie aux Morts*, the bugle call that the Garde Républicaine played for their dead. When the last three notes faded away, Bruno began to count in his head for the full minute of silence, his arm growing heavier so that he had to make a deliberate effort to keep his hand from quivering. Finally it was over. He lowered his hand and dismissed the parade.

Sergeant Jules was the first to come across and shake his hand, and then each of the Gendarmes, male and female, followed suit as they filed back into the Gendarmerie. Bruno went across to Jean-Michel and thanked him, and then walked in silence along the Rue de Paris back towards his office in the Mairie and the safe where he would lock away his pistol for another year. He crossed the main square and turned in at the narrow iron-studded door, avoiding the public entrance with the modern elevator and preferring to climb the ancient stone steps. At the top he found the Mayor filling his pipe and waiting patiently for his arrival.

'Thank you for being there,' Bruno said. 'I saw you in the crowd.'

'Thank you for doing this, Bruno, and the music was a lovely touch. It will be a sad day if France fails to honour those who fall for the Republic. I saw Capitaine Duroc had once again managed to extract himself from an embarrassing situation.'

'Well, sir, luckily I only have to answer to you, not the government of France.'

The Mayor's eyes twinkled. 'Ah, Bruno, how very nice of you to say so. If only it were true.'

CHAPTER ONE

It felt like the first morning of spring. The early sun was chasing the mist from the wooded hollows that sheltered the small streams flowing busily down to the river Vézère. Drops of dew sparkled on the new buds that seemed to have appeared overnight on the bare trees. The air smelled somehow different, fresh and hopeful, and enlivened by the tuneful notes of a dozen different birdsongs. Excited by the change in scents and season, even after his early morning walk through the woods, Gigi the basset hound thrust his nose at the open window of the small police van that descended the steep and curving lane from his master's home. At the wheel, Bruno was singing a half-remembered song about springtime in Paris, vaguely thinking of the duties of the day that lay ahead, when rounding the last bend he was suddenly forced to brake.

For the first time in his memory, the quiet road ahead was blocked by a line of cars and tractors, their engines running and their drivers' heads poking from windows. Some were out of their cars, looking at the road that led to St Denis. Several were talking urgently into cellphones. In the distance a car horn sounded, swiftly joined by others in discordant chorus. As Bruno surveyed the scene his own phone began to ring. He checked the screen, recognised the name of Pierre, a neighbour who lived further up the road. He ignored it, assuming Pierre would be calling to complain at being stuck in the jam ahead. There had to be an accident of some sort.

Bruno pushed aside the thought that he could have avoided this delay if he'd stayed the night with Pamela, the Englishwoman he'd been seeing since the autumn. She had called off the arrangement that he would dine with her and stay the night, saying she'd finally secured an early morning appointment with the *maréchal*, the travelling farrier who was to reshoe her horses. Pamela postponed their meetings too frequently for Bruno's comfort: he never quite knew whether she was cooling on their relationship or simply wary of commitment. They were to meet again that evening, he reminded himself, without feeling greatly reassured. He parked the van and climbed out to investigate. The best view of the long traffic jam was commanded by Alain, who kept a dairy farm further up the road to Les Eyzies.

'Geese – the road's full of ducks and geese,' he called down to Bruno from his perch high on a tractor. 'They're all over the place.'

Bruno heard the sound of rival honking as the geese called back in response to the car horns and he clambered up beside Alain to peer ahead. The traffic jam stretched as far up the road as he could see. Darting between the stalled cars were dozens, perhaps hundreds of ducks and geese, streaming through the woods on the side of the road and heading across it to settle in a broad pond that spread across the meadow, swollen by the spring rains.

'That's Louis Villatte's farm, behind those woods,' said Alain. 'A tree must have come down and broken his fence, let them all escape. There's over three thousand birds in there. Or rather, there used to be. Looks like he's lost a few to the cars.'

'Have you got his number?' Bruno asked. Alain nodded. 'Call him, see if he knows his birds have escaped. Then go through those woods and see if you can help Louis block the gap in his fence. I'll try and sort this out here. Join you later.'

Bruno went back to his van, released Gigi, and took his dog down the road, brushing aside the angry queries of the car drivers. A driver he knew was looking mournfully at a broken headlamp while a wounded goose lay half-pinned under his car, honking feebly.

'You grew up on a farm, Pierre,' Bruno told him, rushing past. 'Put the poor devil out of its misery.' Looking back, he saw Pierre bend to grip the goose behind its head and twist. The bird fluttered wildly and then went limp. Even when the farm boy grew up like Pierre to work in an accountant's office, he hadn't lost the skill.

When he came to the main grouping of birds, advancing in a raggle-taggle column from the woods, Bruno saw that the road ahead was blocked by some stalled cars coming the other way. He briefly considered using Gigi to turn the birds back, but they would only go and cross the road elsewhere. There was no stopping this exodus, so he might as well try to speed it up and clear the road. He persuaded the leading cars in each queue to reverse a little to make a broader passage to let the birds pass freely across to the pond. Some drivers tried to argue, but he pointed out that the sooner he could stop the supply of ducks, the sooner the road would unblock. He left them grumbling and took Gigi into the trees, trotting past the trail of ducks and geese that was still pottering and waddling its way from the Villatte farm. Bruno smiled to himself, wondering if the birds felt a sense of escape or curiosity, of adventure triggered by the coming of springtime.

Louis and his wife were already at the huge hole torn in the fence. No tree had fallen, no tractor had ridden through the sturdy barrier of wooden posts and chicken wire that ringed the farm. Instead, whole fence posts had been hauled from the earth and the wire cut. With boards and old doors and cardboard boxes stuffed beneath an ancient tractor, Louis was trying to plug the gaps in the fence. His wife and eldest son were flapping their arms and their dog was barking to shoo away the ducks and geese following their fellows towards the freedom of the woods.

Without being told, Gigi darted forward to help drive the birds back from the fence and Bruno helped Alain to haul some branches from broken trees to seal the remaining gaps in the wire. Once the makeshift barrier was in place, Louis came forward to shake their hands. Gigi and Louis's dog sniffed politely at one another's tails and then sat beside one another, staring at any bird that dared to approach.

'We've been at this since daybreak,' Louis said. 'But you see how big this gap is? Some bastard ripped this fence down deliberately and made a proper job of it.'

'And we know who,' added Sandrine, his wife. 'Look at this, stuck on the bits of the fence they didn't tear down.' She handed Bruno a photocopied leaflet, sealed inside a transparent plastic envelope.

'STOP – cruelty to animals. Boycott foie gras,' he read. There was a smudged photocopied image of a duck held down in a narrow cage. A flexible tube hanging from above was thrust into its mouth by an unidentified man who was stretching the duck's neck taut. At the bottom, it read: '*Contactez PETAFrance.com.*'

'Who's this PETA?' asked Alain, peering over Bruno's shoulder.

'People for the Ethical Treatment of Animals,' said Bruno. 'It's an American thing, maybe British, but it's growing in France. They made a big fuss up in Paris about battery chickens and veal, those calves kept in pens. Looks like they've started running a campaign against foie gras.'

'But that's our livelihood,' said Sandrine. 'And we don't make foie gras, we just raise the birds.'

'And look at this,' said Louis. 'The wire's been cut with proper cutters. This was organised.' He showed Bruno the snipped strands of wire. 'Then they pulled it away somewhere, hiding the lengths of wire they cut. I sent the other boy out looking for it in the woods.'

'City bastards,' grunted Alain. 'Don't know the first thing about the country and they come here like a bunch of bloody terrorists and try to ruin people.' He turned aside and spat. 'You find out who they are, Bruno, and we'll take care of the rest.'

Bruno ignored Alain's outrage on behalf of his fellow farmer. 'All the birds seem to be heading for that pond on the far side of the road,' he told Louis. 'Have you got some way to collect them and bring them back?'

'I'll ring the food bell. That brings most of them running. And for the rest, I've got some netting. That's how we usually round them up. I'll put them in the trailer and bring them back once I've got this fence fixed.'

'Sooner the better, because they've blocked the whole road into town,' said Bruno. 'That's what brought me here.'

'Daft birds,' said Louis, grimacing in rueful affection. 'They've got a perfectly good pond back in the field, but give them a sniff of someplace new and off they go.' He gestured back beyond his house where already some of the ducks, frustrated in their efforts to escape through the newly sealed barrier, were splashing and paddling serenely in their old familiar pond.

A young boy of about ten laboured towards them from the woods, proudly hauling a section of wire fence.

'I found it, Papa,' he shouted. 'And there's more. I can show you where.' His face broke into a grin at seeing Bruno, who taught him to play rugby in winter and tennis in summer. 'Bonjour, Monsieur Bruno.' He dropped the fence and came forward to shake hands.

'Bonjour, Daniel. Did you see or hear anything when this happened?'

'Nothing. The first I heard was when Papa woke us all up to come out and save the birds.'

'I heard something, a duck call, a single one and then repeated, just before the cockerel started,' said Louis. 'So it must have been a bit before dawn. I remember thinking that's odd, because the ducks don't usually stir until after the hens.'

'Could it have been a lure, one of those hunter's calls?' Bruno asked. 'Whoever cut the fence must have had some way to wake the birds and tempt them to move. They'd have wanted them out before you and the family were awake.'

'It must have been something like that,' Sandrine said. 'The birds tend to stick around the barn, waiting to be fed. They've never gone off before, even when we had that storm that knocked part of the fence down.'

'I'd better get back to the road and see that jam is cleared,' said Bruno.

'Before you go, what do you know about this PETA?' asked Sandrine.

'Not a lot, but I'll find out,' Bruno replied. 'I think you've lost one or two birds to the cars, but not many.'

'Those birds are worth six euros each to us,' said Sandrine. 'We can't afford to lose a single one of them, what with the bank loan we have to pay until we sell this lot. What if those PETA people come again?'

'I'll shoot the bastards,' Louis said. 'We'll take turns keeping watch, sit up all night if we have to.'

'You have a right to protect your property with reasonable force, according to the law,' said Bruno. 'But people interpret "reasonable force" in different ways. If you hear anything happening again, it's best you call me. Whatever you do, don't use a firearm or any kind of weapon. The best thing is to photograph them so we can identify who they are. If you have any lights you can rig up, or one of those motion detectors . . .'

'A camera won't do any good,' said Alain. 'Even with photos the damn courts will take their side. They're all mad Greenies, the magistrates. Then there's those food inspectors and all the other rules and regulations, tying us up in knots.'

'I think I know who it is,' said Sandrine. 'It's those students at the archaeology site who came in last week, working on some dig with that German Professor, over towards Campagne. They're all staying at the municipal campground. This time of year, they're the only strangers round here, and you know what those students are like. They're all Greens now.'

Bruno nodded. 'I'll check it out. See you later.' Along the fence he saw the fluttering of another of the leaflets inside a plastic bag, one of the kind that could be sealed and used in freezers. He took out a handkerchief and gingerly removed the pins that held it to the wire. Forensics might get something from it. There were several more attached along the fence and he took another. He nodded at Alain. 'Do you want to come with me? You'll have to move your tractor.'

As he reached the road, where the jam was steadily clearing itself, Bruno's phone rang again. He checked the screen, saw the name 'Horst', and this time he answered.

Horst Vogelstern was the German Professor of archaeology in charge of the student volunteers at the dig. For over twenty years Horst had spent his vacations at a small house he owned on the outskirts of St Denis. He ran digs in the valley of the river Vézère that the local tourist board liked to proclaim as the cradle of prehistoric man. The first site of Cro-Magnon man had been found up the valley over a hundred years earlier, and the famous cave paintings of Lascaux were further up the river. It was a source of pride to Bruno that he lived in this valley that could claim the longest continuous human habitation of anywhere on earth.

Bruno had attended a couple of Horst's lectures, delivered in excellent if strongly accented French. He had visited his digs and read a couple of articles Horst had published in the popular monthly *Dossiers d'Archéologie*. Normally a quiet man, Horst became passionate when he talked of his subject, the great mystery of the replacement of the Neanderthal humans by the Cro-Magnons, some thirty thousand years ago. Had it been violent? Did they interbreed? Were the Neanderthals wiped out by some plague or disease? It was, so Horst believed, the crucial question over our human origins. Whenever he spoke Bruno caught a sense of the excitement that gripped the scholar.

'Horst,' he answered. 'How are you? I was just on my way to see you at the dig.'

'Good, we need you here right away. And you'd better bring a medical doctor with you. We've found a body.'

'Congratulations – isn't that what you wanted to find?'

'Yes, yes, but I want skeletons from the distant past. This one is wearing a St Christopher around his neck and I think that he's also wearing a Swatch. This is your department, Bruno, not mine.'

CHAPTER TWO

As Horst led him past the parallel trenches and the chess-board pattern of white string that defined the work of the site, Bruno was struck as always by the careful dedication of the team. Using fine brushes to tease away the soil from a possible find and sifting each handful of earth through a sieve, they barely looked up as he passed. Some of them were in trenches so deep that he had to peer down to see them, provoking them to look up as his body blocked what little sunlight they had.

He heard a shout – 'Bruno!' – and turned to see a pretty girl with fair hair and a slim build jumping across the trenches toward him.

'Dominique,' he exclaimed, as he received the embrace of the young woman he had known since she was a child. Her father, Stéphane, was one of Bruno's regular hunting partners. He ran a small dairy farm in the hills and made the *tomme d'Audrix* cheese that Bruno loved. Each winter since Bruno had arrived in St Denis he had been invited to the killing of the family pig, and he and Dominique always had the job of rinsing out the intestines in the freezing water of the nearest stream. Now at university in Grenoble, she was a militant but very realistic member of the Green party. 'I was coming up to the farm to see you. Your dad invited me to Sunday lunch.'

'You're here for the body?' she said, hanging on to his arm.

'Right. I'd better get a look at it but I'll probably see you Sunday.'

'No, I'll see you tonight at the museum. You have to come to the Professor's lecture. It's a big announcement, but we're all sworn to secrecy. Now I must get back to sieving soil.'

She darted off, leaving Bruno to cast his eyes over the site. Close to the overhang of rock, the trenches gave way to a large pit, at least four metres square and three metres deep, with metal ladders propped against the sides. At the bottom, a large flat rock with curious cup-shaped holes in its surface was being worked on by three archaeologists. They were using brushes so fine they could have belonged to portrait painters. Even from this height, Bruno could see the brown smoothness of newly exposed bones. He looked inquiringly at Horst, assuming this was the skeleton that had prompted the call. The people working with the brushes did not look up. Their continued concentration struck him as even more remarkable, given the ghoulish nature of the discovery that had caused Horst to call. Maybe archaeologists were accustomed to bones and death.

'Sorry this grave is so crowded, but your body is this way, to the side of the main dig,' said Horst. His beard was a little whiter than last year, his hair more sparse, and he was still wearing the English tweed jacket with the leather elbow patches that Bruno remembered from last year and many years before. 'Those bones down there are from three bodies over thirty thousand years old. Your skeleton is over here.'

Steering Bruno past a small winch with a system of pulleys attached to a tripod, Horst led Bruno across to a long, narrow trench, perhaps two metres deep. Beside it an attractive girl and an older woman with red hair, wearing what looked like a man's shirt in green and white stripes, were standing to watch their approach.

The girl, her glossy dark hair tied in a loose bun held together by what looked like an antique TV antenna, had a hand on the shoulder of a burly young man with long hair. He was kneeling, head bowed, over the trench. A small trowel lay beside him. The red-haired woman smiled politely as Bruno approached. It was one of those delicate moments of French meetings; he wasn't sure he knew her well enough for the *bise*, the kissing of cheeks.

'*Bonjour*, Clothilde,' said Bruno, opting for the handshake. She was director of one of the departments of the National Museum of Prehistory in Les Eyzies. She used his outstretched hand to pull him forward to exchange kisses in a determined way, as if to declare that no mere corpse was going to deter her from the social niceties. One of the most eminent archaeologists in France, Clothilde Daunier was a friend and colleague to Horst, and they had once been lovers. Over a bottle of German wine he had brought as a gift to Bruno, Horst had once confided that Clothilde had been the love of his life, though their affair was said to be long over.

Bruno wasn't so sure; he distinctly remembered seeing Horst in the green and white shirt Clothilde was wearing.

'Bruno, this young lady is Kajte, from Holland, and I hope I pronounced that correctly,' Clothilde said. The girl gave her a cool smile and proffered a hand for Bruno to shake. She looked a self-confident young woman, her grey eyes appraising him with a raking glance. Even though she wore the khaki slacks and denim shirt that were almost a uniform among the students on the dig, hers looked expensive. Maybe it was the way she wore them. 'And this is Teddy who found the body. He's British and he's understandably somewhat upset.'

'When was the body found?' Bruno peered down into the trench to see a skull, two shoulder blades and what he assumed were arm bones. The hips and legs were still covered in dirt. The skeleton seemed to be lying stretched out and face down. Scraps of what might been a leather jacket were mingled with loose earth and stones on the body's back. Some strands of hair were still attached to the skull and there was a glint of gold from what had been the neck, the St Christopher medal that Horst had mentioned. The bones of the wrists and hands were still intact, but twisted together behind the back and tied with some faded red electrical wire. A Swatch was still attached to the long bone of a forearm.

'Sweet Jesus,' said Bruno. 'With his hands bound like that, do you think he was buried alive?'

'That's what got to me,' said Clothilde. 'I know I'm going to have nightmares about this grave, just thinking of that. I suppose this makes it murder.'

'Certainly it's a matter for the Police Nationale as well as for the medics. I'll have to inform them and they'll be sealing off this place as a crime scene. They'll want to know exactly when and how the body was found.'

'Teddy found him soon after we started, so not long after seven-thirty. Before eight, certainly, which was when I called you,' said Horst.

'*Bonjour*, Teddy,' Bruno said to the young man. 'Do you speak French?'

'Yes, but not too well,' said Teddy haltingly. He looked up and Bruno saw a pair of very bright blue eyes and a pronounced, almost jutting chin. 'I called the Professor immediately I found him.' He had a very deep voice and a strong accent that Bruno could not identify, too melodic to be English or German.

'Do people usually dig alone? I though you worked in teams,' Bruno said, recalling previous digs he had seen.

'That's true, but Teddy had an interesting idea he wanted to follow up,' said Horst. 'He was looking for the midden, the latrine and the place where people threw their rubbish, and he assumed it would be away from the water supply. It makes sense – if that stream was running in the same course thirty thousand years ago, which I doubt.'

'We always look for the midden because it can tell us a lot about the food they ate from the bones and seeds,' said Clothilde. 'Teddy is a careful worker, so we let him follow his idea. He's been digging that trench for three days now.'

'I'd better call in the doctor. The death may be obvious but we need a medical certificate.' Bruno turned away and pulled his phone from the pouch at his belt to call Fabiola at the clinic. Not only was she a friend, she also knew a lot about forensics.

As he waited for her to answer, Bruno looked up at the high cliff that loomed over the site and the way it sloped inwards towards the ground, creating a narrow space that offered some shelter. A stream ran down the wooded slope, passing perhaps fifteen metres in front of the sheltered space. Beyond the stream was a stand of trees and then another cliff, but this one descended without an overhang. The stream ran for roughly a hundred metres, alongside the track the archaeologists had made with Horst's 4x4, before it reached the narrow back road that led to Les Eyzies. Despite the narrowness of the sheltered space and the height of the cliffs on either side, this place that the prehistoric people had chosen was sited to catch the sun for most of the day. Idly, he wondered how much the landscape had changed over thirty thousand years, and whether the ground at the site had risen with the generations of silt the stream must have brought down. He wasn't convinced that Horst was right to think the route of the stream might have changed; the gap between the cliffs looked like a natural watercourse.

When Fabiola answered, Bruno explained the reason for his call and gave her careful instructions on how to find them. Then he turned back to Horst and Clothilde.

'You've seen a lot of digs over the years, both of you. Any idea how long the body has been dead?'

Clothilde shrugged. 'We deal with the very long dead,

and I don't know much about the rate of decomposition. Different soils can affect the speed of the process, but it must have been there at least ten years, but not before 1983.'

'Why do you say that?'

'The Swatch.' She held up an advanced cellphone and gave a sly and lively grin that took ten years off her age and made Bruno understand Horst's love for her. 'I just used my phone to check the internet. Those watches weren't introduced until 1983.'

'What about the soil over the body? Did that look undisturbed?'

Horst shook his head. 'It was just like the rest of the site, as though nothing had been touched since Peyrony's day.'

Bruno raised his eyebrows. 'Somebody dug here before?'

'Denis Peyrony, eighty, ninety years ago. He was a local teacher who became the father of French archaeology,' said Clothilde. 'He discovered a lot of the main sites like Les Combarelles and Font-de-Gaume back before the Great War and he founded the museum where I work. He drew up a catalogue of all the known and likely sites, including this one. But he only had time to make a brief exploratory dig, found nothing and moved on. Horst and I thought this one deserved another look.'

'Any particular reason?'

'Informed instinct,' said Horst. 'Plus the fact that the site and location are very similar to La Ferrassie.'

The nearest national monument to Bruno's home, La Ferrassie was less a cave than another shallow shelter formed by an overhang of rock. But it was famous as a graveyard of Neanderthal man. The bodies of eight people, men, women and children and two foetuses, had been buried there some 70,000 years ago. The skulls and skeletons were supposed to have been important, but Bruno couldn't remember why. With the overhanging cliffs forming a shelter and a stream running nearby, the similarity between that site and this new one was obvious. He cast an envious glance at Clothilde's phone, thinking how useful it would be to look up La Ferrassie on the net without having to go back to his office computer. But he couldn't see the Mayor dipping into the town budget to provide one.

'When did you start digging here?' Bruno asked.

'Just over ten days ago when the students got here,' Horst said. 'But you remember we did a preliminary dig at the end of the season last year, which was what made us come back. Word must have got around that we were on to something, because we were flooded with applications for this year's dig.'

'You can't keep secrets in this business,' said Clothilde. 'Even the smallest hint and the buzz goes round the world.'

'Sounds interesting.' Bruno wondered how to ask an informed question when he had so little idea of what these experts might think important. 'I presume those really old bones down in the pit are quite a find. It's been a while since you've come across any burials. You said over thirty thousand years – would they be Neanderthal or Cro-Magnon?'

Horst and Clothilde exchanged looks.

'It's a little early to be definite,' Clothilde said carefully. 'We'll say more at the lecture Horst is giving at the museum.'

'You are coming, I hope,' Horst added.

'It sounds like you've found something important,' said Bruno. 'But I was coming anyway. By the way, what's the winch for?' He pointed at the tripod structure.

'It's to lift that big flat stone at the bottom of the pit,' Horst said. 'It has the same little hollows carved into it as the one at La Ferrassie, although that was forty thousand years earlier.'

Bruno wondered briefly how Horst kept all these dates in his head. 'Fascinating,' he said politely. 'But today my main interest is this new body.'

'I think we can safely say that it has no connection with our archaeology,' Horst said, with a smile. 'Except, of course, that it was one of our diggers who found it.'

Teddy heaved himself onto his feet, towering over the rest of the group. He must be nearly two metres tall, thought Bruno, with shoulders to match. The Dutch girl barely came up to his chest. His nose had been broken, and looking at his imposing figure, Bruno felt a sudden curiosity.

'Do you play rugby?'

Teddy smiled for the first time. 'Of course. I grew up in Wales, *Pays de Galles*, you call it. We all play rugby. I played at school and university.'

'Gareth Edwards, Ieuan Evans,' said Bruno, naming the two recent greats of Welsh rugby. In this region, the cradle of French rugby, the two players were esteemed almost as highly as they were in Wales. And Wales explained Teddy's unusual accent. 'I saw Evans play, but Edwards only on TV. If you want a game while you're here, we can bring you into a practice session at the club.'

Teddy nodded eagerly. 'That would be great.'

A horn tooted from the road and Bruno headed down the track to direct Fabiola. Parking her car on the road rather than risk the bumpy route to the dig, she handed Bruno her medical bag to carry before kissing him on both cheeks.

'Is this your day off?' he asked, noting her jeans and sweatshirt rather than the neat trouser suits she invariably wore to work.

She shook her head, and explained she was helping clean out the store cupboard at the clinic and ditching pills and lotions that had been there for a decade and more.

'I'm glad of the break,' she said, 'even if it is a body. There were things in that cupboard growing mould. They'd been there since I was a schoolgirl and planning to be a ballerina rather than a doctor.'

Bruno raised his eyebrows; he'd never heard that before. He introduced Fabiola to the group around the trench, marking the way their eyes first noted and then carefully avoided the long scar on Fabiola's cheek, the legacy of a mountaineering accident. Bruno was no longer aware of it and Fabiola simply ignored it. Her dress and demeanour boldly asserted that this was a self-confident and attractive woman who knew her own worth.

Fabiola peered into the trench at the body. She pulled a small digital camera from the pocket of her jeans and photographed the scene from all sides. Then she looked at the narrow steps cut into each side of the trench.

'Can I stand on those ledges to examine it?' she asked.

'That's why we cut them,' said Horst. 'We had to brush away some of the soil. Here, take my arm.' He leaned forward to help Fabiola clamber carefully into the grave. Bruno placed her medical bag on the lip of the trench.

'Can I have someone else down here, a proper archaeologist, to help clear away some of this earth?' Fabiola called. 'I want a good look at that skull.'

'You might see if there's a wallet or anything that might identify the body,' Bruno suggested. He knew of no missing persons in St Denis in the ten years since his own arrival and there were no unsolved cases of missing persons in the files.

Horst stepped down and Teddy handed him a brush, a trowel and a plastic bag for the dirt. While Fabiola took more photos, Horst carefully exposed the top half of the skull. He handed the filled plastic bag to Teddy, who handed him a fresh one.

As Horst began to clear away more soil, Fabiola told him to stop and clambered down into the pit. She looked intently at the base of the skull, then took the brush and worked gently at the soil.

'I'm pretty sure that's a bullet hole,' she said, and looked up at Bruno. 'At least he wasn't buried alive, but it's still murder.'

Bruno thumbed the speed-dial number for his friend J-J, Jean-Jacques Jalipeau, chief of detectives for the *Police*

Nationale in the region. While waiting for the answer, he wondered how he could explain to Horst and Clothilde that once their precious dig was a crime scene, whatever the demands of scholarship, much of the area would soon be closed off to them as the forensic specialists began the search. Perhaps J-J could be persuaded to limit the restrictions on the dig, since the killing was hardly recent.

J-J's phone told him to leave a message after the beep. He did so, then hit zero to reach the police switchboard. He reported the find and Fabiola's certification of death, and was asked to secure the site and to detain all possible witnesses until a murder team could reach the spot. Bruno asked how long it would take and was told it could be a couple of hours or more. He rang off, and then called Sergeant Jules at the Gendarmerie and asked him to send someone in uniform to hold the fort, since Bruno had appointments elsewhere.

'I'll need a list of names of all the students on this dig, along with their identity card numbers or passport numbers,' Bruno said, not sure whether he should address Horst or Clothilde. It was Horst's dig, but Clothilde would be officially in charge of the site, since it was on French soil.

'If you can come back with me to the museum, I have a list there,' said Horst. 'And I found nothing like a wallet, but I didn't want to disturb things too much.'

Bruno shook his head. 'I'm sorry, but nobody can leave until the detectives get here from Périgueux and take over custody of the site. That's the law. Even I can't leave until a Gendarme gets here to replace me.'

'What's your email?' Clothilde asked, tapping at her phone. Bruno gave it. She tapped again and looked up at him with that cheeky grin. 'I just emailed the list to your office, names, ages, passports and universities for all eighteen of them. Can I go now?'

'Sorry, not quite yet. Can you tell me if any of the students are involved in the animal rights movement? We had another crime here last night. Someone ripped down a stretch of farm fences and let out a lot of ducks and geese. They left leaflets behind, and since your students are all strangers, I'll have to ask about their movements last night.'

'If they're anything like students in my day, they'll all be able to give each other alibis for the night,' said Clothilde, nodding towards Teddy and Kajte.

CHAPTER THREE

Sergeant Jules was as good as his word and arrived quickly to stand watch at the dig, so that Bruno could leave in time to make his appointment at the Château de Campagne. The Brigadier was not a man to be kept waiting. Even though he held no formal authority over St Denis and its chief of police, Bruno and his mayor knew that the orders of this senior but shadowy figure in French intelligence were best obeyed. He had summoned Bruno to a meeting at the decayed gem of a castle whose pointed turrets and battlements the state had been promising to restore for as long as Bruno could remember. But as Bruno turned in through the tall iron gates, now gleaming with black paint, he was surprised to see its courtyard bustling with life. He could barely find a place to park. There were furniture vans, vehicles of plumbers and electricians, a catering van and a large truck loaded down with fresh-cut turf for a lawn that gardeners were laying below the broad balcony. There was a smell of fresh paint, the sound of electric drills, cheerful voices of decorators and the blare of tinny radios from the open windows. But there was no sign of the black limousine Bruno had expected; the Brigadier had not yet arrived.

As he looked around at a building project that seemed almost complete, his phone rang, and J-J's name appeared on the screen.

'I'm on my way, be another thirty minutes.'

'I won't be at the site – I'm tied up with the Brigadier,' Bruno replied. 'But we've got no missing person on file that could fit the body, let alone explain the way he was executed.'

'I know, it's a forensics job. What does the Brigadier want?'

'Apart from a welcoming glass of Monbazillac and some foie gras he hasn't told me.'

'He can't get that in Paris?'

'Isabelle told him he had to try my own pâté, so I have a cooler in the van with a bottle of Tirecul La Gravière, and a fresh baguette from Fauquet.'

'What year for the Tirecul?'

'The '05.'

'That should do it. Call me when you're done. We can have lunch and I can tell you about the new nightmare that's coming into your life. Her name's Annette Meraillon and she came top of her class at the magistrates' school in Bordeaux last year. She's right up your street. She's a vegetarian feminist and she spent her last summer vacation in Paris working for some rights group for Muslim women. She's just been assigned to the sub-Prefecture at Sarlat, which means she'll be your new magistrate.'

'A vegetarian magistrate for St Denis? They must be mad. What does she think about hunting?'

'She's against it. She wants all guns out of private hands. Unless they're Muslim women, I suppose. Remember that young inspector of mine in Bergerac, Jofflin? He met her doing a course at law school and said she didn't even drink. Not a glass. And she's going to hate foie gras, even yours. You're in for a fun time with this one, Bruno.'

As a municipal policeman employed by the Mairie, Bruno seldom sought to bring prosecutions under criminal law, so he'd have a great deal less to do with the new magistrate than the Gendarmes and the Police Nationale. But she could call on him to help her with local inquiries, take up his time and interfere endlessly in his business. Bruno had so far been lucky, since the main magistrate for St Denis and the neighbouring communes had been for the past decade and more a genial fellow, a keen hunter and former chairman of the rugby federation for the Department of the Dordogne. He was also a *Prud'homme* of the *Jurade de St Emilion*, which since the twelfth century had defined when the grapes should be harvested and had kept jealous guard over the branding iron that marked each barrel of the renowned wines of St Emilion. These days it was an honorary role for local worthies and the occasion for some spectacular dinners. But it meant that he took his wine and the pleasures of the table and local tradition very seriously. Bruno could hardly imagine a more appropriate principal judicial officer for the region that saw itself as the gastronomic heartland of France. This new woman sounded as if she'd be very much less accommodating.

'There's a chopper coming in, probably the Brigadier,' said Bruno. 'I'll call you back if he's finished with me in time for lunch.'

Bruno rang off and walked out of the courtyard and into the park where the commune of Campagne held an open-air antiques market every summer. For the first time he saw the newly erected windsock and the big whitewashed circle, marked for a helicopter to land. He put his hand on his hat against the sudden rush of air as the chopper swooped in for its landing on the marked patch of grass. Two tough-looking men in dark suits were the first out, one carrying a FAMAS submachine gun and frowning as he scanned the nearby hillsides, the second with his hand casually inside his jacket. He nodded into the darkness inside the helicopter and two more men appeared in the doorway. Bruno recognised the Brigadier, and watched him invite the other man to precede him. Trust the Brigadier never to turn his back, Bruno thought.

Officially a senior office in the Gendarmes, but long attached to the RG, the shadowy *Renseignements Généraux* intelligence arm, the Brigadier was now on the personal staff of the Minister of the Interior. Bruno had known him involved in monitoring militant ecologists, the extreme right, Asian gangs and networks that smuggled illegal immigrants. He had wide powers, a very loosely defined job and access to a helicopter whenever he wanted. Since Bruno was employed by the Commune of St Denis, the Brigadier had no formal authority over him. The Brigadier overcame this technicality by bringing a formal request to the Mayor from either the Prefect of the Department or the Interior Minister himself for Bruno to be seconded on special duties. And if that failed to work, Bruno had few doubts that the Brigadier would activate his army reserve status and have him conscripted.

Bruno felt a wary respect for the man. He had also been in command of an operation in which Isabelle Perrault, a woman with whom Bruno had had a truncated love affair, had been seriously wounded. She had been a police inspector when Bruno had met her, before being lured away to the Brigadier's staff in Paris. The Brigadier had informed Bruno that a similar job awaited him in Paris should he choose to take up the offer. Bruno noted that the Brigadier now wore the small red button of the *Légion d'Honneur* in his lapel. That was new. He wondered if it had been awarded for the operation to intercept a shipload of illegal immigrants when Isabelle's thigh had been shattered by a bullet from an AK-47.

The man accompanying the Brigadier was so tall that he had to stoop unusually low as they scuttled under the slowing rotor blades. As the stranger straightened up, Bruno saw a fit-looking man in his forties with thick and rather long hair of a deep glossy black, and the kind of dark shadow on his chin that meant he would shave twice a day. His mouth was thin and his jaw thrust almost arrogantly forward. It would have been a cruel face, but for the alert way he looked around him and the easy smile he flashed when he saw Bruno.

'*Bonjour*, Bruno,' said the Brigadier. 'Meet Carlos Gambara, deputy head of counterterrorism for the Spanish Ministry of the Interior. For this job, he's my counterpart in Madrid, but he's going to be here for a few days before attending the summit. Carlos, this is the man I told you about, Chief of Police Courrèges, but I think you can call him Bruno.'

'Summit?' asked Bruno, sketching a hasty salute despite feeling rather odd doing so while holding a plastic bag in his left hand, and very conscious of the silent bodyguard standing behind him with a submachine gun at the ready. They'd probably want to search his bag. 'In St Denis?'

'A little summit,' said the Brigadier, lowering his voice as the rotor blades coughed to a halt behind him. 'The Spanish Interior Minister and our own will be signing a new cooperation agreement on Basque terrorism – intelligence sharing, joint staffing of a common office for cross-border liaison, joint firearms permits and rules of engagement. Now they've killed one of our cops here in France, the gloves are off.'

'Sir, I'd rather you all moved inside,' interrupted the bodyguard whose hand was still inside his jacket, but his eyes were trained on the hills. 'It's a bit exposed here. Don't want you falling into bad habits.'

The Brigadier nodded and gave a half-smile to the man. A sign of a good unit, Bruno thought, when the bodyguard could tease the boss a little.

'Welcome back to St Denis,' Bruno said, handing the Brigadier the bag. 'Isabelle told me you were hoping to taste some foie gras, and there's some Monbazillac to go with it.'

'Very kind, Bruno. It's been a long time since breakfast.' He handed the bag to one of the bodyguards. 'Maybe we can introduce our Spanish friend to a real French *casse-croûte*, once we've done the inspection.'

'The Brigadier has told me a lot about your shared adventures,' said the Spaniard, stretching out a large hand for Bruno to shake as they walked into the shadow of the château walls. Bruno took that with a pinch of salt; nobody could hear themselves speak inside a military helicopter. 'In the name of my government, we thank you for your help.'

'Welcome to the commune of St Denis, or rather Campagne,' Bruno said. 'When do the ministers plan to meet?' He scanned the wooded hills around them, seeing any number of places for a sniper to hide. Next week the trees would still be bare enough to give both cover and a decent field of fire. They'd need screens to cover the move from the helicopter to the château. But what kind of screens would stand up to a helicopter downdraught?

'Next week, final restoration work permitting,' said the Brigadier. 'That's why we're here – a quick inspection and I wanted to bring you into the picture early and get to know Carlos. He'll be staying for a few days, getting the lie of the land and checking the secure communications set-up. Bruno, I'd like you to draw up a patrol plan to secure the immediate perimeter and all roads and tracks within a reasonable radius. I can deploy a company of Gendarmes and another of CRS for roadblocks and a platoon of special forces for patrols, probably from the *treizième paras*, your old unit. You know the drill and the terrain so I'll leave it to you.'

Bruno sensed the Spaniard watching him as he cast his eyes around the hills. When he looked back he saw Carlos was grinning at him.

'We think alike, Senõr. A good place for a rifleman. But the ETA prefer their bombs. And we have good solid screens that don't blow over. If we're still worried, we can have the ministers take a limousine into the courtyard direct from the helicopters.' His French was accented but good.

'Who picked this place?' asked Bruno, with a funny feeling that he already knew the answer.

'Isabelle suggested it,' said the Brigadier, with a half-wink. 'And of course she sends you her warmest regards. She's taken a liking to this area and when she heard the renovation of the château was almost finished, she thought the summit would be a good occasion for the formal opening. And maybe our Minister owed the Minister of Tourism a favour.'

'Why not hold the summit in our own Basque region down by Biarritz?' Bruno asked. 'If you want the symbolism of government cooperation . . .'

'Security,' said Carlos. 'This is as close as you can get to the Basque country without having any Basques.'

'I wouldn't say there aren't any,' Bruno said. 'There are some second- and third-generation . . .'

'I know,' said Carlos. 'The ones who came to France in 1939 as refugees after our civil war.'

'Some of them made up the hard core of our Resistance,' said Bruno. 'They hated Fascists and Nazis. Most of them moved back to the Basque district near the frontier when the war ended but one or two married local girls and stayed.'

'We know. Commies most of them, some anarchists. We kept an eye on them and we're not worried about them.

They're mostly dead,' said the Brigadier. He opened his briefcase, took out an envelope and handed it to Bruno. 'Here's a letter to your Mayor from the Minister. As of now and until the conference ends, you're attached to the joint security coordination committee, which Carlos and I run. You'll treat his orders as my orders.'

'What about my usual duties?' Bruno described the discovery of the body at the archaeological dig.

'An execution? In St Denis? How recent?'

'From the state of the skeleton, at least twenty years old,' Bruno said, and saw the Brigadier relax his sudden tension. 'But we have to find out who it is. J-J should be at the scene by now.'

'I understand, but this takes priority,' said the Brigadier briskly.

'I imagine that keeping an eye out for strangers means doing your usual patrols and inquiries. You can probably combine some of the work, and I'm grateful for your help,' said Carlos. 'I'm looking forward to spending some time in the district. I've seen our own prehistoric cave paintings at Altamira, so I'm hoping to see some of your famous ones while I'm here.'

Bruno smiled to himself at the transparency of the old routine of hard cop, soft cop. But the Spaniard was playing it the wrong way round; it was the Brigadier with whom Bruno had already built a relationship. Grudging respect on his own part, along with the kind of conditional trust that soldiers give to officers who know what they're doing. But Bruno was less sure what the Brigadier thought of him, beyond being a useful local tool and on occasion a reluctant subordinate. Carlos was a new factor in the mix.

'What's your own background, Monsieur, if I may ask?' he said, with the blend of forthrightness and deference that he knew officers liked.

'I've something in common with you,' said Carlos, looking Bruno in the eye. 'I believe you're an orphan, like me. I went into the military early, like you. I was a combat engineer, and served a year with the Eurocorps in Strasbourg. That's where I learned my French. Then I was attached to military intelligence when I was with the Kosovo force back in '99. So we both served in the Balkans, and I got to know your old commander, Colonel Beauchamp. I transferred into counterterrorism after we were pulled out of Iraq.'

'It sounds as though the Brigadier has shown you my file already. So they brought you in after the dirty war?' Bruno asked. There had been a series of scandals followed by a massive purge of Spanish intelligence after state-sponsored death squads had been exposed for assassinating a number of Basque militants. Bruno was vague on the details but he knew a lot of heads had rolled and a former interior minister had been jailed. He wanted none of that in St Denis. It was bad enough thinking of that gangland-style killing back at the archaeological dig without contemplating some shadowy state officials plotting unlawful executions.

'Long after,' said Carlos coolly. 'Those GAL killings were back in the 1980s, even though the scandal broke later. *Grupos Antiterroristas de Liberación* – we're not like that now.'

'The terrorists haven't changed. ETA has killed over eight

hundred people, half of them civilians,' snapped the Brigadier. 'If those Basque murder squads thought they could take out a French and a Spanish minister with one attack, they'd jump at it, even if they do claim to be observing a ceasefire. That's why it's going to be top security here.'

Bruno said nothing. The Brigadier, he knew, was the kind of ruthless operator who would not shrink from putting a couple of ministers at risk if it meant luring a terrorist squad into the open. Carlos was an unknown quantity, but Bruno had few illusions about the way counter-intelligence worked and he bridled at the prospect of this kind of danger being invited into St Denis.

'I'll have to explain to my Mayor about holding the summit here. Are you planning to announce it?'

'Oh yes,' said the Brigadier, almost casually. 'There's to be a press conference after the agreement, TV cameras present for the signing. You can't keep that kind of thing secret. So we may as well make an announcement. It depends on today's inspection whether the conference chamber and facilities will be ready.'

The Brigadier gestured to his security men to stay outside and led the way up the steps to the balcony, which was flanked by a long line of French windows. He tried several in turn, not sure which was the main door. Finally he tapped on the window and a man in painter's clothes looked up, waved and came forward to open the last window in the row. The Brigadier nodded thanks and shepherded them all inside, over the dustsheets. He stopped to gaze at the long room.

'This is where the formal meeting will be held, and the final press conference.'

A Spanish and a French flag were propped neatly against the far wall. Carlos walked the length of the room to unfurl the Spanish banner, as if to examine it for blemishes. He let the folds fall and walked back, studying the space as if he sought to commit its contours to memory.

'Where will the furniture come from?' he asked, opening a door that led into a small cupboard.

'Government stores,' said the Brigadier. 'Usual things, conference table, signing table, chairs – they're supplying some decent antiques. Maybe a statue or two and a couple of sideboards for the walls. They're probably in that furniture van in the yard.'

'Upstairs?' Carlos asked.

'We'll have the whole place checked, but upstairs will remain unfurnished apart from a couple of bedrooms in case the ministers want to rest. Nobody's staying overnight except the security teams. And Isabelle, of course,' the Brigadier added in an aside to Carlos, carefully not looking at Bruno. 'You remember from Paris, the young Inspector on my staff who got shot, walks with a cane.'

'When is she expected?' Bruno asked, his mouth suddenly dry. He suspected it always would be, at the mention of her name. He wondered what the need for a cane might do to that shining self-confidence of hers. He'd been there when Isabelle left the military hospital for the convalescent centre outside Paris, still on a stretcher.

'Tomorrow, I think, when the communications systems

start being installed. Maybe the day after. She persuaded the doctors that she was fit enough to return to light duties, so she'll be here, running the base. We're taking over the local hotel.'

'So I report to her?' Bruno asked.

'Of course. Usual procedure, a morning staff meeting at nine, evening review at six. If I'm here, I'll take it, if not then it will be Isabelle and Carlos. I see you're still using that secure phone we gave you.'

'Have you selected a back-up location in case anything goes wrong?'

'What makes you think we'll need a back-up location?' Carlos asked.

'I've worked with the Brigadier before.'

'Come on out to the balcony,' the Brigadier said. 'The sun's out and we can take our *casse-croûte* there.' He turned to his bodyguard. 'Can you find us some plates and wine glasses?'

'Already taken care of, sir. Philippe went to the hotel across the road to borrow some.'

'Enough for the bodyguards to have a bit of the foie, Bruno? They won't drink on duty.'

'Enough for everybody,' said Bruno, pulling the rubber seal on the glass jar to break the vacuum and then levering up the wire catches to open the lid. The Brigadier picked it up to sniff. 'Try that, Carlos,' he said, as Bruno took his Laguiole knife from the pouch at his belt, levered up the corkscrew and opened the bottle of sweet golden wine. He cut the baguette into five portions and brought out a small pot of onion marmalade he had made the previous autumn.

'*Bon appétit*, and welcome to the gastronomic heartland of France,' he said to Carlos. He took some of the yellow duck fat he had used to preserve the foie and spread it on the baguette before adding a healthy slice of pâté and a small dab of marmalade.

'This is wonderful,' the Spaniard mumbled through a mouthful of fresh bread and foie gras. He took a sip of wine and his eyes widened. 'Magnificent. They were made for each other.'

Bruno found himself smiling broadly as the Brigadier sniffed at his Monbazillac and said, 'Spring sunshine warming the stone of an old château, a wonderful foie gras and a glass of the perfect wine to accompany it. What do you say, Carlos? Counterterrorism isn't always like this, eh?'

CHAPTER FOUR

Lunch with J-J was late, but Ivan offered them an omelette with the fresh, tender buds of the first *pissenlits* and brought them a carafe of his new house wine from the Domaine down the valley. His *plat du jour* was one of the happier memories of his disastrous love affair with a Belgian girl from Charleroi, *endives au jambon*. Bruno well remembered Ivan's three months of summer bliss and a crashing, drunken winter of heartbreak when she left him and his Café de la Renaissance almost went under.

'He does a good béchamel sauce, your Ivan,' said J-J, wiping the last of his empty dish with a crust of bread. He chewed with enthusiasm, took a sip of the young red wine and sat back content, his big, square hands resting on his portly stomach. 'You don't know how lucky you are here in St Denis. No fast food, a couple of real bistros, wine from your own valley. Half my coppers up in Périgueux seem to live on takeout pizzas and hamburgers.'

'Talking of your lads, can you get them to run this for fingerprints?' Bruno asked. He handed across an envelope containing the animal cruelty pamphlet that he'd taken from the Villattes' farm. 'I used a handkerchief but there may be one or two of mine smeared on.'

J-J took it with a grunt. 'The priority is going to be identifying that corpse, at least once we get the Brigadier and those damn ministers out of the way. They'll demand the use of half my force for security.'

'So what's next?'

'I'll wait for the forensic report. What they told me after the initial examination was pretty obvious – youngish male, dead at least twenty years, probably shot while already in that grave, but that's not certain. If we get a good estimate of his age and the length of time since death, then we'll run through missing persons. But over two hundred thousand people go missing in France every year, so it's a long shot. And we've no idea where the dead man's from. One of the forensics men said the teeth suggested a foreign dentist.'

'He's not from round here. I know our own missing persons file,' Bruno said. 'But there has to be a local connection, if only through the killer. Only someone from round here, or maybe an archaeologist, would know about that site.'

'Not necessarily. They could have been driving round, interrogating him in the back of a car, hands behind his back. They decide to do him in, and it's a quiet, sheltered place.'

'It's not that sheltered. And there would've been a gunshot. Then they had to bury him. If they wanted somewhere deserted, they could've found better places up in the woods.

Maybe there's a reason they picked that spot. If so, there is a local connection – and it's the killer, not the victim.'

'But until we know who he was . . .' J-J said, as Ivan brought their coffee and the bill. He stared at the total, blinked in disbelief, and slipped a twenty-euro note under his saucer. 'It's like time travel, coming here. Lunch for two and change from a twenty. Now I know why you like this place.'

'I'll see if Joe recalls anything. You remember him, he had this job before me?' Bruno pulled out his own wallet. J-J waved it aside, muttering 'Expenses,' and putting Ivan's bill into his notebook.

'Keep me informed, particularly if Joe has anything, and I'll send over the forensic report as soon as I get it. The best clue might be the watch. One of my lads says there'll be a batch number in the mechanism somewhere that could give us a better time frame.' He looked at his own watch, and lumbered to his feet. 'Got to go. By the way, you'll be getting a call from the new magistrate about the body. I sent a notification through of a suspicious death and she wants to see the site. Just remember, Bruno, she's feminist, vegetarian and very Green – in both senses of the word.'

There were three places in town for photocopying, and he started at the nearest, the Maison de la Presse. Patrick shook his head when Bruno asked about recent batch jobs. Most of Patrick's customers just wanted a single sheet, or to make a copy of an ID card or wedding certificate. Nor did he recognise the crude leaflet when Bruno showed it to him. Then Bruno went to the Informatique, where they repaired computers and sold office supplies and charged twice as much as Patrick for a photocopy. Locals knew this but strangers might not. Finally he tried the most obvious, the tourist information centre down by the river, where Gabrielle, a tennis club friend, ran the small internet centre, sold rail tickets and looked after the photocopier.

'No, I don't recognise that leaflet, but then I never really look,' she told him.

'Any batch jobs?'

'We did do a lot for those students at the archaeology dig yesterday, maybe the day before. Cooking rotas and work-sheets and other paperwork, she said. Nice young girl, Dutch. It must have been fifty or sixty sheets.'

'Did you see what it was she was copying? Did you load the machine?'

'No, someone came in for a ticket to Bordeaux and she knew how to run it. I just checked the number counter at the end and charged her.'

'You'd recognise her again?'

'Certainly. She was here for ages, used the computer for her emails.'

'Has it got one of those history buttons, tells you which websites you've visited?'

'Yes, but I don't know how long it goes back. Mind you, it hasn't been busy. No tourists this time of year. That's why I let her stay so long on the computer. Usually it's an hour maximum, thirty minutes if we're busy.'

Gabrielle fired up the computer and clicked open Internet Explorer, but the 'Delete Browsing History' function had been applied. Damn, thought Bruno. Maybe this won't be so easy.

'Wait a minute. She was saying she didn't like Explorer,' Gabrielle interrupted. 'She has a Mac at home, she said, and she likes Apple and hates Microsoft. So maybe she'd have used another browser . . .'

Her voice trailed off and she opened the Firefox browser, waited for it to load and clicked 'History'. The fourth item was petafrance.com and the fifth was peta.nl for the Netherlands.

'Can you print that page out for me please, Gabrielle, and sign and date it?' He waited until she was done and then clicked the petafrance webpage. As he expected, it was connected to a page on foie gras. *'Ecrivez au ministre de l'Agriculture pour protester contre cinq années supplémentaires de cruauté du foie gras.'* – Write to the minister of Agriculture to protest against five more years of foie gras cruelty.

Bruno considered the contrast between the good sense of a civil appeal to ministerial reason and the pulling down of fences. He had no problem with writing to a minister. Criminal damage to the property of a perfectly legal and not very prosperous farmer was another matter, quite apart from the squashed bodies of ducks and geese he recalled from the morning.

'And print that out too, if you would.'

He clicked on the Peta site for the Netherlands. He couldn't read the Dutch but he read the names of celebrities and movie stars who seemed to be lending their names to its campaigns. Then there was what looked like a vegetarian recipe to make some kind of foie gras substitute. It seemed to be mainly mushrooms. He might try making it some day.

'What's this about, Bruno?'

'The Villattes. Somebody pulled down their fences last night and let the ducks and geese out. It seems your nice Dutch girl may have been involved.'

Gabrielle put her hand to her mouth and stared at him. 'What are you going to do? Arrest her?'

'Well, I'd have to be sure it was her first. And I don't think she acted alone, so I'll have to find out who else was involved. Was she alone when she came here?'

Gabrielle nodded. 'She was at first, then a bunch of other students came in and took some of the tourism leaflets. She left with them. And I remember now, they called her Katie. But she was very polite, thanked me when she paid for the photocopies and the computer time. I hope she's not going to get into trouble.'

'What would you do to her, Gabrielle, if you were sure it was her? You know the Villattes, decent, hard-working people. You know their boy, Daniel, good little tennis player. What happens to him if his parents lose their livelihood?'

Gabrielle looked at him, considering. 'I'd make her go and confess to them and say she was sorry. I think she should put it in writing. Then I'd make her pay for the birds and repair the damage, and then pay some more compensation for their trouble. And I'd hope she learned her lesson.'

Bruno pondered the difference between Gabrielle's thoughtful reply and the blunt avowals of vengeance that he'd heard that morning from Alain. Maybe the difference was that Alain was thinking of some anonymous, face-less enemy; Gabrielle knew the Dutch girl and had warmed to her.

'She's very young,' Gabrielle went on. 'Maybe she just got carried away. You know young people and their causes. And some of this animal cruelty business is nasty stuff. It turns my stomach to see those poor whales and those baby seals that get clubbed on TV.'

'Well, we don't eat baby seals,' Bruno replied. 'We do eat duck, and foie gras, and a lot of our neighbours make their living from it, and they're the ones who pay my wages. And yours, come to that. They've got rights, too. Thanks for your help, Gabrielle. I'll let you know how this develops.'

The municipal campground of St Denis had a pleasant location beside the river. The town's open-air swimming pool flanked one side and the rear opened onto a large sports field with a running track and a playground for children Between the campsite and the main part of town were some of the tourist attractions of St Denis: a small aquarium that was closed for repainting, a wildlife museum and a beach where canoes were rented in summer. Behind them were the town's handsome municipal gardens, a less ambitious attempt to repeat the gravel walks and chequerboard lawns and topiary of Versailles. It wasn't greatly to Bruno's taste.

He walked quickly through the gardens to the iron-studded wooden door in the garden wall that was partly hidden by a boxwood hedge, and used one of the many keys on his belt to let himself in. Bruno always enjoyed this place, where time seemed to slow a little and in summer butterflies swarmed. He paused as he relocked the door and gazed around at the walled garden with peach and apricot trees espaliered symmetrically against the old bricks, faded now from their original red to a dusty orange that made a pleasing backdrop to the bright green of the new leaves. Inside the walls were herb gardens and beds for unusual plants, continuing an old tradition that went back to medieval times, when there had been a nunnery on this land and when Jean Rey, a local natural philosopher, had written an early book on using plants as medicines. St Denis was the only commune Bruno knew that employed its own herbalist, who turned a decent profit for the town by selling seeds and plants to the homeopathic trade. There was no sign of Morillon, the old gardener, but Bruno was only using the garden as a short cut to the town's campsite and let himself out quickly by the rear door.

Dominated by the shower block at one end and the reception building at the other that housed office, shop and bar, the campground was a large field criss-crossed by gravel paths and parking stands. In one corner stood perhaps a score of multicoloured tents, one very large but mostly small, huddled together close to the river bank. There was no sign of life except the thin sound of radio music leaking from the office, where Bruno found Monique. She was sitting and smoking while she toyed with the crossword in that day's *Sud-Ouest* and hummed along to the pop songs on Périgord-Bleu. Married to Bernard, who managed the campsite and did whatever odd jobs were required, Monique looked after the campsite shop and the town pool. They lived rent-free in a small apartment above the office, shared two modest salaries, and worked like slaves from the start of the tourist season in May until the end of September. For the rest of the year there was little to do other than maintenance.

'*Salut*, Bruno. You fancy a coffee?' She got up and presented her plump cheek to be kissed. Her hair was bottle blonde, black at the roots. He nodded and she began fussing with a small machine that looked new.

'Trying it out on approval,' she said. 'I like the coffee it makes, but Bernard prefers the old way, stewed on the stove top. What brings you round here?'

'The students who're camping; are they all from the group that's here for the archaeology?'

'They'd better be. That's why they get the special rate. But they all had the right paperwork from the museum. Why, is there trouble?'

'I don't know, but the Villatte farm was done over last night by some animal rights people. They let all the birds out. There are no other strangers around so I thought I'd better ask if you heard anything from the youngsters.'

'No, they keep themselves to themselves, cook their own food down by that big tent they use as a living space. They don't even shop here any more, once they saw the prices are cheaper at the supermarket. They've been no trouble, except for the noise late at night, but you have to expect that.'

'It looks like more tents than people. Do they each have their own?'

'In theory, but you know what youngsters are. Most of them are paired off now and sharing.' The coffee machine made gurgling noises and started dripping coffee into the two cups Monique had put under the spout. She slid a sugar cube and a spoon onto his saucer and added a small biscuit wrapped in cellophane. 'It's like the United Nations here every Easter – Dutch and Polish and Belgians and English. I don't know where Horst rounds them up. Some of them come back two and three years in a row.'

'There's a Dutch girl called Katie or something like that. Do you know her?'

'She's the one always entwined around the big English boy. Her own tent's empty now.'

'Mind if I take a look?' He finished his coffee.

'Official, is it?'

'Not yet but it could be. You'd better come with me, keep an eye on me in case I try to walk off with her underwear.'

'I wouldn't put it past you. Keep an eye out for anyone coming is what you mean.' She grinned at him. 'Come on then. Let's go make a security check.'

Kajte's tent was empty apart from a couple of plastic bags filled with clothes and some paperbacks resting on a flat stone. Teddy's tent contained two sleeping bags zipped together into a double and two rucksacks aligned neatly side by side. Two towels hung from a thin rope strung between the two tent poles. He'd built a small shelf of a plank of wood resting on stones to hold a couple of tin plates and mugs and two toilet bags and what looked like textbooks. Bruno thumbed through some papers in a small briefcase, but from what he could read of the English they seemed mainly photocopies of articles from archaeology journals. There was nothing about animals. The rucksacks held only more clothing, and he found nothing more when he felt around the side pockets.

He was backing out of the tent, shaking his head at Monique, when his phone rang.

'Monsieur Courrèges?' It was a young woman's voice, very brisk. 'This is Magistrate Annette Meraillon. I'm told a dead body has been found that I'll need to see. I can be in St Denis in thirty minutes. Where should we meet?'

'*Bonjour*, Mademoiselle, and welcome to the Périgord,' he said. 'You know the body has been removed by the Police Nationale and taken for forensic examination?'

'What? Without my seeing it in place?' Her voice had risen a notch.

'That's something you'd better discuss with Commissaire Jalipeau, the chief of detectives. But I gather it's quite routine, particularly when there's a problem of identification.'

'We'll see about that. I still want to see the site. Where will you meet me?'

'In front of the Mairie in thirty minutes. I'm in uniform, so you can't miss me, and you can park there. But you might want to bring some boots or walking shoes. It's some way off the nearest road.'

'Right. Thirty minutes.' She rang off. Bruno looked at his watch. He had a little time, so he turned back to Monique.

'Can I take a look in the big tent, the one you called their living room?'

About five metres square, with a peaked top and a large canopy, the main tent contained a couple of the bench-and-table units that the campsite provided beside the barbecue stands. There was a small stereo-radio on one with a pile of CDs beside it, a five-litre box of cheap red wine and some empty pizza boxes. On the other were some cooking pots. Piled on a ground cloth beneath the bench were several boxes of vegetables and cereals and a dilapidated wicker basket containing some tools. Bruno noted a hammer and small saw, a couple of screwdrivers and a large pair of wire-cutters.

CHAPTER FIVE

A small blue Peugeot circled too fast around the roundabout. It beeped its horn to deter a mother with two children in a pushchair from setting forth on the pedestrian crossing before parking with a jerk across two of the marked spaces in front of the Mairie. The front bumper stopped within a hand's breadth of Bruno's leg. The young woman at the wheel, clad in a grey woollen suit, threw him a swift glance and then began collecting papers from a briefcase on the passenger seat. From down the street, he heard a siren. The Peugeot was freshly washed but far from new, with dents in the bumper and scratches on the rear wings, and the wide tyres he'd only previously seen on cars used for rallying.

Bruno tapped on her window. 'Your papers, please, Mademoiselle.'

She turned from her briefcase and looked at him coldly. The sound of the approaching siren grew and a blue Gendarmerie van came into view, Sergeant Jules at the wheel.

'You're Courrèges, the village policeman, right?'

'Correct. You are illegally parked and about to receive a citation for failing to stop for a pedestrian crossing,' he said.

He realised that this was the new magistrate, but the traffic in St Denis was one of his responsibilities. He pulled out his notebook as Jules parked the police van behind the blue Peugeot, blocking its exit.

'You got her, too?' called Jules, heaving himself from the car. 'We clocked her at seventy-eight coming into town.' He began to fill out a speeding ticket.

'Meet our new magistrate,' said Bruno. 'Annette Meraillon. Mademoiselle, this is Sergeant Jules of the Gendarmerie.'

'*Putain*,' said Jules. 'I've started to write it now. Can't tear it up, they're all numbered.'

'I'm sure Mademoiselle Meraillon believes that the law should always take its course,' said Bruno. 'Where was she doing seventy-eight?'

'Going past the vet, just where the limit goes down from fifty to thirty. That'll be three points off her licence.'

'Plus the pedestrian crossing,' said Bruno. 'That's four. And the fines, not including the twenty euros for parking across two spaces.'

'If you two have finished,' the young woman said, 'I'm on official business, and have an appointment – with you.'

Jules and Bruno looked thoughtfully at one another.

'Urgent official business, Mademoiselle?' Jules enquired.

'Of course.'

'Mademoiselle Meraillon wants to see a crime scene from which she knows the body has already been removed,' said Bruno. 'It may be official but it's not exactly urgent. And I don't know of any provision for magistrates to break the traffic laws when there is no crime in progress.'

'This is ridiculous,' she began, then came an interruption.

'Well, I'm glad you've got the stupid woman,' said Florence, putting the brake on her pushchair. The two children sitting inside, safely buckled in, waved at Bruno. He waved back. Florence, the science teacher at the local college, kissed him quickly as he bent to say hello to the children. She put her hand on the roof of the blue Peugeot and looked in.

'You're a dangerous driver,' she said. 'I'd started crossing that road and it was my right of way. You have no right to drive like that in town.' Florence turned to Bruno and Jules. 'Take my name. I'll be happy to be a witness.'

The woman in the car glanced at the children as if seeing them for the first time. She swallowed hard, looked at Florence and then back at the children. She gripped the steering wheel, braced her shoulders against the car seat and lowered her head.

'I'm sorry,' said the magistrate, raising her head to look directly at Florence. 'And I'm sorry if I frightened your children. I didn't mean to and I apologise. I was in too much of a hurry.' She reached into the bag on the seat beside her, pulled a driving permit from her purse and handed it through the window to Jules. Then she leaned across to open the glove box and took out a plastic folder with insurance documents and *carte grise,* the car registration. She also handed Jules a laminated ID card with the red, white and blue stripes of the *République Française* across her photograph.

'You were right, Monsieur Courrèges. I'm a magistrate. The law should take its course. Please take this woman's statement and then I will give mine. I freely admit that I was driving too fast and should have stopped for the pedestrian crossing.'

Florence looked down at her. 'When did you start this job?'

'Monday. First job out of magistrates' school.'

'Well, in that case . . .' Florence paused. 'Just be careful in future.' She unlocked the pushchair and wheeled her children off toward Fauquet's café, promising them ice creams.

'I think I lost my witness,' said Bruno. 'But the parking fine stays.'

'And the speeding ticket,' said Jules. 'But I'll put it in the fifty zone. That won't be too bad.' He filled out the ticket and handed it to her. 'I'll see you, Bruno.' He got into his van, reversed smartly and drove out of the parking lot.

'Shall we start again?' Bruno said. 'I'm Bruno, not Monsieur Courrèges, and we're supposed to be colleagues. May I call you Annette?'

'Yes, please do, and I'm sorry about this.' She ventured a hesitant smile. It made her look even younger. Fair-haired and slim, with a thin face that looked pretty now that she was not trying to be fierce, she could have been a teenager. The suit seemed incongruous, as if she were dressing for a role as someone older, a businesswoman perhaps.

'I understand,' said Bruno. 'I was very nervous when I started and probably tried too hard to make an impression. But I don't think I was foolish enough to try doing it with a car.'

'That woman with the children, is she a friend of yours?'

'Yes, but then most people in this town have known me for years and I try to get along with everybody.'

'It's just ... you have this reputation, Monsieur ... I mean, Bruno.'

He raised his eyebrows. He could imagine what young magistrates might think of him, an ex-soldier who hunted and drank and who tried never to arrest anyone and cared little for the subtleties of modern law enforcement with its counselling and political correctness.

'Let's go and have a coffee, and you might want to pay for those ice creams Florence promised the kids,' he said. 'She's a good woman, a teacher and single mother, and worth getting to know. I presume you haven't many friends yet in the area.'

She swung her legs out of the car. The skirt of the suit was tight and rather short, and her legs were shapely. He handed her back the car keys and she made to lock the door. Bruno coughed.

'Perhaps you could fit the car into a single space, Annette,' he said.

She grinned, got back into the car, reversed and straightened up. 'Anything else, before those ice creams?'

'I hope you have some spare clothes in the car. That suit won't look so good after we get to the site.'

'I brought walking shoes, as you advised. And I've got a snowman in the back of the car,' she said, referring to the white plastic coveralls that were worn by forensic teams. 'What more does a girl need?'

'This,' he said, handing her the parking ticket.

*

Now that the skeleton had been taken away, the grave site had reverted to being an archaeological dig. Bruno noticed that the winch had been placed over the large pit. He told Annette to be careful to follow his footsteps between the trenches and led the way to the place that was still marked off with crime-scene tape. Teddy and two other students were digging just beyond it, extending their ditch and still looking for the midden. Bruno leaned over the yellow tape and looked into the empty grave.

'There's nothing to see,' said Annette, sounding irritated.

'The forensics people have been doing their job,' Bruno said.

'They even took some of the soil, probably wanting to see if the body bled in place,' said Teddy. 'They sieved it first, which was decent of them, but nothing found.'

'Not even a bullet?'

'I heard them talking,' said one of the other students; good French, but with a strong accent. 'They said it might still be in the skull.'

'And you are, Monsieur?'

'Kasimir, from Poland, University of Krakow.' He had dark hair, clear blue eyes and wore a T-shirt featuring some Polish artist Bruno had never heard of. Kasimir leaned against the side of the ditch, pulled a pack of tobacco from his pocket and began to roll a cigarette. 'They put a black cloth over the grave and sprayed something. Then they shone a light down, and said they were sure he'd been killed right here.'

'What did you think, Kasimir? Hear anything else that might help the magistrate here?' Bruno recognised the standard forensic test for blood, although he'd be surprised if traces had lasted so long.

'They said they thought they might get a rough date of death from the shoes he was wearing. They were trainers, or at least they had been.' He shrugged. 'Other than that, the skeleton looked intact, what we could see. They put screens up.'

'People must be upset,' said Annette. 'Would you like me to arrange for some counselling?'

'Counselling?' asked Kasimir, snorting. 'We're here to find bodies. Skeletons are what we do.'

'Something else I wanted to ask,' Bruno said, turning to Teddy. 'Where were you in the early hours of this morning, around dawn?'

Teddy looked startled. 'In bed, fast asleep, back at the campsite.'

'And Kajte? That girl I saw you with?'

'She was with me.' A touch of bravado in the statement. 'She was there when I woke up. We all had breakfast together. Kas was there. You remember this morning?'

'I'm not good in the mornings, but we were all there today, drinking the worst coffee in the world,' Kasimir said, lighting his cigarette. 'Why do you ask?'

'Some animal rights militants tried to liberate a farm full of ducks and geese. Some of the birds were killed when they wandered onto the road, which seems a funny way of protecting animals.'

'Maybe no worse than the alternative,' said Teddy. 'But you're all into foie gras around here.'

'Not all of us,' said Annette suddenly animated. She turned to Bruno. 'What happened?'

'A nearby farm had its fences pulled down and PETA leaflets were stuck on the bits that were left. It stands for People for the Ethical Treatment of Animals,' Bruno said. 'The farmer has kids to raise and he barely makes a living as it is, without losing a few ducks and geese and having to repair fences. And round here, we believe in the ethical treatment of farmers.'

Teddy said nothing, but Kasimir looked at him curiously.

'You ever tried foie gras?' Bruno asked, his tone conversational, rather than challenging.

'Of course,' said Kasimir, as Teddy shook his massive head. 'We have it in Poland as well, always at Christmas. We have a sweet white wine from Hungary with it, a Tokay.'

'So the cruelty these PETA people talk about, it doesn't worry you?'

Kasimir grinned. 'If there's any cruelty, blame Mother Nature. Ducks and geese always stuff themselves to swell their livers before they fly off on winter migration. That's how they store their energy. Everybody knows that.'

From the look on Teddy's face, it didn't appear to Bruno that he knew that *gavage*, the force-feeding of the birds, was also a natural process. He glanced at Annette. She also looked surprised.

'Well, if you hear of any of your chums making plans to attack more farms, talk them out of it. Or I'll be making arrests for criminal damage. And Annette here will have to bring charges. That's her job.' Bruno turned away, then looked back at Teddy.

'One more thing. Rugby practice tomorrow evening at six, if you're interested, and again at nine on Saturday morning. We have spare kit at the stadium – you know where it is? First left after the Bricomarché, and you'll see the rugby posts.'

'Thanks,' said Teddy, looking surprised. 'I'd like that.'

'You might want to bring Kajte along,' Bruno added. 'And tell her to be careful where she does her photocopying.'

Teddy's cheerful face suddenly clouded and he looked away.

'What was that last remark about?' Annette asked, as they headed back to Bruno's van.

'I made a few inquiries. Kajte was doing the photocopying for the dig, work rotas and stuff. I think she photocopied the leaflets that were left on the wire, and I checked the websites she was using. She was looking up PETA slogans and campaigns.'

Annette stopped in her tracks, her expression horrified and her voice suddenly shrill. 'You searched her private computer?'

'No, I looked at the public computer she used in the tourist centre,' said Bruno equably. 'She hadn't cleared the cache. No privacy was breached, and the computer is owned by St Denis, so I have every right to consult it.'

Annette nodded, but still looked troubled. Then she looked at him challengingly. 'But if you have a case against some-body, why give them a warning like that? It's not as though you share their sympathies about animal rights. And I should let you know that I do, and if there are any cases of wanton cruelty to animals, there are statutes against it that I would want to enforce.'

They were walking side by side, amiably enough, although there was a sharper tone in her voice. But she seemed ready to listen. Bruno was reminded of times in the army when a new officer had come to take over the squad. It was always Bruno's job as sergeant to educate him, buff away the officer-school polish and teach him how to make forty tough young soldiers obey their orders cheerfully. He wondered if Annette would be amenable to some gentle coaching, after making such a disastrous entry into St Denis. He'd have to try. Nobody would benefit from a constant tension between town and magistrate.

'I want to stop it now before it gets any worse,' he said. 'You must have seen angry farmers on TV, dumping cart-loads of manure on the steps of a Mairie, blocking roads with tractors, throwing bureaucrats into the river. That's what could happen here unless we can defuse the situa-tion. It would hurt the museum and mean trouble for my friend Horst, a German Professor who runs the dig.'

'He wasn't there today?'

'No, he's giving a public lecture at the museum tonight, so he was probably preparing that. I'm looking forward to it. He's a good speaker, he's passionate about prehistory, and I've been getting some hints that he has something big to say. If you have nothing better to do, you might want to come along and listen, meet some of my friends and start to understand what's so special about this valley.'

CHAPTER SIX

Bruno recognised the image on the giant screen, the deep
pit he had seen that morning at Horst's dig, the flat stone
with the strange cup-shaped depressions and the smoothness of bone. A small ruler, in red and white with grada-
tions for each ten centimetres, lay alongside what Bruno
could now identify as a human femur. The red spot of Horst's
laser pointer picked out the details he chose to highlight
on the enlarged photograph as he spoke from the podium.

'A new prehistoric burial site in this region is always a
remarkable discovery, and this one with its two adults and
child may be very special indeed.'

The auditorium at the new National Museum was filled,
with some of Horst's students standing at the back and
more listening to his lecture through a loudspeaker in the
hall. Bruno counted well over a hundred seats, another score
or so against the walls, and with the overflow there must
have been two hundred people in attendance, the largest
audience Bruno could remember. Nor did he recall ever
seeing TV cameras at the back of the hall before, and for
once Philippe Delaron from the local *Sud-Ouest* newspaper
was not the only reporter present. Bruno sat between Pamela

and Fabiola, with his tennis partner the Baron next in row and Annette the new magistrate beside him. She had changed into jeans and a white silk shirt that looked expensive. Pamela was wearing a light green sweater that Bruno guessed was cashmere. It set off the hints of red in her bronze hair.

The skeletons, Horst was saying, were around thirty-three thousand years old. That meant they came from the pivotal period when the Neanderthal humans were being replaced by the Cro-Magnons, modern mankind. Horst paused, and then stepped out from behind the podium towards the front of the stage, face suddenly illuminated by the light from the projector, his shadow falling thick and long on the screen behind him. It was a deliberately theatrical move. His eyes must have been blinded by the projector light, but he swivelled his head slowly as if to look at each part of the audience before he spoke again.

'This is the great mystery of modern man. How did our ancestors live and prevail while the Neanderthals disappeared? Was it war or disease that wiped them out?' Horst paused again, and raised his arms and slowly let them fall, as if in bafflement. 'Or perhaps it was simply evolution, or maybe the inability of the dwindling Neanderthal gene pool to adjust to rapid and repeated changes in climate. Perhaps they could not compete for limited food supplies. Each of these theories has been proposed.'

Horst paused again, his delivery given gravity by the way the light of the projector, playing on his white beard and casting stark shadows on his cheekbones, gave him something of the look of an Old Testament prophet. He stroked his beard thoughtfully before lowering his voice to speak in almost conversational tones.

'But we do know that almost every creation myth in human culture keeps alive the terrible and haunting possibility that our ancestors prevailed though deliberate violence, that they destroyed their competitors. It is indeed possible that modern humankind was born through an act of genocide. Some scholars have suggested this might be the real original sin.'

Bruno found himself sitting forward, almost on the edge of his chair, unexpectedly captivated by Horst's narrative. This was not like the other talks by Horst that Bruno had attended, one on cave art and the other on the diet of the people who had produced it. They had been interesting but somehow passionless, as if Horst were playing the role of scholar. Now, however restrained his delivery, Horst seemed to be afire.

Behind Horst on the screen the image appeared, side by side, of two early humans. One was squat and hairy, with a thrusting forehead, a barrel chest and long arms. This was the image of the Neanderthal, of the brutal caveman that Bruno recalled from schoolbooks. The other was taller, slimmer, with a narrow skull and features that were somehow more familiar as a human, despite the clothes of fur. Bruno felt a sudden chill, thinking of other contrasting images he recalled from his school days, the way Nazi propaganda had depicted Jews as alien and thuggish creatures, to make the contrast with the Aryan as some human ideal.

Was it so easy to indoctrinate through images, he wondered, or was Horst right to suggest some human archetype at work from thousands of years ago?

'Almost wherever we look in the human past, we find the two great narratives of our origins, of a gigantic flood, and of a fratricidal killing or a civil war,' Horst went on. 'Amid all the mystery that still shrouds the birth of humanity, those two myths stand out in the folk memory of people after people, tribe after tribe, culture after culture. But now, we have a scientific revolution. We have forensic genetics and the ability to read DNA from bones.'

Horst explained the latest genetic evidence that the Neanderthals did not disappear entirely. Some Neanderthals shared the type O blood group of so many modern humans, and all shared the FOXP2 gene, which is what gives speech and language. So there must have been inbreeding. He spoke of the collection of Neanderthal DNA from the El Sidrón cave in Spain where a dozen Neanderthals died some 49,000 years ago. Cut marks on their bones suggesting they had been butchered with stone tools.

Horst paused, clicked his remote, and the photograph of the dig that Bruno had seen that morning reappeared on the screen.

'And some of what we are about to learn will come from these three bodies at the burial site outside St Denis that I am describing in public for the first time this evening,' Horst said. 'And it is at this point that we enter the field of speculation, and probably of controversy.'

Bruno narrowed his eyes to concentrate as Horst explained

the orthodox theory that Neanderthals and modern humans shared a common ancestor some four hundred thousand years ago, after one of the great migrations from Africa. A minority of experts thought there might also have been some limited interbreeding about a hundred thousand years ago. There was an alternative theory, called hybridisation, that Neanderthals and their successors lived together and interbred and shared their skills and their culture as recently as thirty thousand years ago.

There were three kinds of evidence for this, Horst explained. The first was fossil evidence, at sites such as Arcy-sur-Cure, where Neanderthal bones were found along-side tools and cultural signifiers and personal ornaments usually associated with their successors. That suggested trade and interaction between the two groups. The second evidence was genetic from the FOXP2 gene, which should have produced many more mutations had it come from a common ancestor as distant as 400,000 years ago. Finally there was archaeological evidence from the Lagar Velho cave in Portugal, discovered in 1998, which contained the bones of a four-year-old child – the first complete Palaeolithic skeleton ever unearthed in Iberia. Horst cited leading scientists who judged that the child's anatomy could only have resulted from a mixed ancestry of Neanderthal and early modern human.

'But more evidence is required to turn this hypothesis into something closer to historical fact,' Horst said. 'We may now have further important evidence of this kind from St Denis.' He clicked his remote to display a photograph of the pit that Bruno recognised, but this time with the covering flat stone removed from the three bodies. Suddenly revealed, the two adult skeletons lay side by side, each body bent in almost foetal position. They were tucked into one another like three spoons, Bruno thought. The largest adult, presumably the father, lay to the right, and then his mate and then the bones of the child.

'Preliminary anatomical studies,' Horst said, raising his voice above the gasps that came from the audience, 'and now confirmed by leading scientists here in France, in Germany and in the United States, suggest that St Denis may have preserved for us through the millennia something extraordinary. We may have here the first modern family, a Neanderthal male, his Cro-Magnon mate and their child ...'

His words were drowned out by bursts of applause and cheers from the back of the hall, where Horst's students gathered. As the implications of Horst's remarks began to sink in, Bruno noticed Clothilde, seated to the side of the stage, rise to her feet and join the applause. Bruno rose from his chair, and with profound thoughts of the origins of mankind mixing with prosaic assessments of the impact on the local tourist trade, he began to clap his hands. A thunderous applause came from Jan, a Dane who had settled nearby and become the local blacksmith, his big hands and massive shoulders producing a level of volume that drove everyone else to their feet. Bruno felt rather than saw Pamela and Fabiola rise beside him, and then it seemed everyone in the hall was standing to applaud, their eyes shining and fixed on Horst, who stood now silent before them, his gaze fixed on some distant place or time. The entire hall seemed energised, as if all present were aware that they were sharing a historic moment.

'And to think I nearly didn't come this evening,' Pamela was saying as the applause died away and people began to sit down again. 'What a remarkable discovery.'

'It makes you wonder what else is lying out there under the earth, waiting to be found,' Bruno replied, musing on the irony of the new corpse at this ancient site. It made for a crowded grave.

'Spoken like a true policeman,' said Pamela, amusement in her voice.

'Perhaps, but I was thinking more of the price we might pay for ignorance if some things are never found. I was trying to remember what I was taught in school about the Neanderthals, savage brutes, speaking in grunts like apes. Did you have lessons like that?'

'I think we all did. But I also remember seeing a photo of a flint tool in some textbook that was shaped like a perfect leaf, and how it struck me as beautiful. I made a drawing of it and kept it in my purse for years. I think I still have it somewhere. For a while, I wanted to be an archaeologist, and I have that same feeling again now.'

She glanced at him, and their eyes met. Bruno felt a surge of affection for her, seeing suddenly in her enthusiasm the little girl who found beauty in a flint that had been shaped and made many millennia ago. He reached down and squeezed her hand as Horst spoke again.

'Let me end with a warning. These are preliminary and hesitant conclusions, or rather suggestions,' Horst said. 'There is more research to be done, and however well we think we understand the differences in bone structure, we can still be mistaken in our identifications. And like all scientists, I am human and can be carried away by emotion, by the yearning to see something that may not truly be there. So I leave you with this image of a family, a long-dead man and woman and their child. We do not know how they died, or who buried them, or who made the ornaments of shells that we think we have found around the woman's neck. We know only that at one time they lived, that perhaps they loved, and that some other humans cared enough about them to bury this family with respect and ritual. And that, if nothing else, connects us to them across the generations as human beings. I know that I speak for all my colleagues on this dig when I say that we share that respect for these people, along with a deep gratitude for what they can tell us from this grave they have shared for so long.'

He bowed and walked off to the side of stage, where Clothilde embraced him before he was swallowed in a knot of journalists and students and a fusillade of camera flashes. Bruno could see Teddy's head towering above the rest of the admirers. Jan, one of Horst's closest friends, used his great strength to keep some space for him in the throng. Having seen Jan take on and defeat all comers at arm-wrestling in the annual St Denis fair, to raise money for the local infants' school where his wife used to teach, Bruno was glad to be out of his reach. As the hall lights came back up, people began to rise from their seats and shuffle along their rows, some animated and talking among themselves about the lecture, others deep in private thought. From the far side of the hall his hunting partner Stéphane, his head bowed as he listened to his daughter Dominique chattering into his ear, waved a salute. Bruno waved back, surprised to see the big farmer at such an event. Dominique must have brought him along, proud to show off the fruits of her time at the dig.

In the front row, Bruno's own Mayor, Gérard Mangin, was beaming in delight as he chatted with his counterpart from Les Eyzies, home to the museum. Bruno could imagine the mental calculations that his Mayor would be making about tourism and tax revenues, the need for a car park and visitors' centre and the prospect of new jobs. Bruno had already checked the *cadastre*, the map that showed every property in the commune of St Denis, and knew that the site of the dig was part of an abandoned farm on which no taxes had been paid for years, which meant that ownership had reverted to the commune.

'That's the place where Bruno took me today,' he heard Annette telling Pamela and the Baron. 'The place where the much newer body was found.' She turned to Bruno. 'I wish you'd told me. We could at least have peeked in and had an advance look at the skeletons.'

'I had to trek out there to see the body and Bruno didn't tell me either,' said Fabiola.

'Because I didn't know,' Bruno protested. 'Horst and

Clothilde were very cagey about it when I looked into the pit this morning, and all I could see were some bones. They dropped some hints that it was a big discovery but that was all. I think they wanted to make an impact with the lecture.'

'They certainly achieved that,' said the Baron. 'You saw the TV camera?' He looked at his watch. 'But it's time for dinner. Bruno, you were making some arrangement?'

'I booked us a table at the Moulin,' Bruno said. 'We have to stay in Les Eyzies because Horst and Clothilde will be joining us for coffee, after they go off for a celebration pizza with their students. And Horst asked us to save an extra seat for his friend Jan, that Danish guy who's the black-smith in St Chamassy.'

'He's sweet,' said Pamela, turning to Fabiola as they all waited in the crowd at the exit. 'He made those candle-sticks you admired, the ones in the dining room.'

'I'm so glad I came,' he heard Annette telling the others as they emerged into the expanse of the entrance hall with its time lines on the wall of the stages of human develop-ment from six hundred thousand years ago to the present.

'I wonder if Horst takes any volunteers on his digs,' Pamela said. 'I'd love to be more involved in this, but I suppose he only wants archaeology students who have some training.'

'Well, you can ask Horst when he turns up after his pizza. You'll never find him in a better mood.'

'I'm in a good mood, too,' she said, turning her head to kiss his cheek and then nestling into his shoulder, their steps keeping time. 'So I hope we don't stay too long here tonight. I want to get you home.'

'It must be spring,' said Bruno, smiling.

'Play your cards right and you'll think it's Christmas,' she whispered, and then he felt her lips brush tantalisingly against his.

CHAPTER SEVEN

As the chestnut woods began to thin and the early morning sun suddenly appeared over the far slope, Pamela tapped her horse's sides with her heels. The stately trot became a canter and she whooped aloud with the joy of it. Bruno grinned widely as flecks of mud spattered him from her horse's hoofs and he felt the smooth stretching of his own horse as they kept pace and broke into the open field. A startled hare bounded back for the cover of the woods, rabbits took to their burrows and a great cloud of birds rose from their morning feast of worms and took, complaining loudly, to the sky.

They cantered on up the slope to the sunlit ridge. As they topped the rise, the wide plateau lying magnificent and green before them, Bruno saw Pamela lean forward over Bess's neck, urging her into a gallop. Bruno felt the tautening of great equine muscles beneath him as Victoria gathered her strength to follow. His mare moved easily into the new rhythm, her neck reaching out and her nostrils wide, as if eager to butt aside the clods of earth that were being kicked up by the horse ahead. Bruno sat forward, giving her free rein. He lowered his own body to urge her on and felt the rush of wind in his ears and the tattoo of hoof-beats. Movement by car or bike or any machine was slow and lifeless compared to this.

Pamela reined in and slowed Bess to a trot and then a walk as the plateau began to fall away into the valley of the river Vézère below them, the distant red rooftops and the church spire of St Denis nestling into the great bend of the stream. Victoria slowed of her own accord, whinnied softly and then edged up to stand beside Bess. Bruno gazed down on the gentle valley and the town below. The sun's rays gleamed gold on the cockerel atop the war memorial. They breathed warmth into the honey-coloured stone of the buildings. The eddies of the river danced in the sunlight as they rippled beneath the arches of the bridge that dated from Napoleon's rule.

He could never leave this place, Bruno thought. St Denis owned him now, the only place he had ever thought of as home after his years of travels with the army. Seeing it now from horseback had opened fresh perspectives and a new sense of the terrain that he had previously known only in his van and on foot as a hunter. He felt a rush of gratitude to Pamela for teaching him to ride, knowing him well enough to be sure that he'd take to it and enjoy the strange, beguiling intimacy across species that connects a horse and rider. She was a fine woman, he mused, handsome and spirited and sure of herself and the life she wanted to lead.

Pamela had made it clear that she wanted neither husband nor children, nor even a lover who would share her home. He was her friend for life, she had said one night soon after their affair had begun, but he should know that she saw him as a guest in her home and in her bed. The invitation was hers to bestow. And while Bruno was as jealous as she of his own privacy and equally devoted to the familiar comforts of his own home, he felt puzzled by Pamela. His previous love affairs had been consuming and over-whelming, like diving into a rushing river and being carried headlong with little thought for course or destination. With Pamela, he felt that he took his place amid her horses and her *gîtes* and her morning ritual with the BBC World Service and her English magazines and all the other furniture of her life. It was all very pleasant and sometimes marvellous, but not what he thought of as love.

'You're riding well,' she said, her breathing back to normal after the gallop. 'I don't think there's much more to teach you, not unless you want to start jumping fences.'

'You're a great teacher. Six months ago, I couldn't ride at all,' he said. 'A great way to start the day.'

'After a wonderful night,' she said, smiling in that private way of hers that had so confused him in the early days of their affair. He could never tell whether the smile was for herself or whether he was included. She reached out to put her hand on his thigh. 'I feel I'm glowing with energy.'

He took her hand. 'I'm going to need all the energy I can get today. There's that foie gras problem I mentioned, plus a security meeting over some big minister's visit that's coming up, and the Mayor and council want to pay a visit to Horst's dig. And there'll be journalists arriving, catching up on the story they missed at last night's lecture. They'll

want to visit the site, which means organising the parking
and telling Horst to set up barriers so they don't all fall
into the trenches.'

'Can't you get the Gendarmes to do that?'

'Yes, but knowing Capitaine Duroc, he'll probably set up
speed traps to nab the reporters.'

Pamela squeezed his hand but her eyes were serious. 'In
this blizzard of information I can't tell whether you're trying
to tell me something or hiding something.'

'I'm not hiding anything, but after tomorrow those security meetings will be taking place twice daily,' he said. 'And
it seems that they'll include Isabelle.'

Pamela's face went very still, and then she removed her
hand and turned to pat her horse's neck. 'I thought Isabelle
was still convalescing,' she said quietly.

Her horse picked up a step and moved ahead of Bruno
so he could no longer see her face. He remembered her
outburst of anger at the children's Christmas party when
some busybody had told her of seeing Bruno and Isabelle
together at a hotel in Bordeaux. It had been an innocent
meeting, but that flash of jealousy made Bruno wonder
whether Pamela herself was at ease with the controlled inti-
macies of their own affair.

'She was supposed to have six months' leave to recover,
but she got bored doing nothing,' said Bruno, talking to
Pamela's back. 'I'm told she's now walking with a cane and
is coming down to do something about communications
and security. It's her minister who's running the meeting.'

'What brings the Minister of the Interior to St Denis?'

Bruno shrugged, then realised Pamela couldn't see the gesture. 'Some meeting with a foreign colleague and a photo-op,' he said, raising his voice so it would carry.

'A foreign colleague?' Her voice was mocking. 'So St Denis joins the ranks of international conference centres?' She was sitting very upright in the saddle, her back stiff. 'Two meetings a day. I suppose she'll try to lure you to Paris again. Isabelle has always impressed me as the kind of woman who gets what she wants.'

Carlos the Spaniard was sitting on the uncomfortable chair outside Bruno's office and filling in the blank numbers in *Sud-Ouest*'s Sudoku game when Bruno arrived. He looked up and caught Bruno glancing at his watch. It was two minutes short of eight.

'Give me a moment,' Carlos said. 'I'm almost done.' He scribbled another number as Bruno went into his small office, put his hat on the table, turned on his computer and sat in his revolving chair. It gave the usual, almost welcoming squeak. He rang Claire, the Mayor's secretary, and asked for two coffees for a special guest and then tapped in his username and password and began dealing with the accumulated email. Most were routine but two made him pause.

They both came from Isabelle. The first was a formal note from her ministry email address, attaching a list of 'families of interest.' Bruno scanned it, found no surprises and sent it to his printer. The second came from her private Hotmail address.

'It's good to know we'll be working together again. Still a lot of convalescing to do, but the doctors are pleased with me. More important, my karate teacher says I'll be back to normal by midsummer. Isabelle xx.'

Bruno pondered his reply, trying to catch the same tone that she had used, of friendly colleagues rather than old lovers. He wasn't satisfied with his reply, but as Carlos pushed open the door, he hit the 'Send' button anyway. 'Happy to hear you're recovering and fit enough to be back at work. *La République* can breathe easily again. Always a welcome for you in St D. See you soon, Bruno xx.'

Carlos held up the front page of *Sud-Ouest* with the photo of Horst's first modern family. There was a smaller photo of Horst, and the headline made Bruno smile – 'First Family Found in St Denis'.

'What did you think of the lecture?' he asked.

'I can't stop thinking about it and what Horst was saying about murder as the first act of modern man, the original sin,' Bruno said. 'It makes me wonder who was the first policeman.'

Carlos pulled two sheets of paper from his inside pocket and laid them on Bruno's desk.

'Families of Spanish origin in this region who may be of interest,' he said. 'Your records may be better than ours.'

Bruno handed him the printout from Isabelle's attachment. 'Most of the names are the same. We have a couple more, but none that rings my alarm bell.'

'What about this old corpse you found? No possible connection to our business?'

Bruno shrugged. 'I'll save you a copy of the forensic report, if you like. I should get something today.'

'This other matter, the animal rights militants. Can we check them out? In my experience, being a radical in one thing makes it more likely to be a radical in another.'

'I can give you a full list of all the students, names, addresses, passport numbers. I was going to ask the Brigadier to check them out with the various home countries but you can probably do that.' He turned to the computer, clicked open Clothilde's email to him of yesterday and printed out two copies of the attachment.

'Email it to me at this address,' Carlos said, handing across a business card that bore simply the arms of Spain, his name, an email address and phone number. 'Then I can forward it direct. It will be faster. But I'd like to take a look at the archaeological site, if that's possible. It's mainly for my own interest but I'd like to be able to report that I'd checked the site of the grave, if this dead man turns out to be interesting. And I'd like to take you to lunch, but perhaps you have other plans.'

'We have the security meeting at the château this evening,' Bruno said. 'I also want to go and have a quiet talk with the old man who did this job for thirty years before me. He knows everybody, so I was going to ask him about Basques, as well as the mysterious corpse. You're welcome to come along, but be careful of any wine he offers you. His red *pinard* is terrible, but his *vin de noix* is worth the detour.'

Carlos smiled. 'Thanks for the tip. I suppose we all have friends like that.'

'I've got one question for you,' Bruno said, leaning back. His chair squeaked again. 'How serious is the security threat? I realise this meeting makes an inviting target, but ETA has been on the defensive for years. You must have some idea of what resources and capabilities ETA still has.'

'We know they used the ceasefire to rebuild some of their networks,' Carlos said. 'And we know they have now determined France to be an enemy state and a legitimate target. We think they have two, perhaps three active service teams available, at least one in southern France. We've already passed on everything in our files to your Minister of the Interior, including what few photos and records we have on the members, and I'll be providing daily updates.'

Bruno nodded and rose. 'I'm going to the site of the dig, if you'd like to come.'

The Spaniard pointed to his computer and said he'd work on his emails. As Bruno trotted down the stairs to his van, his cellphone rang. Bruno looked at the screen, and saw the name of Maurice, a friend from the hunting club. He clicked the green button to take the call.

'Bruno, it's Maurice. You'd better get here quick. I'm in trouble. I think I've shot somebody.'

CHAPTER EIGHT

Maurice Soulier's farm was on the lowest slope of the hillside below Coumont. On the flat land that stretched down to the busy stream that joined the Vézère near St Denis he kept the ducks that he fattened by hand in the old-fashioned way. Lacking a permit to slaughter them, he had the ducks collected twice a week by a cousin who was a local butcher. He paid Maurice a fair price for the foie but kept all the money from selling the meat and carcasses. Of course, the entire hunting club and their extended families bought Maurice's foie gras and his *magrets* and the *confits* made by his wife Sophie. This meant that Maurice was still killing a couple of dozen ducks a week with his grandfather's axe on the old stump in the barnyard, and Bruno was not the only citizen of St Denis who slept under a magnificent eiderdown made by Sophie from duck feathers. So it was with considerable alarm that Bruno pulled into the farmyard to find Sophie weeping in the kitchen and Maurice trying to comfort her.

Bruno sized up the situation, went to the familiar cupboard in the corner opposite the stove, removed the bottle of cognac that Maurice kept to fill his flask before each hunt, and poured a glass for each of them. They drank, and then husband and wife began to speak at once.

'One at a time.' Bruno held up a hand. 'Maurice, you first – tell me what happened.'

Maurice explained that it was about 5 a.m. and he was asleep when the dog started barking in the yard. He went downstairs and saw nothing but then heard a noise over by the barn where he kept the car. Then the ducks started making a racket. Maurice thought they must have been startled by a fox, so he grabbed the shotgun and went towards the duck barn. He heard glass breaking in one of the cold frames he used to plant early seeds. He had shouted and heard another frame break. When he turned the corner he saw something moving low down by the fence and was sure it was a fox, so he fired. He heard a scream and someone shouting in a foreign language and the sound of running. That was all.

'Tell him about the blood,' said Sophie, hiccuping now rather than sobbing.

'I looked around and saw the fence had been partly cut through, so I patched that with some twine. Then I went to see if Sophie was all right because she'd been woken by the shot. I saw to the ducks and took the dog out to see what was what. He stood barking just where I'd patched the fence, but it wasn't until after dawn that we came out to look and then we saw the blood.'

'I said we should call you,' Sophie interrupted. 'But he's a stubborn old devil and he said you wouldn't be in the office until after eight and it wasn't fair to call before then.'

Bruno rubbed his jaw and pondered. It was a strange time for a shot to be fired, and somebody might have reported it, or gone to a hospital where a doctor might already have called the Gendarmes.

'I'm going to take a statement right now, get your version down. It's important to say that you really believed it was a fox and only later thought it might be a human attacker. Give me some writing paper.'

'We had that fox dig his way in last December, you remember,' said Sophie, getting up to pull a writing pad from a drawer. She seemed calmer with something to do. 'No wonder that's what he thought. But then I remembered what happened to the Villattes and thought about those animal cruelty people. Do you think it was one of them he shot, Bruno?'

'Right now, we don't know what was shot. Please can you make us some coffee, Sophie, while I take Maurice's statement?'

Bruno led Maurice carefully through the statement, suggesting phrases and sentences and putting the best possible face on Maurice's account that after the previous fox invasion, he had fired at what he thought was another fox to protect his livelihood. Then he had heard what might have been human voices, but he could not be sure because the sounds were in no language he could understand. It was only when it was light enough to see the bloodstains that he had called the Chef de Police, who was taking his statement.

Bruno drank his coffee and got Sophie to make a brief

corroborating statement before he went outside to look at the patched fence and the blood.

'Just one thing,' he said, standing at the door. 'Whoever else comes here, whether it's Gendarmes or a magistrate or the President of the Republic, say nothing. You've made a sworn statement to me. I'll get it registered and that's all you have to say. If anyone makes threats about charging you, say you insist on your right to a legal adviser and ask them to send for me.'

Sophie looked even more frightened, but Maurice nodded and led the way to the rear of the old barn where the vegetable garden was protected by a wire fence. Just inside the fence was Maurice's row of cold frames, two of them broken, and Maurice's careful watering the previous evening had preserved a very clear footprint of what looked to Bruno like a small training shoe. He went to his van, pulled out a roll of yellow police tape and fastened it around and across the cold frame, then covered the useful footprint with one of Sophie's plastic bags. The small patch of blood was beside the cold frame. As he bent to examine it, he saw a couple of what could have been wormholes in the wood of the barn. But the holes were fresh, so he guessed they must be pellets from Maurice's shotgun. They were below waist height. That would support Maurice's claim that he thought he was shooting at a fox.

'What kind of shell were you using?'

'Just birdshot. It was what was in the drawer when I fetched the gun.'

'Can you show me where you were standing at the moment you fired?'

'About here, I reckon. I'd just turned the corner,' Maurice replied, from the angle of the old barn that he used as a garage. Bruno paced out the distance, taking thirty-six long steps. He sighed in relief. At that range, the birdshot would have spread. Then he went back to the cold frame.

There wasn't much blood, a small patch roughly ten centimetres across. It was maybe ten metres from the woods. At the spot where the vegetation was trampled down he found some more blood on the crushed leaves. The trail continued through the woods towards the track that led up the hill to Coumont. Attached to the thorns of a bramble bush he found a crumpled copy of the leaflet he had first seen at the Villatte farm. Using his handkerchief, he removed it from the bush and noting some smears of dried blood on the paper, he placed it carefully inside a plastic bag. On a small pile of dead leaves nearby he found two more smears of blood. He tied his handkerchief to a twig to mark the spot, and then called Maurice to examine them.

'If that was a deer, what would you say?' he asked Maurice.

'I'd say it wasn't badly hurt, maybe a flank shot.'

Bruno nodded. 'So put your mind at rest. You haven't killed anybody. It was an accident and you can't even be sure it was human.'

Maurice nodded dully, and Bruno saw that he was feeling too guilty to be reassured.

'I'll have to take the gun, they may need to run tests,' Bruno said, thinking that even at a range of over thirty metres birdshot could do a lot of damage. 'I'll borrow your hunting permit, make a copy and get it back to you. Don't worry, Maurice, the gun's legal, your permit's in order and you very reasonably believed you were shooting at a fox to protect your property.'

'What about those cuts in the fence?' Maurice asked, his voice quavering. He suddenly looked very old.

'Nothing about them in the statement. I'll add a note to say we just found them and patched them now.'

'I don't like this, Bruno. It feels like deception.'

'Trust me, Maurice. This could turn out badly unless you do what I say and never utter a word that's not in your statement. And make sure Sophie does the same.'

Back at the house, Bruno asked Sophie to write out a copy of both statements. He and Maurice went out and put a saucepan over the patch of blood to protect it for the likely forensic tests. Back inside, Bruno signed and dated the statement copies. Then he called the medical centre and asked for Fabiola.

'Anybody been brought in with gunshot wounds?'

'No, and I was on night call for the whole district, so I'd have heard. Why, should I expect somebody?'

'Looks like some animal rights people got up to their tricks last night and the farmer thought they were a fox. There's a small bloodstain, about the size of a saucer.'

'Doesn't sound too bad. I'll keep my ears open. You might want to try the pharmacies, see if anybody's buying bandages.'

'Bandages and tweezers – they're probably trying to pull out birdshot pellets right now.'

'Some girls carry tweezers to pluck their eyebrows. Stick

with the bandages and surgical gauze. And maybe bleach or something, to get the bloodstains out of clothes.'

Bruno scribbled down *Pharmacie* in his notebook, then added the names of the Baron, J-J, Jules, the Mayor and Hervé, the insurance broker. He was that year's President of the hunting club, which paid an annual insurance premium in case its members needed legal assistance. J-J could recommend a good lawyer, which Maurice would probably need.

The first call was to the Baron, to come and sit with Maurice and Sophie and be prepared to stand up to the Gendarmes and to Annette the magistrate, if they turned up while Bruno was elsewhere. J-J reported that the case did not sound too serious to him, if nobody had reported being hurt, and gave Bruno the name of a reliable lawyer in Périgueux. In any event, the incident had now been officially reported to the Police Nationale, which meant that the Gendarmes would not have jurisdiction. Nonetheless, Bruno called Sergeant Jules on his personal number, who told him to bring in Maurice's shotgun for safe keeping, and he promised to warn Capitaine Duroc that the Police Nationale has taken over the case. He rang the Mayor and gave him the details, and finally told Hervé, who confirmed that the club's insurance was both up to date and well funded.

The Baron arrived in his veteran Citroën DS, greeted them all and proceeded to distribute more cognac, on the inventive principle that anything Maurice might say thereafter could be dismissed as the ramblings of someone who had taken a little too much alcohol for the shock.

Bruno took the shotgun to Sergeant Jules at the Gendarmerie, and then went to the general office in the Mairie to make more copies of Maurice's statement. He faxed them to J-J and Hervé, and to the general number at the magistrates' office in Sarlat, with a covering note addressed to Annette. That gave Bruno an idea. Rather than call the lawyer in Périgueux, he went into his own office to track down a number for Louis Pouillon, Annette's predecessor, now retired.

As a devoted hunter and an occasional customer of Sophie's foie gras, the old chief magistrate was delighted to take the case. He assured Bruno he would be at Maurice's house within the hour. Bruno read aloud to him Maurice's statement, and it was pronounced 'most helpful'. The problem would be, the former magistrate noted, if someone reported having been shot. Bruno replied that he was making inquiries.

He phoned both of the pharmacies in St Denis, and drew a blank each time. Where else would students, relative strangers to the area, know to find a pharmacy? The one other town they knew was Les Eyzies, where the museum was located. Bruno called the pharmacy there, and was told that a tall young foreigner had been waiting at their door when they opened. He'd bought bandages, antiseptic wipes, surgical gauze and sticking plaster, and had paid with a credit card. They gave Bruno the name and number; issued by a British bank, Barclays. Its owner was Edward G. Lloyd.

CHAPTER NINE

By the time Bruno arrived at the site, Clothilde had installed a security guard from the museum, roped off a field for parking, and announced a thirty-minute photo-opportunity followed by a press briefing back at the museum. He was impressed. She was standing by the site entrance where the cellphone reception was better, talking fiercely into her mobile and dressed in another shirt that he remembered seeing on Horst. She'd been wearing a skirt the previous evening and was in khaki slacks now and working boots. Bruno found himself hoping she'd spent the night with Horst; he deserved it, after the triumph of the lecture. And so, perhaps, did she.

'Congratulations,' he said, as she slammed the phone shut and swore, looking round crossly at the site, where the students were all at work. Then she noticed him.

'Oh, Bruno, those bastards at the Ministry!' she said, giving him a resounding kiss on each cheek. 'They demand to know who authorised me to lend the name of the National Museum to such a publicity-grabbing hypothesis. I told them it was the same people who gave me my doctorate and elected me to my chair and if they gave me any more shit

I'd take up Yale's offer of a professorship and triple my salary. That shut them up.'

'You've taken care of everything: parking, security, photo-op and press conference,' said Bruno. 'You've done my job for me, as well as being part of the biggest breakthrough in history. And you look wonderful.'

'Thank you, *mon cher*. I just did the things you said needed doing, while fending off those idiots in Paris and half the archaeologists in Europe. And who is this?' she asked, as Carlos came up the path, after parking his rented Range Rover behind Bruno's van.

Bruno introduced them briefly, describing Carlos simply as a Spanish colleague on liaison duties, and pointed Carlos towards the empty grave, still circled with yellow police tape.

'I was most impressed by the lecture yesterday,' Carlos said. 'It seems you have a historic discovery here.'

'We hope so, thank you,' she said. Her phone rang again. She looked at the screen and ignored it. 'Those idiots at the Culture Ministry again,' she said, fishing her car keys from her bag. 'I have to get back to the museum.' She waved a vague farewell.

Bruno led Carlos toward the fluttering yellow tape, but first he wanted to look at the pit where the three prehistoric bodies lay. Bruno recognised the Polish student, Kasimir, working on a subsidiary trench off to one side and nodded a greeting. Carlos gazed down into the deep hole, where the three skeletons were now covered in a sheet of thick plastic. Two students were at work with brushes on one of the walls. Carlos looked up at the overhanging cliff and off to each side, as if trying to imagine how the place might have been, thirty thousand years ago.

'It might be an idea for the two ministers to come here, after the signing,' he said. 'France and Spain, Lascaux and Altamira, the two great centres of prehistoric art, coming together again at the place where modern man emerges, maybe even a joint visitors' centre. It could be an interesting initiative.'

'You sound more like a publicity man than a security expert,' Bruno said, making a joke of it. 'It would double the security problem.'

'It's the kind of things that ministers like,' Carlos said. 'It makes them seem like more than just politicians; a touch of history, a reference to art. You've seen the papers. This is big news, and I think they might be wondering how to get some of that attention for themselves.'

Bruno nodded; he could see that. He looked around at the site. Some police on the cliff above, with a security cordon down at the road, would probably suffice to secure the place. The cliffs themselves were part of the protection. And here at the site of the pit, they were even protected from the cliffs on the far side of the river. It would be an extraordinary sniper who could hit something from that far away.

Carlos moved on to the trench where Teddy had found the body. There was nothing to see, but Teddy rose from his search for the midden, stretching his back. There was no stiffness in his movements, no bulge of bandages under

his jeans. He had gone to the pharmacy on behalf of somebody else.

'I'm looking forward to the rugby to get my muscles
stretched,' Teddy said, and then paused, looking at Carlos.

'Hi, we haven't met,' Carlos said, stepping forward to
shake Teddy's hand. 'My name's Carlos, on a liaison mission
from Spain. Bruno is kindly showing me round.'

'From Spain?' said Teddy, looking mystified.

'Where's Kajte?' asked Bruno.

'Back at the camp. She's on cooking rota today.' His voice
was normal, but there was something wary in his eyes.

'Why are you digging so far away from the others?' Carlos
asked.

'I'm looking for the midden. Most settlements have them,
if people lived there for any length of time.' He shrugged.
'I'm beginning to think I may be wasting my time.'

'I don't think anyone at this site is wasting their time,
not after last night's lecture,' said Carlos. 'Have you found
anything at all?'

'Other than the body of the murdered man, nothing I'd
call significant, just some shards of modern pottery and
half an old clay pipe. A few recent bones, the usual stuff
you tend to find in a field.'

'What's that black strip in the earth, down by your knee?'
Carlos asked.

'Probably a forest fire, but it's a bit thick for that. It could
have been people making charcoal. I found some charcoal
shards.'

Bruno had had enough. 'I'm afraid it's not archaeology

that brings me here. Where were you in the early hours of this morning, at about 5 a.m.?'

'Asleep at the campsite,' Teddy replied.

'And Kajte?'

'She was asleep beside me.'

'I'm now questioning you formally, Teddy. Think about your answer because if you lie to me, I can arrest you. Where were you at eight o'clock this morning?'

'Going for a walk. We'd just had breakfast, all together, and I walked here.'

'Have you got your credit card with you?' Bruno pressed. 'Are you sure it hasn't been stolen?'

The young man took out his wallet, removed a credit card and held it up. It had been issued by Barclays.

'That card was used this morning to buy bandages and medical supplies at a pharmacy in Les Eyzies,' Bruno said. 'Roughly three hours earlier some intruders at a local duck farm were shot at by a farmer. I found blood at the scene and I'm pretty sure we'll identify it as coming from your friend Kajte, just as I'm sure we'll find the bandages you bought wrapped around her legs. Do you still want to lie to me?'

His eyes fixed on Bruno, Teddy's mouth hung open. He swallowed hard, his hand tightened on the handle of his spade, then his eyes darted from side to side as if thinking of escape.

'I think this young man needs a lawyer,' Carlos said.

'He needs to answer my questions and tell the truth,' Bruno snapped, keeping his eyes on the young Welshman.

'Come on, Teddy. Kajte may be more badly hurt than you know. We ought to get her to the medical centre.'

Teddy looked, almost desperately, at Carlos once more, as if in appeal. But Carlos remained silent. Teddy's head then slumped in defeat and he nodded, swallowed again and seemed about to speak when there was the sound of a police siren in the distance.

'It looks like you'll either speak to me or the Gendarmes, and they'll ask their questions in the cells,' Bruno said. 'Come on, man, speak up and tell me where we'll find your girlfriend.'

'Are you going to arrest him?' Carlos asked, a strangely hesitant tone in his voice. Bruno looked at him. 'Obviously, you could and perhaps you should arrest him. But I learned long ago that one should think about the consequences of an arrest, and I was wondering what it might do to the dig, to the museum, to your Mayor's plans.' Carlos's voice tailed off.

Bruno's thoughts had been moving along parallel lines. He looked back towards the road where the sirens were now very loud, but the entrance to the dig was hidden by a bend in the track. He heard a car door slam and made up his mind.

'Stay here with him, would you?' The Spaniard nodded, and Bruno trotted back to a point where he could see the entrance to the dig. The security guard seemed to be arguing with a tall, thin man in the uniform of a Gendarme. His blue van, light flashing, was parked blocking the entrance to the path, with a familiar small blue Peugeot behind it.

A troop of four Gendarmes lined up beside the van, shuffling their feet and not looking happy to be there. To Bruno's dismay, Sergeant Jules was not among them.

'*Merde*,' said Bruno, and sprinted back to Teddy's trench. 'It's Capitaine Duroc and our new magistrate,' he told Carlos. 'Can you do me a favour? Walk down to them and introduce yourself, delay things and buy me some time? Tell them I'm here but say I'm checking something at the site. I'll explain later.'

Carlos raised his eyebrows. 'A little conspiracy against the Gendarmes? OK. I'll look forward to your explanation.'

Bruno spoke urgently to Teddy, still gripping his spade and now looking completely mystified.

'Can you get in touch with her?'

Teddy tapped the mobile phone at his belt and nodded. 'But why . . .'

'No time to explain now. Call her and tell her to get away from the campsite. That's where they'll be looking for her next. Tell her to go across the river to the rugby stadium and you'll meet her there. I'll need time to try and fix this.'

'What do you mean, fix this?'

'We both know she printed up those leaflets that were left at the duck farm and that she was shot this morning. I've already got enough evidence to arrest her, and probably you too, since I know you helped. But if I can sort out a private settlement with the farmers, we may be able to stop this being a criminal matter.'

Teddy bit his lip, started to speak but then stopped. He threw down his spade.

'I'm not saying she did anything, but she's the kind of girl who believes in things,' he said. 'She might want the publicity of being arrested, being shot, being a martyr.'

'It's not just herself she's putting at risk, and not just you. It's Professor Horst's reputation and Clothilde's and the museum, and it's going to cast a shadow over this discovery of yours if some of the archaeologists get arrested. Try to impress that on her and I'll meet you both at the rugby stadium in an hour or so. Here . . .'

Bruno gave Teddy a business card that carried his mobile phone number. 'Call me if you can persuade her. Meanwhile you'd better make yourself scarce. Can you sneak up the stream and over those cliffs rather than take the road? There's a marked ramblers' path about fifty metres back from the top of cliffs that'll take you to a short cut back to St Denis.'

'You mean, leave right now?'

'Absolutely right now.'

Bruno walked briskly back to the entrance to the dig as Teddy darted away past the overhang and into the trees that fringed the stream. Carlos was leading a small knot of Gendarmes slowly up the path, chatting amiably with Annette and Capitaine Duroc. Bruno stopped, waved cheerfully and awaited their approach. He noticed Annette hanging back with her head down. She glanced at him and gave a shrug and something that was half-grimace, half-smile, as if trying to excuse herself. What persuaded her to bring Duroc and the Gendarmes into this? Bruno wondered. The previous day she had seemed ready to let Bruno handle it in his own way.

'I see you've met my Spanish colleague,' he said. 'But if you're looking for the people I'm trying to find, the birds have flown.'

'A Dutch female called Kajte?' said Duroc in his Normandy accent. When he swallowed, his Adam's apple seemed to bounce over the stiff collar of his blue shirt. 'Are you looking for somebody else as well?'

'I don't think she could pull out fence posts on her own,' Bruno replied. 'She may have had help.'

'Does anyone know where she is?'

'Yes, she's not digging today,' Bruno replied. 'She's on the kitchen rota, so she could be shopping or she might be back at the campsite. That's where I was planning to go next.'

'Do you want to come with us?' Duroc asked, in a reluctant way that suggested he would rather not share the arrest.

'I'll let you handle the paperwork,' said Bruno. 'It could be complicated, her being a foreigner. You might want to check with Doctor Clothilde Daunier of the National Museum in Les Eyzies. She's in charge of this dig and she's responsible for the students. I'm sure the magistrate will agree.'

'That's seems the right thing to do,' Annette said in a small voice, avoiding Bruno's eye.

'So you'll leave it to me?' Duroc asked, a hint of suspicion in his voice.

'I have a security meeting with Monsieur Gambara here.' Bruno nodded at Carlos. 'So she's all yours.'

'I was just asking Monsieur Gambara what brought him here to St Denis.'

'We have a liaison meeting coming up nearby and I asked Chef de Police Courrèges to show me round the district,' Carlos said. 'And after the lecture last night, I particularly wanted to see this famous site.'

'What's this lecture?' Duroc demanded. 'Nobody told me about any lecture.'

'Perhaps the magistrate can explain,' said Carlos. 'But the Chef de Police and I have an appointment elsewhere. Capitaine, Mademoiselle, I hope to see you again.'

Without looking at Bruno, he led the way down the path to the cars. With an apologetic gesture, Bruno hastened after him.

'Since I have no idea where we are meant to be going for this security meeting you mentioned, I'll follow you,' said Carlos when they reached the road. Then he lowered his voice. 'They don't seem to know about the shooting yet.'

Conscious of Duroc's eyes following him, Bruno took the road for Les Eyzies and then turned off at the railway crossing and followed a farm track to the back road through the woods to reach the St Denis rugby stadium, avoiding the town centre. As he skirted St Chamassy, his cellphone beeped that he had a message. He pulled in to the side of the road to read it. In the mirror, he saw Carlos pull his Range Rover in behind and gestured from the window that he needed to answer a call. Carlos waved back, and raised a thumb.

'We are at rugby stadium,' it said, and Bruno breathed a sigh of relief. Then he made a call to Dominique. He had not seen her at the dig, but when she answered she said that she was working on cataloguing at the museum.

'Can you get away for an hour or so? It's important,' he asked her. 'It's about two of your colleagues at the dig, Teddy and Kajte. I think I'm going to need your help.' Quickly he explained what had happened.

'There's a lot of rumours flying about those two,' she said, but promised to come.

Bruno drove on and parked behind the tennis club, where his van would not be seen by any passing Gendarme, and waited until Carlos drew in beside him.

'Thanks,' he said, when Carlos climbed out. 'I owe you for this.'

'It's always fun to tease Gendarmes,' said Carlos, grinning. 'But can you tell me who or what are you trying to protect, and why?'

'Two young fools who've got mixed up in the animal rights movement and did that raid on the duck farm. You wanted to talk to them anyway, when you said that one kind of militant can easily become another. Now's your chance, they're hiding out at the rugby stadium.'

'Why don't you want them arrested?'

'Because I don't want two young lives ruined and I don't want the farmers here getting angry with the archaeologists and the museum. Horst is a friend of mine,' Bruno said, as his mobile phone buzzed on his belt. He checked the screen; it was Annette. He ignored it and led the way across the field to the tiny gate that led from the tennis club to the rugby pitch and its stadium, where two distant figures sat huddled together.

CHAPTER TEN

The town was very proud of its small covered stadium, which still gleamed with the coat of paint it had been given in the autumn for the start of the new rugby season. The changing rooms, built of cinder blocks by local volunteers and painted white, were at one side and on the other were small kiosks that served beer and grilled sausages on match days. Kajte and Teddy sat hunched together on the stadium steps. The girl's face was white and drawn with pain. Bruno checked his watch. Nobody would be coming for the training session for hours yet.

'I know you've been shot,' he said to Kajte. 'Can you make it into the changing rooms where you'll be out of sight? If not, we can carry you.'

'I got here on my own legs,' she said in excellent French. 'I'll just lean on Teddy.' She grimaced as she got to her feet, and then limped down the steps and followed Bruno, who had his own key to the building. Inside, between the two changing rooms for the home team and the visitors, was a passage that led to the big communal bath, a row of showers, and to a small medical room. A massage table stood against one wall.

'Get out of these slacks and let me look at your injuries,' Bruno said. 'Don't worry. I've treated worse gunshot wounds than yours.'

'I told her you said you wanted to fix this, if you could,' Teddy said to Bruno, helping Kajte onto the table and easing the khaki cargo pants over her bandages. There were two spots of blood on the bandages, none on her trousers. Bruno took a pair of scissors from the medical cupboard, cut the knot and then unrolled the thick bandages, and gently peeled away the medical gauze. Kajte bit her lip but remained silent.

The damage could have been worse. There were three small pellet wounds in one calf and about a dozen in the other leg, on the back of her thigh and her calf, some of them so close together that they almost met. She must have been turning to run when the birdshot hit her.

'I'm surprised you could run after that,' Bruno said, bending her knee carefully to see the play of the ligaments.

'Adrenalin,' said Teddy, and almost at the same time Kajte said, 'He carried me.' They looked at one another and smiled. Bruno felt a rush of sympathy.

'You've been lucky,' said Bruno. 'Nothing near the knee and the ligaments look to be OK.' He turned to Teddy. 'You sure you got all the pellets out?'

'Every one. I counted, one pellet for every hole.'

'Some of them are so close . . .' Bruno muttered, peering to see. But none of the wounds seemed deep and they'd stopped bleeding.

'I used a magnifying glass. We all have them at the dig, part of the basic kit,' Teddy said.

'You've cleaned her up well,' said Bruno, turning at the sound of footsteps on the gravel outside. A girl's voice called, 'Bruno?'

'In here, Dominique,' he shouted back. 'These two you know,' he said as she stood by the door, looking into the room. 'And this is Carlos, a colleague from Spain who's been very helpful,' Bruno went on, explaining what had happened while Dominique's surprise turned into something that looked like disapproval. It troubled him, and so he tried to find the words that would make her want to help. 'If we can't find a way to settle this amicably Maurice could be in deep trouble. The farmers are going to react angrily and I suspect your dad will be one of them. Why not explain to your two friends here what that might mean while I treat these shotgun wounds.'

Bruno went back to the cupboard and came back with a bottle of iodine and a tube of antiseptic lotion that contained an antibiotic. They used it for the serious cuts and grazes on the rugby field.

'Dad was talking about it last night,' Dominique said. 'All the farmers were upset after the attack on the Villattes, and a lot of them blame us at the dig. Some of them wanted to go and fill the dig in, so that's why I dragged Dad along to the lecture, so he could understand how important it was. But all he could talk about on the way home was blocking off the way into the museum with piles of manure, like they did with the Prefecture over milk prices.'

The lid of the iodine bottle was a rubber bulb, with a long tube beneath. Bruno warned Kajte that the iodine would sting, but she bit her lip and said nothing as he used the rubber bulb to squeeze a drop of iodine onto each of the fifteen pellet holes. Some of the brown liquid overflowed and trickled down her leg.

'I hadn't heard about the shooting,' Dominique went on, watching Bruno at work on Kajte's leg and then looking at Teddy. 'But everybody knows it's you two and that other Dutch couple who let the ducks out from that farm. We heard you arguing with Kasimir on the way back from the dig yesterday.'

Bruno applied antibiotic cream to each wound, and covered them with adhesive strips. There were only two places where the pellet holes were so close together that Bruno thought a bandage would be needed, though not the thick layers that Teddy had applied.

'You should be able to walk more easily now,' he said. 'But remember, you're still in shock. Rest here, stay warm and take lots of liquids.'

'You sound more like a doctor than a policeman,' Kajte said, trying to smile as Teddy helped her roll her jeans back on.

'I'm a local policeman, not a Gendarme. It's different. Now, this business cannot be hushed up. I had to take a statement from Maurice, the farmer who shot you. He thought you were a fox. That was why he fired so low. He's devastated to think he hurt somebody and so is Sophie, his wife. They are poor people who barely make ends meet, just like the Villattes, where you and Teddy released the ducks yesterday.'

He held up a hand when she started to protest. 'Don't try to deny it. I've got witnesses to your printing the leaflets and the peta.com website you visited, and I assume it's your blood at Maurice's farm. I'm going to give you a choice.'

'What do you mean?' she asked, taking Teddy's hand.

'You can both be charged with criminal damage and you'll probably spend some time in jail. I don't think you'll have much of a career in archaeology after that. Worse still, the museum and Horst and Clothilde will be held responsible by the local farmers, who are furious about these attacks. You heard Dominique.'

'I'm very angry about what they do,' Kajte said.

'I understand that. And you're entitled to your beliefs, but I live here, I know the farmers and I know the foie gras trade and I think you're going after the wrong target. These duck farmers you attacked are the ones who raise their ducks the old-fashioned way and feed them by hand. They're not the big factory farms and industrial plants where the ducks are kept in cages and force-fed with pumps. How much do you know about foie gras anyway?'

'I've read up on it,' she said defiantly.

'So what's the difference between the male and female ducks when it comes to foie gras?'

'What do you mean? There's no difference. They get force-fed and then they're killed.'

'Not quite. In most places, the female ducklings are killed right away, because their livers are different, too many veins. The customers don't want that. But at Maurice and Sophie's farm they don't do that. They raise the female ducklings, too, although they make no money out of it, and they do so in the open air and in good conditions.'

'They still kill the birds eventually.'

'That's true, but I think you're going after the most decent people in this business. It's cowardly because you're attacking the soft targets, the poor farmers who have no security and no alarm systems, rather than the really bad places where the ducks are caged and slaughtered by the thousand.'

'Bruno's right,' Dominique said. 'I'm as much of a Green as you, but you've picked the wrong targets. Also I don't think you understand just how angry the farmers are. I'm angry too because you've blundered into something you don't understand. I'd say you should be punished and thrown off the dig.'

Kajte locked glances with Dominique and then looked up at Teddy. 'I'm sorry I got you into this,' she said, and turned to Bruno. 'What was the choice you mentioned?'

'There's no guarantee, but let's try to make this work. I'll take you to the farmers, first the Villattes and then to Maurice and Sophie. You apologise to them, and you pay the Villattes for the cost of the birds that were killed and some compensation to make it clear that you're sincere. Then you apologise to Maurice and Sophie for the grief and guilt you have caused them. Maybe you should spend a day at each farm to see what they do and how they do it. I don't care if you remain a member of your animal rights group but you should know what you're talking about.'

'How does that fix things? I'm still going to be arrested.'

'Not if the farmers decide not to press charges and if the magistrate finds that acceptable.'

From his perch by the medical cupboard, Carlos suddenly spoke, addressing Teddy as if he were the more malleable of the two. 'It sounds like a good deal to me. I'd take it, if I were you.'

'You said we should pay compensation,' Teddy asked Bruno. 'How much are you talking about?'

'The Villattes lost about half a dozen ducks at six euros each and a couple of geese, and they had to repair the fencing. Say eighty to a hundred euros. And Maurice lost a couple of cold frames. Buy him some new glass and a good bottle of wine and get Sophie some flowers. Can you afford that?'

'Kajte can afford a lot more than that,' said Dominique. 'She's been telling us she became Green because she feels guilty about her dad, who's some sort of high-up with Shell Oil.'

Kajte looked daggers at Dominique.

'I think we should take Bruno's advice,' Teddy said, kneeling down to be at eye level with Kajte. 'I didn't get into this to get shot at and hurt some poor farmers.'

'I can't say I'm thrilled at being shot, either,' Kajte retorted. She looked up at Bruno. 'What happens to this trigger-happy Maurice if we do what you say?'

'There'll be an inquiry, but he's got a good lawyer and he's already given a statement. You were an intruder, at night, and under French law he has the right to defend his property. What's more, he called the police in, which is more than you did. Maurice should be in the clear.'

'You're getting off lightly,' snapped Dominique.

Bruno sighed. It had been a mistake on his part to invite her. She and Kajte clearly disliked one another. But it had been worth a try, to bring in a local and a colleague of their own age who might be able to convince them to follow Bruno's plan.

'What now?' asked Teddy.

'I have to make a few phone calls, and then take you in my van to the Villattes. I'll arrange for Maurice and Sophie to be there.'

'I haven't agreed to anything yet,' said Kajte. Teddy's face fell.

'You'll have a few minutes to make up your mind while I make these calls,' Bruno said. 'When I come back, either you do it my way or I arrest you both and take you to the Gendarmerie and charge you with criminal damage. Carlos, will you kindly stay here with them while I use the phone?'

Bruno walked out onto the rugby pitch, thumbing in the number of Annette's mobile phone.

'I just got your message,' he said. 'I was out on patrol in a place with no reception.'

'I was calling to apologise,' she said. 'I didn't want to interfere with your attempt to settle things, but Capitaine Duroc insisted.'

'How did he find out about it?'

Annette explained that when Duroc had visited her office that morning, making conversation over a cup of coffee, she'd mentioned what Bruno had told her about tracking the students down through the computer. A crime is a crime,

Duroc had said, and insisted on her accompanying him to St Denis to make an arrest.

'Duroc doesn't seem to like you,' she added. 'I'm sorry if this makes things difficult.'

'What's done is done,' Bruno said. Annette had let herself be bullied by Duroc, a man who made no secret of his belief that country policemen like Bruno were an anachronism in modern France who should be replaced forthwith by Gendarmes. 'Have you got the fax I sent you?'

'No, I haven't been to the office yet. What's it about?'

'Those students went after another duck farm in the early hours of this morning, and the farmer thought it was a fox and fired his shotgun. Then he called me. There was some blood at the scene so one of them may have taken a few pellets.'

'You mean someone has been shot?' Annette's voice was shocked. 'This is awful. Duroc was right, I should never have listened to you. If we'd arrested those students yesterday this would never have happened. And why do you only tell me this now rather than when I saw you at the dig? Are you doing some kind of cover-up?'

'Hold on, Annette. Let's be sure of our facts. Nobody has reported in to the medical centre with shotgun wounds. But you were informed as soon as it happened. I took the farmer's statement and faxed a copy to your office in Sarlat. It's not my fault if you don't check your inbox.'

As soon as he said it, Bruno knew that the last sentence had been a mistake. After all, she had called him to apologise.

'I've been hearing from Capitaine Duroc about the way you operate,' she said, her voice crisp. 'He told me that you're always taking the law into your own hands, looking out for St Denis and your Mayor first. You're not going to get away with that with me.'

'It's St Denis that pays my salary,' he retorted, irritated that she was listening to a fool like Duroc. Then, making himself speak normally, he asked, 'Where are you now?'

'I'm in St Denis, at the campsite, waiting for this Dutch girl to turn up so Duroc can arrest her. I'd have thought you wanted your precious foie gras farmers protected. Does this shooting involve the same farmer?'

'No, they went for another farm. But this one's a prominent member of the local hunting club, which includes the Mayor and the sub-Prefect, so he has some well-placed friends.' Bruno felt that he at least owed her the warning that this could get complicated. Any local magistrate would understand that kid gloves were required. But Annette was not local and worse still she was inexperienced, not knowing the importance of personal networks and friendships in country areas.

'The hunting club has legal insurance, so you can be sure he'll be well defended,' Bruno said. 'You'd better handle this by the book.'

'And you'd better understand that I always handle things by the book,' she said briskly. 'But if he's wounded somebody then your farmer's going to be in very serious trouble, whoever his friends are. I shall call Duroc.'

'If you do, warn him that the Police Nationale have already

taken the case. They won't take kindly to the Gendarmes butting in. You'll find all the details in Maurice's statement, and there's a copy with Sergeant Jules at the Gendarmerie, who also has the gun. I took it in there this morning when the farmer voluntarily surrendered it. He has a hunting licence so the gun is legal. If I were you, I'd wait until I'd checked the statement and wait to see if anybody has called in with a gunshot wound. Otherwise you could be bringing a case with no victim.'

'I don't need a victim. I'm the magistrate and I know the law. And I'm not impressed by local worthies trying to bend it.'

'Very well.' He gave it one more try. 'Please remember this looks like your first case in your new district. For your own sake, you'd better make sure it's a success. I'll call you as soon as I know whether any of the local doctors have seen anyone with shotgun wounds.'

'I'll expect your call.'

She rang off, leaving Bruno staring at his phone and asking himself how he could have handled Annette so badly. Could he still try to resolve this case amicably when the magistrate was on the warpath? It sounded as if Annette was now prepared to drop everything and focus on the shooting. He called the Baron's mobile, and found him still with Maurice and Sophie. The Mayor had already been and gone, and Louis Pouillon, the retired magistrate, had just arrived. Could he get them all into the cars and over to the Villattes' farm, where Bruno would join them shortly?

Telling the Baron that he planned to try settling the

affair without formal charges, he asked him to warn Maurice and Sophie that he was going to bring two very apologetic young students to apologise for all the trouble they caused. Then Pouillon took the phone.

'Bruno, I have the statement and I've looked at the scene,' said the retired magistrate. 'I think we'll be fine. I can tell you there's no way that this would have led to any charges in my day.'

'I'm not sure your successor will take the same view, I'm afraid. That's why I want to get everyone together and agree no charges will be brought by anyone. I'll be bringing the two culprits, a pair of foreign students, and they are going to apologise and pay compensation for the ducks.'

'That makes sense.'

'It might not make sense to the new magistrate, nor to Capitaine Duroc. You remember him.'

'The big one from Normandy with the Adam's apple? I remember him always trying to boost his arrest record, trying to file charges that I'd then have to drop.'

'I expect him to turn up at Maurice's farm any minute with the new magistrate, so I suggest you all follow the Baron to another farm, the Villattes' place these two young fools hit the previous day. I'll meet you there in a few minutes.'

CHAPTER ELEVEN

They had stopped briefly at the florist's, where Kajte had used her debit card to buy two imposing bouquets. But the moment he saw Sophie clucking and fussing like a mother hen over the limping Dutch girl, Bruno felt confident that his plan might just work. Her youth and good looks were half the battle with the men, and Teddy helped when he said that he hoped this incident would not mean he would be unwelcome on the rugby field. Responding instantly to Sophie's genuine good nature, Kajte managed to display the combination of humility, apology and grace that was required to win over the less gullible Sandrine. Pouillon and the Baron quickly announced their satisfaction at this solution and the flowers and the compensation money helped seal the deal. The Baron went out to his car and returned with a bottle of his home-made *vin de noix* to toast the agreement.

Bruno checked his watch and declined. He and Carlos had a number of families of Spanish origin to visit, a chore that Bruno felt would pay few dividends but he wanted to be able to report it done at that evening's security meeting. He'd see J-J at the meeting and tell him the matter had been resolved. Annette, Bruno hoped, could be left to Pouillon. The important thing would be to keep Maurice and the students away from Duroc and his insistence on formal arrests. Maurice and Sophie agreed to stay at the Villatte place rather than go home, and the Baron suggested that Kajte and Teddy come back to his small château.

'Is this how you usually work?' Carlos asked, after leaving his rented car at the hotel in Campagne and squeezing his long legs into the modest space of Bruno's police van.

'Depends what you call work,' Bruno said. 'My job is to take care of local matters that don't need the Police Nationale or the Gendarmes. It's better when we can settle things among ourselves. That's the way Joe taught me to operate, and it seems to work. We'll start with him because he knows everybody.'

Joe's farmhouse was in a small hamlet just beyond the outskirts of St Denis. Over the years, he had converted some of the barns and outbuildings into houses for his own children and his nieces and nephews, the children of his elder brother who had died in the Algerian war. Now well into his seventies, Joe still tended the largest vegetable garden in the district and a small vineyard, while his wife ran a modest drapery in St Denis.

Bruno led the way into the familiar courtyard with the long table where Joe held court at the obligatory Sunday lunch for his extended family and whichever friends he happened to meet and invite at the Saturday market. Joe's elderly hunting dog, Coco, stirred from dreams of rabbits to sniff Bruno's trousers and give his hand an amiable lick.

Bruno tapped the small iron bell that hung from the side of the kitchen door and let himself in, smelling the woodsmoke from the fire that Joe kept burning until the first of May. White-haired but spry, Joe put down his pipe and looked up from his examination of a seed catalogue to greet his successor and to shake hands with Carlos.

'There was one Basque family, but they moved off to Argentina or somewhere just after the war. I can think of only two families that still speak of being Spanish in anything but the most sentimental way,' said Joe, once Bruno had explained the reason for the visit. 'And the youngest one left in the Garza family is almost as old as me.'

'Garza is a Gallego name,' said Carlos. 'They come from Galicia in the far north-west. Even without the age factor, they're not likely to be involved with Basque affairs. How about the other family?'

'The Longorias,' said Joe, pouring out three glasses of his *vin de noix* without asking if anyone wanted a drink. He reached into a sideboard behind him and pulled out a bowl of olives and another of nuts. 'I don't know where they came from but they're proud of what their family did in the civil war. Anarchists, if I remember right. When I was a kid they told stories of how they used to be miners and used sticks of dynamite instead of hand grenades.'

'*Dinamiteros*, they were called, from Asturias,' said Carlos. 'They were the shock troops of the Republic. But again, they're not Basques.'

'When they settled here they started as farm labourers and fruit pickers. Now they're plumbers with a nice little business in central heating,' Joe said. 'They call it Lebrun, because they married into the family firm, but father and his sons still use Longoria as their middle name. The old grandad and his brother died years ago, and the brother's kids moved to Lorraine after the war to get jobs in the mines. Big in the Resistance, both of them, and lifelong communists, even when they had their own business. The young ones, it's just business. You know Lebrun, Bruno. He was on the council a few years ago, called himself a Gaullist. His little sister was the radical, the one that went into TV up in Paris.'

'Any of them still got family they visit, back in Spain?' Carlos asked.

'Not the Spaniards, not that I know of. The Portuguese, now, they're different. Always going home and saving money to build houses back home. They still call it home, some of them. But the Spaniards, at least the ones round here, were determined to make themselves French as soon as they could.'

'Any names you recognise?' asked Carlos, handing across the list that he and Bruno had looked at earlier.

'This is a good one, Joe,' said Bruno, raising his glass as Joe went through the names. 'What year is it?'

'The '99, a good hot April and May so I picked the walnuts early, first week of June. And I had that *eau de vie* from all those peaches we had the previous year, so I held back on the sugar. I've still got a few bottles left.' He looked up at Carlos and handed back the list. 'There's nothing here worth bothering about.'

'Is there nobody else you've heard of, maybe outside this immediate region, who still talks about Spain and politics?'

'Just that old comrades group from the civil war that used to meet in Périgueux every year, some time around the end of March. I think it was the anniversary of the fall of Madrid. The old Lebrun brothers used to go. But I haven't even heard about that in twenty years and more.' Joe paused. 'It's a long time ago.'

'Not for some of them,' Carlos said. 'The ones with long memories who think it was less to do with Franco than with Spanish domination.'

Very long memories indeed, thought Bruno, doing the sums in his head. Anybody who'd fought in the Spanish Civil War would be in his nineties by now. And modern Spain had been a democracy for as long as Bruno could remember. He sipped at his drink, wondering what made people into militant separatists in a democracy. In France maybe there were still a few hotheads left in Corsica and maybe one or two in Brittany, but mostly it was about dressing up in regional costumes, re-enacting folk dances and publishing poems in languages that fewer and fewer people spoke.

'The only person I ever heard talking about Basques round here was Anita, that schoolteacher who came from Perpignan. You remember her, Bruno, she taught at the infants' school and then lived with Jan the blacksmith, the Danish guy. She used to talk about Basques and Bretons and Rwanda and Kosovo and I don't know where else. She was a great one for causes.'

'There was some talk of Breton militants having links with ETA,' said Carlos, perking up.

'Not this one,' said Joe. 'She wasn't so much a leftie, more on the environment and human rights and getting up petitions for political prisoners all over the place. Died of breast cancer, must be four or five years ago. She was a nice woman, all the kids liked her.'

He held up the bottle, offering another glass. Bruno shook his head and Carlos followed his lead and rose, thanking Joe for his time. As they left, Joe poured himself another glass and went back to his seed catalogue. In the courtyard, his dog opened a single, watchful eye as they walked past him and then went back to sleep.

After three useless visits to families who had almost forgotten their Spanish roots, Bruno dropped Carlos at his hotel and drove to the rugby stadium. Some thirty or so young men, the first and second teams and reserves, were trotting back and forth along the pitch, warming up. Teddy was jogging alongside Laurent from the post office, the tallest man in the St Denis team and a line-out specialist. The Baron rose from his perch next to some cronies and joined Bruno in the changing room to watch him slip into a tracksuit and trainers.

'Where's the girl?' Bruno asked.

'She's been asleep all afternoon. Best thing for her,' the Baron replied. 'Your Welshman looks useful. He borrowed a spare pair of boots from Laurent, the only feet big enough to fit him.'

'No word from the farmhouse?'

'Nothing. I rang just before we left, and all was quiet. Pouillon has gone home, but he's arranged a meeting with the new magistrate in Sarlat tomorrow.'

Bruno waved at the group of small boys from his training class who were practising place kicks behind the posts, ran onto the pitch and caught up Teddy and Laurent. He trained for the pleasure of it and the camaraderie of the club. In matches, he was linesman and sometimes a referee. Nearly ten years older than the oldest member of the first team, he only played at this level in emergencies.

'It's good to be on a rugby pitch again,' Teddy said, panting. 'I thought I'd be waiting until the next season. Laurent here says there'll be a practice match.'

'Papi Vallon is running this session,' Laurent said as a whistle blew. 'He always likes a practice game, and he said he was expecting you to turn up, Bruno, and be the ref.'

Papi, fifteen years older than Bruno and still as fit, broke up the two teams, sending the forwards of the first team and the backs of the second to one side of the pitch, to play against their counterparts. They were still a man short, so Teddy was sent to play number eight with the second team forwards. Papi handed Bruno the whistle, muttering, 'Don't stop play unless you have to,' and jogged back to the touch-line to watch.

Usually in these practice games the first team forwards won possession, but their running backs were then stopped by the backs of the first team. But this time the teams seemed more evenly matched. One man could not make a great difference in a team of fifteen, but Bruno noted that Teddy was adding something to the second team pack. It was old rugby lore that you never saw a good forward, he was too much in the mêlée. But Teddy's height made it easy to spot him always in the thick of things, stiffening the resistance and then using his weight and speed to break out of the rucks. And he played thoughtfully. When the other team's scrum half was a little slow in passing to the fly half after a scrum, Teddy broke away fast from the back row, intercepted the pass and ran for the line. He waited until the full back was committed to the tackle and then passed the ball smoothly to his wing forward, who went over for the try.

'Wouldn't mind having him with us next season,' Laurent said as they lined up behind the posts for the place kick.

'You're right, but he's a student, just here on holiday for the archaeology. He'll be back at university soon,' Bruno replied.

'It's a good practice,' said Papi, as they waited for the try to be converted. 'I want to see if our pack can learn to control this Welsh guy.'

Bruno recalled the standard drill for neutralising a good forward. Two men to mark him, a short one going low and one of his own size going high. It could be brutal, but this was a friendly practice, so Bruno kept a close eye on the mauls. The first time it worked. One of the burly prop forwards hit Teddy hard on the knees going one way and Laurent piled in high from the other direction. Teddy somehow managed to keep control as he fell, curling his body round the ball so his forwards could keep possession. The next time Teddy watched for the double hit, sprinted hard with his knees pumping into the prop's face and ducked beneath Laurent's dive to break through again for a try.

Putain, thought Bruno, as Papi ran onto the field with a sponge for the prop's bloodied nose. This boy's a natural. Teddy ran back from the posts where he had scored and helped the prop to his feet, shaking his hand and slapping him on the shoulder as if to say now they were even.

'Do you think he'd play for us Sunday?' Papi asked when the practice was over. 'With him and Laurent together we'd murder Sarlat in the lineouts.'

'I think he'd be delighted to be asked,' Bruno said as he turned to head for the showers. Sarlat was a much larger town with a fine team, currently top of the league, and expected to beat St Denis easily. He saw Papi lead Teddy aside, talking quietly into his ear until the young Welshman nodded eagerly. Sarlat was in for a surprise.

But so was Bruno. As he emerged from the changing room, back in his uniform and heading for the security meeting in Campagne, Capitaine Duroc was standing by the gate to the stadium and looking even angrier than usual.

'Did you put Commissaire Jalipeau up to this?' he demanded.

'Up to what?' Bruno asked, straight-faced. His relations with Duroc had been strained from the outset, since the Gendarme officer had been blessed with more ambition than common sense. He was jealous of his status, impatient and unpopular with his Gendarmes. Bruno had some sympathy for him. The Gendarmes were being relegated increasingly to traffic duties, all except their elite units, known as *les Jaunes* from the yellow stripes on their epaulettes. Duroc, whose epaulettes carried white stripes as a member of the ordinary *Gendarmerie Départementale*, was one of *les Blanches*.

'You know exactly what I'm talking about – taking this shooting case for the Police Nationale.'

'I'm not responsible for the cases the Police Nationale chooses to investigate. You know that.'

'You and Jalipeau have always been thick as thieves. You're not going to get away with it this time,' Duroc snapped. 'The magistrate has opened a dossier and we have a blood sample and the gun.'

'You only have the gun because Maurice voluntarily surrendered it.' Bruno kept his voice reasonable, while freshly showered rugby players eyed them curiously as they headed for the clubhouse bar. Bruno hoped Teddy would be a long time in the shower. It would be tricky if he were arrested now. 'I handed the gun in to the Gendarmerie myself.'

'I want that Dutch student you tracked down. I don't suppose you'd know where she might be.' Duroc's voice was heavy with sarcasm.

Bruno shrugged. 'Which case are you investigating – the shooting or the pulling down of the fences at the Villatte farm?'

'You don't think they're connected?' Duroc asked, his voice mocking.

From the corner of his eye, Bruno saw Teddy emerge from

the changing rooms, chatting eagerly with Laurent and the prop forward whose nose he had flattened. They were heading for the bar, which meant they would walk right past Duroc. Bruno was not certain if Duroc yet knew Teddy by sight, but he didn't want to risk it. Casually, he stepped to one side, forcing Duroc to turn to keep him in sight. Now the path to the clubhouse was out of Duroc's view.

'I have a security meeting about this summit that's coming up,' Bruno said. 'What do you want me to do if I see the Dutch girl, arrest her?'

'I want to find out who got shot.'

'So you've had the blood tested already? It's human and not a fox?'

'It's human. Type O.'

'Have you informed Commissaire Jalipeau of this? You'd better do so fast, because I'll be seeing him at the security meeting and I'll be sure to let him know.'

'Annette, I mean the magistrate, will doubtless be informing him, now that she has opened her own dossier on the case.' Duroc coloured slightly as he spoke of Annette.

Could the upright Duroc, never known to flirt or be at ease around women, finally be falling for the charms of the new magistrate? Duroc in love would be something to see, but Bruno found it hard to imagine Annette returning his stiff-necked affections.

An alarm bell went off. Annette would not open a dossier unless she thought she could bring a prosecution beyond the shooting that J-J was pursuing for the Police Nationale. That spelled trouble.

'What dossier is that?' Bruno inquired innocently. If it was connected to the shooting, the solution he had crafted could yet unravel.

'If the magistrate thinks it's any of your business, she'll doubtless inform you,' Duroc said, with a smile that indicated he knew all about it and was delighted that Bruno did not.

'Have you been briefed about these security meetings?' Bruno asked, raising his voice over the first sounds of revelry from the clubhouse.

'No,' said Duroc, his Adam's apple suddenly bobbing as he swallowed, not liking to admit that Bruno was part of the inner circle and he was not. 'The Gendarmerie is being represented by the General from Périgueux. I've simply been ordered to stand by for security duties and cancel all leave for the day.'

CHAPTER TWELVE

Bruno had never seen Isabelle like this. He'd known her in passion and in moments of quiet contentment. On one occasion he'd even seen her in tears as she concluded that there was no hope for their affair. He'd seen her handle a weapon as easily as she worked a computer and had watched her fight with forensic but brutal efficiency in a political brawl. He'd seen her elegant and beautiful over a grand dinner that he could barely afford. And had seen her waking in laughter and mock outrage as his dog clambered into their bed to show his own affection for this woman who had won his master's heart.

And now he watched Isabelle as coolly she chaired a committee of men who were themselves accustomed to command. She drove the meeting briskly, letting each man be heard and ticking off the points on her agenda. She was pale and looked tired, and once Bruno saw a spasm of pain pass across her face as she shifted position in her chair. The bullet she had taken on the beach at Arcachon in December had left her with a titanium implant in her thigh. Slim as she always had been, she was now thinner, with hollows in her cheeks and shadows under her eyes.

A cane leaned on the arm of her chair and she had not risen to greet him when Bruno entered the long room at the château, now painted a pale grey. A handsome table with curved gilt legs, at least four metres long, dominated the centre of the room. Burgundy-coloured velvet curtains were draped at the row of windows that looked out onto the terrace and the open field where the Brigadier's helicopter had landed.

'*Merci, mon Général*,' Isabelle said as the chief Gendarme for the Department concluded his report on the number of security teams he could provide. They had already heard from J-J on the Police Nationale, from the specialist VIP escort unit, from the communications team and the ministry's facilities group who were in charge of preparing the château. The meeting had opened with a report from Carlos on the latest Spanish intelligence, which was much as Bruno had heard it that morning. Suddenly she looked across at him, not a trace in her voice or her eyes of what they had been to one another.

'Chef de Police Courrèges, anything you wish to say on local concerns and developments?' Her voice was as anonymously official as it had been throughout the meeting. Her eyes were fixed on a point somewhere above Bruno's head.

'Very little, Mademoiselle,' Bruno said. 'We have recently come across an unidentified corpse, shot some twenty or so years ago. There's been a case of animal rights vandalism, some foreign students from a local archaeology dig seem to be behind it. But there's nothing so far to suggest any connection with our summit. And at Senõr Gambara's request interviews have been conducted of local people with Spanish connections without significant result.'

Bruno disliked the way he sounded in official reports, the way the bureaucratic phrases came to his lips as they had in his days in the army. The words felt lifeless as he spoke them, just as they had done when he listened to the reports from the others around the table.

'Keep us informed of any developments in those two cases you mentioned,' Isabelle said. 'But let's make sure we check everything, particularly those foreign students. If you could let me have a list of names and passport numbers I can make the usual inquiries. Any of them Spanish?'

'No,' said Carlos. 'It was the first thing I checked.'

'I'll email you the list,' Bruno said.

'I have a liaison meeting with the Prefect in Périgueux tomorrow, so we won't bother with the morning meeting. If there is no other business we'll convene again at six tomorrow evening, Messieurs,' Isabelle said. She closed the file in front of her and put away her pen. She did not rise, but sat back in her seat and closed her eyes as the men shuffled to their feet and began to file out to their cars, talking in low voices. Bruno delayed rising, hoping to exchange a private word with Isabelle, but the large figure of J-J loomed into view, his expression unusually grim.

'Why have you got me taking over this minor case of accidental discharge of a firearm?' J-J asked. Carlos had perched on the edge of the long table beside Isabelle and had said something to make her smile. Bruno felt a surge of something that he hoped wasn't jealousy; perhaps it was just pleasure at seeing her face come alive.

'Because my Mayor and your sub-Prefect are members of the same hunting club as the guy who fired the shot,' Bruno told him. 'And because it's in your interest to keep Capitaine Duroc from blundering into the scene, which would ruin the first case of that new magistrate you warned me about.'

J-J pursed his lips as Bruno briefly explained the informal agreement that he had brokered between Kajte and the farmers. J-J would be sympathetic to anything that could reduce his paperwork.

'Any chance of persuading the Dutch girl to head back to Holland on the next train? That would make it a lot easier.'

'We can try it,' said Bruno. 'But if she's set on a career as an archaeologist, this is the place to be.'

J-J's phone trilled, and after a quick glance at the screen he answered, mouthing the word 'Duroc' at Bruno. There was a pause as he listened, keeping his eyes fixed on Bruno.

'You've heard of the new security alert in the region, Capitaine, because of this high-level international meeting coming up?' J-J said. 'That's why all firearms and other potentially suspicious events are being handled by me during this period. I was just discussing these special measures with your General at today's security meeting.' J-J gave Bruno a broad wink, and continued: 'Would you like me to put him on the line so you can explain why you want an exception in this case? No? Very well, and I'll be sure to let you know whatever action I decide to take.'

'I hope that's not my General whose name you're taking in vain, J-J,' Isabelle said. She had suddenly appeared at J-J's side, walking more easily than Bruno had expected and with the cane held loosely by her side rather than used as support. She leaned forward to kiss her old boss, but J-J threw his arms around her, saying the Périgueux detectives had not been the same since she left. Bruno too was kissed lightly on the cheeks, but the hand that was not carrying the cane discreetly squeezed his own.

'So many damn generals around me these days I'm bound to upset someone,' J-J said.

'Carlos has just been telling me about his introduction to your own methods of policing here in St Denis,' Isabelle said, grinning at Bruno. 'It seems to involve rugby and hunting, foie gras and a pretty girl, archaeology and gun-play – have I left anything out?'

'Guilty on all counts,' Bruno replied, laughing and raising his hands in the air in surrender. 'But you left out the Mayor and my dog.'

'And how's Gigi?' she asked eagerly. 'I hope you'll bring him along to tomorrow's meeting. He'll be more fun than the generals.'

'Why are we standing here talking about dogs when there's a perfectly good bar at the hotel across the road?' J-J demanded, leading the way to the door. 'These committee meetings are thirsty work.'

Maurice's call came to Bruno just as the first glasses of Ricard were emptying and thoughts turning to dinner.

Maurice and Sophie had returned home to feed the ducks, and had found a curt note from Capitaine Duroc ordering them to appear next morning at the Gendarmerie. Bruno assured them that he'd be there and suggested they call Pouillon and ask him to attend. Just before ringing off, leaving Bruno no time to protest, Maurice added that he'd left a cooler with some fresh foie in the second-hand refrigerator Bruno had installed in his barn. With that, the question of dinner was solved, and Bruno led the way by the back road skirting Les Eyzies and through the woods to his home.

'I love this road. It feels almost magical, like something in a fairy story,' said Isabelle as he turned off by the disused quarry along the single track where the flanking trees leaned inwards so that their branches met and intertwined above the road, making a dark and mysterious tunnel. At each bend, the eyes of watching animals gleamed in Bruno's headlamps.

Bruno's heart had given a little leap when she led the way from the hotel and installed herself in the passenger seat of his van, leaving Carlos and J-J to follow in a separate car.

'Happy birthday for tomorrow,' she said, kissing his cheek before sitting back to fasten her seat belt. 'Don't be surprised that I remembered. You Pisces, me Leo.'

He smiled, recalling the way they had celebrated her birthday with a champagne breakfast in his bed in what he recalled as the happiest summer of his life. He had teased her then about the way she checked her own horoscope each day in a newspaper. It didn't seem to matter which one, and she liked to read his aloud over their morning coffee. It was one of the little rituals of their affair that he missed.

'Your leg seems to be healing well,' he said. 'Do you still need the cane to walk?'

'Not really, but it's useful,' she said, twisting and lifting the silver handle so that Bruno could see the gleam of steel beneath. 'It's an old sword cane, a gift from the Brigadier. It could come in useful, walking home at night in Paris.'

'So he does feel guilty about sending you into that fire-fight,' Bruno said. 'And so he damn well should. There was no need for you to be there.'

'I volunteered,' she said crisply. 'And as you can see, I'm making a complete recovery. But enough of that. Tell me about yourself. Are you happy? Is your Englishwoman looking after you? I always found it hard to read your face.'

'I've become a horseman, thanks to her. She taught me to ride and I love it. Perhaps we appreciate skills more when we learn them when we're older. I had to work at riding, and it gives me enormous pleasure.' He looked across at her, leaning back into the corner of the car seat, studying him with fond amusement. 'Do you ride?'

'No, but then I'm not in the rural police,' she said. He could hear the gentle teasing in her voice. 'I like the thought of you patrolling the far reaches of St Denis on horseback, like an old-fashioned garde-champêtre, or perhaps like a sheriff in a Western. Bruno, the fastest gun in the Périgord.'

He laughed. Two could play at this game. 'And now you're

the queen of the committees, a rising star among officials, with Generals and Prefects deferring to your leadership,' he said. 'A woman with a future.'

'A woman with a career,' she said quietly, as he turned up the lane that led to his home. 'I'm good at it and I'm proud of it. And I'm not going to let this leg slow me down.'

Bruno nodded, giving what he hoped was a reassuring smile. Inwardly he sighed. This was the irony that governed them and which had doomed their affair. Everything that made him love her, Isabelle's courage and her drive and self-confidence, was locked inextricably into her job and her determination to excel. And that meant living in Paris and working at the headquarters of the Ministry of the Interior on Place Beauvau. If she gave that up and returned to live with Bruno, she'd probably succeed J-J as chief detective for the Department, but diminished by the curtailing of her own ambition, she'd no longer be the Isabelle he loved. And if he accepted her offer to move to Paris, giving up his hunting and his garden and all his friends and roots in St Denis, he knew he'd no longer be the Bruno that she loved. He wasn't made to live in a city. He'd be unhappy and resentful in a way that would slowly but certainly undermine whatever happiness they found together. He had pondered it and thought it through to the same bleak conclusion on dozens of solitary evenings and walks in the woods with Gigi. But it didn't stop him thinking of might-have-beens.

As he rounded the last bend Isabelle opened the car window and poked her head out, shouting 'Gigi, it's me,' and opening the door before Bruno had fully stopped to welcome the galloping basset hound, his short legs pounding and his long ears flapping as he leapt into her lap and licked passionately at her neck.

Bruno left them to their reunion, musing how much easier such encounters seemed to be for dogs than for humans, and took the packet of foie from the barn. He let himself in the back door and opened the front one for his guests. Isabelle laid the table and J-J made more drinks from the supply Bruno kept in his kitchen. Carlos, who had brought two bottles of Rioja from a case in the back of his Range Rover, leaned against the window frame to watch.

Bruno put a kettle on to boil and from his larder took a large glass jar filled with an *anchaud de porc* he had made earlier in the winter, a fillet of pork cooked and preserved in duck fat and garlic. Usually he served it cold, but the night was fresh so he spooned the duck fat into a frying pan to melt on low heat, sliced the fillet and put it into the oven to warm, along with four plates. He peeled and sliced some potatoes, threw in some salt and added them to the boiling water. Then he cut thick slices from the fat round loaf of *pain de campagne* and put them under the grill. Without being told, Isabelle took the cheese from the refrigerator, half of a *tomme d'Audrix* that Stéphane made and some *cabécous* of goat's cheese from Alphonse. She put them on a wooden board and took it into the dining room.

'Making your special foie?' she asked on the way out. When he nodded she said, 'I'll come back to watch. Anything I can do?'

'Peel and slice those shallots,' he said, and for a moment it was as though she had never left, each of them falling into the familiar kitchen rhythms, neither getting in the other's way.

'Then we'll make the pork the usual way, in red wine with the dried *cèpes*?' she asked when the shallots were done, the potatoes parboiled and dried and set to sauté in the duck fat. Bruno grunted confirmation as he bent to the delicate task of slicing the raw foie to just the right thickness. She warmed the shallots, on a low heat, added the dried mushrooms and a glass of wine and joined Carlos to watch Bruno's next step.

'No fat for the foie?' Carlos asked as Bruno put a jar of honey alongside a heavy black iron pan that had been heating for some time.

'It contains all the fat it needs,' Isabelle said.

Bruno laid slices of the foie in the pan, so hot that the surface of the foie was seared to keep in the juices, but its own fat seeped out steadily into the iron pan. Carlos looked up as he noticed Bruno humming to himself.

'That's how he times his cooking,' said Isabelle. 'It takes Bruno forty-five seconds to sing the *Marseillaise*, and thirty seconds if he stops before *Aux Armes, Citoyens*. Steaks get the full version but the foie needs only thirty seconds a side.'

Bruno turned the slices of foie and began humming again, using a spatula to keep moving the liver around the pan. As the first tendrils of smoke began to rise, he stopped singing to himself, removed the pan and poured out the excess fat into a waiting jar. He slid the foie onto a hot serving dish and then took a bottle of balsamic vinegar, poured in a couple of spoonfuls. The spatula scraped back and forth with the heating vinegar to cleanse the bottom of the pan and then he added three large spoonfuls of honey and swirled it into the thickening sauce.

'So simple,' said Carlos. 'Yet it smells so good.'

Bruno took the toasted bread from the grill, quickly scraped a clove of garlic over each slice and put them on the warmed plates. He draped two slim slices of cooked foie over each piece of toast, drizzled the honey-vinegar sauce over each one. Isabelle took the plates to table as Bruno put the portions of *anchaud* into the red wine and shallot sauce and left them on a very low heat alongside the potatoes. Finally he took an opened bottle of Monbazillac from the refrigerator, four fresh glasses and joined his guests around the big table that took up one side of his living room.

'A glass of this with the foie,' he said, pouring out the rich, golden wine of the Bergerac. 'And *bon appétit.*'

'I always thought of foie gras as a pâté, something you ate cold,' said Carlos. 'This is amazing, not just smooth but silky.'

'*Putain*, but this is good, Bruno,' said J-J. 'I never heard of it being done this way with the honey and vinegar, but the fat balances the sweetness. You've got the foie crisp on the outside, and this toast with the juices . . .'

'I used to sauté the foie with a tiny knob of butter,' Bruno said. 'But then someone with a stall at the night market in Audrix made it this way and I liked it so much I watched him and learned how to do it.'

Bruno briefly left the table to turn the *anchauds* and the potatoes, and came back to sip at his Monbazillac when he saw Isabelle raise her glass to him across the table. She was sitting in the wheelback chair she had always used when they were together. She had bought it for him as a gift, soon after they had become lovers, at an antiques market where they had spent a happy summer afternoon. Seeing her there, he might fleetingly imagine that nothing had changed. From the corner of his eye Bruno noted Carlos observing the interplay and history between them.

She looked down to where Gigi had been waiting patiently at her side until she fed him the final morsel of her toast, rich with the juices of the foie and its sauce. J-J used his bread to wipe his plate clean, and the others followed his example as Bruno brought in the *anchauds*. Carlos's Rioja, a Torre Muga, was sampled and pronounced excellent and Bruno looked with pleasure at the scene around the table. Entertaining his friends in this house that he had built, with food he had grown in his garden and cooked at his own stove, gave him a deep satisfaction. J-J was an old friend, Carlos seemed to be a promising new one, and Isabelle – well, Isabelle was special in the way that only an old lover can be.

'Excellent sauce, Isabelle,' said Carlos. 'And delicious pork.'

'Knowing Bruno, this pork fillet will have come from a pig he killed with Stéphane a couple of months ago,' she said. 'And his freezer will be filled with rillettes and ribs, sausages and trotters. Nothing ever goes to waste from a good farm pig.'

'Let's not go into that, or we'd have to arrest him,' said J-J. 'You know those idiots in Brussels have made it illegal for our farmers to kill their own pigs.'

'If we carried out that regulation, we'd have to arrest half of Spain,' said Carlos. 'Our police aren't fools, most of them know when to turn a blind eye. In the end it comes down to judgement.'

'Unfortunately, good judgement is in much shorter supply than new laws,' J-J said. 'Let's hope this summit meeting doesn't produce any new ones, because I can't keep track of all the laws on the books already.'

'Tell me if I'm wrong, but this summit sounds to me like a political meeting about cosmetics,' said Carlos, pouring out the second bottle as Isabelle passed the cheeseboard. 'We've already got all the cooperation we need with France, both police and intelligence.'

'And yet the bastards still seem to keep a step or two ahead of us,' said Isabelle. 'The one thing that could make a difference out of this summit will be to agree joint staffing of the *écouteurs*. We haven't got enough Basque speakers monitoring the phones.'

'But that's not on the agenda,' said Carlos, looking thoughtful.

'Not explicitly,' Isabelle agreed. 'But it's what my minister wants. Read between the lines of the draft agreement and it's there.'

'Talking of cooperation, we might need some from you,' J-J said to Carlos. 'I got the forensic report on that skeleton, Bruno. They say that from the shoes and the Swatch it's twenty to twenty-five years old, one shot to the back of the head with a nine-millimetre Beretta. They found the bullet in the eye socket, squashed against a stone, so he was shot in place. The dentistry is poor but they think it's Spanish, Portuguese or possibly Moroccan. We're sending it out on the Interpol wire, but perhaps you can cut some corners.'

'Email me the report and I'll try,' Carlos replied. 'Anything else?'

'Yes, the report claims he was tortured,' J-J went on. 'The finger bones were crushed and splintered with what they think was a pair of pliers. That makes it look like gangland, maybe drugs.'

Carlos winced and took a deep breath. 'Poor devil, whoever he was.' He pointedly looked at his watch, and J-J picked up on the cue.

'Early start tomorrow, so no time for coffee,' he said, rising, and looked at Carlos and Isabelle. 'I'll drive you both back to the hotel and let Bruno do his washing up.'

Isabelle looked at Bruno and raised her eyebrows slightly, before leaning down to stroke that spot she knew behind Gigi's ears. He told himself that he detected a touch of regret in her gesture, but he might have been flattering himself.

She looked up from the dog, noting quickly that J-J and Carlos were chatting together, and said quietly to Bruno, 'Thank you for the books. We must talk about them some-time.'

When she had been convalescing, Bruno had spent a while considering what books to send her in hospital. He knew she had a taste for American detective stories, but knew too little about them to make a thoughtful choice. But in the brief time they had been together he had seen her reading a couple of his own history books, and so he sent her the three volumes of Pierre Nora's *Les Lieux de mémoire*. He'd devoured them, fascinated, after reading an essay in a popular history magazine about Nora's analysis of some of the iconic French sites like Verdun and Versailles and the difference between reality and the memory and myth attached to them. Two months later, he had received a short note of thanks from her and a book of Jacques Prévert's poems. Her gift had been doubly thoughtful. She knew that one of Bruno's favourite films was *Les Enfants du Paradis*, and Prévert had been the scriptwriter. The note said the book had been her first purchase after leaving hospital.

'And my thanks for the poems,' he said, although he'd already sent her a note. They were at the door, Carlos and J-J standing back to let Isabelle go ahead. He remembered the first time she had come to his house. When looking at his books she had gone unerringly to the volume of Baudelaire's poems that had been a gift from a woman he'd known and loved in the war in Bosnia. Now Isabelle's gift stood beside it on the shelf.

'Gigi has to go out and patrol the grounds first, and we'll meet again tomorrow,' he said, as he turned on the porch light and saw them out. Gigi looked mournfully after Isabelle and then up at his master.

'She's still our friend, Gigi,' he said. He grabbed his coat and led the dog into the shadows around the enclosure where he kept his ducks and hens. 'And that's all she is.'

CHAPTER THIRTEEN

Bruno had learned to worry whenever Capitaine Duroc looked triumphant. As he stalked out of the Gendarmerie pulling on his gloves against the early morning chill, Duroc looked very smug indeed. Following him, clad in a dark blue trouser suit beneath an open black raincoat, Annette's face was impassive. She still looked astonishingly young, almost like a schoolgirl dressing up in her older sister's clothes. Alongside her was a stranger, a small, dark-haired man in blue overalls and rubber boots with some sort of badge on his chest pocket and a large black bag in his hand. Pouillon emerged from his warm Citroën, its engine purring to keep the heater going. Still glowing from a jog through the woods with Gigi followed by a brisk shower, Bruno barely felt the cold. But beside him Maurice was shivering despite his greatcoat.

'You're probably aware that temporary security precautions have delayed my investigation into the shooting and wounding that took place at your farm,' Duroc told Maurice. 'In the meantime, the magistrate has asked me to investigate reports of breaches of the hygiene regulations at your farm. You will now accompany us while Inspector Varin here from the INRA office in Bordeaux makes his report.'

Damn Duroc, Bruno thought, and damn Annette too. They had planned this carefully. The inspector from the Institut National de la Recherche Agronomique had either got up very early to reach St Denis or had been called in late yesterday. They were determined to get Maurice for something, and once Duroc had him in the Gendarmerie they could put pressure on him over the shooting.

Bruno felt Annette staring fixedly at him. Any hint of that understanding he thought they had reached was gone. Beside him, Maurice looked ashen. Bruno's heart sank as he thought of that gift of foie that Maurice had left at his house the previous evening. He must have killed the ducks some time that afternoon, but he only had a licence to rear them. Although few farmers observed the rule, animals for human consumption were supposed to be killed in a licensed abattoir.

'Aren't they supposed to give some kind of notice of an inspection?' Bruno asked Pouillon in a whisper. The lawyer shook his head. Bruno had another worrying thought. The insurance company would pay Maurice's legal fees if he was accused on the firearms charge, but not for illegal killing of his own ducks. Maurice had no money for lawyers.

'The inspector and the magistrate and Monsieur Soulier will come with me,' Duroc said, pausing to escort Annette to the Gendarmerie van. 'The rest of you may follow, as you wish.'

Bruno called out to Pouillon, who was about to climb into his car, to ask if they could drive together. They needed

to talk without Duroc or Annette being able to overhear.
This latest gambit by Annette and Duroc, Pouillon warned
as they followed the Gendarmerie van, was something for
which he had not prepared. He had read the relevant parts
of the *Code Criminel* on firearms, and he believed they could
mount a strong defence. But the hygiene regulations were
different, complex and constantly being updated. The most
dangerous provision of the law for Maurice would be the
clause prohibiting unlicensed slaughter, even for personal
consumption.

'You know what always worried me most when I was a
magistrate, Bruno?' Pouillon went on. 'It was the fear of
doing something so stupid that the public felt justified in
taking the law into their own hands. You know the kind of
thing, blocking roads with their tractors, sending flocks of
sheep into official buildings, dumping strategically placed
heaps of manure. Nothing really violent, of course, that
might justify the state in taking strong action.'

'You mean the kind of spontaneous public demonstration that makes the law look like an ass and the authorities look worse?' Bruno said, as he began to understand.
'Like enforcing an unpopular law that is widely ignored?'

'Exactly,' Pouillon replied. 'Particularly if there's some
humour attached to the protests, and an elected public official or two among the protesters. Perhaps a Mayor wearing
his tricolour to show that the politics of this are going to
be much more complicated than people first thought.
Naturally, the power of such public opposition is magni-
fied if the media happen to be present. And what always

scared me the most was the thought of demonstrations led by women.'

Pouillon glanced across at Bruno, a twinkle in his eye. Bruno was grinning as he reached for his cellphone.

'Any public official found using his phone to foment such events could be in big trouble.' Pouillon said, taking his hand off the wheel and putting it over Bruno's phone. 'But I happen to have my young granddaughter's cellphone in the car. She forgot it the other day.'

He pointed, and Bruno opened the glove box and took out a small pink phone with a cartoon figure of a smiling kitten on the screen when he turned it on. He opened the address book of his own phone to get the right numbers and began to dial. His first call was to his friend Stéphane, his second was to the head of the *syndicat*, the farmers' equivalent of a trade union, and his third to the St Denis cooperative where the farmers bought their supplies. He asked each one to make more calls and round up more people. He then called his Mayor, followed by Philippe Delaron, the local photographer and news reporter. By the time they turned into Maurice's farmyard, he was on his last call to Nicco, his counterpart as municipal policeman of nearby Ste Alvère.

'Have you called the Villattes?' Pouillon asked. 'They live pretty close and they know everybody in this valley.'

'I'll delay matters here a bit,' he continued, as Bruno began urgently punching more numbers into his pink phone. Pouillon parked the car, climbed out and shouted to the impatient Duroc, 'Just a minute, I think I may have broken something.' He bent down to peer behind his rear wheel, and then raised his head to shout again. 'And I don't want any questions or any word to come from Maurice unless I'm standing beside him.'

He winked at Bruno as he bent again, evidently enjoying his foray onto the other side of the law.

But for Sophie, coming to the door of the farmhouse and drying her hands on an apron, there was only cause for fear in the scene before her. A tall Gendarme was holding her husband's arm, flanked by a woman who looked both stern and official and a man in overalls who looked like a farm inspector. Sophie's hands flew to her mouth as Maurice tried to go to her and Duroc held him firmly back.

'*Mon Dieu*,' she cried, stretching her hands out to Maurice, making Bruno wish that he'd also called Father Sentout. Perhaps the Mayor would ensure the local priest turned up, as a symbol of civic unity.

'Inspector, do your duty,' said Duroc, in tones that would have graced the highest court in France rather than a muddy farmyard that echoed with the cackling of ducks who assumed this gathering meant they were about to be fed again.

Bruno kept his eyes on Annette. Conscious of his accusing gaze she bit her lip and turned to watch the inspector, who knelt to open his black bag and pulled out a small camera and a tape recorder. The camera went in a pocket. The tape recorder was hung around his neck and he made the usual sounds of testing to check that it was working. Then he began a muttered monotone, describing the farmyard and the date and time as he took photos.

The inspector led the way into the paddock where the ducks clustered, shooing them away as he squeezed through the gate. Annette, Bruno and Pouillon followed him. Duroc remained, Maurice still pinioned. The inspector checked the tall barrels, heaped with dried maize, and the low huts where the ducks sheltered at night, long gutters filled with water and feed running through them. There were few droppings; the ground had evidently been swept earlier that morning. Thank heaven for that, Bruno thought. The inspector examined the funnels that Maurice used to feed the ducks and then took photographs. They were the old-fashioned type, the narrow end made of leather, and well oiled to minimise any damage to the ducks' gullets.

He put the camera away and picked up a duck at random, opened its protesting beak to peer down its gullet, probed its stomach and lower back with skilled fingers and then did the same with three more plucked from different parts of the flock.

He looked into the storage cupboards where Maurice kept his gardening tools and his additives for the feed. He examined all the labels, dictating them into his tape recorder. He checked the flow of the taps, probed the dunghill where Maurice raked the droppings and then waded into the wide pond to scoop up mud from the bottom, which he sniffed before tossing back into the water.

Bruno stole a quick glance at his watch. The longer the inspector took, the more time for his plan to take effect. For the first time that morning, he began to feel a surge of hope.

With a courteous 'Pardon, Madame,' the inspector squeezed his way past the silent Sophie into the kitchen, opened the refrigerator and checked the contents. He opened the cupboard beneath the sink to look at the garbage pail. He went out to the barn, ignoring the neat ranks of preserves that Sophie had canned and bottled, and went straight to the big freezer, pulling out each item and checking the handwritten labels. Finally he went to the old oil barrel with holes punched into its sides that Maurice used as an incinerator and sifted through the ashes.

And then the inspector turned to the one item Bruno had willed himself not to look at: the wide stump of some long-felled tree. He photographed it from every angle, and then took close-ups of the flat top, scarred with decades of axe blows. He took a small spatula from a pocket on the side of his overalls and scraped gently at the surface. He carried the scrapings to his black bag, pulled out two small glass jars, one empty and one filled with a colourless liquid. He put the scraping into the empty jar, added some drops from the liquid, sealed it and shook. The clear liquid turned a very pale brown.

He turned to Maurice. 'Monsieur, where is your axe, please?'

Maurice pointed back to the barn. The inspector led the way back inside and there the axe hung on the wall above the workbench, with all the other tools. He took it down, studied it and turned to Maurice. 'You cleaned it.'

'I clean all my tools after I use them,' Maurice said, pride overcoming his nervousness.

'And you scrubbed the stump with Eau de Javel,' the inspector said, a touch of pride in his own expertise. He gave Maurice a look that Bruno interpreted as grudging respect. Bruno felt a growing confidence.

'Thank you for summoning me here,' the inspector said to Duroc. 'It's been a long time since I had the pleasure to see such a well-kept duck farm. The ducks are healthy, their quarters clean and their diet and additives are entirely as they should be, perhaps better. Even their pond has been recently dredged. The place is a model.' He turned to Maurice. 'I congratulate you, Monsieur, and I shall use my photographs in training sessions to show my students how a duck farm should be run.'

Still on the doorstep of her home, Sophie's legs gave way and she sat down in surprise. Annette let out a short laugh before looking down at her feet. Duroc let go of Maurice's arm and his Adam's apple began to bob over the edge of his collar.

'However,' the inspector went on, 'it's clear that some animals have been killed on this stump within the last few days. I'm told that you don't have a licence to slaughter your own ducks. Perhaps you can tell me what it was you killed.'

Duroc seized Maurice's arm again and Annette looked up at Bruno. Pouillon stepped forward. 'Leave this to me, Maurice,' he said. He turned to the inspector. 'My client has no statement to make at this time. He will naturally want to consult his records to see if he can be of assistance, and he is of course grateful that his exemplary stewardship of his farm has met with such extraordinary official approval.'

'He killed ducks on that stump, so he broke the law,' Duroc said stubbornly.

'I didn't say ducks had been killed, and I found no evidence of recent duck carcasses,' the inspector said quietly. 'Animals was the word I used. It could have been rabbits, or he could have been chopping up a deer. Blood is blood. I gather the Monsieur has a hunting licence. I cannot confirm that ducks have been illegally slaughtered here.'

Annette walked across to the stump and looked down at the scarred wood.

'These feathers in the stump, they look recent, surely?' she said.

The inspector shrugged. 'It's a duck farm, Mademoiselle. Feathers are to be expected.'

Annette's eyes were casting around, at the stump, at the axe, at Bruno. She looked fiercely towards Sophie, still squatting in the doorway of the farmhouse, and it was as if a light had suddenly been turned on in her eyes. She sniffed. Her eyes widened and she sniffed again.

'*Mon Dieu*,' she said softly. 'Bouillon. She's making duck bouillon,' Annette went on and led the way into the farmhouse, stepping around Sophie, whose face was now hidden in her apron.

'Follow me, *Monsieur l'Inspecteur*, and I'll show you your fresh-killed ducks.'

She advanced on the venerable wood-fired cooking range of black iron that had been there since Maurice's grandfather's day, and took a dishcloth to lift the lid from the enormous *fais-tout* that simmered on its top. She looked around for some kitchen tool, spied the breadknife on the table, and plunged it into the simmering stock to spear and haul out the unmistakable carcass of a duck.

'Voilà,' she cried, her eyes blazing in triumph. 'And I don't think she'd be making stock from ducks that died of disease.'

CHAPTER FOURTEEN

Duroc informed Maurice and Sophie that they were both under arrest when everything seemed to happen at once. Bruno's phone rang, the small pink phone with the kitten began to signal another incoming call with an electronic version of a cat's miaow, and the sound of a large tractor was heard approaching up the lane.

'Bruno,' came J-J's urgent voice as Bruno handed the pink phone to Pouillon. 'We've just had a report from the quarry outside Les Eyzies. Their explosives store was broken into overnight and a case of dynamite has gone. I'm on my way and I'll see you there.'

'It's for you,' Pouillon said, holding out the pink phone.

'I assumed you wanted me to call you back on this number,' the Mayor said. 'Has Villatte arrived yet?'

'I think I hear his tractor.'

'He's there to delay matters until we can round up enough people at the Gendarmerie. We'll need another half-hour. What's the situation with Maurice?'

'The idiot has arrested both Maurice and Sophie?' said the Mayor in disbelief, once Bruno had explained. 'He must be mad.'

'I have to get to the quarry outside Les Eyzies for a real crime – dynamite's been stolen.'

'And the Gendarmes of St Denis are all tied up over a farmer's wife making soup,' said the Mayor.

'Here's Villatte now,' said Bruno, as an elderly tractor hove into view at the end of the narrow lane. As it got to the gate, the engine coughed twice, a puff of black smoke came from the vertical exhaust, and it died.

The tractor stopped between the stone gateposts, blocking the way from the farmyard. Villatte stepped down, opened an inspection panel and peered into the engine. Bruno saw him slip something from the engine into his pocket.

Duroc pushed Maurice into the back of the Gendarmerie van and motioned Sophie to follow, but she seemed incapable of movement. Annette moved across to help her but Sophie edged away, terror in her eyes at the thought of being arrested.

'Get that tractor out of my way,' roared Duroc. Villatte turned and waved a spanner at him and then plunged his head back into the innards of the engine. Duroc stalked across the farmyard. 'Can't you push this thing out of the gateway?'

'Not with a couple of tons of manure in the trailer,' said Villatte, gesturing at the rear of the tractor. 'That's why I'm here, but the tractor's a bit temperamental.'

Bruno used his own phone to call Carlos, tell him of the theft of dynamite and ask him to drive to the end of the lane so they could go to the quarry. He closed the phone, and went across to where Annette was vainly trying to persuade Sophie to get into the Gendarmerie van.

'You aren't going anywhere as long as that tractor's there,' he told Annette. 'Let her sit down in her kitchen while you're waiting. You could even make her some coffee. I'd do it myself but I have a real crime to get to at the far end of the Commune.'

'How convenient,' Annette said. 'This is also a real crime. Food hygiene is a major issue for me.'

'This is nothing to do with crime. It's a petty act of vengeance, Annette. I'm surprised that you've let yourself be manipulated by Duroc in this way. Surprised and disappointed.'

Bruno went across to Sophie, sat her down at the kitchen table, poured her a glass of water, told her not to worry and to pull herself together because Maurice would need her support. He strode out, ignoring Annette, spoke briefly to Pouillon to explain why he had to leave, and then with a wink at Villatte he squeezed his way past the tractor and began walking to the end of the lane.

'Sorry I took so long,' said Carlos, when he arrived. 'Seems to be a demonstration at the Gendarmerie and it held me up. Is there another way back?'

'Yes, but it's no faster,' Bruno said, taking off his képi so he'd be less easy to recognise. 'And I ought to take a look at the demo.'

The traffic was reduced to single file as they came off the side road, one of Sergeant Jules's Gendarmes controlling the flow. Already they could hear the bullhorns. When it was their turn to creep forward to the bend that opened onto the Place de la Gendarmerie, the whole space seemed filled with tractors and farm equipment and a pungent smell of manure hung in the air. The *Chasseurs* party had brought out some of the old 'Hunters are the Real Greens' banners from the last election. Bruno saw Alphonse from the local hippy commune with two of his goats in the back of his truck, Dominique standing beside her father waiting to take the bullhorn and the Mayor in his tricolour sash talking to Philippe Delaron, who was taking photos for the regional *Sud-Ouest* newspaper.

'What are they protesting about?' Carlos asked, grinning as Bruno explained. 'Anything I can do to help?'

'Call Isabelle,' said Bruno. 'Ask her to complain to the Prefect that you can't do your job because St Denis is blocked by a protest against the local Gendarmes arresting farmers. Make sure she tells the Prefect that the Mayor is leading the protest. Then ask her to call that Gendarme general you met yesterday and complain to him.'

'Here, take the wheel,' said Carlos, pulling the Range Rover into the side of the road and thumbing his cellphone as he walked round to take the passenger's seat.

J-J was already at the quarry, squatting outside the small blockhouse with the iron door where the explosives were kept. With him were Jeannot, the site foreman who had done twenty years in the army engineers, and a worried-looking man in a grey suit which carried traces of the yellow-gold limestone the quarry produced. The system of deadlocks and padlocks on the door seemed intact, but around the side of the low building lay a pile of broken breeze blocks beneath a large hole in the wall.

'The explosives were secured according to the regulations,' the man in the suit was saying.

'You can have all the locks in the world but they're useless if they can crowbar their way through the bricks,' said J-J, ignoring the man in the suit to address his words to Bruno and Carlos.

'What did they get away with?' Bruno asked.

'There were sixteen sticks left in the case,' said Jeannot. 'We only ever keep one case at a time in the store. The rest are at the secure depot at Périgueux.'

'Let's hope it's more secure than this place,' said J-J. 'The stuff could have been taken any time from six last night until Jeannot here opened the quarry at eight this morning. They were blasting yesterday and had a permit to continue blasting today. Forensics will be here soon but I'm not confident of finding much here. They also used wire cutters on the fence that seals this place off from the road. I say "they" but it could have been a single man. The dynamite wouldn't weigh much and my grandma could break through those breeze blocks with a good crowbar.'

'We reckon four sticks weigh a kilo,' said Jeannot. 'It's the usual stuff, ammonium dynamite, fifty per cent strength, stabilised with gelatin and sawdust.'

'What about blasting caps?' Carlos asked.

'We use the electric match type, and store them separately in the safe in the office. That wasn't touched.'

'So either it was a thief who didn't know what he was doing, or one who knew perfectly well where else he could get some blasting caps,' said Bruno.

'I've checked the employee list,' said J-J. 'Everybody has worked here at least six years, and no connections with any of the names on that list you sent me.'

'How often do you have dynamite stored here?' Bruno asked Jeannot.

'Every second or third week. But it depends. For the big blasts, we drill a ten-metre hole, ten centimetres wide, fill it with about fifty kilos of ANFO and then tamp it down with a couple of metres of gravel. But then we have to do secondaries where we use dynamite, and we also use dynamite where the rock formation is tricky. We blast, then we quarry until we have to blast again. As I say, it depends on the rock formation, but we usually do two or three days blasting at a time.'

'So anybody who knew the routine would have heard the blasting yesterday and could assume you'd be storing dynamite overnight?'

Jeannot nodded. 'It's the way most quarries operate these days, ever since the restrictions came in on storing explosives on site.'

'What's that ANFO you mentioned?' J-J asked.

'Ammonium Nitrate Fuel Oil,' said Jeannot. 'It's cheap and it does the job. But that's stored at the depot and we only bring it in on blasting days.'

'I have a copy of all our licences and permits,' said the man in the grey suit. 'Everything is in order . . .'

'Except that you've lost enough dynamite to blow up a bloody battleship,' said J-J.

Jeannot looked mournfully at the hole in his blockhouse.

'I always said we needed concrete, but the company never got around to it.'

'That's enough,' said the man in the grey suit.

Jeannot rolled his eyes at Bruno, then turned to J-J and asked, 'I presume you'll bring dogs in, give them a sniff?'

'Some time later today,' said J-J, and led the way back down to the road and the cars, where he paused and looked at Carlos. 'What do you think? Could this be your guys?'

'ETA prefer explosives to anything else, and they've used dynamite before, stolen from quarries. But there's no shortage of Semtex on the black market. Still, I think we'd better assume that it's them. And if they're here they'll need a base.'

'If they're using explosives, then they need to place them,' said Bruno. 'Our ministers are coming in by helicopter direct to the château, so they can't mine a road. The château is under guard round the clock and there'll be dogs. Where and how do they plant the stuff?'

'We'll thrash it out at the evening conference,' said J-J, thumbing his way through messages on his cellphone. 'By then I'll have a preliminary forensic report on the quarry. In the meantime I have a bank robbery suspect in custody back in Périgueux ... and what the hell's going on in St Denis? I've just got a message saying that traffic is backed up halfway to Périgueux, the Gendarmerie's asking for reinforcements and the Prefect wants to know what's going on.'

'Duroc,' said Bruno. 'And the new magistrate. They make quite a combination. They arrested a popular local farmer and his wife for killing and cooking their own ducks and the other farmers are demonstrating for their release.'

'*Merde*. Shouldn't you be there?'

Bruno sighed. 'When the Brigadier seconded me to the security team he said this takes priority.' He took the opportunity to check his own text messages. There was one from Pamela, saying, 'Happy birthday; see you tonight,' and another from Stéphane that said, '*Saint Denis bloqué. Tout le monde à la bataille.*'

'I can report to Isabelle on the dynamite theft,' said Carlos. 'We can do without you until this evening's meeting. Come on, I'll take you back.'

Once in the car, Bruno rang his Mayor, to learn that St Denis was at a standstill. Since it was the intersection for roads running both east–west and north–south that meant a large part of the Department's traffic was now stalled. Duroc's van was surrounded by immobilised tractors, so close that he couldn't even open the doors. Maurice, Sophie and the magistrate were all still inside with Duroc, and children were clambering over the tractors to taunt him. Women gathered on the pavements were demanding Sophie's release, and Father Sentout was with them. It was all, the Mayor stressed, completely peaceful, extremely noisy and great fun.

Even if Duroc made it to the Gendarmerie, its entrance was blocked by a large heap of steaming manure, the Mayor gleefully reported. The *pompiers* had been called to use their fire hoses to wash it away, but their fire engines were also stuck and were adding to the traffic jam. Sergeant Jules, who understood the difference between duty and folly, had apparently taken one look at the gathering storm on his way to begin his shift and gone home to call in sick with a convenient migraine. And as luck would have it, a TV crew from TF1 had been making a programme at Horst's dig and was now filming the besieged Gendarmerie and its reporter was about to interview the Mayor.

'Wonderful,' said Bruno. He wished that he'd been there to watch this mobilisation of St Denis. 'For the media, let's play up the absurdity of it all. You might tell them that a farmer's wife has been arrested for making bouillon,' he suggested. '*L'affaire bouillon* has a certain ring to it, the kind of phrase the headline-writers like.'

'It invites them to add that the Gendarmes are in the soup as a result,' said the Mayor, chuckling. 'I think this is our chance to get Duroc transferred out of St Denis.'

'You might want to give Radio Périgord a call. They'll put you straight on air and it's crucial to get our side of the story out first,' Bruno said.

'By the way, Bruno,' the Mayor added. 'Happy birthday. We'll have a drink when we see you tonight.'

The blockade of St Denis was all over by midday, as Bruno expected, when the thoughts of all good Frenchmen turned to lunch. Several of the farmers stopped for a *petit apéro* of Ricard to celebrate their victory on the way home, and he waved away a dozen invitations to join festive groups at the bars as he headed along the Rue de la République towards the Gendarmerie. He wanted to ensure that Maurice and Sophie were released as the sub-Prefect had insisted.

'Want a lift, Bruno?' came a voice from the road. It was Albert, the chief fireman, making room on the wide running board for Bruno to step up and join him. 'Now the road's clear we're off to the Gendarmerie to hose the manure from the steps. Is Maurice OK, do you know?'

'That's why I'm going to the Gendarmerie, to find out. Sophie was the one who seemed most upset.'

By the time they reached the square in front of the building, Duroc's van was already parked inside the yard of the Gendarmerie. A heap of manure, not nearly as large as the Mayor's description had led Bruno to believe, was tumbled over the steps but the armoured glass entrance door to the building was only partly blocked. Bruno stepped down with a wave of thanks to Albert. A few seconds later he heard the hydraulic pump of the fire engine and the spluttering inside the hose that meant the water was on the way. Ahmed had the hose pointed directly at the steps and Bruno saw, in a moment of appalled anticipation, the handle of the door start to turn.

Events then seemed to happen in slow motion, but unfolded in an inevitable progression as Duroc held the door open for Annette to walk through. She paused above the steps, obviously surprised to find the manure still there. Not expecting her to halt, Duroc bumped into her as he came through the door in turn. Then with one hesitant initial burst the full force of the fire hose hit the manure and sprayed it powerfully up the steps in a pungent brown flood, over Annette and Duroc and into the Gendarmerie through the still open door.

CHAPTER FIFTEEN

Clothilde's call came as Bruno was driving back to the Mairie after dropping Maurice and Sophie back at their farm. The presence of Stéphane and the Villattes and other well-wishers, all proudly recounting their various feats of traffic disruption, had delayed him. Before collecting Maurice from the Gendarmerie, Bruno had stopped to buy some shampoo and shower gel for Annette. He couldn't see her relishing the harsh industrial soap that was on offer in the shower that served the Gendarmerie's cells. Along with the smallest pair of overalls that he could borrow from the firemen, he thought the toiletries a wise peace offering, making up a little for the laughter that had him and Albert leaning help-lessly against the fire engine as Duroc and Annette stood and dripped manure. Still stunned by the shock of her foul drenching, Annette had barely recognised Bruno's gesture, but he was glad he'd made it. Duroc could fend for himself.

'*Salut*, Clothilde,' he answered when she rang, pulling in to the side of the road to take the call.

'Bruno, I'm worried about Horst. Have you seen him? He's not at home, not at the museum and not at the dig. Nobody's seen him since he left the dig yesterday afternoon.'

Bruno explained about the traffic jam in St Denis and Clothilde objected that being stuck in traffic would not stop him answering his mobile phone. Calls for him were still coming in from archaeologists around the globe. Clothilde had phoned his neighbour, who hadn't seen him, and there was no answer when she went to knock on his door. The woman who did Horst's cleaning used her key to let herself in, and had told Clothilde the place looked as if there'd been trouble. Furniture had been knocked over.

'I'll go and check his house and call you back,' he told Clothilde. He rang off and then he tried Horst's mobile number, but there was no reply, so he set off for Horst's home. The neighbour let him in and at first Bruno thought she must have exaggerated when she'd told Clothilde the house was in disarray. One of the chairs at the big round table had been knocked over and some papers had been spilled on the floor.

'You might want to accompany me while I look around,' Bruno told her. 'I think we'd both feel reassured.'

Horst had many years earlier bought a small and half-ruined house, one of a row of cottages just outside St Denis on the road to Ste Alvère, and by the time Bruno had arrived in the town he'd restored the place in a way that was both functional and lavish. The downstairs was one large room with a big round table where Horst worked and ate, a couple of armchairs and an expensive stereo system, its power light glowing red. The walls were lined with shelves for books, CDs of classical music and files and papers.

Horst's laptop was open on the table, its power cable

trailing down to a plug in the floor. The screen was dark, but it lit up when Bruno pressed the 'Enter' button, open at the front page of *Die Welt*. Bruno checked the date; it was yesterday's. He noted with surprise that it was still connected to the internet. Horst was paranoid about viruses and had often warned Bruno never to leave a computer connected when not in use. The commands were all in German but he moved the cursor to the place where the History button was usually found to see what Horst had been looking at. Another surprise; he'd been looking at peta.de sites on foie gras and animal cruelty.

Upstairs looked tidy, the big double bed neatly made and the bathroom clean, towels hanging folded on their rails and toothbrushes and toothpaste in their jar. The bedroom was large, and the bathroom was the most luxurious Bruno had seen in St Denis, with a large jacuzzi bath and a separate shower stall with nozzles spraying water from every possible direction. With a smile, he remembered one evening over dinner when Clothilde had joked she had only started her affair with Horst so that she could use his bathroom. The kitchen seemed like an afterthought, a lean-to attached to the rear of the house but filled with expensive German appliances. The kitchen door led to Horst's small terrace and garden and the space where he parked his car. Unable to park in front of the cottages, Bruno had driven into the alley and parked beside Horst's familiar black BMW with the Cologne registration. He checked that the doors were locked.

It was the kitchen that worried Bruno, the chopping

board with an onion half-sliced, a splash of olive oil in an empty frying pan, and the refrigerator door was ajar. A bottle of Château de Tiregand 2005 was open on the counter, a half-filled wine glass beside it. Horst was careful about his wine. He'd never have left a decent bottle uncorked. Horst's overcoat was hanging on the rack by the front door and his leather gloves were in the pockets. The morning had been cold enough that he'd have worn them if he'd been going out.

The wooden floorboards, golden with age and layers of wax, were highly polished by the conscientious cleaner, and Bruno knelt down to see if there were any marks that might suggest a scuffle. There were some smears on the wax by the round table and more by the kitchen door. On the kitchen floor were two thin black parallel lines leading past the refrigerator to the back door. It could have been feet being dragged. On the side of the half-open refrigerator door was a reddish-brown smear that might have been a meat sauce, or it might have been blood. The back door was closed and locked, but it was a Yale, so it would have locked itself.

'Don't touch anything,' said Bruno, when he saw the woman take a cloth from her apron. 'Have you done any cleaning since you looked in when Clothilde called?' She shook her head.

'When did you last see Horst?'

'Yesterday morning, quite early,' she said. 'He came in to give me my week's money and then he and Clothilde left in his car. I didn't see it come back last night but it's there now.'

'You heard nothing unusual?' She shook her head again.

'Do me a favour,' he said. 'Go and ask the other neighbours if they heard or saw him come back any time after
he left yesterday morning, if they heard anything, or if he
had any visitors.'

Bruno used his handkerchief to open the back door for
her, blocked it open with a stone and went to his van to
get a pair of rubber gloves. A couple of plants had been
half-wrenched from the ground beside the terrace, and there
were two more lines dragged in the thin grass that led to
the pounded patch of gravel where Horst's car was parked.

Back indoors, he examined the papers strewn across the
floor. They were printouts in German, heavily corrected and
annotated in Horst's spiky handwriting. Bruno recognised
the words *Archäologie* and *Neandertal* but that was all. The
bookshelves ran from floor to ceiling but one of them had
a cupboard where the lower shelves should have been. Inside
were more files marked 'Bank' and 'Tax', and another
marked 'Clothilde' which contained letters and photos.
Beneath them was an old photo album, and as Bruno leafed
through he saw pictures of Horst as a young man getting
his university degree and as a student with long hair and
one of those curved moustaches that had been popular
back in the Sixties. The photos were chronological, so as
Bruno turned the pages back he saw Horst as a schoolboy
and as a child. There were family snaps of Horst with an
older woman, presumably his mother, and several in which
he had his arms around the shoulders of another boy, a
year or two older.

There seemed to be no pictures of a father, until he turned one page and stopped in surprise at a family group, of Horst as a baby in his mother's arms. The older boy was sitting on the knee of a man in black uniform with a swastika armband. On the lapels were the two jagged lightning flashes that Bruno knew stood for SS.

Horst was in his mid-sixties, and had already stayed on at his university beyond the usual age of retirement. He'd have been born close to the end of the war, so Bruno shouldn't be surprised at Horst's father, if that was indeed who he was, being in uniform. Being in the SS was somewhat different.

He and Horst had never talked about the war, nor had Horst discussed his parents, although once or twice he'd remarked on the occasional incident of anti-German prejudice. But he seemed to understand it as the result of the ferocity with which the local Resistance had been crushed by the Wehrmacht. Bruno leafed back quickly through the remaining photos. There was one, clearly a wedding day with a younger, prettier version of Horst's blonde mother holding the arm of the same man, still in uniform and with an Iron Cross around his neck.

Bruno eased the photo from the little corner tabs that held it in place, and on the back was a faded stamp of a photographer with an address in Friedrichstrasse, Berlin. There was no date, but tucked beneath it was another photo, the same man sitting on top of a tank with some other men in overalls, all of them grinning for the camera. Behind them was a burning house and one of the old French road signs. Bruno strained to read the words on the concrete arrow, and was pretty sure it was Dunkerque.

This could put a different perspective on Horst's disappearance. Some local with long memories might consider it as a motive to do Horst harm, although Bruno had never understood those who sought to blame young Germans for the sins of their fathers. He'd have to get an expert to look at the photos to see if they could identify the units Horst's father had served in. Some of them, like the SS Das Reich panzer division, were infamous in this part of France for the atrocities they had committed while heading for the Normandy beaches to attack the Allied beachheads after D-Day in June 1944.

Bruno closed the family album and went to the printer but the out-tray was empty. Beside it on the wide shelf was a tray where Horst kept his keys for house and car and museum, and they were still there, along with his mobile phone, his passport and wallet, cash and credit cards inside. Whatever had happened was no burglary. He pulled out his own phone and called Clothilde at the museum.

'I'm at the house now and I'm worried. His wallet and passport and keys are all here, along with the car. When did you last see him?'

'Yesterday morning. We spent the night together and had breakfast at Fauquet's, then he drove me to the dig where I saw you, and he went to the museum to deal with all the phone calls. He was out somewhere for lunch and when I got back to the museum he'd gone to the dig.'

'Had you been cooking? There's an onion half-sliced and an open bottle of wine.'

'That's not like him. Horst is positively anal about corking his wine and leaving his kitchen clean. And I told you, we went to Fauquet's for coffee and croissants.' She sounded as if she were going to add something but then remained silent.

'What is it, Clothilde?'

'I suppose you ought to know. We had a row over breakfast, about that damn girl who caused all the trouble, the Dutch one. I wanted her sent home, off the dig, but Horst said I was overreacting. Her professor back in Leiden is a close friend of his and he didn't want to offend him.'

'It doesn't sound too serious.'

'It got serious. It was my fault. I said he was giving her a break because she was young and pretty. It wasn't fair, but I suppose I was worried about the farmers doing something to damage the dig or the museum. It had been on my mind overnight and I raised it when we woke up. We started to argue and it got worse in the car and over breakfast. By the time we got to Les Eyzies we were hardly speaking.'

'So he was upset?'

'Yes, but he was much calmer than me. I tend to get emotional and he doesn't, or at least he doesn't show it. When we have rows he usually goes off to that friend of his for a few hours and lets me cool down.'

'What friend?'

'The Danish guy, Jan. You know him.'

'The blacksmith?' Bruno asked.

'Yes, they're pretty close. But I called him before I called you and he said he hadn't seen Horst since the night at the museum. That was when I got worried.'

'Anything else that might have upset him?'

'Not that I know of. I'm worried sick now. If I hadn't got so worked up ... And that damn girl has gone anyway.'

'You mean the Dutch girl? Gone where?'

'Back to Holland, according to Teddy. She's on the train to Paris now. She had a blazing row with some of the other students when she turned up at the dig this morning because she hadn't done the cooking and it was her turn. And then Kasimir had a go at her about the animal rights stuff and somebody else complained they'd had to buy pizzas last night because there was no food and she tossed a fifty-euro note at them. Then it was "poor little rich girl" and she stormed off. Teddy persuaded one of the boys to give them a lift to the station.'

'Has he gone, too?'

'No, just her. She wasn't much use anyway. But Teddy's good, in fact Horst and I had talked about offering him a research post at the museum once he graduates.'

'Time for a visit to Jan, I think. See if he can throw any light on Horst.'

Jan had been in the district for twenty years or so, much longer than Bruno, and his smithy had become a modest tourist attraction. The credit should go to his late wife, a local schoolteacher, who had started taking schoolchildren to watch a blacksmith at work and arranged for the Department's educational budget to pay a small fee to Jan for each visit. Then she began running guided tours of the smithy in the tourist season, with herself as guide. She had pushed him to make candlesticks and boot scrapers, table lamps and crucifixes and name plaques for houses, items that the tourists would buy. They soon started bringing in more money than the horseshoes and plough repairs and door fittings for house restorations that had so far made Jan a bare living. Eventually Jan realised that Anita had made herself so indispensable to his life that he'd married her.

He still lived in the small farmhouse that he had bought and restored when he first arrived, but it had been Anita who had cajoled and bullied him into restoring the huge barn so that it looked like a smithy of the nineteenth century. The fire was stoked with a vast bellows that Jan could operate with a foot pedal. Jan was about Bruno's height, but heavier, with massive arms and shoulders from his work, and with a healthy belly that looked as firm as rock despite his age. He wore wooden sabots on his feet and a heavy apron of cow hide, black with age and scorch marks. A black bandanna kept the sweat from his eyes and the great bucket where he cooled the red-hot iron was made of wood and leather.

The only modern item in the barn was the computer that Anita had installed in the small office behind the show-room of his work, where she had kept the accounts and taken care of orders that came in over Jan's website. Bruno had known Anita only briefly before her death but admired her bustling energy. Jan probably had to do all that for himself, these days.

Bruno could understand why Horst enjoyed his visits, the tap-tap-tap of Jan's hammer as he worked, the throat-catching sharpness of the coke dust in the air, the sudden bursts of Danish curses that mixed with Jan's accented French. Bruno had not been to the place since Anita's funeral some years earlier. Jan had always worked alone, so Bruno was surprised to find beside him in the smithy a slim, dark-haired young man whose arms so far showed few signs of the bulging muscles that Jan's work had developed.

'This is Galder, one of Anita's relatives,' Jan said by way of introduction, wiping his hands clean on a towel before greeting Bruno. The young man seemed tense, but nodded coolly and murmured a greeting in mangled French. 'He wants to learn the trade.'

'I've come to see if you've heard anything of Horst since yesterday,' Bruno said. 'Clothilde rang me, worried because she couldn't find him. I went to the house and it looked a bit suspicious, as though there might have been a scuffle.'

'I haven't seen him since the night of the lecture in Les Eyzies,' Jan said quickly. He didn't sound worried. 'Nothing wrong then. Maybe he was called back to Germany. That lecture made quite a stir.'

'His passport and wallet are still at the house, so I don't think he can have gone far.'

'Maybe he had a row with Clothilde and went away to cool off,' Jan said. 'It's one of those relationships, up and down, hot and cold.'

'Clothilde said that you're his closest friend here and when they had a row he usually came to see you.' Bruno felt the young man watching him carefully. Given his poor command of French, the lad was probably trying to work out what Bruno was saying.

'Yes, often enough,' Jan said, looking down at the iron bar he had been hammering when Bruno first arrived. 'But not this time, I haven't seen him.' He took the rag, picked up the iron bar and thrust it back into the brazier as if he wanted the conversation to end so that he could get back to his work.

'Did he ever talk to you about his family?' Bruno asked, thinking of the photo album.

Jan shook his head. 'Mostly we just drank and played cards. Sometimes he said he missed speaking German and was glad that we could talk German together.'

'But you're Danish. Isn't that your mother tongue?'

'Yes, but I'm from a place just over the border and we all speak German, just like a lot of Germans on the other side speak Danish. Schleswig-Holstein, it used to be Danish until the 1860s.'

'Is that where Horst comes from?'

'No, he's from further south, near Hamburg.'

'So you talked about that, his childhood, where he grew up?'

'No,' said Jan, looking impatient. 'It was just something that came up. You know, in conversation, how come you speak German? And I say I'm from the border and he says he comes from near Hamburg. It was my wife introduced us. She'd taken her schoolkids to one of his archaeological digs and got to know him that way.'

'Do you know anything about Horst's family?' Bruno asked. He kept his tone conversational, but felt determined to press the issue. Jan was not reacting as Bruno had expected. There was no sign of concern about his friend, no evident readiness to help. It didn't feel right. Maybe he'd better check on Jan's *permis de séjour* when he got back to the Mairie.

'No, I said so. I'm pretty busy here, Bruno, so if you . . .'

'Did you know Horst's father was a Nazi, in the SS?' Bruno interrupted.

Jan looked as if he'd been hit by his own iron bar. He seemed to stagger, and then glanced quickly sideways at the young man before looking back at Bruno.

'No, I didn't know. How could I?' he said. 'That's quite a shock, learning something like that about a guy you've known for so many years.' Jan paused. 'No wonder he didn't want to talk about his family. It's not something I'd want to talk about either. Nor would you.'

'Did Horst ever talk about having any enemies here in the district, someone who hated Germans, maybe someone who might have known about his father?'

'No, that never came up,' Jan said. 'How do you know about this? Did he tell you about it?'

'I can't remember him ever saying a word about his own past,' Bruno said. 'Which is odd when you think his entire life as an archaeologist was about the past.'

'So how did you find out?' Jan said, looking sharply at Bruno. His big hands were twisting the rag he'd used to grip the hot bar.

'Looking around his house today when he was reported missing, I found a photo album with lots of snaps of Horst as a young man and as a boy. And there were pictures of his mother and father and brother. I can't imagine either of his parents is still alive so I'll have to get in touch with the brother back in Germany. Would you have an address or a phone number?'

'I didn't even know he had a brother,' said Jan, with another quick glance at the young man beside him.

'I'll have to go through his university, they should have something on his next of kin,' said Bruno, and then added in a casual tone, but watching Jan closely to assess his reaction, 'If not, I'll have to go through the German police.'

There was no reaction from Jan. He was looking down at the iron bar in the brazier, its tip glowing a fierce red. There was sweat on his face, but there usually was from working so close to the brazier. There was nothing to put his finger on but Bruno felt Jan was hiding something. It could just be the understandable worry of a foreigner confronted with the French police, but Jan had been here too long for that.

'I'll get the Embassy on to it, since Horst was an eminent man even before this latest discovery of his,' Bruno added, still probing to get some reaction from Jan.

'If I hear from him, I'll let you know,' said Jan.

CHAPTER SIXTEEN

Bruno had never paid much attention to birthdays, since nobody had ever deemed his own worthy of attention. As an orphan, left at the door of a church and then raised by cousins with too many children of their own and too little money ever to bother about anniversaries, such events had never marked his memories of childhood. So he was partly delighted and partly alarmed by Pamela's insistence that he present himself at her house, showered and shaved and neatly dressed, at 7 p.m. sharp. This time, she had announced when he confided that he had never blown out a birthday candle nor ever had a birthday cake, his birthday was going to be properly celebrated. Especially, she had declared while standing at the foot of his bed clad only in a very small towel and brandishing a toothbrush, a Big Birthday.

But the casual comment from his Mayor that he would see Bruno this evening had triggered a certain concern. Bruno had assumed that Pamela's idea of a proper cele-bration meant a splendid dinner for two, followed by a particularly romantic evening. With this, he would have been more than content. The presence of the Mayor, however, suggested something less intimate and probably more formal; two reasons for disappointment. Moreover, Bruno had not the slightest idea how the English marked their birthdays. He had been stunned to learn from Pamela that the French song *Joyeuse Anniversaire* had been stolen from their neighbours across the Channel.

Apprehensive behind the bunch of flowers he had thought it wise to bring, Bruno counted an unusual number of cars parked in the courtyard and along the lane that led to Pamela's house. He noted that there was no welcoming light in the courtyard, no comforting glow in the windows and indeed no sign of any life at all. Was this some English joke that he would have to pretend to understand and appreciate?

The kitchen door was locked and he groped his way along the rose bushes, calling out the occasional '*Allô*,' until he reached the front door that neither he nor Pamela ever used. Its handle turned at his touch, but the hallway within was dark. Sounds of 'Shhhh' and smothered giggles led him into the main room, when the lights blazed on and champagne corks popped and a score or more of people erupted from behind chairs and sofas to call out 'Surprise' and begin singing *Joyeuse Anniversaire*.

Pamela, looking magnificent in a long green dress, was first to embrace him. Fabiola and Dominique were quick to follow, then Florence and the wives of Stéphane and the Mayor and Sergeant Jules and Albert the chief *pompier*, who were quickly replaced by Françoise from the Gendarmerie, Fat Jeanne from the market and Nathalie from the wine cave. The various husbands came next and some friends from the hunting and tennis and rugby clubs and Julien from the vineyard and Alphonse in his hippy dress clustered around to shake his hand, kiss him and pound him on the back. One particularly enthusiastic blow came from the meaty fist of J-J.

A camera flashed, and Bruno turned to see the inevitable figure of Philippe Delaron, which meant that a photo of this event would find its way into the pages of *Sud-Ouest*. Then Ivan appeared, wearing his white chef's blouse and toque. He must have dashed here from his restaurant to attend.

The Baron gave Bruno a glass of champagne and then they all stood back, expectant grins on their faces, and Bruno realised with embarrassment that he was now expected to make a speech.

He raised his glass to them all. 'I'm ambushed, stunned and overwhelmed. And I'm deeply grateful to you all for your friendship, and particularly to Pamela, our charming and beautiful hostess this evening. I suppose the great merit of birthdays is that with each succeeding one, we have more opportunities to make good friends like you all. So thank you for making this the most memorable birthday of my life.'

Bruno lifted his glass in salute, first to Pamela, whose eyes were glowing, and then taking in the entire company. Speeches did not come easily to him, but emotion did, and he felt a stinging in his eyes that suggested tears were not far away. He blinked to hold them back, and then shook his head, surprised at how moved he felt.

'This is just the friends I had room for,' Pamela said. 'But many more wanted to come, and they have all signed this.'

She led him to the far end of the room that stretched the full width of her ancient farmhouse, where a large card, a metre square, was covered in signatures. Some were accompanied by tiny smiling faces or small sketches of Bruno done by childish hands, and he recognised names of the boys and girls he taught to play rugby and tennis. The town's rugby teams had signed, and the staff of the Mairie, and here was a cluster of names of stallholders in the market.

'We kept it hidden in the coat cupboard in my office,' said the Mayor. 'We had a warning system every time you were in your office. I'm amazed we kept the secret.'

'And we took it to the rugby match with Lalinde when you were away on that course,' said Joe.

'Unbelievable,' said Bruno, blinking hard again as the Baron refilled his glass.

'I took it up to Périgueux, so you've got most of the cops and the Prefect,' said J-J. 'I wanted to get it up to Paris, but there wasn't time, so we've stuck this piece of paper on the corner.'

Bruno bent down to see, and there were the signatures of the Brigadier and Isabelle. He understood why she wasn't here, but felt a pang at the thought that she was alone in a hotel just down the road.

'And now it's time for your present,' Pamela announced. 'Baron, the blindfold, if you please.'

Bruno felt a black cloth being tied around his head and laughed nervously. He felt someone remove his champagne glass and then a firm grip was taken of each of his arms and he was steered out of the house and into the cool evening air, the crunch of gravel under his feet. From the sound, everybody else was coming too.

He summoned up his mental map of Pamela's property. They were turning left, away from the swimming pool and the tennis court and towards the separate *gîte* where Fabiola lived. But no, that was more to the other side of the courtyard, so they were heading to the old barn where Pamela kept her lawnmower, and beyond that was the stables and the kitchen garden at the rear of the farmhouse. It must be something hidden in the barn. Some special wine, he thought, remembering that Hubert and Nathalie were there from the *cave* and Julien from the vineyard.

Then he picked up the scent of roasting meat on the faint breeze. Had the hunters caught a wild boar and were roasting it in the open air? But it didn't smell like boar, nor like venison, and there was no smell of woodsmoke that would have signalled an open fire. He felt the ground change under his feet from gravel to what felt and sounded like concrete and then he smelled the stables and suddenly he knew. They have bought me a saddle of my own, he told himself, something that would have been beyond his own slender purse.

Bruno felt straw under his feet and the smell of horses was very strong. Through the blindfold he sensed a glare of light. He was steered forward and then turned, and he heard the rest of the party lining up behind and around him.

'This is the one,' he heard Pamela say, and someone took his hand and placed something round and smooth in his palm. He felt a stalk. It was an apple. Then the blindfold was removed and he was temporarily blinded by the flare of light.

'Bruno, this is Hector,' Pamela said. 'Hector, this is Bruno, your new master, and he's going to give you an apple.'

A soft muzzle brushed against his hand as Bruno's vision cleared and he found himself looking into the intelligent eye of a horse the colour of a perfectly ripe chestnut. Its ears were alert and pointed, its mane dark and its teeth white and strong as gently it took the apple from Bruno's paralysed hand.

'You can stroke him,' came Pamela's voice. 'You can even ride him if you want. He's yours. Happy birthday, dear Bruno, from all your friends.'

'We began collecting at Christmas, just after you got those Chinese kids out of the fire. Everybody who signed the card contributed to your gift,' said the Mayor, as they took their places around Pamela's table, every leaf installed to stretch it to the fullest extent.

A generous serving of pâté de foie gras studded with truffles lay before each guest, with a glass of chilled Monbazillac to accompany it. There were two more plates beneath the foie, two more wine glasses at every place, and from the array of knives and forks and spoons that surrounded his plates Bruno knew that a feast lay in store.

There was an empty place, and then Ivan bustled in from

the kitchen to fill it, sweeping his chef's toque from his head and sat down, raising his glass to Bruno. From the look of him Ivan was doing the bulk of the cooking.

'No,' he said when Bruno began to speak. 'I'm not allowed to tell you the menu. I can say it's half-English and half-French, but that's all.'

'The foie comes from the cupboard full of preserves that our friend Hercule left to me in his will, and I'm pleased that something of him is with us tonight,' the Baron said. 'And that's Hercule's wine in the carafes, a Château Haut-Brion '89.'

'Hercule bought four cases through me *en primeur* when I told him it was going to be one of the great wines,' said Hubert from down the table. 'Back then, I got it for him at three thousand francs a case. Then that American Robert Parker gave it a hundred points, and the prices went through the roof. These days, if you can find it, the prices start at a thousand euros a bottle.'

Bruno looked down the table, where places were set for twenty people and a row of carafes of the richly dark wine stood glowing before them. Most of a case of Haut-Brion, he thought, and looked across at the Baron and raised his glass.

'To Hercule,' he said. 'Would that he could be here with us tonight.'

He savoured the foie gras and its truffles, the creamy, refined richness of the foie and the earthy perfume of the truffle blending warmly together, two opposites that attracted one another and together created something much grander. He sipped the last of his Monbazillac as the plates were cleared and then Ivan brought in the first of five large tureens, each with its own ladle, and began by serving Bruno.

'*Ecrevisses à la nage*,' Ivan announced, crayfish atop a broth of celery and fennel, onions and carrots. 'I used the same Bergerac Sec that our friend Julien has provided to drink with this course.'

'It's the one I made with Hubert's advice,' said Julien, piling freshly opened bottles onto the table. He looked years younger than the dispirited man he had become when his wife was dying, and before the Mayor had arranged for the entire town to invest in his vineyard. 'We're calling it *cuvée Mirabelle*, after her. It's sixty per cent Sauvignon Blanc, thirty-five per cent Sémillon and five per cent Muscadelle. At the Domaine we'll be making twice as much of it this year.'

A spoon was being tapped on a glass at the far end of the table. Bruno looked up to see Ivan standing there.

'Now for the English course, courtesy of Pamela,' he announced, and on cue, Pamela entered bearing a giant silver dish on which steamed an entire shoulder of beef.

'Courtesy of Ivan's ovens,' Pamela said as she put the dish down on the table. 'Mine wasn't nearly big enough.'

With a theatrical flourish, Ivan waved a huge Sabatier knife and began to carve.

'The roast beef of old England,' said Ivan. 'With Pamela's own *raifort*, which the bizarre English called the radish of horses, so it is very suitable for tonight.'

Dishes of roast potatoes and *petits pois* appeared on the table as Ivan piled slice after slice of perfectly done beef, still pink in the centre, onto big serving plates that were passed down. Ivan's server went back to the kitchen and returned with a tray filled with gravy bowls. Hubert rose to start pouring out the Haut-Brion and Pamela returned to Bruno's side. She looked cool and serene, not a hair out of place, as if the vast joints of beef and the gravy had all appeared by magic and without the slightest effort on her part.

'This is magnificent, what you've done for me,' Bruno said, taking her hand.

'It's not every day you have a big birthday,' she said, squeezing his hand in return.

'This is the first time I've really had a birthday at all,' he said. 'I never knew what I was missing.'

'Well brace yourself, because next year won't be quite so special. And besides, it's not over yet,'

'How can there be more, after such a gift, such a feast, such an evening?'

'Well, I presume you'll want to ride your new horse in the morning. That means you get to spend the night here,' she said, releasing his hand to run her fingertips up his thigh. 'And now behave, because your friends want to drink another toast with the Haut-Brion and I can't wait to taste it.'

CHAPTER SEVENTEEN

Bruno and Pamela strolled arm in arm through the early morning light to the stables as she told him of his horse. Seven years old, it was of the breed known as Selle Français, the best-known sport horse in the country and a national legend since it had won a gold medal for France at the Seoul Olympics. The Selle Français was mainly of Anglo-Norman breed, which Pamela explained had combined English thoroughbreds descended from Arab stallions with the medieval warhorses of Normandy. The result was a classic show-jumper and hunter, easily trained, sturdy and of calm disposition. Hector was a gelding and had been a good jumper, but a little slow for steeplechasing, and so had spent the last three years in a riding school that was cutting back because of the recession. One of Pamela's friends had heard that Hector was for sale at a bargain price, and she and the Mayor and the Baron had decided this would make the perfect gift for Bruno.

'I've ridden him and he's intelligent, safe and very strong,' she said. 'He won't get you into trouble and he'll probably manage to rescue you from anything stupid.'

'He sounds rather like you,' Bruno said, and kissed the

side of her neck. Despite last night and this morning, he still felt amorous.

'Not in the stables,' she replied, hugging him quickly before pushing him away. 'Now, Bruno, this is serious. This is your first ride on Hector and it will define your relationship. Remember what I told you.'

Repeatedly and softly murmuring his horse's name, Bruno let himself into Hector's stall, a carrot in his hand, and waited for the horse to approach him. Hector ambled across, took the carrot and stood still for Bruno to caress his head and neck, to run his hands over the back and chest and legs and get the horse accustomed to his touch. Hector meanwhile was turning his head to watch and sniff at Bruno, probably smelling the extra carrots he carried in his pocket.

Bruno carried out the full inspection as he had been taught – eyes, mouth and ears, hoofs and fetlocks. He gently put on the bridle, led the horse out to the yard and walked him round while Pamela saddled Bess and Fabiola emerged yawning from her *gîte* to attend to Victoria. Once the other two horses were saddled and mounted, Bruno brought Hector back into the stable, saddled him and walked him out to stand between the others. He kept patting Hector's neck and murmuring into his ear and waited until the horse settled before mounting him.

'We'll just walk around the paddock at first,' said Pamela, leading the way.

Hector was a couple of hands taller than Victoria, Bruno's usual ride, so he felt much higher in the saddle. The spring of the ribs was about the same, so his thighs and knees were comfortable and Hector felt well balanced beneath him. He responded smoothly when Pamela led them into a trot, showing no signs of impatience or tugging on the reins. Pamela paused by the gate to watch as Bruno took Hector on a couple more circuits and then she opened the gate from the paddock and led the way out to the open land that stretched up to the ridge above St Denis.

From the trot she raised the pace to a slow canter and for the first time Bruno felt the power of Hector's muscles as his horse stretched into an easy rhythm that was as familiar as if they had been riding together for years. He could sense Hector's enjoyment of the run, the open land and the feel of the wind going past them, the effortless way the horse ate up the distance, his pace not slackening as they took the slope to the ridge.

'I told you he was a good horse,' Pamela said, laughing with pleasure as he reined in beside her atop the ridge.

'He seems happy,' Bruno replied. He looked at Pamela and felt a rush of tenderness. Hector walked in slow circles around Pamela and Bess, as if eager to start again as they waited for Fabiola to catch up on Victoria. Hector's breathing was normal, but plumes of mist came from his nostrils as his warm breath reached the chill morning air. Bruno leaned down to pat Hector's neck. 'And I'm a very happy rider.'

'We'll walk them round the edge of the woods and then try a gentle gallop,' Pamela said. 'I don't want him going through trees until you know each other better.'

She took them from a trot to a canter and then as the

last of the trees passed behind them she bent over Bess's neck and loosened the reins and urged her into a gallop. Beneath him, Bruno felt the surge as Hector followed, running well within himself but seeming to bound forward as if he'd been yearning for this. In a few strides, he drew level with Bess and then pulled ahead as if all Hector wanted to see before him was open ground.

From the wind around his ears Bruno knew he was going faster than ever before, but Hector's stride was smooth and his seat felt as steady as rock. A fleeting thought struck Bruno that he might almost be able to hold a full glass of wine without spilling a drop. *Putain*, but this was a marvellous horse. Moving as one with another living creature, sharing the same rhythm and the same movement and feeling the play of strength and muscle of another being merging with his own, was an exhilaration. What was it that made him feel so close to animals, Bruno wondered. With his dog when they hunted, it was almost as if they could read one another's mind, and now with Hector he felt the promise of a similar intimacy.

'I can see it in your face,' Pamela said, when he finally reined in and she and Bess caught up before the slope that led down to her home. Her smile was wide and her eyes bright, even as her chest heaved from the gallop. 'You felt it. You were at one with your horse. And on your first ride together, you lucky man. And now comes the hard part, rubbing him down and mucking out his stall. It's not all thrills and gallops, Bruno. Just like love.'

*

Bruno was drying off from his shower in Pamela's bathroom when he heard the town's siren start its eerie whine,
just before his phone rang. It was Albert, the chief *pompier*,
telling him there had been some kind of fire at Gravelle's,
the small foie gras canning plant on the road to Les Eyzies.
Bruno dressed in a hurry and skipped his shave, telling
himself he should get one of those travel razors to keep in
his van. He downed a coffee while explaining to Pamela his
need to rush, kissed her goodbye and was on the road
within three minutes. At least this could not be blamed on
the Dutch girl, he told himself. She should be in Amsterdam
by now.

'I found it when I came to open up,' said Arnaud Gravelle,
when Bruno arrived. He was the grandson of the founder
of the family firm and now the manager since his father's
retirement the previous year. He was white-faced and
shaking. 'I said it was a fire, but all this damage, I don't
know . . .'

The entire showroom at the front of the small factory
was demolished, the windows gone and the remains of the
flat roof sagging. Scores and perhaps hundreds of tins of
foie gras and the other delicacies were scattered around
the car park amid broken bricks as if they had all been
tossed by a giant hand. Gravelle also sold wine and the floor
of the place was awash with broken glass. By his foot Bruno
saw a spiral of metal, like a spring. Whatever could that
have been?

There were scorch marks on the walls of the factory and
some of the wood of the shattered window frames was still

smouldering, but the inside of the place looked as if it had been destroyed by something more violent than fire.

'Have you looked around the whole building, or is the damage just here?' he asked.

Arnaud shook his head helplessly. 'I got here and saw this and rang the *pompiers*.'

'Come with me, tell me if there's anything unusual,' Bruno said. They set off to make a circuit around the outside of the plant. The wall nearest the road was clear apart from scorch marks and the rear of the plant looked untouched. On one side of the building, he was not greatly surprised to find that someone had used an aerosol paint can to write '*Arrêtez foie gras – PETA.fr*.'

'Ever heard of these PETA types?' he asked.

Arnaud shook his head. 'Heard of them, yes, but that's all. We've had some nasty letters, but that was some time ago.'

'What are all these bricks doing, scattered around everywhere?' Bruno asked, hearing the siren of the fire engine coming down the road from the bridge. 'Your showroom was mainly wood and glass.'

'We had a stack of bricks round the side for the extension we were planning,' Arnaud explained. 'We hadn't started building it yet, and now we're ruined.'

'Are you insured?'

'For the building, yes, but not the stock. *Putain*, that was a bad mistake.' He turned away, putting his fist to his mouth as though to prevent himself being sick. The sound of the siren stopped and the fire engine pulled into the yard.

'You might be all right,' Bruno said. 'This looks like more than just a fire to me and you can get compensation for criminal damage.'

'I thought I told you to keep away from fires,' Albert said to Bruno by way of greeting, before peering into the wrecked showroom and looking curiously at the collapsed roof. He scratched his chin beneath the strap that secured his helmet, more like a habit in reflection than to relieve an itch.

'*Merde*, this is a mess. But there's not much of the fire left. In fact, I'm not sure this was a fire at all. See the way those tiles from the roof have been scattered out to the sides, rather than fallen into the room. And most of the glass has been scattered inward.' He turned to Arnaud. 'Did you have any explosives stored here? Propane gas tanks, dynamite, anything like that?'

'Explosives?' he looked bewildered. 'Why would we need explosives?'

Ahmed climbed down from behind the wheel of the fire engine and he and Albert clambered through what had been a window, trying to keep their balance on the small tins of foie gras that lay underfoot. Albert turned back to Bruno, sniffing. 'It smells a bit like cordite. Can you call Jeannot at the quarry? I think we need his expertise.'

Bruno called him and asked Jeannot to come as soon as he could. It was no comfort that Albert shared his suspicions.

'How come you didn't hear anything?' Bruno asked. 'That's your house round the back.'

'I didn't spend the night there,' Arnaud said, hesitant.

'Well, I hope she's not married because I'm going to have to check with her.'

For the first time, Arnaud smiled. 'It's not like that. It's Mireille, from the florist's, and we're engaged. I'm at her flat in town most nights.'

'Congratulations,' Bruno said. 'You kept that quiet. I hadn't heard.'

'It's my dad. He's against it, you know, that old family thing.'

Bruno nodded. Arnaud's grandfather had been wounded when serving with the Resistance in the war and Mireille's grandad had been a *collabo*. There were families where this still mattered.

'I think it was dynamite, and they certainly knew what they were doing,' said Albert, clambering out of the ruined showroom. 'See those bricks and those metal springs?'

Bruno nodded. 'I was wondering . . .'

Albert held up a bit of scorched rag. 'I think it was a mattress. They used it to tamp down the explosion, covered with those bricks to weigh it down. It would direct the force of the explosion. That's why the roof tiles were blasted off to the sides.'

He turned to Arnaud. 'You must have some pretty serious enemies. Any idea who it could have been?'

Arnaud shook his head, hands in the air and mouth agape. 'This is crazy. Who'd want to . . .' He broke off and turned to Bruno. 'You saw that slogan on the wall. We get some of our ducks from Maurice. Do you think . . .?'

'Let's hold our horses until Albert's sure of what happened,' Bruno said. 'We might need a forensic report.'

'I'm pretty sure right now,' Albert said. 'But I'd still like to hear what Jeannot has to say.'

'Hey, *chef*,' Ahmed called from the side of the wrecked storeroom. 'Come look at this.'

They walked across. Ahmed's discovery was the scorched and badly bent face of a small clock. Albert bent down to examine it more closely.

'See that little hole drilled there?' he said, looking at Bruno. 'That's the give-away. This was the timer. They drill that hole for the contact and when the minute hand comes round and touches it, *boom*.'

As Bruno pulled out his phone and punched in the speed-dial for J-J, an all too familiar Peugeot pulled into the parking lot and Philippe Delaron appeared, camera in hand.

'Do you never mind your own camera shop?' asked Bruno, tiredly.

'*Maman* can do that. I make more money from the papers, these days,' Philippe replied. 'Great evening last night, Bruno, and thanks for inviting me. So what's this? I heard the siren and went to the station to ask where the trouble was, but it doesn't look like your usual fire.'

'It's not,' said Ahmed before Bruno could stop him. 'It was a bomb. Somebody tried to blow the place up with dynamite.'

'*Bordel*, dynamite? After those attacks on the farms? Somebody's declared war on foie gras,' said Philippe, snapping away. 'Hey, that's not a bad headline.' Camera around his neck, he turned to Arnaud, pulling a notebook from his pocket. 'So what's this going to do to your business?'

Meanwhile, Bruno heard the tinny tones of J-J shouting into his phone and quickly stepped away out of hearing. Philippe knew far too much already. 'Sorry, J-J, an interruption. We've had an explosion here, looks like dynamite. Nobody hurt, but it was a bomb with a timer. We're at Gravelle's foie gras canning plant, the one off the side road by the bridge as you head for Ste Alvère. There's an animal rights statement painted on the wall and the press are here already, talking about a war on foie gras. This is getting serious.'

'Any sign who did it?'

'There was nobody here and it's quite a way from the nearest house. You might want to give all the students an explosives test,' Bruno said. 'But if they're all clear we'd better start thinking about the Basques.'

'Get the press out and seal off the whole area. We'll need a fingertip search, so you'd better call Isabelle. She can get the Gendarmes to round up all the students. I'll be there in thirty minutes. Maybe a bit more – I'll collect that Spanish guy, Carlos, bring him with me. He's been with the Prefect.'

Before hanging up, J-J said he'd get a coach to take the students to Bergerac airport. 'It's only thirty minutes away and all the airports have explosives-testing gear for their security checks these days.'

Bruno called Isabelle to report the news and then went to his van for his roll of crime-scene tape, steering Delaron and Arnaud out of the area. He'd barely finished sealing off the scene when Jeannot arrived in a small truck. Albert took him into the wreckage of the showroom, showed him the scraps of mattress and the clock face, and they began sketching likely blast patterns.

Bruno sat in his van, and began calling from memory every house he could think of that might have been close enough to hear the blast. He tried three without success before he remembered Manchon, who ran a couple of taxi-ambulances that took out-patients to the hospitals in Sarlat and Périgueux. He might have been up early, and might even have been close enough to hear something.

'Didn't hear a thing, Bruno,' Manchon replied. 'But my lad said something over breakfast when he came back from his run. He's training for the Bordeaux marathon and said he heard something that sounded like an explosion just after five. He thought it was the quarry, starting early.'

Bruno sat back, thinking. He didn't see the students resorting to dynamite, however many PETA enthusiasts might remain after Kajte's departure. Nor was it likely that they'd know how to use it and tamp it down. But somebody certainly wanted to make it look that way.

He tried to put himself in the shoes of a terrorist group, isolated and trying to put together a hurried operation in unfamiliar territory, with no military-grade explosives to hand. They raid a quarry for some dynamite, knowing it will bring a massive police operation. It might be worthwhile to use a stick or two to mount a distraction, to send some of the security forces chasing after the students on a false trail—

Bruno slammed a fist into his hand. He was the one being distracted, and not by any terrorist group but by his own foolishness. He'd been thinking of horses and of Isabelle, of Pamela and of Maurice and the Villattes and his own people. Were there really Basque terrorists so short of explosives that they had to raid a quarry within shouting distance of the château where the summit was taking place? ETA had been in business for forty years, despite everything the Spanish state could throw at them. They weren't a bunch of amateurs. They'd have access to Semtex or some other plastic explosive. They could get hold of a sniper's rifle on the black market. They might even have shoulder-launched missiles to attack the helicopters. Sticks of dynamite and cheap clock timers seemed like kids' stuff, rather than the work of an experienced and professional terrorist organisation. None of this felt right to Bruno, unless he and Isabelle and Carlos and the whole security operation were being deliberately encouraged to underestimate the opposition.

Putain de bordel, he'd been lazy and irresponsible, Bruno told himself. He'd forgotten the first rule he'd been taught in the army: know your enemy. He hadn't even sat down to do some basic research on ETA and their methods here in France, let alone in Spain. He'd been going through the motions, content to let the Brigadier and Carlos and Isabelle and the other specialists set the agenda and do all the work, while he sat back and thought about his farmers and that worryingly inexperienced new magistrate. He took a deep breath, and picked up the phone to call Isabelle and ask her what intelligence data she had on ETA that she could share with him.

'It was dynamite, sure enough,' came a voice. Jeannot

was coming towards him, Albert by his side. He was waving something in his hand. It fluttered as he walked. 'And what's more, it's mine.'

'We walked around the perimeter and stopped where the slogan was painted,' Jeannot said. 'Seemed a funny place to put it, away from the road where nobody would see it. But it would be the right place to put a bomb together, out of sight. They could even have used a torch to see what they were doing. We found this.'

He held out a strip of waxed brown paper, about twenty centimetres long. It had numbers stamped on it.

'It's wrapping from a dynamite stick. They pulled this end off when they put the detonator in. And those numbers are from the same batch that we had stolen yesterday. I should know – I spent half the day filling those same numbers into a stack of insurance forms.'

'Looks like we've solved your case, eh Bruno?' said Albert, looking pleased with himself.

'Could be,' said Bruno. 'A pity you didn't use gloves when you picked it up. It means we'll have to fingerprint you, Jeannot, just to eliminate your prints from the inquiry.'

His doubts about this whole business redoubled. He could just about accept that a terrorist group might in desperation raid a local dynamite cache, but he couldn't see them leaving such helpful clues scattered around the landscape. Somehow he was sure they were smarter than that.

His phone rang again. This time it was his Mayor.

'I've just heard Philippe Delaron live on Radio Périgord talking about some animal rights bomb at the Gravelle place,' the Mayor said, but almost as soon as he began to speak Bruno's phone signalled another incoming call. 'And now Claire tells me I've got France-Inter asking questions on the other line about a war on foie gras. That's our bloody livelihood, Bruno. What the hell's going on?'

Bruno ignored the other call and briefly explained, promising to return to the Mairie as soon as his security meeting was over. Then he checked the number of the call he had missed. It was Pamela and he called her back.

'I've just had a call from Edinburgh,' she said, sounding distracted. 'It's Mother, she's had a stroke. My aunt said it doesn't look too serious but I have to get to Scotland.'

'I can drive you to Bergerac for the afternoon flight,' said Bruno, knowing how the coming of the daily Ryanair flights to the once-sleepy nearby airport had transformed the lives of the British in Périgord.

'Let me check connections to Edinburgh and call you back. I want to get there tonight so I may have to go via Bordeaux or Paris. I don't know how long I'll be gone,' Pamela said, her voice tense with dismay.

'Have you managed to speak to the hospital?' he asked.

'No, just to my aunt so far, but she had a brief meeting with the doctor and she's at the hospital. It's so unfair. She's only in her sixties, never had a day's illness and now this. Can you look after the horses? It might be easier if you and Gigi moved into my place ...'

'Don't worry, we'll work it out,' he said, trying to calm her. Bruno had never heard Pamela like this, her voice gabbling, jumping from subject to subject. She must be in shock herself. 'The important thing now is to get you there. Let me know about the flight times and I'll drive you wherever you need to go.'

Part of his mind was wondering whether he'd be able to keep that promise, with security meetings and bombings, foie gras and Jan and Horst's disappearance, Mayor and horses all clamouring for his attention.

'I'm very sorry about your mother. I hope she recovers soon. What time did it happen?'

'That's just it. We don't really know,' said Pamela, her voice cracking. Bruno heard her swallow hard down the phone. 'They think it was some time yesterday evening. She was in her normal clothes and her bed hadn't been slept in. If my aunt hadn't arranged to visit her for coffee this morning she might have been lying there another day.'

'Are you alone now?' he asked.

'Yes, but I'm OK. I'll get onto the internet and call you back.' Pamela rang off and Bruno, ignoring the buzz of an incoming text message, quickly rang Fabiola at the clinic to tell her the news and ask if she could go and keep Pamela company. Fabiola promised to go as soon as her last morning appointment was finished, probably not long after eleven.

CHAPTER EIGHTEEN

Although it was the smallest of the security committee meetings so far, for the first time the video conference link with the ministry in Paris was being used, and Bruno looked at the Brigadier's familiar face on the screen with interest. Most unusually, the Brigadier was smiling.

His voice was normal but his image on screen kept jerking in a disconcerting way as he explained that Horst's name had raised an alarm in Berlin. Bruno was startled to learn that the quiet archaeologist had been a student militant in the Sixties, and a suspected sympathiser with the Red Army Faktion in the Seventies. Isabelle gasped when the Brigadier said that Horst had a brother called Dieter, now believed dead, who was an associate of the Baader-Meinhof group and possibly even an active member. The brother got out into East Germany and the Stasi files reported him dying of a heart attack in 1989, the year the Wall came down. There were no specific links to ETA from his known record, although ETA and the Red Army Faktion were known to cooperate.

'This Dieter was known to have attended a Palestinian training camp in the Beka'a Valley in the Seventies, at a time when several ETA militants were there,' the Brigadier said, and looked up from the file. 'I think we have a connection.'

'Perhaps Señor Gambara can get us some more information on this,' Isabelle interjected.

'We never came up with much on this so-called cooperation,' Carlos said. 'There were personal contacts and some visits, stemming from those training camps in Libya and Lebanon, but no real collaboration. No joint operations, no sharing of munitions, nothing useful that we could get hold of. Remember those Palestinian training camps were over thirty years ago. But if you can get me the name of the camps and the dates, we'll check from our side.'

'Our German colleagues have also tracked the father's war record for us,' the Brigadier went on. 'He was Waffen SS, the military arm, and served his entire war in the Totenkopf armoured division, which spent most of its time on the Eastern front.'

'But there was a photo of him in France, on a tank with a Dunkerque signpost,' Bruno objected.

That had been in 1940, when Heinrich Vogelstern was a junior officer, an *Untersturmführer*, the Brigadier explained. After the fall of France his unit was stationed down south of Bordeaux near the Spanish frontier until April 1941. Then they were moved to the East, to take part in the invasion of Russia, where they stayed until the end of the war. By 1945 he had risen to be a *Standartenführer*, the equivalent of colonel, and was killed in Hungary at the end of the war, in March 1945.

'Anything known of his time in France, anti-Resistance operations or anything that could have made his son a target for vengeance?' Bruno asked.

'There wasn't much Resistance at that time,' the Brigadier said drily. Until quite late in the war, the communists had dominated the Resistance. And until Hitler invaded Russia in the summer of 1941, the French Communist Party had been under orders from Moscow to accept the German occupation. So the Brigadier saw nothing relevant from Vogelstern's time in France. And although most of the Totenkopf division came from concentration camp guards, Horst's father had come from a different unit, the SS-VT or *Verfügungstruppe*, a special force that trained alongside his *Leibstandarte* bodyguard. He had been a devoted Nazi from the beginning, but as a soldier, not in the death camps.

The Brigadier looked up. 'These German records are remarkably thorough. It makes me quite envious. Horst's university hasn't heard from him and nor have his neighbours in Germany and there's been no activity on his credit cards ...' The screen and the audio went blank and then cleared, and Bruno heard the Brigadier's voice, sounding distorted, saying ... 'because it seems like there's no obvious connection. But we have to assume there is a connection here somewhere that could be relevant to our security mission. The coincidences are too strong.'

'I've got another coincidence for you,' said J-J. 'I got the forensic report this morning on that unidentified corpse at our German Professor's dig. They did a DNA analysis and there's a better than eighty per cent probability that he was a Basque. Don't ask me how they know but apparently there are some distinctive genetics.'

'Anything on the identity?' asked Isabelle.

J-J shook his head, leafing through the file. 'No, but they think he was shot sometime between 1984 and 1987.'

'And once again our German Professor is the connection,' said the Brigadier. 'His brother, his dig and now his disappearance.'

'This Basque guy, the unidentified corpse, wasn't he shot at the time of the dirty war?' Bruno asked the flickering video image, and then he turned to Carlos. 'Remember, we talked about it the day we first met. If he was a victim of the dirty war, maybe there is something that could identify him in the Spanish records.'

'Not many records were kept, for obvious reasons,' Carlos said, scribbling a note to himself. 'And then they were very thoroughly sanitised. The commission of inquiry into the *Grupos Antiterroristas de Liberación* had a terrible job trying to reconstruct it all. But I'll check with Madrid, see if they have anything.'

'I'll email you the forensic report,' said J-J. 'There's some detail on the clothing, but nothing that really helps us beyond giving us a rough date, like the Swatch he wore. His nose had been broken in childhood, that's about it. And the electric wire that was used to bind his hands was made in Germany, but it was on sale all over Europe.'

'And I'll arrange a search of our own files,' said the Brigadier. 'A lot of those killings took place on French soil. I remember we even arrested four of your agents in Bayonne,

Carlos, trying to kidnap somebody they claimed was the head of ETA. Some of their colleagues then kidnapped somebody else to secure their release.'

'José Mari Larretxea,' said Carlos, his voice sombre. 'He was the head of ETA at the time. It was a very embarrassing operation.'

'Our German Professor could be a kidnap victim,' said Bruno, thinking that nobody else seemed much concerned about Horst's fate. 'You saw my report on the scene at his house, the bloodstains and the marks of someone being dragged.'

'All that could have been staged,' said Isabelle. 'But what worries me most about all this is our almost complete lack of intelligence on this ETA active service unit. It's said to have been based in France for months now, and all we have is one name, Michel – I can't pronounce this – Goikoetxea, and a photograph of him at age eighteen. He's now what, almost forty.'

'Mikel Goikoetxea, he's named after his father, one of the ETA leaders,' said Carlos, 'killed by a GAL sniper in Bayonne in 1983. The son is forty next year, and we've never laid eyes on him since he was arrested at a student demo. What can I say? They have very good security. It's almost impossible for a non-Basque to infiltrate them.'

'And now we come to the latest drama,' said the Brigadier. 'Bruno, what do you know about this morning's bombing? There was something on my car radio about a war on foie gras, but Isabelle emailed me that there could be a connection.'

'There's certainly a connection with the dynamite theft from the local quarry,' Bruno replied. He explained that the dynamite that was used had come from the batch that was stolen the previous day and there was a scrawled slogan about animal rights on the side of the building.

'Is anything more known about any of these students?' asked the Brigadier.

'We put through a routine inquiry to all the relevant foreign police, but nothing of significance came back,' Isabelle said. 'I'll do it again with a priority code, and with a special request under your name asking for a full security readout on the two students directly involved in the earlier attacks.'

'The Dutch girl was supposed to have been back home in Holland by the time the bomb went off,' Bruno said.

'We'll get the Dutch police to do an eyeball, make sure she's there.'

'What I really want to know is how and when the information about this summit meeting leaked out,' Bruno went on. 'How did the ETA group find out it was taking place? If we're sure they do know, that is.'

Isabelle and Carlos looked at each other, as if sharing something on which Bruno had not been briefed. But knowing the Brigadier, he felt a suspicion begin to dawn.

'That comes under the category of need to know,' said the Brigadier, his image flickering so that Bruno could not read his expression. But his words confirmed Bruno's thoughts.

Bruno looked from the Brigadier to Carlos and Isabelle

at the table. A controlled anger was building inside him at the way these people worked, at the job Isabelle had chosen to do, the job that she had preferred to him and the life he offered in St Denis.

'I think you leaked it deliberately, setting a trap for this ETA cell to fall into,' Bruno said, his voice deceptively calm and his manner as restrained and philosophical as he could conjure. 'You're using this summit as a lure. You're putting my town at risk of a terrorist attack and you're even using your own minister as bait.'

'*Putain*,' said J-J. 'He'd better not be right about this. That's two top ministers' lives you're playing with.'

'The ministers are in full agreement with this operation,' said Carlos.

'In the meantime, you all have your to-do lists,' said the Brigadier coldly. 'And if you breathe a word of this to anyone outside that room, Bruno, I'll have your job, your pension and I'll feed your damn dog to your new horse.'

He leaned forward and pressed something and the video screen went blank.

'A useful meeting,' Isabelle said briskly, gathering her files and folders. 'I think it went well, considering. We all have our jobs to do and we meet again to report back at six. By then, let's make sure we have some results, shall we?'

She began to stalk out, but her bad leg failed and she stumbled. Carlos steadied her by the arm and led her out, neither one of them with a backward glance.

'*Putain de merde*,' said J-J, looking after them as they left the conference room. 'What do they do to these people?'

CHAPTER NINETEEN

The text message that Bruno had ignored since the start of the security meeting had come from Annette. It was politely worded but uncompromising. His presence at the Gendarmerie was required as soon as possible. On arrival he asked Sergeant Jules if he knew what she wanted.

'She's been with Duroc in his office most of the morning,' Jules said, shrugging. 'I know they went to Gravelle's place to see the bomb damage and then I saw her give a radio interview outside.' He jerked his thumb at the small radio on the side of the counter, its volume turned low. 'It hasn't been played yet, but I'll be listening.' He gave Bruno a quizzical look. 'There's a disposable razor and some soap in the shower room downstairs. I'd use it, if I were you.'

Bruno took the advice, and a few minutes later, cheeks stinging slightly from the crude soap, he straightened his uniform, tucked his hat under his arm and knocked on Duroc's door. Without waiting, he entered and greeted them both formally. Annette was sitting at the desk, a sheaf of what looked like witness statements before her, and Duroc rose quickly from where he had been leaning over her, his arm on her shoulder. He coloured slightly.

'I hope I wasn't interrupting anything,' Bruno said innocently. 'You asked me to come as soon as I could.'

'You're in the shit this time,' Duroc said. Annette grimaced, visibly irritated by his coarseness in what she intended as a formal occasion. Bruno raised his eyebrows at Duroc's remark but said nothing. Duroc looked down at Annette and stepped back, as if letting her take the lead.

'I've asked you here to inform you formally that I am initiating disciplinary proceedings against you on charges of unauthorised entry, obstruction of justice and incitement to riot,' Annette said, reading from a paper before her rather than meeting Bruno's eye. 'I have signed an order to retrieve your phone records and have asked your Mayor to suspend you from duty while these charges are pending.'

She lifted her head and looked him in the eye. 'Do you have anything to say?'

'No,' said Bruno. 'But I have some questions to clarify matters, and I'd like to have a witness present.' He turned back to open the office door and asked Sergeant Jules, who was standing suspiciously close to the door, to join them. Briefly he explained the situation and asked Jules to take note of his questions.

'First, which was the riot in question? Second, which were the premises I'm supposed to have entered without authorisation? Third, I'd like a detailed account of the supposed obstruction of justice. Fourth, what was the Mayor's response? Fifth, have you informed the office of the Minister of the Interior of your attempt to suspend me? I should add that I'm currently attached to his staff, with my Mayor's approval. Finally, the Sergeant here will kindly note that I freely give approval for my phone records to be examined. I have nothing to hide.'

'You know perfectly well which riot we're talking about because you organised it,' Duroc snapped. 'The unauthorised entry was to Professor Vogelstern's home. The obstruction of justice was protecting your damn farmers and aiding and abetting two students suspected of criminal damage to escape arrest by me and my men. I personally delivered the letter of request for your suspension to the Mairie earlier this morning. We'll see what the Interior Ministry has to say when we send them these charges.'

'So you haven't talked to the Mayor?' Bruno wondered how Duroc had learned of the help he'd given to Teddy and Kajte.

'We haven't yet had a reply,' said Annette, in a voice that sounded a little uncertain, as if confused by Bruno's reaction and Sergeant Jules's presence.

Bruno pulled out his phone, speed-dialled the Mayor and explained the reason for the call.

'Put this on speaker so that they can hear this as well as you,' the Mayor said. Bruno complied, and watched stony-faced as Annette and Duroc listened to the Mayor.

'I have your letter before me and I reject the request,' said the tinny voice over the phone's speaker. 'Chief of Police Courrèges has my full confidence, but I am writing to the head of the judicial office in Sarlat, Mademoiselle Meraillon, to say that this Mairie has no confidence in you. We will in future withhold all cooperation with you and I formally request your transfer to a less demanding post. Were it not for your youth and inexperience I would have requested a formal disciplinary hearing against you. I have also written, Capitaine Duroc, to the Prefect and to the General of Gendarmerie in very similar terms. I should add that the sub-Prefect has sent me a copy of the highly critical report he has filed on your unprofessional behaviour in St Denis yesterday.'

The Mayor disconnected and Bruno closed his phone. Duroc's face was white and Annette looked up at him nervously as his Adam's apple began its usual dance.

'I think that covers everything, for the moment,' Bruno said. 'But to save you some embarrassment, you might want to drop the charge about unauthorised entry. The owner of the house, Professor Vogelstern, entrusted me with a key some time ago, along with a letter asking me to inspect the premises in his absence and collect his mail and forward it to him in Germany.'

'So why did you ask the neighbour to let you in?' asked Annette, pulling a witness statement from the file before her.

'Because I wanted someone else present when I searched the premises, in the course of an investigation into his disappearance, requested by the curator of the National Museum,' Bruno said. 'Anything else?'

'I'll want to see this alleged letter,' Annette said.

'You'll have a copy later today,' Bruno replied. 'You will understand when I say that in view of the personal malice that I believe is part of these proceedings, I'm not prepared to entrust you with the original. You may, of course, make an appointment to come to my office in the Mairie and examine the letter in the presence of me and the Mayor. Might I also put on record that I request Mademoiselle Meraillon to recuse herself from this case on grounds of partiality and transfer it to a colleague.'

He put his hat on his head, turned and marched out, Sergeant Jules following behind and closing the door on Duroc's office. When he reached the main entrance, Bruno felt Jules pluck at his sleeve and beckon him to follow. He led the way across the road and into the Bar des Amateurs. Jules ordered two coffees, unbuttoned the breast pocket of his uniform and took out a folded sheet of paper.

'We've got them both by the balls,' Jules said, unfolding the paper so that Bruno could see it was a photocopy of his charge book, with its carbon of the original speeding ticket that he'd written against Annette.

'He's sweet on her, so Duroc fixed the ticket. The copy that should have gone to the main office was never sent, and Françoise is prepared to swear that she saw him take it out of the box of outgoing mail and tear it up. I've got my charge book in a safe place, but I reported it lost. So we've got the evidence that the speeding ticket was issued, which means that she as a magistrate is in trouble because she hasn't paid it. And Duroc faces an internal investigation and that could mean a court martial.'

'Did Françoise really see him tear it up?' Bruno asked. 'She's never liked him.'

'Françoise is straight as a die. She wouldn't lie about this.

She's also made a sworn statement that she saw him do it, and I've got a copy.'

'I presume she dated the statement, so you can't sit on it too long before doing something about it,' Bruno said.

'I can say I was making inquiries about it but mislaid my charge book. We've got a few days. It's your call, Bruno. Either I can report this to the internal investigations branch and get them both in trouble, or you can use it to make them drop these crazy charges against you.'

Bruno shook his head. 'It's gone too far for that, now that she's sent the letter to my Mayor and he's filed his own complaints in return. This inquiry's going to go all the way. Besides, if I tried to use it discreetly, Duroc would know that you and Françoise were both conspiring against him. He could make your lives a misery and you'd have no comeback. I think this is one of those times when justice has to take its course.'

Back in his office, after briefing the Mayor, Bruno rang Pamela's home. Fabiola answered, and said Pamela was packing her suitcase and was taking the afternoon train to Bordeaux from Le Buisson for a flight to Edinburgh. Bruno checked his watch. He could leave at two and take Pamela to the station. That gave him a little time.

He went to the dusty registry of the Mairie, a long, thin room lined with shelves and filing cabinets, to look up the copy of Jan's *carte de séjour* in the Mairie's registry. All foreigners, even citizens of another European country who had the right to live in France, had to file registration papers.

Jan Olaf Pedersen had established residency in the Commune in December 1985. His date of birth was September 1942, in Kolding, Denmark, and there was a photocopy of his passport in the file. Jan's *taxe foncière* and *taxe d'habitation* and water bills were paid on time. The registration papers for his company were up to date and there was an *avis* from the Conseil Général for Jan to be an approved *instituteur external*, authorised to demonstrate and teach technical skills outside of school premises. He had married Juanita Maria Zabala, a French citizen born in Perpignan, in May 1993, years before Bruno had arrived in St Denis. Bruno reflected that he'd been in Bosnia on the day Jan had married, as a member of the UN force that was keeping Sarajevo airport open.

Everything was in order as Bruno scanned the slim file, but as he dragged his thoughts back from those days of living in a bunker and sheltering from the Serbian artillery barrages, his eye went back to the wife's name, Juanita. Everybody had referred to her as Anita. And Joe had said something about her talking about the Basques. He went to the office, checked his watch again and rang Joe at home.

'Joe, that woman who married Jan, the blacksmith. You said you remembered her talking about the Basques. Do you remember her name?'

'Anita, but she talked about human rights for everybody, Bosnians, Rwandans, Palestinians. She was always taking up collections and getting people to sign petitions. A heart of gold but a pain in the neck, if you know what I mean. She was the sort of woman you admired but you ducked when you saw her coming.'

'It's just that she's listed as Juanita in the registry, and I'm interested in any Spanish connections.'

'Everybody called her Anita,' Joe said. 'She came from Perpignan, already had her teaching diploma when she arrived. I don't recall ever hearing her called Juanita. Try the Mairie in Perpignan, they should have something. I think she was born there.'

The Mairie at Perpignan took his number to check that he was indeed calling from the Mairie of St Denis, and a sergeant of the town's municipal police called him back almost immediately, claiming that Bruno had met his brother on a legal training course in Toulouse. He was happy to help, and called him again with details from the birth certificate. Juanita Maria Zabala had been born in Perpignan in April 1950, daughter of Joxe Asteazu Zabala, a naturalised French citizen, and Marie-Josette Duvertrans of Perpignan.

Bruno thanked him and went to his computer, called up Google.fr and typed Joxe Asteazu into the search box. The first item that came up was *Sculpteurs Basques en Espagne* and the second was in Spanish that he could understand, *Lista de atentados del GAL*, a catalogue of the assassination attempts on Basque militants during GAL's dirty war. So Juanita's father was a Basque. Bruno then ran a search of her father's full name plus Perpignan, in French web pages only. He was directed to a list of people awarded the *Médaille de la Résistance*. Bruno called Perpignan again and asked the helpful sergeant to look up any details of Zabala's naturalisation papers, adding that the man had served in the Resistance.

'Naturalisation was granted in 1946, and there's a note about special recognition for Resistance services, despite his internment record. He was in Camp Gurs, that was the big one for the Spanish Civil War troops who fled to France when Franco won. That's all it says.'

Bruno then called the Centre Jean Moulin in Bordeaux, the Resistance archive named after the man who had tried to unify the Resistance under De Gaulle and had died while remaining silent under Gestapo torture. Bruno asked for the Curator, whom he knew from a previous case, and asked if there was any place that collected details of naturalised Spaniards who had been awarded the Resistance medal. The Curator asked for details, took Bruno's email address and promised to find out what he could.

Then Bruno called Rollo, headmaster of the local college, to ask when Anita had first started teaching in St Denis, and who among the other teachers might have been close to her. He was given two names, but while neither one knew of Anita as Juanita, he learned that Anita had been a member of the Communist Party, and that she had arrived in town and started work in 1985. Bruno's next call was to Montsouris, the only communist on the St Denis Council, and his inquiry was met with the usual suspicion.

'I'm trying to find Horst, that German archaeologist,' Bruno began. 'He's disappeared and he was a great friend of Jan, the blacksmith. Jan said that he'd met Horst through Anita, so if I was wondering if there were any other old friends he might have known through her. I'm clutching at straws here so any help you can give . . .'

'Horst wasn't in the party, I can tell you that. Nor was Anita, really. She paid her dues, but it was no secret she was a member out of sentiment because her father had been a lifelong member. I think he was in the International Brigades, or something in the Spanish war. I remember she said her dad came into the party through the Resistance, when he was in the FTP. But that's all I know, and she's been dead for years now.'

Bruno knew that the FTP were the *Francs-Tireurs et Partisans*, the communist wing of the Resistance. He called Bordeaux again to tell the Curator of this extra snippet of information.

'I could have told you that,' the Curator replied. 'We've found a fair bit on our friend Joxe. He escaped from Camp Gurs in 1940, like a lot of the internees did. It wasn't well guarded and he had relatives in France, among the Basques in Bayonne. They probably wangled him some identity papers. He was in the FTP from the beginning, after Hitler invaded the Soviet Union in 1941, and with his Spanish experience he did a lot of training of the young lads in the Maquis. He also helped organise the Spanish refugees. The citation for his medal says he fought at Tulle and Terrasson in the summer of '44 and was wounded.'

'I knew I could count on you for this,' Bruno said. 'Thank you, it's a great help.'

'Hang on, there's more,' the Curator said. 'He joined the French army when he recovered and fought his way into Germany in '45. That's how he escaped being rounded up and sent back to Spain like so many of the other war refugees.

The British and Americans were worried about these Resistance-trained Spaniards going back to overthrow Franco and replace him with a communist regime. So they handed a lot of them back to Franco's tender mercies.'

'I never knew that,' said Bruno, his satisfaction at tracking down the information suddenly chilled.

'Not many people do. The Cold War started a lot earlier than most people think.'

CHAPTER TWENTY

Although the sun was out, Pamela was wearing a heavy woollen coat in black, a cream cashmere shawl around her shoulders and black boots that somehow looked both elegant and sturdy when Bruno raced into her courtyard, scattering gravel. She waved goodbye to Fabiola and climbed in beside him, pulling her carry-on bag onto her knees and looking nervously at her watch after she kissed him.

'I checked the *météo*. It's cold in Edinburgh,' she said, gesturing at her coat as he drove off. She began to wrestle with the strap of the seat belt.

'Just that small bag?' He wished he could have driven her all the way to Bordeaux.

'I have clothes there at Mother's house. Are you sure you can take care of the horses?'

'Fabiola will help,' he said. 'Don't worry about things here. Have you had any more news about your mother?'

'Yes, from my aunt, who saw her and said that it's her left side that's affected. But she recognised my aunt. She just can't speak much, but the doctor says that should come back in time.' She was twisting the black leather gloves in her hands as she stared through the windscreen. 'Will we be in time for the train?'

'Comfortably,' he said, but pressed the accelerator a little harder, glad that his new police van had a better turn of speed than the old one. 'Have you eaten?' he asked.

'Fabiola made me eat an omelette and an apple and drink some tea. She put a sandwich and a bottle of water in my bag. I'll be fine.' She looked at her watch again. 'I'm worried about the train.'

'If I have to, I'll put the siren on.' He tried to make light of it.

'This is the time I should be processing all the bookings for the *gîtes* this summer,' she fretted. 'I'll go broke if I can't get them all settled and the deposits in the bank.'

'There are bound to be internet places in Edinburgh where you can attend to that. I can check your mail and pay cheques into the bank,' Bruno said, looking both ways before turning onto the busy main road toward Le Buisson. He understood that she was saying these things as a way to make a mental list of things to be done, an effort to impose control over her life again after the shock of the news about her mother. She needed reassurance.

'These things can all be resolved. Right now, your concern is your mother, so don't worry about anything to do with St Denis. We can take care of things here. I can send you reports by email.'

'I can't leave it all to you, Bruno,' she said, rummaging in her handbag to check that she had her passport and the printout of her boarding pass. 'You have more than enough on your plate as it is, and now this dynamite and the corpse at the dig and the foie gras and Horst disappearing . . . Oh God, this is all happening at the worst possible time. And now there's Charles.'

Bruno hated taking his eyes off the road when he was driving, but he looked quickly across at her, not sure what she meant.

'It means I'll have to see my husband again,' she said, her voice flat and almost dull. She was looking fixedly at the road ahead, not meeting Bruno's eye. 'He stayed very close to Mummy even after the divorce and she always thought the world of him. She was furious when I left him, barely spoke to me for ages. He still visits her from time to time.'

'That's to be expected,' he said, not sure why she was telling him this. Pamela had always spoken of her mother with great affection, even though Bruno had sometimes wondered why she never came to visit her daughter in France. 'An illness in the family, it brings people together.'

'It's not that,' she said. 'It's just that knowing I'll see him will bring back all the things I disliked about marriage, not just him but the institution, the way it forces people into roles.' She paused, and then said almost to herself, 'I hate depending on people, or their depending on me.'

Bruno wondered whether she was talking about their relationship, rather than her former husband. She was still twisting her gloves in her hands, her knuckles white. He slowed at the last bend before the Stop sign and the turn onto the bridge over the Dordogne. Small drops of rain spattered his windscreen.

'I don't know why I'm talking about this,' she said. 'The thought of seeing him again just adds to all the pressure, I suppose. And my mother will be so pleased to see him, probably more than she will to see me. I'm the daughter who let her down, with no grandchildren and a failed marriage.'

'It's a difficult time for you,' he said. Pamela had always made it clear that she had no desire to settle down and was determined never to have children. They had never talked seriously about it, but it was something that Bruno knew placed a limit on their relationship. He sometimes asked himself if it had been a mistake to break his traditional rule of never starting an affair with someone who lived in St Denis.

'He'll probably expect to stay at the house when he comes up and I'll have to be polite to him,' she said, her voice cold. 'God, I hate that kind of acting.'

Perhaps unconsciously, Bruno thought, she had timed her last remark to end just as he turned the final bend that led to the train station. They still had a few minutes before the train left.

'Just think about your mother. She's the only thing that matters now.' He brought the car to a halt outside the station. 'Would it help if I came to Scotland?'

'No, absolutely not. That would just make everything much more complicated and it's much more help to me that you'll be living at my place and looking after the horses. But it's sweet of you to offer. I know this is a busy time for you, but I don't want you to start living on pizzas and sandwiches.'

He laughed. 'You know me better than that.'

'Fabiola will keep an eye on you. She said she'll invite you round for meals.'

He opened the door, climbed out and walked quickly round to help her with her bag, then held open the station door for her. 'Have you got your train ticket?'

'I'll get one on board – no, don't wait for me.'

He ignored her, went to the ticket counter and greeted Jean-Michel, who played for St Denis and whose nose was still swollen from his encounter with Teddy at the rugby practice. He bought her an open return, exchanged a jest about Jean-Michel's bruises, punched Pamela's ticket in the required yellow box and led the way across the rails to the platform for Bordeaux.

'I have no idea how long I'll have to stay,' she said as they walked across the wooden pathway over the rails that led to the far platform for the Bordeaux train. 'I suppose it will depend on her recovery and whether she can continue to live alone.'

'You could bring her over here. You have plenty of room.'

'She'd hate it, being away from Edinburgh and her friends. She's always wanted me to move back there.'

Bruno hadn't known that. He could see the train coming in the distance. They were the only people on the platform. He took her hand, still gripping the mangled gloves. He looked her in the eye, raised her hand to his lips and kissed the inside of her wrist. She looked back, her lip trembling.

'I'll miss you, but we'll take care of everything here. Don't worry. And if you need me . . .'

'God, this is like a scene from *Brief Encounter*,' she said, looking behind her at the approaching train.

'From what?' He spoke loudly over the squeal of the train's brakes and the rumble of metal wheels.

'It's an old film that always makes me cry,' she said. 'It's very British, about a doomed love affair and a railway station. Only it had steam trains.'

'I like steam trains,' he said, pressing the little green button on the gleaming blue and silver door that slid back with smooth, electronic grace. He put her case aboard, turned back and took her in his arms to kiss her firmly on the lips and then lifted her onto the train as the guard blew his whistle. Her bronze-red hair spread out, tumbling over the cream cashmere on her shoulders, and there were tears in her eyes. As he watched, one spilled over and rolled down onto her cheek.

'*Bon voyage*, my beautiful Pamela, and I hope your mother is soon better and don't worry about the horses, or anything.'

The train doors slid together, leaving her standing behind them, one hand to her eye, the other raised in an uncertain gesture that might have been a farewell wave or she might have been reaching to him through the glass. The train began to move and he stood immobile, watching it diminish down the track.

'*Ça va*, Bruno?' It was Jean-Michel. 'Can I help you with something?'

He shook his head. 'A woman,' he said. 'Saying goodbye.'

Jean-Michel looked at him quizzically. 'But that was your Mad Englishwoman. She lives here. She'll be back.'

'She's not mad,' said Bruno, quietly. 'And she's from Scotland.' He crossed back over the rails to the ticket hall and out to his van in the forecourt.

Bruno was putting down the phone after telling Clothilde there was still no news of Horst when the Mayor called his name. Along with most of the rest of the employees of the Mairie, the Mayor was looking at the small TV set in the staffroom beside the kitchen, and peering over the heads of others Bruno could see on the screen a shot of Gravelle's wrecked showroom with a headline 'War on Foie Gras?'

The next image was the scrawled slogan on the wall of the factory, and then a short interview with a tongue-tied Arnaud Gravelle. A brief cheer went up as they saw their Mairie on screen, and then a close-up of the Mayor standing beside the old stone pillars of the market hall.

'There's no excuse for these attacks on innocent farmers and shopkeepers going about their normal and entirely legal duties,' the Mayor was saying. 'Foie gras is one of the glories of French cuisine and a pillar of our economy and only crazy militants would resort to this kind of violence, bombing a quiet country town. We count on the police to bring these extremists to justice.'

Another brief cheer greeted the Mayor's remarks, but then the TV reporter, standing on the bridge with the river Vézère flowing placidly behind him, said not all the local authorities agreed. And some maintained that foie gras was indeed cruel to animals. The image shifted again, to Annette, their new magistrate, standing on the steps of the

Gendarmerie. She looked calm, attractive and highly professional in neat white blouse and trim blue jacket.

'There have been other non-violent attacks protesting against this cruelty to animals,' Annette said. 'Two demonstrations have taken place against local duck farms, and on the second occasion the farmer fired his shotgun and we found blood at the scene. Perhaps in an understandable response to this violence, it seems an escalation has taken place. But I note that it was a bombing against property in which nobody was injured. As the investigating magistrate I take this very seriously, but I regret to say that the local authorities seem more concerned with protecting their foie gras industry than with seeing justice done.'

'Do you mean that your investigations have been deliberately obstructed?' the interviewer asked. The staffroom of the Mairie was silent in shock.

'I mean precisely that, and I will be filing a complaint to the competent authorities,' Annette said. 'There are laws against cruelty to animals and I'm convinced that foie gras is not just cruel, it's barbaric.'

The camera cut away as the dozen or so people in the staffroom erupted in jeers and booing.

'If not a war on foie gras, it looks like a war over foie gras, here in St Denis, in the Périgord, where a bomb destroyed a local factory producing the famed delicacy this morning,' said the reporter, signing off.

'And now sports,' said the news announcer and the Mayor stepped forward, turned off the TV, ejected the videotape and turned to the staff.

'This is a serious situation and I'll be convening a full council meeting to discuss our response,' he told his staff. 'All media questions, and any inquiries from the magistrate, will be referred directly to me until further notice. Bruno, please join me in my office.'

'This is war,' said the Mayor, once inside his office with the door closed. 'What grounds might she have for complaint against us?'

'Capitaine Duroc has made sure that she blames me for that demonstration when the farmers blockaded the Gendarmerie,' Bruno said. 'So now she thinks I organised it and she's demanded my phone records to prove it.'

'What will those records show?'

'Nothing. No calls that morning. I said I was happy for her and Duroc to look at my phone logs.'

'Good.' The Mayor paused, then looked at Bruno quizzically. 'I don't want to pry into your emotional life, but is there anything personal that's gone on between you two that would explain this vendetta? Hell hath no fury like a woman scorned, that sort of thing?'

'No, not at all, though I gave her a parking ticket once,' he said with a grin. 'She may try to blame me for the disappearance of the chief suspect, the Dutch student at the dig, who has apparently returned home to Holland. But since the magistrate has filed no charges against the girl, and has just made it publicly clear that she is in sympathy with the allegations of cruelty against animals, she's on weak ground. Remember, she used the word "barbaric" about foie gras, a dish that's eaten in two-thirds of French households.

When it comes to a battle for public opinion I don't think she can win.'

'Are you sure that's the right terrain?'

'No, that's our last ditch,' Bruno said. 'We have to do two things. First, we have to separate her from Duroc. And you don't want to know, but I think I have a way to do that. Second, and this you do want to know because you'll have to be part of it, we attack her credentials in this case.'

'How do we do that?'

Bruno explained that he'd already asked her, in front of Sergeant Jules, to recuse herself from the case on grounds of partiality. In view of what she'd just said on TV she'd have no choice. It was unfair to have a magistrate investigating an affair where her prejudice was so public.

'Most people already think the magistrates are just a bunch of lefties,' said the Mayor, nodding in agreement.

'True, but we mustn't say that,' Bruno insisted. 'The last thing we want is to get all the magistrates rallying to her side in solidarity.'

The Mayor looked at him keenly, a half-smile on his face. 'You want us to speak more in sorrow than in anger.'

'Precisely,' Bruno replied. 'We love French justice, we want a magistrate. We just maintain we have a right to be investigated by a magistrate who hasn't already told the French public that we're a bunch of barbarians because we make a food that France loves.'

'Meanwhile, we'd better get some allies standing with us. I'll get the Société de Gastronomes de France to complain to the Justice Minister,' said the Mayor, his eyes lighting up.

'We can ask the great chefs of France for their views on foie gras. I'll get my old friends in the Senate to pass a resolution on foie gras as part of our national heritage. I'll get all the other mayors in the Périgord to join us. The farmers' union, the *vignerons* of Monbazillac and Sauterne, the *députés* of the *Assemblée Nationale* – we'll build a coalition, Bruno.'

'And we have to make sure that no coalition rallies around her. Bring in Alphonse,' Bruno said. 'He's a Green, but he's one of our own councillors and he likes his foie gras. We get him on our side and we split the Green movement. We have to think where she might get support, and work out how we can neutralise it in advance. We have to leave her with no allies but the extremists.'

'Leave this to me,' the Mayor said, rubbing his hands together with glee. 'This is my speciality. This is politics.'

CHAPTER TWENTY-ONE

The Danish student was named Harald, and being short, plump and dark-haired he could hardly have looked less like Bruno's mental image of a descendant of Vikings. But he spoke good French, his eyes were keen with intelligence and he was not lacking in self-confidence.

'That guy's not a native Danish-speaker,' said Harald, settling back into the passenger seat of Clothilde's car as she climbed in. She handed a wrapped brown paper parcel that contained a shapely wrought-iron candlestick to Bruno, who was sitting in the back seat.

'You're sure?' Bruno asked. 'This is really important.'

'His Danish is OK, but he'd never fool another Dane. I'd say he was originally German, probably from Hamburg or somewhere,' said Harald, swivelling in his seat to look at Bruno. 'What's this about?'

'I'm not sure yet, but your Professor has disappeared mysteriously. Jan was his closest friend in these parts and now it seems there's something suspicious about him. I'll take this candlestick he wrapped and check his fingerprints, see if we can find out anything else. How much do I owe you for the candlestick, Clothilde?'

'If it helps find Horst, consider it a gift,' she said, starting the car and heading back towards St Denis. 'This all seems a bit cloak-and-dagger, you hiding in the back seat.'

'Better not to raise Jan's suspicions,' said Bruno. 'It seemed natural enough for you to bring along a young Danish student to meet the only other Dane in the district. Just so long as it didn't make Jan think he was being checked out.'

'No, I was pretty casual, just asking him what he liked about the area, why he'd stayed, if he missed going back to Denmark, that kind of thing,' said Harald, who had evidently enjoyed his brief foray into police work. 'And I asked him if he knew who'd won the Danish soccer final – just friendly chit-chat.'

'Did he know?'

'No. He said he sometimes got *Politiken* to keep up with the news, but he didn't follow sports much. That surprised me a bit because he had a copy of *L'Equipe* in front of him when I saw him in a café early this morning. That's your sports paper, isn't it?'

'It is indeed,' Bruno said. 'Could Jan's accent come from being born on the border? He said everybody round there spoke German as much as Danish.'

'He's right about that, but they're still Danes. I had a girl-friend from down there once and visited her a few times. They speak Danish like me, and he doesn't. I'm sure he's not one of us.'

'Anybody else there?'

'Some young guy. We weren't introduced and he didn't

speak, but I was pretty sure he didn't understand the Danish we were speaking.'

'I'm not even sure he understood my French,' added Clothilde.

Bruno nodded, remembering the young relative of Juanita he'd met at the smithy when he called, the one that Jan had said was learning the business. The name escaped him. When Clothilde dropped him at the Mairie, Bruno took the wrapped candlestick in his own car to the château at Campagne. The workmen had been replaced by armed security guards who called up to Isabelle before letting him enter.

Isabelle had installed herself in what must have been the master bedroom. It was vast, with high ceilings and three tall *portes-fenêtres* that opened on a broad balcony overlooking the gardens. Beyond the château wall, Bruno could just see the windsock of the helicopter pad. Inside the room was an old-fashioned four-poster bed draped in great swoops of heavy cream damask.

'Apparently there was a lovely scene of nymphs and cherubs on the ceiling, but they couldn't save it so they had to paint over it,' she said from the Louis Seize armchair at the elegant desk that stood before the central window. A huge bouquet of flowers dominated the desk.

'You could get used to living like this,' Bruno said.

'Not really,' said Isabelle, gesturing at the small and functional folding table beside her desk. It held two mobile phones and a military radio. Leaning against it was a cork board thumbtacked with security rotas, phone numbers and call signs. 'I seem to bring this chaos with me.'

'Are you sleeping here?' he asked.

She shook her head. 'The bed isn't even made up. I stay at the hotel over the road, but I hate working out of a hotel bedroom. This is perfect.'

She looked at the parcel in Bruno's hands, smiling, and surprised him when she asked, 'Is that a present?'

'Yes, of course,' he said, recovering swiftly. 'But first we have to get it checked for Jan's fingerprints and see if the Danes or Germans can trace him that way.'

In the courtyard, Isabelle had a mobile police unit at her disposal that could deal with fingerprints. She directed Bruno to it, saying that she would need the prints scanned and emailed to her so that she could forward them. While that was being done, she rang Danish police colleagues in Copenhagen and asked them to check on the details of date and place of birth that Bruno had taken down from Jan's *carte de séjour*. When he returned to her room, Bruno sifted through the reports that had come in from other national police units on the background of the various archaeology students.

Nothing seemed to stand out, except for young Kasimir, who was supposed to have been fulfilling his duties as a conscript at an army camp for his Easter vacation, rather than digging in the soil of Périgord. Bruno grinned. He could imagine Kasimir talking his way out of that problem.

Bruno picked up the report from the British police saying that nothing was known on Teddy, no arrests or driving offences, not even a parking ticket. There was a photocopy of the passport, and then suddenly Bruno stopped. Teddy was short for Edward, the name on his credit card and pass-port. But the British police record listed him as Todor (Edward) Gareth Lloyd. But Todor was not a name Bruno recognised, which made him curious. What did the British mean when they put the name Edward in brackets? Why did the passport give his name as Edward? Could he have changed his name?

Bruno asked Isabelle for the use of her laptop. He went into Google.fr, and typed in the name Todor. A blizzard of Bulgarian and Hungarian names came up, variations on Theodor, which left him scratching his head. Then on a hunch he added the word 'Basque' and again a flurry of names emerged, but this time full of Basque connections. So Todor was a Basque name. Bruno opened his notebook and looked up the brief remarks he had scribbled after visiting Jan at the smithy. The name of Juanita's taciturn relative was Galder. He typed that into Google and again up came a blizzard of Basque references.

Coincidence was piling improbably upon coincidence, and he needed more data. He called Isabelle and showed her the British police report and the Google pages. She moved her chair alongside his and took over the computer, going into her own database, and clicked on the file of documents marked 'Campagne' and then on a sub-folder marked 'Etudiants'. As he moved aside to make room for her, he could not help but see a large card attached to the bouquet of flowers on her desk. It said, 'In thanks and admi-ration, Carlos.'

What could that mean? Bruno felt the sly curl of jealousy start to unfurl in his mind, and tried to stamp on it. Isabelle had no obligation to him. She was a free woman with her own life to lead. Perhaps he was being more sensitive after recently saying goodbye to Pamela, he told himself. *Putain*, he had to stop this. He was going round in circles while there was a job to do. Come on, Bruno. Focus.

'I asked the various police forces for more detail on the students and dumped it all into this file,' Isabelle said, unaware that he had noticed the card. She began searching through the assorted pdf files until she came to a further sub-file marked RU for *Royaume-Uni*, United Kingdom. Two more clicks and she brought up Teddy's birth certificate. He had been born in Swansea on 26 March 1986. His mother was listed as Mary Morgan Lloyd, and her occupation as Student. The father was listed as Todor Felipe Garcia, occupation Mechanic. Teddy had been born in Swansea maternity hospital.

'Felipe Garcia are Spanish names, but not Basque,' said Bruno.

'I know,' Isabelle replied. 'Let's do some more checking.'

She went into her own secure Interior Ministry database and put in the name Todor Felipe Garcia with a date range from 1984 to 1986. Three items came up. The first was a *carte de séjour* issued in Biarritz in September 1984, for a Spanish citizen of that name, employed as a mechanic at a local garage. The second was a speeding fine issued in Bordeaux in April 1985. The third was the report of a missing person, filed on 30August 1985, by a British citizen, Mary Morgan Lloyd, employed as an au pair with a French family

in Talence, Bordeaux. She reported that Todor Felipe Garcia
had disappeared from his rented apartment and from his
workplace a week earlier.

'She would have known by then that she was pregnant,'
said Isabelle, counting on her fingers. 'Poor girl, she must
have been frantic with worry about him.'

She clicked on the fourth line on her screen that simply
contained three asterisks. She double-clicked on it and a
pop-up window appeared.

'Turn aside Bruno,' she said. 'This is an Intel database
from the RG files and I need to punch in my own password.'

He looked away until she told him to turn back and the
screen was filled with lists of raw surveillance reports, the
name of Todor highlighted in yellow.

'Todor the father was a Basque militant, sure enough,
and we were keeping an eye on him,' she said, clicking on.
'Here is young Mademoiselle Lloyd, with whom he began a
relationship that summer, and she was checked out but
nothing known. We even checked on her with the British
police but she was clean.'

She clicked back again and followed Todor's trail further.
'Known associates,' she said, and sat back in surprise at the
length and detail of the list that appeared on her screen.
Pedro Jose Pikabea, injured in an attack on the Les Pyrenées
tavern in Bayonne on 29 March 1985. Pikabea allegedly was
a member of ETA. Another associate had been assassinated
the next day in St-Jean-de-Luz, a photo-journalist called
Xabier Galdeano. Another assassination on 26 June, of yet
one more of Todor's known associates, Santos Blanco

Gonzales, in Bayonne, and he too was an alleged ETA member.

'*Mon Dieu*, Bruno, everyone Todor knew was being bumped off that spring and summer, and all of them we suspected were carried out by GAL. You were right to talk about the dirty war, all these killings by Spanish agents, all on French soil. And here's one more, on 2 September, Juan Manuel Otegi, again a suspected ETA militant, killed in St-Jean-Pied-de-Port.'

Isabelle sat back again and looked at Bruno. 'We'll have to pick up this Teddy and interrogate him, find out just how much he knew about his father. And it looks to me as if his father could have been killed by GAL when Teddy was still in the womb, so we'll have to get the British to go and have a talk with his mother.'

'Teddy should be at Bergerac by now with the rest of the students,' said Bruno. 'You'd better get on to the Gendarmes, find out who went with them in the coach and get some more Gendarmes to the airport to make sure they hold him.'

Isabelle picked up her phone and made the call.

'And he was the one who found the unidentified corpse,' she said, turning back to Bruno after asking the General in Périgueux to arrange a Gendarme car to meet Teddy at Bergerac and bring him directly back to the château after the explosives check.

'So the question is, how did Teddy know where to look?' said Bruno. 'Somebody must have told him where the body was buried, and that somebody must have known about the killing of Teddy's father. So when did Teddy become an archaeologist and get himself onto the team going to exactly that site? Could Horst have been involved in that?'

'Who apart from Horst and Clothilde knew where they were going to dig?' asked Isabelle.

'Remember they did a preliminary dig last year, late in the summer. We can find out from Clothilde if Teddy was in that group.' Bruno picked up his own phone and called her, keeping his eyes on Isabelle, and then nodding excitedly at Clothilde's reply. He rang off.

'Teddy was indeed on the dig last summer, and he knew they'd be digging again,' said Bruno. 'But we still don't know how he knew where to look for the corpse.'

'Do you think it could be his father's?' she asked. 'The dates would seem to fit.'

'We aren't sure of that yet. We'll need a DNA check on Teddy, but I'm ready to bet it will be positive.'

A small buzz came from Isabelle's laptop, and she clicked into her secure mail window, again asking Bruno to turn aside while she entered yet another password to open the message.

'It's a reply from the Danish police,' she said. 'There is no record of any Danish citizen by the name of Jan Olaf Pedersen being born in 1942, and no record of anyone of that name being born in Kolding. The Danish passport number that Jan filed for his *carte de séjour* is a forgery. And the Danes would be grateful for any more information, since they would probably seek to file an extradition request.'

'You could send them the fingerprints your mobile team took from the candlestick,' said Bruno.

'Good idea,' she said. 'I'll send them along with a copy to Interpol for a search request.' She looked at him apologetically and closed the special database on her computer, saying, 'Sorry, Bruno. You understand.' She picked up her cane and limped out to arrange for a room, a security guard and a DNA test kit for Teddy's arrival.

Bruno was trying to make sense of all this information and not doing well. His mind did not work that way. So he pulled a piece of paper towards him and drew a box, writing inside it the name of Teddy's father with the date that Mary had notified his disappearance, and then drew an arrow to another box in which he wrote Teddy's name and date of birth. If the gestation period had been the usual nine months, Teddy had been conceived in June of 1985, and Mary should have known she was pregnant sometime in August. Todor had disappeared in the week before 30 August.

Then he drew three more boxes. He wrote down Horst's name in one, with an arrow to another where he wrote Jan's name, and an arrow to yet another in which he wrote Juanita's. Could Juanita, with her Basque background, have a connection to Todor? He drew a dotted line between them. That might even connect Horst's disappearance to the Basques. He put a question mark over his dotted line.

And who was Jan, if he wasn't Danish? Harald had said he sounded as if he came from Hamburg, just like Horst. Horst had a brother, but he was dead. Bruno tried to remember exactly what the Brigadier had said over the video connection. The brother had been reported dead, but by whom? By the East Germans, in the days when their so-called 'Democratic Republic' had been giving sanctuary to some of the Baader-Meinhof group? Could it be that the boxes all connected, Horst leading to Jan, who led to the Basques through Juanita?

Isabelle came back into the room with a phone at her waist starting to buzz. She answered it, listened and said, 'But surely they checked them all onto the bus?'

She listened again, and said crisply, 'So you mean to say that your Gendarme miscounted when they boarded the bus. I was hoping you might assign someone with a minimal level of efficiency, at least sufficient to count.'

She paused once more. 'We'll send you a full description,' she said, 'passport details with photograph and credit card numbers, and we'll get the British to put a stop on his card. With any luck, he won't get far.'

She closed the phone and looked at Bruno.

'They lost Teddy. He never got on the bus.'

CHAPTER TWENTY-TWO

Like any large hierarchical organisation, the Gendarmes were pleased to be given a simple and familiar task. They had a procedure for a manhunt and the routine deployments clicked smoothly into place. Patrols were assigned to each rail station and pairs of motorcycle cops were dispatched to the main roundabouts and the ramps onto the autoroutes. Petrol stations and car-hire firms were visited and banks, ferries and airlines alerted to Teddy's credit-card number. Faxes of Teddy's description and details, particularly his distinctive height, went out to the municipal police of every town in the Department and to the immigration posts at every airport and frontier. Europol was alerted and the staff of the liaison office with the British police were told to expect to stay round the clock.

'What sort of manpower does that leave us for searching for Horst?' Bruno asked Isabelle, once the flurry of phone calls died down. 'There are hundreds, maybe thousands of empty vacation homes and *gîtes* out there and he could be in any one.'

'Let me worry about that,' she said. 'You know the Gendarmes, they can only do one thing at a time. I agree with you that Horst's disappearance is probably connected, but so far it's more hunch than evidence.'

Bruno left Isabelle to her conference calls and drove from the château back to the municipal campsite where Monique seemed to be doing the same crossword and listening to the same radio station as when he'd last seen her. Again he was offered coffee. This time he refused.

'Still looking for that Kajte girl?' Monique asked 'They say she's gone back to Holland. Can't say I blame the girl with half the Gendarmerie hanging around here waiting to arrest her. I almost ran out of coffee.'

'It's Teddy's tent I need this time,' Bruno told her. 'He's done a jump and I need to know what he left behind.'

Monique stubbed out her Royale filter and led the way to the tent, where the two sleeping bags zipped together had been replaced by a single lonely sack, left open to air. Teddy's rucksack was still there. Donning a pair of evidence gloves, Bruno opened it, looking for the toilet bag. He zipped it open and saw with satisfaction that although the toothbrush had gone the hairbrush was still there.

'Do you want a receipt for this?' he asked Monique. 'I'll have to take the whole rucksack.'

'You'd better,' she said. 'Just so I'm covered if there's any comeback. And do you want the envelope he left in the safe? They usually leave valuables with us.'

'Yes, please.' He should have asked her if there was anything else.

Teddy had left a large manila envelope which seemed to contain only papers. Bruno put it into the rucksack, thanked

Monique and headed back to the mobile police unit parked at the château. From a previous case he recognised Yves, one of the forensic experts, and showed him the rucksack. Yves took fingerprints from the hairbrush handle and then used tweezers to take some hairs from the brush itself. Bruno checked that Yves had the DNA data on the unidentified corpse for comparison, and then lugged the rucksack up to Isabelle's stately room.

'Your English is better than mine.' He handed her Teddy's big envelope and started to unpack the rucksack. 'They've already taken Teddy's fingerprints from the hairbrush,' he told her as she slipped on some evidence gloves.

'Routine,' she shrugged, and began shuffling through the papers while Bruno searched the pockets of the rucksack and every item of clothing inside it. He unrolled pairs of socks, looked at name tags and labels and smoothed out scraps of paper, sweet wrappers and old bills that had found their way to the bottom of the sack.

Isabelle leafed through Teddy's papers and found his university transcripts, letters of recommendation from his professor and teachers, certificates from other archaeology digs where he'd worked, the stuff he'd need if the museum wanted to check his credentials.

'All as you'd expect, but what's this?' she said, looking up. 'This isn't his handwriting, at least it's not like his hand on these other papers.'

She held up what seemed like a crudely drawn map, which somehow looked much older than the rest of the papers in the envelope. She took it to the desk by the window, pushed aside the huge vase of flowers and beckoned Bruno across.

'Get rid of those damn flowers,' she said. He smiled to himself as he took the vase to the corner of the room and then joined her, bending over the map. It was a photocopy of an older document, but one of the corners had been covered when the photocopy was made, and the paper was much whiter there.

The map showed a river, joined by a stream, and then some lines that could signify contours and a small track leading from a road. The main feature was a cross, with some thin lines drawn as if to measure its distance from the road, the stream and the start of the contoured slope. Each line had some scrawled numbers beside it and arrows led off the page to other locations, identified only by initials.

'If those letters on the edge are SD, they could stand for St Denis,' said Isabelle.

'That would make these letters look like LE, which could be Les Eyzies, so this is the river,' said Bruno, drawing on his mental map of the district. Suddenly the location jumped into place.

'It's the archaeological dig,' he said. 'And those scrawls beside the lines are distances in metres. The track runs a hundred and twenty metres from the river, and then this cross here is fifteen metres from the stream, eight metres from the start of the contours. I'll need to go back and pace out the distances, but I think this is a map that shows where the unidentified corpse was buried.'

'So this is how Teddy knew exactly where to dig,' said Isabelle. 'And the map must have been drawn by somebody who knew where the body was buried, probably by some-body who took part in the killing. So how did Teddy get hold of it?'

'What's this blank patch?' Bruno asked. 'Why would they want to cover something when they made the copy?'

'That's simple.' She reached into her briefcase to pull out a file with a sheaf of documents inside. 'All bureaucracies work the same way,' she went on, pointing to the stamp of the French Interior Ministry at the top right-hand corner of her own papers, with spaces for a date and different departmental codes to be written in.

'This is a document that's been filed in some kind of registry, possibly official or state-controlled. Then some-body took it out of the files and photocopied it while concealing the registry mark that could identify it, and maybe identify whoever had taken it out.'

She turned the paper over and looked at a small scrawl of numbers on the back, in a different handwriting.

'Could be a phone number,' she said. Bruno reached for his mobile but she shook her head. 'Your number might be known. This one's anonymous.' She picked up a phone from the folding table, punched in the number and waited.

'It's an answer-phone in Spanish. Asked me to leave a message.' She picked up another phone, gave her name and ID code and asked for a subscriber check on the number. Bruno was studying the map.

'There's no writing on it apart from those initials for St Denis and Les Eyzies. It could come from anywhere,' he said. 'French or Spanish or even Russian.'

'Russians would use their own alphabet,' said Isabelle. 'If we assume that Todor was killed by the GAL, then this map could come from the GAL files, or at least from some Spanish file, maybe Ministry of the Interior or police intelligence.'

'Do we bring Carlos into this?'

'I'm not sure,' she said thoughtfully. 'I'd better fax this to the Brigadier and check with him.' She looked at her watch. 'He's going to be here later today and may be on the way. We'll just keep this to ourselves until he gets here. He can decide how far we want to share this.'

'I'll copy those coordinates and go out to the site and check them.' Bruno paused. 'Does this mean that you don't altogether trust Carlos?'

'I don't altogether trust anyone, Bruno. Except maybe the Brigadier, and on a good day, you – unless the interests of St Denis are concerned.' She smiled as she said it, a smile that grew wider as she saw his eyes dart across to the corner where he had put Carlos's flowers.

'Now I see why you want to know if I trust Carlos,' she said, her voice teasing. 'Bruno, I do believe you're getting jealous. And now you're blushing. That's not something I've seen before.'

He shook his head, half laughing, half embarrassed, not sure what to say, confused further by the presence in the room of the enormous bed. He was tempted to scoop her up in his arms and carry her to it, close the big damask curtains and forget about the world. 'You know I still care for you,' he said.

'And I for you,' she said, suddenly switching her mood

in a way that had always disconcerted Bruno. 'So why are you walking around me on eggshells as if you daren't approach? Is it because of Pamela?'

'Partly, not entirely. In fact, Pamela's had to go home. Her mother had a stroke. I'm waiting for news. Maybe it's that you're wounded,' he said. Of course he walked on eggshells around her: he no longer knew the rules of engagement, couldn't read the signals. Were they ex-lovers and still friends? Or colleagues thrown together by duty who had to forget that they had once shared a bed? Or should Bruno act on the question that sometimes kept him sleepless at night, the suspicion that Isabelle was the love of his life? He thrust the thought aside; the last time a woman had consumed him so deeply, she had been dead within the year in the snowbound hills around Sarajevo.

Isabelle was eyeing him coolly, waiting for him to say something else. He floundered for words. 'You shouldn't be back on duty, not yet, not while you still need that cane.'

'I'm not,' she snapped. 'I'm deskbound, light duties only. And I'm not destroyed by this, Bruno. I'm making a full recovery, even if I do have a titanium brace in my thigh. *Merde,* I thought you of all people would be able to understand this. You've been shot, too. It didn't stop you being a man and a bullet hole in my leg doesn't stop me being a woman, so why don't you treat me like one?'

'I'd like nothing better than to touch you, Isabelle. You know that.' He took her hand, pushing back the guilty memory of doing the same with Pamela just a few hours earlier. 'But every time we get together we break apart when you head back to Paris and I have to brace myself to soldier on through it all over again.'

'Doomed lovers,' she said with a wry smile, moving her hand from his lips to stroke his cheek. 'I guess it's never going to work, but we keep hoping that it will.'

A phone buzzed on her desk and she pulled her hand away. 'And we're supposed to be working,' she said. 'Dammit, Bruno, go and check that map and I'll see you at the evening meeting.'

He was going out of the door when she called, 'Wait.' He turned back. She muttered something into the phone and held the line open. 'It's the German police. They checked the fingerprints. Jan is Horst's brother, the one from the Red Army Faktion gang who was supposed to be dead.'

Bruno went to the stack of papers on the desk, looking for the sheets he'd been working on earlier. He pulled out his crude diagram with the boxes and the dotted line from Horst to Jan and the Basques. He showed it to Isabelle.

'This means that Galder, the young guy with bad French who Jan described as a cousin of his wife, is probably connected. Does Carlos have any mugshots of suspected ETA militants I could look at?'

'We have our own as well as theirs, passed on to us under the intelligence-sharing agreement,' she said. He tried to come up with a mental image of the youth. Medium height, slimly built, with dark hair and a prominent jaw. A straight nose and hands with long fingers that looked too delicate for a blacksmith's labours. Not much to go on, but Bruno would know him again if he saw him.

'They're in the file room downstairs, a big red folder on the shelf above the photocopier,' Isabelle said.

'Do you want me to bring Jan in?' he asked, reluctant to believe that Horst could be his brother's accomplice.

'He's ex-Baader-Meinhof, he'll probably be armed. I'll arrange a firearms team. Take a look at the mugshots, and then go and check the map coordinates and I'll have the team ready to go inside the hour. And I'll arrange to use the cells at the Gendarmerie when you bring him back. The Germans are faxing through an extradition order on a Euro-warrant.'

The archaeology dig had been deserted, all the students still going through the explosives checks at Bergerac, but the coordinates on the hand-drawn map were precise. When Bruno paced out the numbers on the sketch he found himself standing at the ever-lengthening trench where he had first met Teddy and first seen the corpse. As he led the way to Jan's smithy, a firearms team from Isabelle's security force in their unmarked van following behind, he wondered at the coincidence that had led a Spanish murder squad to pick the same burial place as prehistoric people had chosen for their dead thirty thousand years before.

Generation after generation, so many bodies must lie scattered in the soil of France, so many battlefields where the bones must lie thickly together. In Normandy and Dunkerque from the last war, at Verdun and the Somme from the *Grande Guerre*, at Gravelotte and Sedan from the Prussian war, the wars and bodies stretched back through the centuries to Spaniards and Englishmen, Normans and Arabs, Huns and Gauls and Romans. France is built on a heap of bones, he thought; we are the sum of all the dead that went before us. And here we are again, a troop of armed men with their weapons ready, heading across the placid Périgord country-side to enforce the will of the French state. He bit his lip to snap himself back to alertness, remembering how in the army he'd often been this way before going into action. He supposed it was some kind of defence mechanism, his subconscious trying to distract him from fear.

Bruno stopped at the turnoff to Jan's smithy and parked his van. He climbed into the back of the second vehicle and struggled into the flak jacket they handed him as they jerked and bounced over the ruts in the lane. The jacket's design did not seem to have improved since his days in Bosnia. It still left the throat and sides exposed, and he doubted if it would stop anything more than a 9mm. He'd seen men killed by an AK-47 round that had penetrated their jackets. Bruno looked at the squad with him. They had the extra armour of ceramic plates slipped into their jackets, front and rear. He raised his eyebrows at the Sergeant of the *Compagnies Républicaines de Sécurité* whose troops made up the firearms team. The Sergeant shook his head and shrugged: no plates for Bruno.

They had discussed the approach and Bruno had said there was no obvious reason for Jan to be alert and armed. He wanted to drive up beside the smithy, to go in himself while the armed team deployed quietly, and make the arrest. The Sergeant had objected, wanting his men in place while Bruno used the bullhorn to call Jan to give himself up. Bruno had won that argument, but as he clambered out of the truck, feeling clumsy from the flak jacket beneath his wind-cheater, he was wishing that he'd listened to the Sergeant.

The place was quiet, no sound of hammer on iron nor of Jan's salty curses, and none of the usual smell of burning coke. The smithy was empty, the tools all neatly tidied away and the fire cold. There was no car in the other barn and the door to the main house was locked, the windows shuttered. Bruno signalled to the truck and men in black with weapons pointed deployed around the rest of the property. As the Sergeant approached, Bruno pointed to the locked door. The Sergeant turned back to the van and returned with a heavy ram. He took one side, Bruno the other and they smashed it into the lock while another trooper stood cover behind them, his weapon aimed into the doorway. The door tore open but no sound or sign came from within.

The Sergeant went in first, flicking the button on the torch taped beneath the barrel of his FAMAS to illuminate the room. Bruno followed, and once the Sergeant came down from upstairs and pronounced the premises clear, Bruno flicked on the switch inside the doorway and the room blazed with light. He felt relieved. He'd begun to expect that they'd find Jan's dead body in the abandoned house.

'I'll search the house,' he told the Sergeant. 'I'd be grateful if your team could search everywhere else. Hold any papers that you find for me, and let me know of any signs that other people have stayed here. There's an office with a computer in the barn by the smithy. Leave that to me.'

Bruno took off his windcheater, wriggled out of the flak jacket and handed it to the Sergeant. 'I'd have thought they'd have improved these things since my day,' he said.

'You ought to see the new German ones,' the Sergeant

said. 'My brother's in the Paras in Afghanistan. He brought one back, light and terrific. Said it would stop anything short of an RPG.' He paused. 'What unit were you in?'

'Combat engineers, then attached to Paras,' said Bruno. The Sergeant raised his eyebrows and nodded slowly.

'You can count on us, then,' he said.

'Check in the smithy for any false walls or trapdoors or anything like a basement,' Bruno said. 'Get two of your lads to take a good look in that lean-to where he stores his coke. Shift some of it if you have to.'

The Sergeant nodded and Bruno went into the house, but there was no study, no box of family files and documents. Jan must have kept everything in the office in the smithy. There was a bookshelf of well-thumbed paperbacks, some in Danish and some in German, and a row of political books in French, presumably Juanita's.

The drawers in the main bedroom contained only clothing, and there were a lot of photos of Juanita standing on the chest. They seemed the only items in the house to have been dusted, which reminded Bruno that he'd always rather liked Jan. There were two other bedrooms, each with two single beds made up with creased and grubby sheets. Another four people had been staying here. In the spare bathroom he found tired towels and the discarded wrapping in Spanish of a disposable razor. In the bottom of the bath was a small, empty plastic bottle of shampoo, marked with the name of a hotel in Bayonne. That might be useful.

Still on the search for documents, Bruno looked in the usual places, the attics and the freezer, the water tank of the WC and beneath the plastic bags of the refuse bins. There was nothing. The smithy office contained paperwork from the business and all the household bills, each loosely stuffed into separate file boxes marked for water, gas, electricity and taxes. He pulled the drawers out of the filing cabinets. Wrapped in plastic and taped to the underside of the lower drawer were three passports, one West German and one East German, each of them a decade out of date, bearing the photo of a much younger and slimmer Jan. Both of the German passports, East and West, named him as Dieter Vogelstern. That settled any lingering question as to whether Jan was Horst's brother. There was also a Cuban passport, still valid with a more recent photo, in the name of Jan Pedersen, the same as the name on the Danish passport he had used to obtain his French residency. Tucked inside it Bruno counted eighty hundred-dollar bills.

He went outside and called Isabelle, asking if she could get a forensics team to Jan's place. There might be fingerprints or DNA traces that could help identify Jan's guests, and maybe even a credit-card number from the stay at the Bayonne hotel. He gave her the various passport numbers, marvelling at the vast international bureaucratic machine that he could summon into action for such an inquiry.

'The fact that Jan left the cash and the Cuban passport suggests that either he thinks he's coming back, or he left involuntarily,' he said.

'Or he doesn't suspect we know about him,' she said.

'Jan's no fool,' replied Bruno. 'He must have known his real identity was likely to emerge once I started asking about Horst's father and brother and said we'd be contacting the German police.'

'So if we assume that Jan's guests were the Basque unit, does that mean that the two brothers are in this voluntarily? You know them both, what's your assessment?'

'My views aren't worth much. I never suspected that Jan wasn't the Danish blacksmith he pretended to be,' said Bruno. 'For what's it worth, and I know him a lot better, I can't see Horst involved.'

Bruno rang off when he heard the Sergeant calling from a small, half-ruined pig barn some distance to the rear of the smithy. Part of the low roof had collapsed and the rest was bowed, a sure sign that the lathes had rotted, and the windows were covered with stout wooden shutters. Bruno hoped this would not be Jan's tomb, but the Sergeant was pointing at the door itself and the sturdy modern hasp and bolt, still shining new.

'It stinks of piss inside and there's a filthy camp bed,' the Sergeant said. 'I reckon someone was held prisoner here.'

Bruno looked in, and paused, taking the Sergeant's torch to shine it upward to see how much headroom there might be. There was one place where he could stand upright. Moving the torch around he saw a bucket, evidently the only sanitation available, and an army surplus camp bed of canvas and thin metal bars. A filthy blanket lay atop it and there was an empty plastic bottle beneath. Bruno switched off the torch and closed the door, trying to assess how much light Horst might have had. There were some cracks in the door and one or two in the apex of the roof, but the sense of darkness was very strong. He must have spent a wretched couple of days in this place, aware that his own brother was his gaoler.

Bruno opened the door again and shone the torch around, trying to see if Horst had left any scrap of paper or any scratch marks on the stones of the wall. He crouched down beside the camp bed, shining the torch into every seam and each pouch where the metal bars fitted to see if some slip of paper had been squeezed into the gap. There was nothing. He was bracing himself to start examining the contents of the bucket when the Sergeant let out an exclamation.

Bruno turned. 'See this?' the Sergeant asked, pointing to scratches on the inside of the door. The marks were only visible now that Bruno had opened the door wide and folded it back against the outside wall. The sinking sun threw the scratches into relief.

'ETA = Jan = RAF,' he read aloud.

It was proof that Jan had been part of Baader-Meinhof and was now working with ETA and the Basques. And further proof that Horst had been kept there, and that whatever protection he'd been prepared to give his brother had been withdrawn. Horst was a victim, rather than an accomplice.

'Sarge,' came a shout from the lean-to beside the smithy. One of the troopers had emerged and was waving, his face blackened with the coke they had moved, much of it now piled on the bare ground outside. 'We got something.'

The floor of the lean-to was made of a solid sheet of cement, except in the rear corner where coke dust in the cracks revealed a large square. The troops must have swept the floor for the cracks to emerge. Bruno was impressed. The Sergeant ran a good unit.

'Let's get a spade and lever it up,' said Bruno. 'It's meant to be opened so it shouldn't be too hard.'

It took two spades, even though the cement in the square proved to be a thin skim over a wooden trapdoor that opened to reveal a hole about a metre square and half that in depth. There were three bundles inside wrapped in plastic.

'Careful,' said Bruno. 'Take a good look for any wires. It could be booby-trapped.'

After a thorough search with torches, they swept off the coke dust and took the bundles outside. The first contained a well oiled Heckler and Koch machine pistol with four magazines taped along the barrel, and a 9mm automatic in a separate plastic wrapping with a box of cartridges, a cleaning kit and a spare magazine. The second bundle contained a wooden box that bore NATO and German markings. It held twelve compartments, four for fragmentation grenades, four for smoke and three for CS gas. The twelfth compartment contained blasting caps wrapped in cotton wool. The final bundle was the lightest, and Bruno recognised it as soon as the final layer was unwrapped revealing the familiar waxed paper.

'Plastic explosive,' he said. 'Enough to blow up a château.' He leaned down for a closer look but the waxed paper was blank. Still, he was pretty sure of the make and so was the Sergeant.

'Semtex?' the Sergeant asked. Bruno nodded.

But for Bruno, the real mystery was why this cache of

arms and explosives was still here. If Jan was working with the Basques, this was exactly the kind of malleable and easily controlled explosive they'd need, rather than the crude dynamite that had been stolen. But the trapdoor under the coke had not been disturbed for years. The coke dust on the wrapping testified to that. So why had the Basques not taken the Semtex? Perhaps they'd been in too great a hurry and had to leave it, planning to return for it later. Or perhaps, Bruno suddenly thought, Jan had never told them the explosives were there. He scratched his head as he pondered the implications, wondering just how long ago Jan had buried the weapons. Bruno made a mental note to keep the place guarded, even though he'd take the guns and explosives. But that meant someone must have warned them a search was coming. Maybe not, thought Bruno. The coke fire of the smithy had been cold, dead for at least a day. They would have had plenty of time to remove the arms cache. That raised another question: was Jan really working with them? Might he be acting under duress, with his brother as hostage? And where was he now?

CHAPTER TWENTY-FOUR

The Sergeant had left two men on guard at Jan's smithy, waiting for the forensics team to arrive. On the unlikely chance that the Basques might return, Bruno had decided against wrapping the place in yellow crime-scene tape. Now in his own van, he led the way back to the château, checking his watch to see if he'd be in time for the evening security meeting.

On his van radio, tuned to Radio Périgord, he heard the familiar tones of Montsouris, the only communist on the town council, defending foie gras as the luxury the working man of France had always been able to afford, and denouncing foreigners and city-slicker animal rights fanatics for daring to question France's culinary heritage. He switched to France-Inter and heard his Mayor saying much the same, except that he denounced 'a biased young magistrate with the ink still wet on her diploma who calls us barbarians for making France's favourite delicacy'. On Périgord Bleu, Alphonse the Green was explaining why his party supported 'the wholesome and organic foie gras of the region'.

As he turned the corner at the church in St Chamassy,

the clatter of a helicopter, almost certainly the one carrying the Brigadier, began to drown out the voices of the council members of St Denis. He glanced up to see the familiar silhouette of a Fennec, the unarmed model the French army used to transport its top brass. It was time for the Brigadier to take charge, Bruno thought. The summit was just two days away. The chopper would certainly beat him to the château.

When Bruno pushed open the door to the conference room, the Brigadier looked coldly at his watch. But then his expression turned to astonishment as Bruno held the door for the Sergeant and two troopers, their arms filled with the weapons from the arms cache. The big box of grenades made a satisfying thud as Bruno signalled one of the troopers to put it on the floor rather than damage the grand antique table.

'You could have called to tell me about this, Bruno,' said Isabelle. 'You didn't have to make an entrance.'

'You wouldn't have heard us, Mademoiselle,' said Bruno's new ally, the Sergeant. 'We were under the flight path of a helicopter.' The Sergeant noticed the Brigadier, in civilian clothes but clearly a military man and very obviously in charge. He saluted.

Bruno explained the origin of the weapons, and suggested the automatic pistol should be given to the mobile forensics unit to see if there were any matches for the bullets. Isabelle looked at Bruno.

'Do you have any particular matches in mind?'

'From the firing pin, it's been used, and more than once,

and cleaned by someone who made a good job of it. It's the right calibre and it looks as if it had been hidden away for the right length of time. So I'd like to know if it could've been the gun used to kill our no longer unidentified corpse,' said Bruno. 'I don't think the Heckler and Koch has been fired since it left the factory.'

'Semtex?' asked Carlos, studying the plastic explosive. 'We'd better check it for tags.'

'It may be too old for tags,' said Bruno. 'I think it dates from the 1980s, or even earlier, original Czech stuff, supplied by the East German Stasi to their allies in the Baader-Meinhof gang. It's been well stored, but at this age I'm not sure how stable it's going to be.'

'Sergeant, take that bloody stuff out to the yard,' said the Brigadier. 'Better still, take it out well beyond the wall and get an explosives expert to check it over. And now perhaps somebody can fill me in on these developments, starting with this corpse you seem to have identified.'

Isabelle took over the agenda, and went through their discoveries of the day, from Teddy's Basque connections to Jan's background in Baader-Meinhof and his relationship to Horst. She confirmed that Bruno had gone through the available mugshots in an effort to identify the young Spaniard who had been seen at Jan's smithy, but without success. She handed over to the General from the Gendarmes, who reported that despite the massive deployment of troops they had not yet located Teddy. Isabelle then said that the Dutch police had visited Kajte's home, and although her mother had said she had returned, the Dutch police were unable to confirm her statement. The Dutch had then checked that Kajte had used her credit card to buy a through ticket from Périgueux to Amsterdam, but the ticket for the Paris to Amsterdam leg on the Thalys train had not been used.

'So the girl is running loose and so is the young Englishman,' said the Brigadier. 'Do we presume they are together?'

'They've both turned off their cellphones, so the last tracking we have of them is Teddy in Bergerac at 1 p.m. today. We don't think Kajte even went to Paris.'

'I thought the first report on this Teddy said he did not board the bus with the other students in St Denis,' the Brigadier said. 'How did he get to Bergerac?'

'It seems he did board the bus,' said the Gendarme General, his face down on his papers, refusing to meet the Brigadier's eyes. 'Somehow he slipped out of the back door when the Gendarme escort at the front of the bus was distracted.'

'Distracted how?'

'One of the young women students. It seems that this Teddy was quite popular and the other students cooperated to help him escape.'

'We're not doing very well, are we,' the Brigadier said, in a way that squashed any attempt to interpret it as a question. 'We've also lost track of the Basque unit and of these two German brothers. And our two ministers arrive the day after tomorrow. So far, our only achievements have been to establish the identity of a twenty-year-old corpse, to find an arms cache and to help our German friends identify a long-lost terrorist from the Red Army Faktion.'

'We have cancelled all leave and I'm bringing in more *moto-gendarmes* from other Departments to help search the roads,' said the Gendarme General. 'We're also visiting all the car-hire firms and garages.'

'We've put a stop on the credit cards of these two students?'

'The Dutch say they can't stop the girl's cards without evidence of criminal behaviour,' interjected Isabelle. 'But we have a watch on the cards. If she uses hers to hire a car, we'll know about it.'

'Not necessarily,' said Bruno. 'Small garages round here will take a credit-card imprint as a deposit, but won't always put the charge through until the hire period is over and the vehicle returned. That's why it makes sense to visit all the garages.'

A silence fell, and after a moment Isabelle broke it to say that the next item on her agenda was a report from Carlos on the Spanish side of the inquiry. He had little to say, and rightly judged that the Brigadier only wanted the essentials. Madrid could not yet confirm the identity of the long-dead corpse as Todor Garcia but were working on it. He had nothing further on the Basques, nor anything on Teddy.

As he paused there was a knock on the door and one of the forensics team came into the room and handed a file to Isabelle. She read it and looked up, eyes shining.

'We can now confirm from the DNA evidence on a hair-brush Bruno found that Teddy is Todor's son,' she announced. 'This means he must have known where the grave was located. I don't know how he knew, but that's now a further reason we need to find him.' Bruno raised his eyebrows a little at her decision not to mention the map, but remained silent.

'Anything else on the agenda?' the Brigadier asked. Isabelle shook her head.

'Our priority is clearly the Basque active-service unit,' the Brigadier said. 'They're the ones who constitute the threat to our ministers. The students are secondary and I suggest the Gendarmes shift their deployments accordingly. Since we don't know the identity of the Basques, we'd better focus on the two Germans who are with them, willingly or otherwise. Have photos and descriptions of these two Germans been distributed?'

'Photos are being printed now, sir,' said Isabelle. Every Gendarmerie in this and all neighbouring Departments, all municipal police and all train stations would have them within hours. The British police were interviewing Teddy's mother and had promised a verbal briefing later this evening.

'Finally, you may want to bring in a media specialist,' she said. 'There's been a leak. The German police have already had one inquiry about the finding of a Baader-Meinhof militant who was supposed to be dead. They stalled it, but we could have a flood of media arriving just as the summit is supposed to start. If the news about the kidnapped archaeologist brother gets out, it'll be even worse.'

'Very well. The Minister's press spokeswoman is travelling here with him, but I'll arrange for someone to fly down tomorrow. Any questions?'

'Yes, sir,' said Bruno. 'What are the rules of engagement? If these Basques are spotted, I mean.'

'Shoot them on sight,' said Carlos. Bruno glanced at him. The Spaniard's face was grim; he wasn't joking.

'This has already been agreed at ministerial level. We use the standard procedure on terrorist cases,' said Isabelle. 'Do not shoot first unless your own or civilian lives are in danger. Use firearms in self-defence. They get one invitation to surrender. All security personnel will be briefed accordingly. Live ammunition is being issued.'

'Any other business?' asked the Brigadier. 'No? Then we shall meet again tomorrow morning, when we had better think about cancelling or postponing or moving this summit. I don't like any of those options, but if we fail to make progress, we may have no choice. Thank you, everybody. Bruno, stay behind, please.'

Bruno recognised that the Brigadier was on parade. There was none of the affable informality of their munching on foie gras, or their sharing of fine Scotch whisky at the conclusion of previous cases. And in official mode, even in civilian clothes, the Brigadier could be as demanding as he was imposing. He sat impassively, hands relaxed on the table before him, waiting until all the others had left the room. Even the General of Gendarmes, who nominally was the senior officer in the room, went quietly with the rest of the security committee. They were, Bruno thought, like so many chastened schoolboys, departing in silence and with sidelong glances of sympathy at Bruno as the remaining victim for the master's wrath.

'It's your patch,' the Brigadier said when they were alone. 'So you'll have a better sense of where these bastards might be holed up than anyone else on this team.'

'There are over fifteen thousand holiday homes in this Department,' said Bruno. 'We'd need at least a thousand teams of armed men to have a hope of checking them all in time. The key to this will be access. Either they have their bombs planted somewhere already, or they have to get here at the right time. I've drawn up a patrol and checkpoint plan for the surrounding area, as you asked. It means sealing off the château in three belts, one five kilometres out, one at a single kilometre and a final cordon on the perimeter.'

'Isabelle sent me your plan, and we're implementing it. But we need to find them and take them, not just block them. And we also want to interrogate the swine, if only to find out who pulled the trigger that killed Nerin.'

'They have to be hiding out somewhere. I suppose we could get each of the Mairies to telephone all the registered *gîte* owners and ask them to check on their own properties. We'll miss those owned by foreigners, and it could be dangerous for them, but I don't see how else we can get much of a search going.'

'We can't have some holiday home owner getting gunned down when he's gone calling at our behest,' the Brigadier said. 'The politicians wouldn't stand for it. They may even have taken over a farm and be holding the farmer at gunpoint.'

'Or in a cave,' said Bruno. 'We've enough of those.'

'I need a Plan B, an alternative place for the summit. I

presume you've thought about it. You mentioned it when we met here earlier.'

'I have a place in mind, just the other side of St Denis. It's a small château, now used as a hotel, and it's also the headquarters of a vineyard. The security is much better, only one road and a couple of tracks. The place backs onto a river, so sealing it off would be a lot easier.'

'Decent rooms for the summit itself?'

Bruno described the Domaine, which he knew well, with its imposing salon for the formal meeting and a ballroom for the press conference. There were side rooms and various bedrooms upstairs, two of them rather grand. With hardly anybody working in the vineyard at this time of year and the vines just starting to show green, there'd be little cover for any approach. The owner, Bruno added, was an old friend who made good wine.

'Right, you can take me there now, but don't speak of this to anyone else, not even Isabelle or Carlos. I'll let them know what I have to when I have dinner with them tonight. You aren't invited, I'm afraid, for operational reasons. I need to talk to those two and you have enough on your plate drawing up a new perimeter and patrol plan for this new place. I want it ready for the morning meeting.'

'Yes, sir,' said Bruno, sighing inwardly. He'd hoped to invite Isabelle to dinner, to try and make up for their depressing talk of the afternoon.

The Brigadier reached into his briefcase and pulled out a printed form and security pass, making Bruno sign each of them. He gave Bruno an enamel lapel badge in blue and

yellow, saying it gave access to all areas and all the security forces would be briefed to recognise it. The pass identified Bruno as a member of the Minister's personal staff.
It was only valid until the day after the summit.

'It gives you authority to tell generals what to do,' the
Brigadier said. 'Don't misuse it,' he added, seeing Bruno's
instinctive grin.

A worried-looking Isabelle was standing by the steps as
they walked out, and asked the Brigadier if everything was
in order, although Bruno thought from her glance of concern
that her question was about him. He winked at her as he
pinned the blue and yellow security badge to his lapel.
Isabelle was wearing one just like it.

'I have a brief courtesy meeting, pure protocol,' said the
Brigadier as he strode past her. 'And I'll see you later.'

'Carlos has kindly invited me to dinner at the Vieux Logis,'
she said, carefully avoiding looking at Bruno, who managed
to keep a deadpan face.

'Cancel it,' said the Brigadier. 'Or call them and make
the reservation for three. I'll meet you and Carlos at the
hotel bar here at eight sharp. Come, Bruno, no time to
waste.'

The Domaine was the centre of St Denis's new wine
industry, but Julien still ran the hotel. The main salon,
decorated by Julien's late wife Mirabelle with some well-
chosen antiques, was given the Brigadier's approving nod
as they walked through on the way to the office. He'd already
walked briskly around the outside of the small château,
mainly seventeenth-century with some unfortunate

nineteenth-century embellishments. Bruno explained their mission to Julien and enquired if there were any guests that might need relocating.

'No bookings until the weekend,' said Julien.

The Brigadier explained to Julien what he wanted, handed over his card, a cashier's cheque for five thousand euros on account, and swore him to secrecy.

'I'll need all the names and ID numbers of all members of staff emailed to me before eight tomorrow morning,' he said. 'Now, I'd like to see your two best bedroom suites and hear about anything of historical interest. The Minister likes that sort of thing.'

'This was Malraux's headquarters in 1944 when he ran the Resistance campaign here . . .' Julien began, still looking dazedly at the cheque in his hands.

'Excellent, just the kind of thing ministers like. Any royal mistresses?'

'No, but Napoleon slept here on his way back from the Spanish campaign.'

'Splendid, give my minister Napoleon's room, but just don't say anything about the Spanish campaign. Not tactful when the summit's with the Spaniards. And now, Bruno said something about your making a decent wine here in the vineyard. Perhaps I could try a glass as you show me the wine cellar, and then we'll take a look at Napoleon's chamber.'

CHAPTER TWENTY-FIVE

It was dark when he finally arrived at Pamela's place, Gigi in the passenger seat beside him and his suitcase in the back of the van. He let himself in with his key while Gigi began looking around the familiar yard, stopping at every corner to mark his territory and explore whatever interesting new scents had developed since his last visit. Bruno quickly changed out of his uniform and donned jeans, a sweater and jacket for his long-delayed evening ride with Hector. As he headed for the stables, Fabiola emerged from her *gîte* across the yard and called to him as she stood silhouetted in the lighted doorway. Fleetingly Bruno saw another figure pass through the room behind her and into the kitchen, but Fabiola closed the door and advanced into the courtyard.

'Hector's already had his evening ride. I assumed you were tied up and took him with me on a bridle,' she said, holding up her face to be kissed.

'That was kind, thanks. I feel bad about not getting here earlier.'

'I know. I assume it's this security alert for the summit that people are talking about.'

'I didn't know it had been announced yet,' he said, surprised.

'It hasn't, but we were told at the clinic to make sure we were fully staffed and had an ambulance on alert for the day after tomorrow. And we expect a military surgeon to join us from tomorrow, an expert on gunshot wounds. So naturally the news spread and the town is filling up with journalists.'

'You can't keep secrets in St Denis,' Bruno said, smiling ruefully. 'I'll take Hector for a walk anyway, just up the lane and back, help him get used to me.'

'I'm inviting you to dinner after that, so shall we say in half an hour?'

Bruno raised his eyebrows. 'Thank you, but you always say you don't cook.'

'I have two dishes, one my mother made me learn and another Pamela taught me. You're having both tonight. And I have some wine, so don't offend me by bringing any. I've eaten enough of your meals and never returned the favour.'

'I'll be delighted,' said Bruno. 'Just the two of us?'

'No, a couple of friends. One of them is Florence from the college, she's just putting her kids to bed in my spare room.'

'Good, I haven't spent an evening with her for far too long. And the other?'

'A new friend, a surprise. And I heard from Pamela. Her mother's had another stroke, more serious this time. She said she tried to call your mobile but you must have been out of range. She left a message on your office phone.'

'I tried calling her but we keep missing each other,' he said. 'I'll try again now.'

'Any news of Horst?' Fabiola asked. Bruno shook his head and turned away, wondering in what grim and makeshift cell his friend might be tonight.

Bruno's thoughts were a jumble as he greeted Hector, fondling his horse's nose and ears before he saddled him and led him into the yard to mount. Gigi appeared from somewhere behind the stable, now quite comfortable with the horse and ready to trot alongside. It was a fine evening, cold but clear, a good night to look at the stars, but there was too much on his mind.

He was concerned about Teddy, whom he liked. Bruno believed he learned a lot about someone from watching them play rugby, and Teddy had been impressive, after the match as well as on the field. He was far more worried about Horst, who was in the hands of people who would hardly shrink from killing him if it served their purpose. He supposed he ought to be concerned about his own fate, with Annette and Duroc launching their vendetta against him, but the Mayor was on his side. Most of all, he was worried about Pamela. He called her mobile, but heard some automated response in English too fast for him to understand.

And as always, when he was in this sombre and fretful kind of mood, Bruno's thoughts turned to the mess he had made of his relationships with women. The affair with Pamela was faltering. In some ways, it had never really begun. Pamela had insisted from the start that her one failed marriage had been more than enough. She wanted neither children nor permanence, which meant that since her commitment was limited, so was his. He doubted whether they would ever be anything more than good friends who happened to sleep together. And while he admired her spirit and enjoyed her company, Bruno admitted to himself that it was a relationship that made him more perplexed than happy.

If only he could be as clear-headed about Isabelle. Equally independent, equally determined to deal with men on her own terms, she had a grip on him that was as powerful now as it had been in that passionate summer when they had met. To see her, even to receive an email from her, triggered a leap in his heart. They had each said time after time that it was over, that it could never work, but where else in his life would he encounter that jolt of electricity that she sent pulsing through his veins? It had been there that afternoon in the ornate château bedroom she used as an office. The wound in her leg didn't stop her being a woman, she'd said; why didn't Bruno treat her like one? Because she wasn't just a woman, she was Isabelle, the woman who kept invading his dreams.

Hector tossed his head as if impatient with this quiet amble up the lane, or perhaps he was disturbed by Bruno's own distracted musings. Horses, Pamela had taught him, were highly sensitive to a rider's mood. Bruno leaned down to pat his neck, murmured Hector's name, and turned him back down the lane towards the paddock. Hector wanted to trot, and so did he, Bruno admitted, hoping to chase away the glooms with a little exercise. They made a few gentle circuits of the paddock together, not enough to warm him, with Gigi loping happily alongside. Bruno didn't want to be late for Fabiola's dinner, so he walked Hector a little and then took him back into the stable.

He'd noted earlier that the stable had been cleaned and the straw changed. He'd have to get Fabiola some flowers. Taking Hector along on the evening ride was kindness enough, but mucking out the stable was beyond the call of friendship. Bruno rubbed Hector down, checked his water and gave him a wizened apple by way of farewell. He washed his hands and face in the stable sink, savouring the old-fashioned smell of the big square block of Marseille soap that Pamela kept there. He pulled out his phone and tried her number again. This time she answered.

'I'm standing in your stables, about to have dinner with Fabiola, and all the horses are fine,' he said. 'How about you? Fabiola says there's been a second stroke.'

'That's right, a big one. She's in a coma, but her entire left side is completely paralysed. I'm just outside the hospital, waiting for my aunt to bring the car round. We'll know more tomorrow, when she's scheduled for a brain scan.'

'I'm sorry. Would you like me to come?'

'No, really. Things are hectic already and now we have to go to the airport and pick up my ex-husband. I'm not sure I could cope with him and you at the same time. And I know you're busy – anyway, here's my aunt with the car. I'll call tomorrow when there's news. Love to Fabiola and the horses, and to you.'

She rang off, leaving Bruno staring at the horses and wondering how long he was going to be staying in Pamela's home. Gigi seemed content with his new surroundings but Bruno missed his own place. Leaving Gigi settling himself in a corner of Hector's stall, he walked across to Fabiola's house and knocked.

Florence opened the door with a smile of welcome, but her eyes seemed wary before she leaned forward to kiss cheeks. Bruno understood her caution when he walked into the room and found Annette setting the table. He was speechless, and he felt his face turning red and his eyes narrowing.

'*Bonjour*, Bruno,' she said hesitantly and tried a half-smile, but then shrugged, as if this evening wasn't her fault. Bruno stood where he was, uncertain how to react, looking around for Fabiola and some explanation when she bustled in from the kitchen, an apron around her waist and the light of battle in her eye.

'You can do better than that, Bruno,' she said firmly. 'This is my house and I have invited friends that I like. I really don't care what arguments you have outside these walls, but in here you'll be courteous with each other.'

'Today she tried to get me fired . . .' Bruno began, but Fabiola cut him off.

'I know all about it, and I think you're both behaving like a pair of idiots and I don't want to hear any more about it this evening. That's an order. And you owe Annette a favour, anyway. She helped me ride the horses this evening, then she cleaned the stables so that I could get on with the cooking.'

'And she helped me bathe the children. She's made the salad and the first course and she brought a nice bottle of wine,' said Florence. 'She and I may have got off on the wrong foot when she drove into town, but we've put that behind us. She's even driven me round the motocross course she uses to practise her rallying. So now it's up to you.' Florence moved to stand beside Annette as if to demonstrate a common front. Florence and Fabiola had planned this, he thought.

'Fabiola's right, Bruno,' Florence went on. 'I don't know all the details of what has passed between you, but I like you both too much to let it go on. And Fabiola feels the same way. So imagine that the two of you are meeting for the first time.'

Bruno took a deep breath, and looked from Florence to Fabiola, two women he respected just as much as he liked them, grimaced and then slowly nodded. They were probably right; this feud with Annette had got quite out of hand.

'*Bonsoir*, Annette, and thank you for cleaning the stables,' he said, stepping forward and holding out his hand. She was clutching a napkin in one hand and a tablespoon in the other and she looked down at them as if unsure what to do with them. Then she set her small chin, put them down on the table beside her, and came forward to take his hand and to offer her cheek to be kissed. Bruno complied, catching a rather pleasant scent from her fair hair.

When he stepped back, Annette handed him a glass of white wine. 'It's from the Domaine,' she said. 'I thought we ought to support our local wine-maker.'

'A good choice, since you're also supporting me,' he grinned. 'I'm a shareholder, and so is Fabiola and lots of other people around here. Has she told you the story of how we saved the vineyard from an American company and how it's now a kind of communal vineyard for St Denis?'

Annette said she hadn't, but would like to hear it. Bruno could almost hear the ice breaking as he told the story, and saw the tension ease in Fabiola's face.

'You haven't mentioned the crime, and my part in it,' said Fabiola. 'It was my forensic work that cracked the case. And I saved Bruno's life into the bargain, when you were going to suffocate in that wine vat.'

With that, Fabiola had to begin the whole story again from the beginning, with the arson and the genetically modified crops and the Canadian girl who worked in the wine store. Then Florence began her own tale of the fraud in the truffle market at Ste Alvère where she had worked and how she had helped Bruno solve the case by getting hold of a vital logbook. By this time they had drunk the first bottle and Annette had opened a second, and they were seated convivially around the table and tucking in to Annette's vegetable terrine.

'I thought somebody told me you didn't drink,' said Bruno, after praising her terrine and taking a second helping.

'You must have been talking to people on the magistrates' course with me,' said Annette. 'I stopped drinking for a while because I was too nervous about failing. I'd been out of university and away from studying for too long and I found it really hard to get back into the discipline of it. So

I stopped drinking just for a while. But when Fabiola and Florence invited me to dinner, I thought how I'd really missed drinking wine with friends. Of course, I didn't know until this evening that you were coming ...' She put her hand to her mouth in embarrassment. 'Sorry, I didn't mean that the way it sounded.'

'So what happened between university and starting the magistrates' training course?' he asked.

'*Médecins sans Frontières*, first in Paris, just doing office work, and then I got interested by the logistics of it and went out to Madagascar to help run the office there and the depot with the food and medical supplies. I was there for three years, which is why I'd forgotten most of the law I'd learned. That's where I took up rally driving. But I found myself getting really concerned about France and politics and migrants and the *Front National* and, you know – the whole mess.'

'We know,' said Fabiola. 'But how did you find out what was going on from Madagascar?'

'I used to be on the internet on this terrible phone connection for hours at a time at night, trying to keep up with the French news. And friends back in the Paris office would make sure they put back copies of news magazines into the supplies that came out. Then I came back to Paris and worked as a legal assistant for an organisation that tried to help Muslim women integrate. Mainly it meant learning to navigate the bureaucracy, which confirmed me in my plan to become a magistrate.'

Bruno nodded, impressed. *Médecins sans Frontières* was an

operation he respected. And he approved of people who wanted to experience something of real life along with their studies. Running a food and medical depot in Africa must have been a challenge for a young woman who still looked barely out of her teens. He could understand her nervousness at her first posting, even understand her suspicion of a local policeman like him who must have seemed prickly and set in his ways. And he'd been a soldier in France's post-colonial wars in an Africa that she knew from a different perspective.

But how could a young woman so obviously intelligent be taken in by the blundering Capitaine Duroc? And why had she been so vindictive against that sweet couple Maurice and Sophie? Worse still, Annette had no idea what would happen tomorrow when she was hit by the counter-attack from St Denis in the media, and she discovered that the story was no longer about foie gras but about her. The Mayor was a veteran politician who knew how this game was played.

Fabiola brought in her mother's dish, a risotto made with fish stock, and *coquilles St Jacques*, brushed with olive oil and grilled, on a separate platter. The rice was perfect, the short-grain Italian variety that was made for risotto. The scallops still had their roe attached. Fabiola hovered over the dishes before serving, looking both shy and proud as she presented her first dinner party in St Denis.

'I used the crayfish shells left over from your birthday dinner, Bruno, to make the stock for the risotto. Pamela showed me how to do it.'

'It's wonderful, Fabiola,' he said, and it was. 'Truly, it's perfection with these scallops. Annette, what do you say?'

'I seldom eat fish but I'll make an exception for this, Fabiola, any time you want to cook it.'

The apple tart from Pamela's recipe was pronounced an equal success, and as Fabiola took the plates away and started to make the coffee, Bruno asked Annette if she had managed to do any more rally driving. Not enough, came the answer, with what she tactfully called the drama under way in St Denis. But Fabiola had shown her the motocross course in the woods nearby that the farmer rented out for weekend races. He was happy for Annette to try it out and she was planning to use it again early the next morning.

'Want to come for a ride?' she asked him.

'Try it, Bruno, it's fun,' said Fabiola, bringing the smell of fresh coffee with her from the kitchen. 'Annette took me on a few circuits. I never thought you could go so fast on forest tracks.'

'I'd love to, but I have to ride Hector in the morning,' he said.

'I'll be riding Victoria tomorrow while Fabiola rides Bess, so we can hit the circuit after that,' said Annette. 'It won't be long, just enough to give you the flavour.'

'In that case, sure, and thank you. But I have to get an early start tomorrow, so I can come if we take the horses out at dawn,' he said. 'I'll skip the coffee, if you don't mind. I have to walk Gigi and then unpack.' He looked across at Fabiola. 'I trust Pamela told you she asked me to stay here while she's away to look after the horses?'

'Yes, and we're going to have a full house. Florence is staying in the spare room overnight rather than wake the children, and Annette's bedding down on the couch.'

'Rather than use a couch there's a spare room in Pamela's house. I'm sure she wouldn't mind,' Bruno said, but as soon as he spoke he wished he hadn't. He and Annette might have declared a truce, but inviting her to sleep in the same house was pushing it a little far.

'I don't think my reputation in St Denis could fall much lower than it has,' Annette said, a twinkle in her eye. 'But it might damage yours. Still, so long as you think you're safe with me I'm prepared to risk it. There's not enough room in the kitchen for all of us, so Florence and I can do the washing up and you and Fabiola take Gigi for his walk. By the time you're back, I'll probably be asleep.'

The other two women agreed so fast, Fabiola already putting on her coat, that Bruno suspected this had been contrived between them. Evidently Fabiola had something to say, and by the time they reached the lane, she was just as ready to say it as Gigi was for his exploration of the paddock. It was a cloudless night with a rising moon, the stars bright and clear and the air still fresh with the new scents of spring.

'Annette is thinking of handing in her resignation and I want you to persuade her not to,' said Fabiola, direct as ever.

'She's pretty much burned her boats with St Denis,' he replied. 'She'll always be known as the woman who accused us of barbaric practices, not just here but all across the

Périgord. It's the kind of label that sticks, and she'll have to live with the consequences.'

'Consequences?'

'She publicly attacked one of the main industries of this part of the world, which means she attacked people's jobs and their livelihoods and they're going to fight back. The Mayor and the council are running a media and political campaign against her and they won't care about her good works in Africa.'

'If she withdrew herself from this whole foie gras case, would that not help? She knows she made a big mistake.'

'Perhaps if she'd done it yesterday, but it may be too late. I've been tied up on this security business so I'm not fully informed, but I think there'll be some nasty stories in tomorrow's newspapers. As far as the Mayor's concerned, St Denis is fighting for its life.'

'Annette said she'd had a call from *Libération* in Paris who were doing some kind of story. She sounded rather shaken by the questions.'

Bruno nodded. The Mayor had sent him an SMS message, telling him to be sure to buy a copy of the paper.

'You can fix this, Bruno, the Mayor listens to you. And once she recuses herself from the case, you've won. What more do you want?'

'He listens, but he makes up his own mind, and he has to get re-elected. So he'll be thinking about the voters, which means the farmers and the people who work in the foie gras trade and the shops and the restaurants, and the

accountants and business people who depend on them –
it's most of the electorate.'

'So what do you think we should do?'

'In her shoes, I'd apply for a transfer to another district,
somewhere urban where she can make a fresh start. I'm sorry,
Fabiola, but short of her agreeing to eat foie gras on TV and
saying she likes it I'm not sure there's an alternative.'

CHAPTER TWENTY-SIX

Strapped in tight, with his feet hard against the floor and his arms braced on the dashboard, Bruno was certain they were going to hit the tree. But Annette twitched the steering wheel and seemed to be braking and accelerating at the same time as the small Peugeot went into a brief skid and then rocketed forward to the next turn. Over the howl of the engine he could hear the stones from beneath the trees being clattered against the untouched tree trunk. He was glad of the helmet that Annette had made him wear, for his head slammed into the roof every time she flew over a bump. His neck muscles tired from resisting the constant G-forces. He was impressed by the obvious strength in Annette's forearms as she kept the car under control at what seemed like insane speeds.

'God, that makes me feel so much better,' Annette said as the car rocked back and forth after a handbrake turn that left Bruno dizzy. 'Would you like to try another circuit or shall we head back?'

'I think I have to get to work,' he said. 'But thank you, it's been a revelation. Where did you learn to drive so fast?' He was delaying the moment he'd have to get out of the car, not sure whether he was too disoriented to stand straight.

'In Madagascar. Most of the roads are like this, and there's a lively culture in rallying.'

'Do you kill many people, pedestrians I mean?'

'None yet,' she said, laughing. Her face was flushed, animated. She still looked as if she were in her teens, but there was a self-confidence in her eyes from the display of her driving skills.

'You love this, don't you?' he asked.

'Absolutely,' she said, grinning. 'For once in my life, it's me that's in charge, with everything depending on me and my own abilities and on the training I've done. And of course it depends on the car, but I'm responsible for that, too.' She turned out of the motocross circuit and onto the lane that led back to the road and then to Pamela's house, where Bruno had left his van. 'Do you mind if we stop in town to pick up a copy of *Libé*? They called me yesterday for an interview on this foie gras business. They were pretty hostile, which surprised me. I thought they'd have been sympathetic.'

'I'd like a copy, so pick up two and I'll buy some croissants and we can have breakfast with Fabiola,' he said.

Annette was tight-lipped and her face white when Bruno came back to the car with his bag of Fauquet's croissants and baguettes. He was feeling rocked himself after looking at a message on his phone that had landed after he'd gone to sleep. From Isabelle, it said she had dropped by his house after her dinner with the Brigadier and Carlos, but was surprised to find it empty and no Gigi. She hoped he had a good night. What had she meant by that, he was asking himself when Annette, silent, passed him a copy of the newspaper and drove away fast before he could even fasten his seat belt.

Fat Jeanne's surprised face whished past as Annette's tyres squealed on the roundabout. Now the whole town would learn within the hour that Bruno had been seen in a car with St Denis's public enemy number one and was buying her breakfast before presumably racing back to the love nest where they had spent a night of passion.

'*Merde*,' he said, but not about Fat Jeanne. He was looking at the front page. It was all about Annette.

It showed a picture of her taken the previous day as she spoke to the TV reporter, looking cool and professional with not a hair out of place, and a screaming headline that read 'Poor Little Rich Girl'.

Beneath the photo was a copy of a caterer's bill for 32,000 euros for a lunch party of forty people. It was made out to a Monsieur Meraillon with an address in Neuilly, the plush inner suburb of Paris. One of the items on the bill, at a charge of 2,800 euros, was for a course of *foie gras aux truffes*. And the newspaper had circled it in red ink. Just below it was an even higher bill for the caviar.

'Billionaire's daughter and magistrate Annette Meraillon has declared war on "barbaric foie gras", but hedge-fund king Papa spends more than the average French annual income on a single lunch, with 2,800 for foie gras alone,' read the caption at the bottom of the page.

Page two was dominated by a big photo of Maurice and Sophie at the door of their farmhouse. 'It takes three months for the foie gras farmer she is hounding to earn as much as Papa spends on the stuff for a single course to treat his fat-cat friends.'

'And rich papa wants YOU to pay for his foie gras fun,' was page three's massive headline. It was all about Papa and his hedge fund, and the tax dispute that had put his luncheon party bill into the public domain as one item in the evidence. Apparently he had charged it against tax as a business expense.

'I don't think I'll join you for breakfast,' said Annette, as he turned to page four's headline, 'War Against Foie Gras', and its long article about PETA's campaign, with a photo of Gravelle's demolished showroom.

'I'm sorry. This is . . . it's unbelievable,' he said. 'It's nothing to do with you, it's guilt by association.'

'I hardly ever talk to my father,' she said. 'I only go home at Christmas and birthdays because of Mother, and he's usually away in New York or London or somewhere.'

Page five had photos of Papa's other houses, one in the Caribbean, his penthouse in London, his chalet in Gstaad and his château in Compiègne, just north of Paris. Each of the photos carried a price tag. The sums added up to over twenty million euros.

Page six had a large photo, which must have been taken by Philippe Delaron just after the hose was turned off, of Annette standing on the steps of the Gendarmerie, doused in manure. Below it was Papa's lunch bill in full. More than half the total was for wine. Bruno could not take his eyes away. He had paid over ten thousand euros for a case of champagne, Krug Clos de Mesnil 1985, followed by a 2006 Puligny-Montrachet Chevalier-Montrachet at over three hundred euros a bottle, and twelve thousand euros for a case of the 1992 Cheval Blanc. Bruno had always assumed that some people must live like this, but he'd never seen it spelled out in black and white. And he wanted a tax deduction for it. He felt the kind of anger at the ways of rich financiers that was probably being felt all across France as people read their paper in disbelief.

'Papa will not be pleased,' said Bruno.

'On the contrary, he'll probably be delighted,' she said as they turned into Pamela's courtyard. She braked hard, and sat with her hands clasped on the wheel, staring straight ahead, much as she had done on the day Bruno had first seen her.

'It's good publicity,' she went on. 'A hedge-fund magnate has to show how successful he is. And he'll be just as pleased at my humiliation. He never wanted me to go to Africa, nor to be a magistrate, nor to have any kind of job except working for him. I suppose he wanted a son to inherit the business and he got me instead. He even hates my being a rally driver.'

She closed her eyes and let her head sink forward to rest on the steering wheel, as if the contact with her car gave her comfort.

'And now I suppose I can never have a life of my own after this. People will never forget it.'

'They will,' he said, patting her shoulder. 'It doesn't seem so now, but people have short memories. And it doesn't matter what they think. It matters what you do, what you achieve, what *you* think. It also matters how you bounce back from this.'

He persuaded her into the house, where Fabiola had coffee ready. She hadn't seen the paper but knew all about it from the daily press review on France-Inter's morning news show. But instead of the sympathy that Bruno had expected, Fabiola stood with a wide grin on her face and a glass of champagne in each hand.

'Well, that'll teach you to call the neighbours barbaric,' she said. 'Come on, cheer up and join in a toast to the most notorious woman in France for the next fifteen minutes – and you didn't even have to sleep with a politician to get the title.'

Annette froze, then shook her head, clenched her fists above her head and laughed. She took a glass from Fabiola and downed it fast.

'Thank the Lord for you, Fabiola,' she said. 'You're right. There's nothing to be done about it now, so we might as well drink champagne.'

'I pinched it from Pamela's cellar,' Fabiola said. 'I thought it probably counted as an emergency.'

'I think she'd approve,' said Bruno. 'If not, I'll buy the replacement bottle.'

Bruno downed champagne and coffee and wolfed his croissant before heading to his van to get to the château for the morning security meeting. After her late-night message, he planned to corner Isabelle to explain before the committee gathered. But as he slowed for the turn at Campagne, his phone rang and he answered automatically without looking at the screen. As soon as he heard the note of vengeful triumph in the Mayor's voice, he responded with a single word.

'Overkill,' he said. 'I'm worried it's the kind of demolition that can do more harm than good. Hell, even I'm feeling sorry for her now.'

'Is that why you were having breakfast with her?' the Mayor asked, his voice grumpy at Bruno's reaction.

'No, I had breakfast with Fabiola,' Bruno said patiently, silently cursing Fat Jeanne, a woman he usually adored for her endlessly cheerful nature. 'I'm staying at Pamela's to look after the horses. Pamela's mother had a stroke so she flew back to Scotland. Annette happened to be staying with her new friend Fabiola. She wanted to buy the papers, I wanted to buy the croissants.'

'You think the *Libé* story was over the top? Everyone else thinks it's wonderful, particularly after France-Inter took it up this morning.'

'We wanted to isolate her, not destroy the girl. Anyway, I think she might have been ready to withdraw from the case even before this. If you get asked about this, you might consider taking the high ground, not visiting the sins of the father on the daughter. We've made our point. Leave the door open for a reconciliation. She'd certainly appreciate it just now.'

The Mayor was silent, but Bruno could hear him chewing

on the stem of his pipe. 'Interesting,' he said finally. 'I'll have to think about that. Meanwhile, am I meant to give a formal welcome to these two ministers tomorrow?'

'I think they're too worried about security for that, and with good reason. I can't say any more.'

'Tell me what you can, when you can,' said the Mayor, and rang off.

CHAPTER TWENTY-SEVEN

Bruno made the 9 a.m. meeting by the skin of his teeth, having to park far from the château because of the military and Gendarme vehicles filling its car park. There was no time to speak to Isabelle. And she was already distracted by the firearms report. Ballistics analysis had confirmed that the 9mm automatic pistol that Bruno had found beneath the blacksmith's coke pile was the gun that had killed Teddy's father over twenty years earlier.

The British police had reported that Teddy's mother had heard nothing from him since they had spoken the day after Horst's lecture. She knew nothing of the discovery of the skeleton of Teddy's father and had seemed truly stunned by the news. She was trying to help a British police artist create an identikit sketch of the only contact she had with Todor's family, a cousin called Fernando who visited occasionally with gifts for Teddy. What she had been able to provide was the information that the authorities in Madrid had not yet been able to deliver, the date and place of birth for her Basque lover.

'We'd better check that thoroughly,' said Carlos. 'It's always possible that he didn't give her the right date. I'm sorry but it seems we're having trouble back in Madrid tracking anything about this guy.'

'False dates of birth are standard procedure for these people,' said the Brigadier, diplomatically trying to spare Carlos embarrassment. His Minister must have insisted the Spaniards be treated with every consideration, Bruno thought.

The Brigadier ran through the arrangement for the security cordons and mobile patrols, giving brief credit to Bruno although the committee had now been joined by a Major Sauvagnac, a tough-looking young paratroop. He'd have been a junior lieutenant when Bruno had served with them, but there was no look of recognition. With a final pep-talk on the need for the Basques to be found before the scheduled summit on the morrow, the Brigadier closed the meeting having said nothing of the back-up plan he had arranged at the Domaine.

'Could the reason why Madrid can't trace this man be linked to the *desaparecidos* from Franco's time?' Isabelle asked Carlos as they headed out the door. Bruno had heard of the 'disappeared ones' in Argentina when people were rounded up and arrested, never to be seen again, but he'd never come across it in the context of Spain.

'I was wondering that myself,' said Carlos, nodding solemnly. He turned aside and asked one of the security guards to bring his car round from the hotel. Then he seemed to notice Bruno's raised eyebrows and stopped to explain. It had happened earlier in the Franco period, after the civil war and the world war, when the Spanish dictator was still terrified of the Left. Women militants who were pregnant would have their babies in prison and they'd be taken away, to Church orphanages or to be adopted. This had been standard treatment for communist militants, but also for the Basques.

'If it did happen that way, the boy would never have been given the name Todor in an orphanage,' Carlos added. 'The Basque children were always given Spanish names to break the link with the real parents. They were usually dead anyway.'

Isabelle nodded and turned to Bruno. 'I saw what the newspapers did to that magistrate of yours this morning. Ugly. Remind me never to take on St Denis.'

'I'm not proud of it.'

'Were you involved? It didn't seem like your kind of strategy, even if she did try to get you fired.'

'It wasn't, but there's no point making excuses. I suppose we're all responsible.'

Carlos shrugged and walked on to the communications centre. Bruno and Isabelle were left alone.

'Sorry I missed you last night,' he said. 'I was staying at Pamela's, looking after the horses. She had to go back to Scotland to look after her mother.'

'Is it serious?'

He nodded. 'A stroke, and now she's in a coma.'

'I shouldn't have come,' she said. 'I was depressed and lonely. It was Gigi I wanted to see as much as you.' She gave a half-smile, but her eyes were fond. 'Brigadier permitting, shall we have dinner tonight?'

'Of course,' he said. His heart gave a lurch. 'Home or restaurant?'

'Home, with Gigi,' she said. 'But it'll have to be quick. This chaos here will get worse all day and later tonight, and probably stay that way until the deal is signed and the ministers have gone.'

If she thought this was chaos, wait until the Brigadier announced the move to the back-up plan tomorrow morning. A voice was calling for her from down the hall. It sounded like the Brigadier. She headed down the corridor, trying not to limp and aware of his eyes following her, suddenly putting out her cane as if about to stumble. Bruno forced himself to turn away, thinking she'd hate him to see her like this.

Suddenly there came a crump and a bang and the sound of breaking glass and car horns. Isabelle tottered and half-fell against the wall as confused shouting came from the stairway. Bruno ran to her but she pushed him away, telling him to find out what was happening. He leaped down the stairs to the front entrance to find the door blocked by a knot of Gendarmes and black-garbed security men. They were looking across the château's park and its railings to the hotel car park across the road where a plume of black smoke rose from a fireball in which Bruno could see the skeleton of Carlos's Range Rover.

'Don't just stand there, get the fire extinguishers,' Bruno shouted, grabbing the only one he could see. 'Somebody call an ambulance and the *pompiers*.'

He forced his way through the throng of confused men and down the steps to start running up the long drive to the main gates of the château. He heard steps pounding behind him and saw Carlos, the only other man who seemed to have found an extinguisher, and they ran on together. The sentry box at the open gates was unmanned, its two guards tumbling from the hotel each carrying a small hand-sized fire extinguisher in one hand and holding a soaked dishcloth against his face with the other. As he approached the searing heat from the burning vehicle, Bruno under-stood their precaution even as he wondered how they were hoping to use the extinguishers with only one hand.

'Was anyone inside?' Bruno shouted.

One of the guards pointed. Behind one of the neigh-bouring cars, its windscreen cracked and bowed by the explo-sion, the innkeeper had covered a heap on the ground with an overcoat and was reaching to turn on the tap of a garden hose. The water sputtered and then spurted out and he pointed it at the overcoat and then lifted the coat to play it on the smouldering form beneath. The form moved, turned over and tried to get to its feet as Carlos turned his extinguisher on the car but it was beyond saving. The klaxon chorus of several car horns all played on.

Suddenly a dozen people seemed to be around them, foam erupting over the wreck of Carlos's vehicle. Now that the man with the innkeeper was standing, Bruno could see that he was the security guard who'd been asked to bring Carlos's car to the château. He was reeling and suddenly bent over to retch but evidently alive. People around him were shouting questions. Was he OK? Did he want to lie down? To stand up? To have a drink? Could he focus on this moving finger?

Bruno looked at Carlos. The Spaniard was standing, arms on his hips and his back hunched, looking grimly at the glowing shell of his car, the emptied fire extinguisher between his feet.

'That was meant for you,' Bruno said.

'I know. Lucky we had one of those remote starters,' the Spaniard replied.

A form materialised beside Bruno, with a scent of something feminine above the acrid smoke.

'They know who you are and where you are,' Isabelle said to Carlos. 'You must be almost as rich a target as the two ministers.'

'Maybe just an easier one,' Carlos said, as an ambulance siren whined in the distance.

'Nobody leaves,' Isabelle said.

She was leaning on her cane, panting. Bruno tried to imagine the willpower that had brought her here so fast from the château. Behind her came the Brigadier.

'All the security teams, the hotel staff, any guests, anybody who could have set that bomb – I want them all double-checked,' he said. 'Where's that damn security chief when I need him?

'Bruno, please call J-J and tell him I need a forensics team and an explosives expert. I want a media blackout on this. Any enquiries and a car simply caught fire with an electrical fault. I want no reference to Carlos nor to the summit. And I want this wreck and any damaged vehicle removed from the car park. I want it all looking normal within the hour.'

CHAPTER TWENTY-EIGHT

A form of panicked calm had descended over the château. The security guard had indeed been spared the full blast of the explosion thanks to the remote with which he had started Carlos's car. The ambulance had taken him, although the *pompiers* had said he was in no danger. One of Isabelle's aides was dealing with the car hire and the insurance and arranging for the delivery of a replacement Range Rover for Carlos.

England was an hour behind French time, Bruno knew, and he assumed Scotland would be the same. It would be a little early to call Pamela. And she'd said she would call him once there was news from the brain scan. Bruno had an appointment with the para Major, Sauvagnac, and the *Mobiles* from the Gendarmes in not quite two hours to walk the grounds and review the patrol system, so he had time to think about Isabelle's supper. It would have to be something he could make quickly, and he'd cleared out most of his fresh food when he moved to Pamela's. And in case some new emergency meant the meal had to be cancelled, it had better be something he could easily save and warm up again.

The house would be cold; he'd have to make a fire. They

had eaten foie and pork the other evening, so he'd go for steak or veal. He had some *soupe de poisson* in the freezer. He'd need bread for the croutons and some spring vegetables, and a visit to Bournichou's *boucherie* for the meat, and at some point he'd have to pick up Gigi, who was evidently the star of the show.

He had time to get to the market, which on this day of the week was held in Le Buisson, where he knew he'd find his regular hunting partner Stéphane selling his cheeses. Stéphane pointed Bruno to Madame Vernier, whose stall across the street carried spring onions, new carrots and *navets*, the small turnips Bruno loved, and even some early green beans. Instantly he decided on a *navarin d'agneau*, a lamb stew with fresh spring vegetables. It would take time, but it was a dish he enjoyed and he'd never made it for Isabelle. He bought his cheese and vegetables and a big *boule* of bread, raced back to St Denis to buy the lamb and quickly went home.

Once in his kitchen, he splashed duck fat into a heavy iron pot and cut the boned lamb shoulder into five-centimetre chunks. While Radio Périgord was playing a talk show filled with callers hailing the charms of foie gras, he browned the lamb on all sides and spooned off the excess fat. Then with the lamb on medium heat, he added his secret ingredient, a large spoonful of honey, and stirred to coat the meat. He sprinkled on some flour to soak up the juices and stirred again. He added a glass of Bergerac Sec white wine, a can of peeled tomatoes, some crushed garlic and a bouquet garni, and then grated in a little nutmeg.

He added salt and pepper and just enough water to cover the meat and brought it to a steady simmer.

He should leave it for an hour, but did not have the time before he had to see the troops who would be manning the cordons. He set the table for two, adding some candlesticks and a vase into which he would put daffodils from his garden when he returned. He took the *soupe de poisson* from the freezer to thaw and then cut some slices from the bread so that they would harden by the evening, making them just right for the croutons. He washed the vegetables and left them ready by the counter.

With another twenty minutes before he had to leave, he went outside to feed his ducks and chickens and check on the fencing and his own *potager*. Up here on the ridge, and with no greenhouse to bring on his early plantings, his own *navets* and carrots were still two or three weeks from being ready, his potatoes and beans even longer. His *mâche* was in fine shape to make a salad and he had some early radishes. He raised his eyes to the view across the slope to the low ridge ahead, and on to the ridges that rolled all the way to the horizon. He never tired of it and it never failed to lift his spirit. As he looked at the land spread out before him he knew there was one thing he had to do today that would make him feel better about himself, more worthy of this place and this view.

He used his phone to call directory inquiries, dialled the number he was given in Paris for *Médecins sans Frontières*, gave his name and rank and asked for the head of the press office. He was put through to a woman who gave her name as

Mathilde Condorcel and asked what she could do for him.

'It's about Annette Meraillon, who used to work for you, in Paris and in Madagascar. You probably saw the story in *Libé* today.'

'I saw it and I didn't like it. We worked together here and she did a great job for us in Madagascar. If she's going to get axed as a magistrate over this we'd all be very glad to have her back.'

'I was hoping you'd say that. Why not put out a press release that says just that and make sure that *Libé* runs it? It's the least they could do after the character assassination they did on her today.'

'That's a very good idea, but why are you calling? Do you know her?'

'I'm the chief of police in St Denis, where she made that silly remark about our foie gras being barbaric.'

'Speaking for myself, I love the stuff, but aren't all you people from St Denis up in arms against Annette?'

'We are, and we think she made a mistake. But that shouldn't take away the fact that she's a fine person who did good work for you. Right now I think she needs some friendship and support.'

'Wait a minute, the chief of police of St Denis. I saw something about you in *Paris-Match*, a photo of you in that fire trying to rescue some children. Why don't you put out a press release? Or we could do a joint one.'

'I wouldn't know how to start.'

'Leave it with me. Give me your email and I'll send you a draft. Have you got a number for Annette?'

Bruno gave her the details. He went back into the house, thought of Isabelle's visit and put clean towels in the bathroom. Telling himself he should stop thinking like a lovesick youth, he looked at the bedroom, which he'd tidied as well as changing the sheets before he left to stay at Pamela's house. Then he drove back to the château to brief the security troops on his soon-to-be-aborted patrol plan. He knew the Brigadier would be angry, but Bruno had been too long in the military to see any sense in fooling his own side, so at the end of his briefing he took Major Sauvagnac aside and warned him in confidence that there was a strong possibility of the summit site being shifted to the Domaine. He pointed it out on the Major's map.

After a bumpy hour in a jeep through the woods with Sauvagnac and two captains from the CRS and *Gendarmes Mobiles*, Bruno came back to the château with his phone buzzing from calls and messages that hadn't reached him. Once away from the vicinity of the château, reception faded fast, and he made a mental note to get the security troops to double-check that their own communications functioned effectively. The first missed call was from Pamela, and he called her back and asked after her mother.

'This second stroke was very bad,' she said tiredly. 'After the brain scan they think there may be brain damage.'

'I'm very sorry.'

'Even if she gets better, I'm going to be stuck here for some time sorting out her affairs.'

'Don't worry about anything here. We'll take care of it all.'

'God, I miss you. And Fabiola, and St Denis,' she said. 'How are the horses?'

He reassured her that all was well with her house and stables and described Fabiola's dinner, remembering to emphasise the success of Pamela's apple pie. Her replies were understandably short and distracted. She had weightier matters on her mind and soon rang off.

The next missed message came from a French mobile phone whose number was not in his own phone's memory. Curious, he called back, and heard a familiar accented voice say, 'Bruno?'

'Teddy? You know half the police in France are looking for you? And where's Kajte?' He went up the stairs to Isabelle's room in the château and put a finger to his lips as she turned from her desk. He walked across as he listened to Teddy and scribbled down the cellphone number the young Welshman was using, then jotted 'Trace this – it's Teddy' on a pad beside Isabelle. She nodded, scribbled 'Keep him on the line,' and left the room.

'She's with me,' Teddy was saying. 'In fact it was her who persuaded me to call you. She borrowed a car from a friend in Paris and came to pick me up. Look, we want to give ourselves up. How can we do that?'

There was no arrest warrant out for either one of them. Skipping from the coach to Bergerac was no crime; the students' agreement to undergo explosives testing had been voluntary. Teddy was wanted solely for questioning about how he came by the map and knowing where to find his father's body, something he could only have learned from someone with knowledge of where the killing had taken place.

'You can give yourself up to me, if you can get to somewhere near me through the various patrols that are looking for you,' Bruno said. 'But you'll still be facing some tough questions. I'll try to see you're treated fairly. Do you want to tell me where you are?'

'We're quite near to you,' Teddy said. 'What sort of tough questions?'

'I think you have a good idea,' Bruno said. 'It's about that unidentified body you found. We've identified it and we know it's your father. That's why you'll be in real trouble if you don't give yourself up and cooperate.'

There was a silence of several beats before Teddy spoke. 'What about Kajte?'

'There's no more against her now than there was when she took the train. I think all the foie gras charges are going to be dropped.'

'We saw that story in Libé,' he said. 'It seems like it's all got way out of control.'

'Particularly your involvement in this Basque business,' said Bruno. 'Tell me where you are and I'll come and get you.'

'When you say this Basque business . . . I just wanted to find my father.'

'Teddy, you know there's more to it than that. And don't think you can get out of this by going home. The British police are now involved. They've interviewed your mother. She's worried sick about you.'

'Will I have to spend the night in jail?'

'You'll have to spend it somewhere. And as long as you give me your parole, you may as well spend it at the camp-site. Your tent's still there and I've got your rucksack.'

'We're driving around now, but in about ten minutes we'll be at that same place where you met us before, remember?'

'I remember,' said Bruno and heard the click of Teddy's disconnect. He went down to the communications room to find Isabelle. She looked up from one of the two phones she was holding.

'They just lost the connection,' she said. 'He's somewhere near here, in a car.'

'I know,' said Bruno. 'I'm going to pick him up now. But I'd like it understood that he's in my custody, please. I think he trusts me. Do you want to come with me?'

'I'll call you back,' she said into both phones at once, put one on the table, the other into her belt pouch and stood up. 'I was thinking that so far there's nothing we can charge him with unless we can use your criminal damage case.'

'I don't think we should charge him at all. We'll do better to treat Teddy as a cooperative witness.'

'Tell that to the Brigadier. Oh yes, and here's the iden-tikit photo of this Fernando who went to see Teddy's mother. It just came in over the fax from London. It's not too helpful.'

Bruno studied the picture as Isabelle got her coat and bag. It showed a man in early middle age with receding black hair, grey at the temples, and prominent ears. His face was very pale and his eyes dark and he had the begin-nings of a double chin. The most prominent feature was the way his eyebrows, which were thick and bushy, met in the middle over the bridge of his nose. It wasn't familiar from the file of mugshots that Bruno had already seen; he'd have remembered a face like that.

Teddy and Kajte were sitting on the same steps of the rugby stadium where he had found them last time. They stood up as he approached, looking warily at Isabelle limping beside him on her stick.

'I haven't brought a SWAT team,' he said, shaking hands with each of them. He introduced Isabelle and told them she was a friend.

'How's the leg?' he asked Kajte.

'It's fine, thank you. You did a good job,' she replied. 'I don't even need the bandage any more.'

'Have you seen a doctor about it?'

'No, nothing since I saw you. I just used that cream you gave me and covered the holes with sticking plaster.'

'Let's take a look.' He led the way into the changing rooms. Kajte slipped off her cargo pants and lay face-down on the massage table. Isabelle's eyes wre riveted on the girl's slim and perfect thighs, Bruno saw, as if she were thinking of the wreckage the bullet had done to her own. He shook his head and told himself to focus. When he peeled the plasters from Kajte's wounds they all looked clean and were scabbing over. Young flesh heals fast. He gave Kajte more plasters from the cupboard.

He turned to Teddy and handed him the identikit picture. 'Do you recognise this man?'

'Yes, that's Fernando, a cousin of my father's. He came

to see us at home every once in a while. And he came to see me at university last year.'

'Was that when he gave you the map identifying your father's grave?' Isabelle asked.

Teddy gulped in surprise, looked down at Kajte, who was clutching his arm, and nodded. 'Yes, he said he'd got it from a sympathiser in the Spanish police who knew my father had been assassinated by the GAL in the dirty war. He said that I was entitled to know my father's fate and to see he got a decent burial, a place where my mother could mourn.'

'Do you know how to get in touch with him? A phone number or an address, perhaps.'

'Only an email address on Yahoo!. He was very cautious about being contacted.'

'So you knew he was ETA?' Isabelle asked.

'I suspected it. It was pretty obvious. He said my father had been an ETA sympathiser, which was why he was killed. He said they'd probably kill him if they could. I didn't know what to think. It's quite something to learn that your father was assassinated for being a member of a terrorist group.'

'And what do you think about that, about terrorism?'

'I don't think terrorism is ever justified in a democracy. Spain these days is a democracy and the Basques have a great deal of autonomy.'

'Have you ever been to the Basque country, looked up your roots?'

'I've never even been to Spain yet,' he said. 'The only Basque roots I know about are the ones I dug up here.'

'How often did you see Fernando, growing up?'

'Every two or three years. He'd come to Wales, and always bought a present for me, a book or something about Basque culture. He always sent something at Christmas, usually posted from France.'

'When did he first talk about finding your father's grave?'

Teddy explained that he emailed Fernando from time to time to keep in touch. He'd sent an email last October, after his summer on the exploratory dig at the St Denis site when it had first become clear they had a potential Neanderthal grave. Soon after that Fernando had appeared at Teddy's room in college.

'He asked a lot of questions about the site and said he really wanted me to go back and work on it again,' Teddy said, smiling as he added that wild horses wouldn't have kept him away.

'Fernando came back to see me in January. This time he had the map and said he thought it was probably my father's grave,' Teddy went on. 'I didn't believe him at first – the coincidence was just too extraordinary.'

But Fernando had been positive, Teddy explained. One of the problems the GAL had in the 1980s was the anger of the French authorities at the way Basque bodies kept turning up on their territory. So GAL had started kidnapping their victims and then burying them to avoid more trouble with the French. One of the killers apparently knew something about archaeology and had known that this St Denis site had already been looked at by the famous French archae-ologist Denis Peyrony and pronounced uninteresting. So he

reckoned it was a safe place for a burial. But now that there
was digging there again, the Spanish police were worried
that the grave was likely to be found and trigger a whole
new controversy over the GAL scandal.

'So Fernando had a source inside the Spanish police?'
Isabelle observed. 'Did he say anything about this source to
you?'

'Only that he had access to the secret archives and had
given Fernando the map.'

'Presumably a new scandal over GAL and these illegal
killings was just what Fernando wanted,' Bruno said.

'I hadn't thought of that,' Teddy replied. 'But it makes
sense.'

'Have you had any contact with Fernando since you've
been in France?' Isabelle asked.

'No, and no reply to the emails I sent after finding the
body. Mum hadn't heard from him either, last I spoke.'

Isabelle took a pen and pad from her bag and made Teddy
write it all down in English as a statement and then sign
it. She checked the wording, and promised to give him a
photocopy.

'Am I under arrest?'

'Have you ever met any other Basques apart from
Fernando?' she asked. Teddy shook his head. 'Have you been
in touch with anybody from outside the dig while you've
been in France this time?' He shook his head again, saying,
'Just Bruno and the foie gras people and now you.'

Isabelle turned to Bruno and raised an eyebrow. She was
going to leave this up to him, which would probably mean

that each of them would spend a very awkward few minutes with the Brigadier.

'I have your word that you won't leave St Denis without my permission and that you'll be available for more questions if we need you?' Bruno asked. Teddy nodded.

Bruno suggested they went to the campsite to drop their things. He'd talk to Monique and also let the magistrate know where they were. He proposed that they return to the dig so he'd know where to find them.

'One more thing. May I have your passports?'

Teddy unbuttoned his shirt pocket and handed his over. After a moment's hesitation Kajte did the same.

CHAPTER TWENTY-NINE

Back in his office at the Mairie after briefing the Mayor, Bruno made calls to Monique and Clothilde about the return of the two students, and had to explain to Clothilde that there was still no news about Horst. He couldn't tell her about the cell they'd found at Jan's smithy; to say that Horst had been alive two days earlier was not much comfort. He put off calling Annette until he heard from Mathilde at *Médecins sans Frontières.*

He opened his emails. Most were dross, but there was one from Mathilde that contained two attachments. The first was a press release from her organisation alone with MSF on its letterhead, praising Annette's record and stating that she'd been the victim of a mugging in print. Bruno grinned, relishing a good phrase. The second one began by saying that MSF was joined in condemning that unfair attack on Annette by 'Chef de Police Bruno Courrèges of St Denis, the town at the centre of the storm over foie gras'. Mathilde had quoted him fairly, made it clear that he disagreed with Annette over foie gras and that she'd been foolish to call it barbaric, but she was sincere in her beliefs. Whatever her father did or whatever he spent on his fancy lunches, it wasn't French justice to condemn someone by association. He emailed Mathilde back saying he approved, although privately he doubted whether much of it would make its way into print.

He cleared the rest of his emails, and took an apple and a banana for his lunch from the big fruit bowl that was kept in the Mairie's kitchen. It had become a feature after Fabiola had come to one of the staff meetings to give them all a lecture on healthy eating. He called J-J to tell him that Teddy and Kajte had returned and gave him a summary of their statement. The forensic team at the smithy had reported back. Fingerprints were being checked against the Spanish files. The Bayonne hotel which had provided the small shampoo bottle he'd found had been contacted, but the guests had paid in cash. Bruno suggested that the hotel staff be shown a copy of Fernando's identikit.

He sat back, hearing the familiar squeak from his chair, and wondered where Jan and the Basques might be now. In their place, he'd look for a remote house that looked modernised but had all the shutters closed, the kind of place owned by Dutch or British holidaymakers who only came in the summer. Here they had the benefit of Jan's local knowledge. He made wrought-iron fittings for wealthy foreigners restoring their properties and he must know of dozens of places that were likely to be empty. With Easter so close and the school holidays starting, that might be risky. But there were hundreds of empty tobacco barns dotted around the fields, many of them far from roads or other buildings.

They would need supplies, he thought. They'd also need at least one car and more likely two or three for the surveillance that would have been required to keep a watch on Carlos, to locate his car and place a bomb beneath it. But cars were easily stolen and number plates changed. What else was essential? As soon as he formulated the thought he was looking at his own computer and answering his question.

They would need communications. Phones were too easily monitored, but they did use email. It was simple enough to concoct a fake address through Yahoo! or Hotmail. They might be somewhere too remote to have online access, but they could be using internet cafés. He called Isabelle at the château, passed on his thinking and asked her to email him the identikit sketch of Fernando and also the one he had done of Galder, the youth at Jan's smithy. Perhaps Gendarmes with the same sketches could be asked to check all the internet cafés and facilities in the region, he suggested. He'd take care of St Denis.

She told him that a police cyber-team in Paris had already got into Fernando's Hotmail account and were locating the various sites he'd used most recently. They'd found one in Sarlat and another in Bergerac used in the last week. The sketches were on their way. Almost at once his computer trilled to signal an incoming message. He printed out the two sketches and was reaching for his cap when his phone rang.

'It's Annette. I'm calling to thank you. I just heard from Mathilde at *Médecins sans Frontières* and she sent me a copy of this press release the two of you concocted. How on earth do you know her?'

'I don't. I just rang the main number and asked for the press office.'

'She spoke as if she'd known you for years. She sent me a scan of the *Paris-Match* article with that photo of you swinging out of the window in a ball of fire.'

'It looked more dramatic than it was. Being in a car with you took a lot more courage,' he said. 'But I'm glad you rang. Teddy and Kajte have come back and surrendered themselves to my custody.'

After telling her they'd be available for questioning, he explained that the corpse Teddy had discovered was his own father, shot by undercover Spanish cops in their war on the ETA movement.

'He dug up his own father's corpse? He must have known where to find it, which means . . . God, I'm not sure what it means. Is he connected to ETA?'

'Only through his father. He's helping us. But since you had opened that dossier on the affair, I thought I'd better tell you that he and the girl are back in the district. Is it still open, on them and on Maurice?'

'Along with my disciplinary proceedings against you, the Maurice matter was dropped on orders from my superior this morning, which means the dossier on those students is also closed. That was Duroc's business, anyway. And have you heard that he's been suspended?'

'Suspended? What on earth for?'

'It happened this morning. I heard about it at the morning

staff meeting because we'll have to assign someone to the case. There was an internal investigation by the Gendarmes and they say he was fixing traffic tickets.'

'I know something about this. I think it was your speeding ticket he fixed.'

'Yes, but I'm in the clear. I paid it, just like I paid your parking fine. I sent off the cheques that very night. But it seems that there were quite a few tickets Duroc took care of and some of the beneficiaries claim they paid him to do it.'

'I don't suppose they'll assign you to the case.'

'No. You're getting another new magistrate. I'm being transferred to the Sarlat office, along with a formal reprimand for my TV interview.'

'I can point you to one or two foie gras factories there that I'd like to see hit with a hygiene order,' he said.

'I think I'll stay away from that issue for a while. But look, thanks for what you did and please tell those two students and Maurice that the case is closed.'

'Thank you,' he said. 'But when you called me in to say you were launching disciplinary action against me, you said I'd helped those two students evade arrest. Wherever did that come from?'

'It was a letter of denunciation handed in to the Gendarmerie. It said you had treated the girl's shotgun wounds in secret and then told them to bribe the farmers to stop them filing formal complaints.'

'Was it signed?'

'I don't remember. That was Duroc's big complaint against you, cheating him out of an arrest. Was it true?'

'Yes, I suppose it was,' he said. 'But I still think it was for the best.'

'Maybe you were right,' she said, and rang off leaving him with the feeling that some little justice had been done. He considered. Who knew enough about what he had done to have written the letter? He couldn't see Teddy and Kajte doing so. He'd have to find the letter. But that meant going through the Gendarmerie, and the thought of Duroc's suspension sobered him. It didn't say much for Bruno's skills that Duroc had been fixing speeding tickets under his nose and Bruno had never caught a whiff of it. He rang Sergeant Jules.

'What's this I hear about Duroc being suspended?'

'First we knew was when a new Captain came in this morning and told us. He's just temporary, from Nontron up in the north of the Department. Apparently they'd had their eye on him for some time. Some guy trying to talk his way out of a jail sentence for repeated drunken driving shopped Duroc a few weeks ago. We're in deep mourning. Come by the bar over the road this evening and you can share our grief. I'm buying.'

'I'm tied up this evening,' said Bruno. 'But drink a glass for me. This security stuff will be finished in a couple of days. One thing you can help me with. There was some kind of letter delivered to the Gendarmerie accusing me of secretly helping those two students evade Duroc. Do you know anything about it?'

'Françoise found it in the postbox, a sealed envelope addressed to Duroc. Give me a minute. Now his office is empty I can take a quick look.'

Bruno waited, wondering whether Kajte had said some-thing to the Villattes or Maurice about his treating her wounds. If not, that left him with Carlos or Dominique as the most likely sources of the letter. Dominique didn't like Kajte, but Bruno couldn't see her wanting to denounce him. That left Carlos. But what possible motive could he have? And could he write a letter in French good enough to fool a French-speaker?

'Got it,' said Jules, coming back to the phone. 'It was in a file in his drawer marked Bruno, and it's unsigned. I'll make you a copy.'

'Is it in good French?'

'It's no worse than half the anonymous letters we get. A couple of misspellings, some odd turns of phrase but nothing out of the ordinary. I can't tell about the accents because it's all typed in capital letters.'

Before he set off on his search of the internet sites, Bruno rang an old contact at the French military archives and asked what their files had on Eurocorps. Carlos had served in it, and been based in Strasbourg, where he'd learned his French. Bruno couldn't see Carlos having any reason to denounce him to the Gendarmes, but the idea of Dominique being responsible was even harder to believe. The old soldier at the archives said the Eurocorps records were remarkably good. He wrote down Carlos's name and the units Bruno could recall and promised to call back. Bruno took the old stone stairs down to the square, heading for the town's tourist office, where Kajte had done the photocopying that had first alerted him to her role in attacking the farms. He showed the sketches to Gabrielle, who looked at them carefully and said she was sure she had seen neither one.

'And what finally happened to that Dutch girl?' she asked.

'It turned out just as you suggested, Gabrielle. She went to the farmers and apologised and paid them compensation and she's now back at work on the dig. The matter is closed, in accordance with your excellent advice. So thank you.'

Patrick at the Maison de la Presse did not recognise the sketches, but the woman behind the counter at the Informatique looked at them carefully, called over a male colleague and they both pronounced themselves convinced that Galder, or someone very like him, had paid ten euros to use their computer for an hour late the previous afternoon, just before they closed at six. In fact, he'd been the last one to use it. Bruno immediately called Isabelle and asked for a fingerprint man to be sent.

'He spoke really bad French,' said the man as they waited. He offered to check the cache to see what sites Galder had used, but Bruno told him that neither the chair nor table nor computer could be touched until the fingerprints had been checked. They remembered little else about him, except that he had paid for the computer time from an impressive roll of fifty-euro notes. He had arrived and left on foot with no sign of a vehicle. They did not recognise Fernando.

Bruno went to the nearest shops, a small supermarket, a gift shop and a property sales and rentals agency, but nobody recognised his sketches. Nor had they served any obvious foreigners the previous day. When he returned to the Informatique, Yves had already arrived with a finger-print man and was shining a bright torch sideways along the keyboard.

'Not a trace,' he said. 'It's been well wiped.' Wearing gloves, he checked the memory cache and declared that wiped, too. He went into cmd and searched for the computer's IP address and scribbled a note of the number. Then he called Isabelle and gave her the number and asked if she wanted him to bring back the hard drive. Bruno couldn't hear her answer but Yves rang off and took a CD from his briefcase and inserted it into the computer, opened a browser and then rang another number. He spoke briefly, and then a small window opened on the monitor screen, asking if the user agreed to surrender control. Yves hit the *Oui* window and then sat back.

'What's happening now?' Bruno asked.

'It's the cyber guys in Paris. They linked in and have taken over the computer. They'll download the lot, saves us having to take the hard drive. And Isabelle says she wants you back at the château.'

Bruno stopped at the Gendarmerie for Sergeant Jules's photocopy and took it with him to show Isabelle. 'This is the letter that made the magistrate try to get me fired,' he said. 'I'm having trouble coming up with any likely suspect other than Carlos. Then there are things that you and the Brigadier tell me not to share with Carlos. Are we sure he's on our side?'

'Now's your chance to find out,' she said, leading the way

down the stairs to the main conference room. 'We were just waiting for you to get here. Carlos asked for a brief meeting before the security committee session, just you, me and the Brigadier, says he wants to make a personal statement.'

Carlos was already waiting, and he rose and inclined his head before sitting, putting on a pair of spectacles Bruno had not seen him wear before, and turning back to a sheaf of papers before him. The Brigadier strode in and Carlos rose again and remained standing.

'I've asked you here to apologise to each of you in person,' he began. 'We Spaniards have been less than frank with you. We haven't shared information with you to anything like the degree that you've done for us. My only explanation is that I was acting under orders and did so reluctantly. Following those orders, I behaved especially badly to Bruno here, who has treated me with kindness and given me his personal hospitality. I repaid this by trying to get him suspended from his work and from this operation, because he was getting too close to creating an embarrassment for my ministry and my government. I'm very sorry.'

Bruno felt the basilisk stare of the Brigadier turning towards him, and nodded briefly to acknowledge the apology. Where was Carlos going with this?

'There are two matters you should be aware of. First, the killing of Todor over twenty years ago and his burial near what is now an archaeology site was an unofficial Spanish operation, one of the extra-legal killings committed by GAL. My superiors took the view that it would be most unhelpful, before tomorrow's summit between our ministers, to have a new GAL scandal exploding into the media and reviving the story of our secret war against ETA. As a result, we dragged our feet on providing information from our files. I promise that we will provide all the information we have, including the names of the killers, once the summit is over.'

'This is a very serious matter,' the Brigadier said. 'You're telling me that you deliberately hindered an operation in a way that could materially increase the prospects of an assassination attempt against a minister of France? You understand that I have no choice but to brief my minister before tomorrow's meeting.'

'I understand, and I trust that the threat to our ministers is not increased, thanks to the impressive security measures you have in train. But let me explain the second matter.' Carlos paused, and took off his glasses.

'This is highly confidential and I tell you this by way of some recompense for our uncooperative behaviour,' he said. 'It is only because of the attempt to kill me today that I have authorisation to share this.'

Carlos claimed to know, from agents inside ETA, that a furious debate was raging in the ETA leadership whether or not to give up the military campaign and declare a cease-fire against Spain. That debate was close to being won by the moderate side, he insisted.

'But the hard-liners have one asset, the active service unit we have failed to penetrate. Again for internal ETA reasons, this terrorist unit needs a success, and we believe that tomorrow's summit is its prime target. This is the team we need to neutralise, in order to swing that ETA debate the right way,' he said, pausing for effect.

Then Carlos drew himself up to his full height and placed his hand upon his heart. He looked the very picture of sincerity, thought Bruno, who could not make up his mind whether to believe all this or not. Glancing at Isabelle beside him, Bruno could see her lips pursed in a way that he knew meant she too was sceptical. Carlos seemed to sense their doubtful mood, and rose to the challenge like an accomplished actor.

'Please understand that the stakes for my government could not be higher,' he said. 'We have a chance to finally put an end to a war that has been under way for nearly fifty years and whose roots go a long way further back. I'm instructed to tell you that this is a matter of the highest national priority, which is why my minister has authorised all my actions. Thank you.'

With a final searching look at the Brigadier, Carlos sat down and closed his eyes, putting two fingers to the bridge of his nose. Bruno and Isabelle exchanged glances before looking to the Brigadier, who was studying Carlos intently.

'I'll explain all this to my minister,' the Brigadier said. 'I acknowledge what you've said without endorsing it. You've flouted every principle of the cooperation tomorrow's summit is supposed to celebrate and I won't forget that. May we count on your full cooperation from now on?'

Carlos nodded wearily and pushed a file across the table. 'This is everything we have on Todor, the man who was killed twenty-four years ago. His father was shot and killed while resisting arrest. His mother died in the Amorebieta prison after giving birth. They were both arrested for their role in one of the first ETA operations, the abortive attempt to blow up a train carrying Franco supporters to a commemoration in San Sebastian in 1961.

'Todor himself was raised, along with many other children of enemies of the state, in the orphanage of Sabinosa, an old TB sanatorium on a peninsula near Tarragona,' he said. They were raised to be good Catholics and good Spaniards, with no knowledge of their family's past, he explained. Basque militants and families knew of the place and tried to track the orphans down after their release. Most of the boys were sent into the military, and some were recruited for ETA while still in the ranks. Todor, along with several others, found out about his past and was an easy recruit for ETA. He took part in their operations in Spain and here in France and that was why he was killed.

Bruno pushed the photocopy of the anonymous letter that he had collected from the Gendarmerie across the table to Carlos.

'Did you write that?'

'Yes,' said Carlos. 'I'm sorry. But after the car bomb, maybe you realise how high the stakes are for us in Spain.'

CHAPTER THIRTY

At the top of the ridge, Bruno slowed his horse and waited for Gigi to catch up. He turned to watch, smiling at the spectacle of his dog's ears flapping and jowls bouncing in that chaotically enthusiastic way peculiar to basset hounds. Bruno had come directly to Pamela's home from the château, and thought he could combine Hector's evening ride with a final check at the Domaine. Later this evening, the Brigadier's security teams were scheduled to arrive there, but Bruno recalled the old army saying that time spent in reconnaissance was seldom wasted.

He gazed down at the wide sweep of the valley, St Denis hugging the broad curve of the river to his right. The ordered precision of the Domaine's vineyards lay below him on the far side of the river. Far off to the left was the old hillside village of Limeuil, with its château watching over the double bridge where the rivers Dordogne and Vézère met. The land was greening with the coming of spring and yellow splashes of forsythia bushes speckled his view. Another month and the stumps in the vineyards would be green and the trees bushy and vibrant with new leaves.

A panting almost beneath his horse signalled the arrival

of Gigi, who began nuzzling at Hector's hoofs. The two animals seemed to have reached a good understanding, and Gigi had been curled up in a corner of Hector's stall when Bruno had arrived. As they started to move down towards the river and the Domaine, Bruno let Hector find his own way while he looked out for the ford. Normally at this point in spring, the river would be too high to cross, but there had been no rain in the past week. Gigi might have to swim.

When he reached the river bank near Gérard's canoe rental centre, the water was not all that deep, but it was flowing too fast for Gigi. Bruno wondered if Hector would accept a novel passenger. He dismounted, picked up Gigi and placed the dog in front of his saddle, making Gigi lie down so that his belly was against Hector's back. He smoothed his dog's back to tell him not to try to stand. Then Bruno patted Hector's neck and swung up into the saddle. One hand on his reins, the other holding Gigi firmly, he let Hector pick his way over the mud and stones of the ford and scramble through the brush on the far bank.

'You've got a good horse there,' came a voice from the bushes. 'I never thought he'd accept that dog on his back.' Bruno looked around and saw nothing, but then came a blur of camouflage and the paratroop Major stepped out from a thicket. He walked forward and began stroking Hector's muzzle, and then looked with amusement at Gigi trying to wag his tail in greeting as he slumped over the horse's back.

'We've been walking the river bank, checking on shallows

and access points,' said Sauvagnac, as a second blur came into view. Bruno recognised the CRS Sergeant who'd found Jan's arms cache with him. 'I saw you coming down the far slope and thought you might be heading this way.'

Bruno dismounted, lifted Gigi and placed him on the ground. He shook hands with the two uniformed men, observing that the security should be easier here, with the open views through the vines, than it would have been in the wooded hills above the château.

'True, but we can't get the jeeps through the vine rows,' the Major said. 'Watching you, I was thinking that it would make sense to put some of the patrols on horseback. Have you got any spare horses we can use? Two or three would do it but I wouldn't mine borrowing yours.'

'I might be using him myself,' said Bruno. 'But Julien at the Domaine keeps a couple of horses for hotel guests. I'm sure he'd be happy to add them to his bill.'

Leading his horse, Bruno walked with the three men to the small stable yard at the rear of the hotel-château and installed Hector in an empty stall where he snorted and then gazed at the two other horses there. Julien was happy to hire them out for the day, and after saddling the two rather elderly mares Bruno and the two soldiers set out to ride the property. The two horses knew their territory and walked slowly through the vines.

They rode back to the river, where Bruno suggested that one squad might be based at Gérard's canoe site on the other bank. After a full circuit of the Domaine, the Major pronounced himself satisfied and they returned to the stable yard. Julien invited them in for a *p'tit apéro* of Ricard, but Bruno said he had to go.

At Pamela's he unsaddled Hector and rubbed him down, then drove back with Gigi to his own cottage to resume his cooking of the *navarin d'agneau*. He lit a fire in the stone *cheminée* and then decanted a bottle of the Pomerol that he and the Baron bought by the barrel. They bottled it themselves with friends on a bibulous autumn afternoon each year. He fed his ducks and chickens and then Gigi, calling him in from his patrol of the grounds, then quickly showered and changed into khaki slacks and his favourite green corduroy shirt.

At the back of his mind, where he endeavoured with little success to keep it, was the question of how the evening would progress. Was this to be a dinner of old friends and former lovers who had exchanged passion for simple affection? Or would Isabelle be offended if he did not seek to invite her back into the familiar bed? Bruno knew which he'd prefer. Isabelle entranced him in ways that were beyond the usual urgings of lust, ways that balanced the sadness that he would feel when she left for Paris again, as she always did. He chided himself for the touch of self-pity that had crept into his thoughts.

A car horn gave a cheerful double beep from the lane, echoed by the joyful yelps of Gigi. Curious, thought Bruno, that his dog was so devoted to Isabelle, while only mildly affectionate towards Pamela, who made just as much fuss of him and saw him far more often. Was there a message for him in that, Bruno thought fleetingly, as he opened the door to greet her and welcome her back into his home.

'What a lovely fire,' she said after hugging him briefly on the doorstep and then advancing into his living room. She shrugged off her coat to reveal a black polo-neck sweater and a full black skirt that came to below her knees. Elegant boots of black leather and a belt of heavy silver chains completed the outfit. 'I've never been here before when it's cold enough for a fire.'

She reached into her bag and brought out a box wrapped in brown paper and sealed with red wax. This was the characteristic sign of one of the better bottles from the renowned *cave* of Hubert de Montignac, which for many Frenchmen was St Denis's greatest claim to fame.

'It was so nice to see Hubert again. When I told him I was dining with you he suggested I get you this, but said it wasn't for drinking tonight. You should really keep it a couple of years.'

'Then we'll save it for a future visit,' he said, breaking the seal and unwrapping a bottle of Pommard Clos des Ursulines '05. 'This is wonderful, thank you.'

'Hubert said it was high time you widened your horizons beyond your beloved Pomerols,' she said. 'I told him how much trouble I always had in getting you to widen them as far as Paris.'

When he offered her a drink, Isabelle asked for mineral water, saying she'd have to drive back, so two glasses of wine with dinner would be her limit for the evening. Well, that seemed to define the evening ahead, thought Bruno. As he poured himself a glass of wine Isabelle turned the conversation to business.

'What did you make of Carlos's little speech?' she asked.

'It was plausible.' He shrugged. 'We know how politicians are, and I can see his minister trying to keep this summit from being overwhelmed by another GAL scandal. But I was surprised he hadn't told us before about this prospect of an ETA ceasefire.'

'There's quite a lot he hasn't told us,' she said, stroking Gigi's ears as he gazed up at her in adoration. 'Maybe I've been lucky, liaising mainly with the British so far. They do share and they tell us when they can't.'

'You've spent more time with him. What do you make of Carlos?'

'He thinks of himself as a ladies' man, holds doors open and sends flowers, but he's too sure of himself and there are little flashes of the predator beneath the good manners. The more I see him, the less I like him and I think he could be a very accomplished liar. That's why I wasn't altogether convinced by his speech today.'

'You noticed the way he put his hand on his heart?'

She nodded, grinning at the memory. 'Quite the actor, our Spanish colleague.' She paused and bent down to attend to Gigi, who had rolled onto his back with his paws in the air, his eyes beseeching for a tummy rub. 'What's for dinner?'

'We're starting with a *soupe de poisson*, followed by *navarin d'agneau* with fresh spring vegetables and then a *mâche* salad with cheese, and I'd better get started on the *rouille*. Come into the kitchen and chat while I do it.'

He began by setting a pot with salted water on the stove to boil for the vegetables, put a spoon of duck fat into his frying pan and tore some of the bread he'd sliced that morning into generously large croutons. Then he grated the rest into bread crumbs, sliced and squashed some garlic and began blending it into a paste with some olive oil and the defrosted red peppers. The croutons were fried until they were golden and he placed them inside the oven for the interiors to dry fully.

'I like watching you cook,' she said, adding a small splash of Bergerac Sec to her fizzy water. 'You never seem to pause, one movement flows into the other.'

'It's just practice,' he said, adding the *navets* and carrots and spring onions to the boiling water and beginning to grate a block of Parmesan cheese. He set his timer to five minutes. 'What do you eat in Paris?'

'I wake up with orange juice, have a croissant for breakfast in a café, a bowl of soup or salad at lunch or sometimes just some fruit if I'm working through,' she said. 'In the evenings, restaurants or dinner parties two or three nights a week and the rest is omelettes, pizzas and takeaway Chinese or Vietnamese. My refrigerator would break your heart, just milk, eggs and orange juice and frozen pizzas in the freezer.'

'What about those things you learned to cook with me?'

'Once a month, I try to give a dinner party, usually all women, and spend a day attempting to read my handwriting from that notebook where I wrote down your recipes.' He turned to her, pleased at the thought of her cooking his dishes. She shrugged in return. 'You'd be surprised how few women still cook in Paris, at least the ones I know, with jobs like mine. When I go to them, it's usually catered or bought in from a *traiteur*. It's the way we live now.'

'Reminds me of that Prévert poem in the book you sent me, *Déjeuner au matin*.'

'I know it, about the guy who sits and stirs his coffee and says nothing and has his cigarette and says nothing and puts on his hat and goes and the girl is left crying.'

'It hardly sounds like France,' he said.

'Paris never was France,' she said. 'Sunday brunches are fashionable now, champagne and orange juice and eggs Florentine and bagels with smoked salmon. Waffles with maple syrup are suddenly all the rage. When I got back to the office from the convalescent home, they'd bought me a waffle maker as a welcome back present.'

She held out her glass for more Bergerac Sec. It was mainly wine now. He took the *rouille* and grated cheese and croutons to the table and began making the *beurre manié*, whisking butter and flour together to make a paste that he added, little by little, to the *navarin* until he judged the sauce thick enough. The buzzer sounded on the timer and he added the vegetables to the stew and left it to simmer gently while he served the soup into two bowls and followed her to the big table in the living room. He brought the glasses, lit the candles and sat.

'*Bon appétit*,' he said, and her lip trembled.

'If you knew how often I remembered you saying that when I lay in hospital,' she said, and tried to laugh. 'Those history books you sent me brought me back to earth, but I'm glad you read the Prévert.'

He stirred *rouille* into his soup, added some cheese and croutons and raised his glass to her.

'It's good to see you at my table again, and I really appreciated the Prévert, even when a poem made me think of you.'

'Which one?'

'"*L'automne*",' he said, and recited:

'*Un cheval s'écroule au milieu d'une allée*
Les feuilles tombent sur lui
Notre amour frissonne
Et le soleil aussi.'

'Yes, that one,' she said, her voice wistful, looking into her wine glass. 'And the one about the sun disappearing behind the Grand Palais, and my heart following it.'

'*Comme lui mon coeur va disparaître*
Et tout mon sang va s'en aller
S'en aller à ta recherche,' he recited.

'How do you remember them?' she asked softly.

'It was the kind of schooling I had, old-fashioned provincial teachers, lots of things to learn by heart,' he said. 'I can still do Napoleon's speech at the battle of the Pyramids about how forty centuries looked down upon them. Come on, enjoy your soup while it's hot,' he said, changing the mood. He knew it wasn't his schooling that made him remember the poems. It was reading and rereading them aloud on wintry evenings as Gigi slept before the fire and thinking of Isabelle in hospital with her thigh smashed by a bullet.

'They weren't crazy, those teachers. A pity we've lost all that.'

'I must have been one of the last generation to be taught that way.' He removed the empty soup bowls and came back with the casserole. He raised the lid and the scent of thyme and rosemary from the bouquet garni he'd made began to fill the room. He excused himself and went out to his herb garden, turning on the outside light to pick some of the new parsley that was emerging. As he returned, Bruno smiled to see Gigi slip out past him to patrol the grounds, pausing by the chicken coop with his ears up and one paw raised, a good sentry going on duty.

He tore up the green leaves to sprinkle them on each of the plates she had served.

'This looks wonderful and smells better,' she said. 'I can't think when I last had *navets*. It reminds me of my childhood. Is that where the word *navarin* comes from?'

'Some say it comes from the battle of Navarino against the Turks, but I prefer to think it comes from the *navets*. You can use any spring vegetables, but if you don't include *navets*, then it's not a *navarin*,' he said, pouring the red wine from the carafe. 'Tell me more of your life in Paris. I can't really imagine it.'

'There hasn't been much of it. Not long after I started in the Minister's office, I was sent to Luxembourg to get into the bank accounts of that mysterious food company that turned out to have been set up by our own Defence ministry. You remember that?' She began to eat. 'This food is wonderful, and this wine. It's your usual Pomerol, no?'

He nodded. 'It's the '03, from the heatwave year, so it won't last much longer.'

'Mmm ... delicious. After a month or so in the office they deployed me to London to liaise on joint operations against illegal immigration, and then I got shot at Arcachon and was in hospital for nearly two months. I could still be on convalescent leave but I was bored and they let me come back to do office work.'

'Friends?' he asked, and offered her a second helping. She shook her head, but held out her glass for more wine.

'Some from school and childhood who've moved to Paris,' she said. 'Some other women who were at the police academy with me and a few colleagues in the office, that's about it. There's a book club at the Ministry that I'm thinking of joining, and I go to a lot of movies, usually the *version originale* to improve my English.'

'And where do you live? You gave me the address, but what's it like?'

'Just a single-bedroom apartment off the Rue Béranger, near the Boulevard Voltaire in the Troisième. But I have my eye on a small house, one of a row of artists' studios with lots of glass, just off the Rue de la Tombe-Issoire near Métro Alésia. I went to a party there and fell in love with the place, but I can't afford it yet. If you come and visit me, I'll take you there to see it and walk you round the Parc Montsouris.'

'Not named after our own communist councillor, I imagine,' Bruno said. 'He always asks after you, by the way. You made a conquest there.'

'A communist admirer, just what my career needs,' she smiled. 'There's another Prévert poem, not in the book I gave you, about two lovers embracing in a tiny second of eternity, one morning in a winter's light in the Parc Montsouris in Paris.'

'A poem for every occasion,' Bruno said, smiling.

She reached across and touched his hand, then sat up, swiftly changing her mood as if by an act of will. 'And I recognise this cheese, it's the one your friend makes.'

'Stéphane's *tomme d'Audrix*, and some *mâche* from my garden to go with it.'

'I haven't eaten like this since last summer. In hospital, it kept me going, remembering dishes you made.' She paused. 'I have to go back in a couple of months. They want to use plastic surgery to make my thigh look better. I can't stand looking at it.'

Bruno nodded, trying to understand. 'Coffee?' he suggested.

'Yes, and I'll have one of my rare cigarettes, if you don't mind.' He gestured permission and she lit a Royale filter. That reminded him and he rose and went to the dresser, opened the drawer and pulled out an ashtray and a half-empty pack of the same brand and put them on the table beside her.

'I found the cigarettes after you left. There were moments when I was even tempted to smoke one.' He took the plates into the kitchen to make coffee. He had barely started when he heard her come in behind him and say his name softly.

He turned, and she raised one side of her skirt. She unhooked her stocking from the suspender and rolled it down to her knee to reveal the savage crimson scar and the crater in her flesh, the thigh markedly thinner than the other, as if the muscles had withered.

'Other than doctors and nurses, you're the only one who has seen this,' she said, a catch in her voice that was almost a sob and an appeal in her eyes that he could not ignore. Her other hand reached out to him. 'Oh, Bruno . . .'

On instinct, he knelt swiftly and kissed the scar, the marks of the stitches still obvious. His hand gently stroked the side of her thigh and he could feel under his fingers the parallel scar of the exit wound on the back of her leg. He felt her hand touch the back of his head, her fingers curling in his hair. She was whispering his name. He rose, and saw that her eyes were closed and her lips were trembling. Very softly, he kissed them, picked her up in his arms and carried her to his bed, aware only of her heart beating fast against him and the passion of her mouth against his own.

CHAPTER THIRTY-ONE

He had woken alone. She had left just before midnight, leaving him to his tousled bed and memories of her rolling the stocking back up and fastening it again to the garter belt so that all he saw was the whiteness of her flesh, the darkness of her eyes and nipples and the glorious geometry of black and white, pubis and stockings, that stretched so invitingly below her trim waist. Before he slept, he had taken down the Prévert and read again.

And now, with Gigi trailing along behind, he was astride Hector, glowing from the gallop that his horse had unleashed along the ridge, as if Hector understood Bruno's strange, almost magical mood of contentment and energy, the pistol he so seldom wore now thudding a tattoo against his hip. Descending to lift Gigi onto his horse's back once more, Bruno again let Hector pick his way across the ford at the river. He waved a greeting to the Sergeant from the CRS who sat high on the back on one of Julien's mares, his machine pistol braced on his thigh.

'We just got confirmation,' the Sergeant said, as Bruno let Gigi down to earth again. 'The meeting's being shifted here. They're putting up the windsock and painting the big

H for the helicopter now. They found a crude bomb in the conference room, behind some new plasterboard. Sticks of dynamite and a digital timer, they tell me. A good job we got that Semtex before the terrorists did.'

Who and how the hell could that have been done? Bruno tried to remember the security arrangements for the château. Carlos and Isabelle had shared the responsibility, but the patrols were mounted by Gendarmes from Périgueux. They'd all have some explaining to do. The Brigadier would have people tearing apart every wall to see what else might have been planted. So far as Bruno knew, only he and the Brigadier knew of the plan to shift the site until the security teams started redeploying last night, so the Domaine should be secure.

Bruno nodded to the Sergeant and spurred forward to the gardens behind the Domaine, Gigi at his heels. The schedule called for the two ministers to meet at Bordeaux airport and then to take two helicopters on the forty-minute flight to St Denis. He checked his watch. They should be arriving in not much more than an hour. He wondered if Isabelle would be told to stay back at the château to clear up the mess torn by the security breach, or if the Brigadier would want her here. His heart gave a gentle lurch at the thought of seeing her again so soon, and he felt a smile come to his face as he turned into the stable yard. It was empty except for two black-clad and heavily armed *Mobiles* from the Gendarmes. He reined in at their challenge and pointed to the Brigadier's metal badge on his lapel. They asked him to dismount and show his special security pass with his photo. Behind them a sizeable pile of horse manure steamed just by the stable door, a pitchfork stuck into it. Gigi ambled up to investigate and then to cock his leg against it. They'd better get that cleared away before the choppers landed.

'Anybody else inside?' he asked, as the Gendarmes saluted and returned his pass after checking it against a very short list of names.

'The Brigadier and the female inspector and a Spanish advance team,' he was told. 'Caterers are on their way, under armed escort. They've already been inspected.'

Bruno put Hector into the stable on a loose rein, and left Gigi there in the stall. Once he was through with the Brigadier, he wanted to ride the perimeter and check the patrols. That was the work he knew, rather than the internal security, and he wanted all the patrolling troops to see him and learn to recognise him before the choppers landed and they went onto hair-trigger alert.

In the main salon of the hotel all seemed chaos. The Brigadier glared at him and nodded while talking fiercely into one phone. Isabelle had a hand over one ear and a satellite phone in the other. Carlos was shouting in Spanish into a third, two armed and serious-looking aides flanking him. All wore the same enamel badge that the Brigadier had given to Bruno. Isabelle turned and her eyes seemed to flash as she saw him. Her cane leaned against the conference table. Carlos ignored him.

Two CRS men stood in the lobby by the far entrance door, another on the landing of the broad staircase and another by the door that led down to the vast wine cellars. Two more black-clad men wearing the enamel security badge and Spanish flags on their sleeves were carrying submachine guns so futuristic that Bruno had never seen one before.

'You heard about the security breach?' the Brigadier called across to him, snapping shut his phone. Bruno saluted, an automatic reaction in this militarised atmosphere. 'Yes, sir.'

'Checked the perimeter patrols yet?'

'Just the river bank so far, sir. Permission to continue?'

The Brigadier waved approval and with a final glance at Isabelle Bruno headed back to the stables, showed his pass again and mounted Hector. The manure pile was still there. He left at a walk, Gigi loping behind, and urged Hector into a trot as he rode up the main lane beside the winery that led to the largest vineyard and to the figure of a mounted man at the far end of the vines. Further up the lane was a parked jeep with two paratroops inside. He slowed as he approached and held his pass at the ready. They checked him and waved him on between the vines where the other horseman was approaching.

'We should never have given up the horses,' said Major Sauvagnac, grinning at the sight of the basset hound as Bruno rode up beside him to shake hands.

'Better not let the Brigadier hear you say that,' Bruno replied. 'He's on the warpath.'

'Quite right, too, after they found that bomb back at the château. The patrols are all in place, my men briefed, and the *Mobiles* and CRS are on static patrol at the key points you suggested. I changed a couple of your dispositions because they sent us two armoured cars from the Limoges barracks. I've got one at the main gate and another at the side of the gardens, commanding the route up from the river. They radioed in. So I've made sure everybody on the radio net knows that a horseman in police uniform is a friendly.'

Bruno nodded an acknowledgement and accepted the Major's invitation to ride the perimeter together. They had deployed just after dawn, Sauvagnac said, and had found the Brigadier's security teams already in place at the Domaine and the winery. Since then, the only arrivals had been the Brigadier's car and the separate Spanish team.

Sauvagnac put his binoculars to his eyes as a large coach turned into the gate of the Domaine. 'What's this?'

'We're expecting the caterers,' said Bruno. 'It's in your brief, along with numbers, names and photographs. They've all been vetted and I know most of them personally.'

'Let's go down, then.' The Major took the opportunity to spur his mare into a reluctant canter. Riding down a parallel row of vines, Hector easily overtook the other horse and Bruno had dismounted at the coach by the time the Major lumbered up. A *Gendarme Mobile* was in the coach, checking the ID cards and passes one by one. Bruno gave his rein to Sauvagnac and climbed into the coach, nodding at the familiar faces from Julien's regular restaurant staff and the extras from the Campagne hotel. No strangers were aboard and he'd known the coach driver for years and taught his two sons to play tennis. All cleared, Bruno climbed out and the coach drove slowly up the tree-lined avenue to the Domaine.

Bruno and the Major followed on horseback, pausing at small knots of two and three paratroops to check that their radio communications were functioning and their orders clear. The men were alert and cheerful, evidently respecting their officer, and even the *Gendarmes Mobiles* and CRS officers seemed to accept his authority without resentment. Gigi's appearance triggered the usual smiles, the men kneeling down to pat him and stroke his trailing ears.

'I'll probably come out again, once the helicopters land and the meeting's under way,' said Bruno. He checked his watch. The choppers should have taken off from Bordeaux ten minutes ago. 'There's not much for me to do inside.'

This time the salon seemed calm. The Brigadier and Carlos were nowhere to be seen. There were large urns filled with flowers at the walls, pads and pencils and mineral water and glasses on the long conference table. The black-clad security men, French and Spanish, were still in place. Isabelle was standing at the passage to the lobby, talking to Julien, who was dressed as if for a formal wedding in pinstripe trousers and coat-tails. She smiled at the sight of Gigi and beckoned Bruno to join them.

'I'm not sure what more we can do, but it's all been very last-minute,' she said, her eyes shining in a way that said much more to Bruno than the brisk tone of her voice.

'The outside patrols are all in place and in good hands,' he said. 'I just rode the perimeter with their commander. Not much will get past him.'

Isabelle's radio buzzed, but there was just a crackling when she tried to listen. 'Damn radios are all out of calibration since we had to move here. They were fine yesterday. I'd better check with the radio room.'

CHAPTER THIRTY-TWO

'Bruno!' came a cry from inside the Domaine. It was Isabelle's voice. He turned and ran up the steps and into the salon, Gigi lumbering up behind. She was standing by the table, the useless radio in her hand, pointing at a black-clad security man standing by one of the giant urns, a Spanish flag on his arm. Carlos was standing halfway down the steps, a cold expression on his face, another burly security man in black beside him wearing a balaclava and one more just emerging from the wine cellar behind her.

Bruno, baffled, scanned from one face to the other.

'I wanted to check the flower urns and he wouldn't let me, and I looked at his face.' She tossed the radio aside in frustration at his slowness and reached for the gun under her jacket. 'Think eyebrows,' she shouted as she pulled out her automatic and pointed it at the Spanish security man.

And then Bruno realised that he was staring at the identikit face of Fernando, but the eyebrows that met in the middle had been shaved away. As Bruno reached for his own gun, Carlos leaped down the remaining stairs to grapple with him and the man coming from the cellar grabbed

Isabelle's arm from behind her and twisted it until her gun dropped, leaving her staggering on her cane and half-falling.

Carlos had his finger inside Bruno's trigger grip to prevent him from firing. Bruno dropped to his knees and used his momentum to turn Carlos over his shoulder, hearing a cry of pain and the crack of a finger breaking as the Spaniard went sprawling. Bruno's gun had been wrenched out of his hand but Gigi jumped at Carlos, going for his throat but yelping in pain as Carlos punched him aside.

As he groped for the gun Bruno heard the rasp of metal. Isabelle had pulled the sword stick from her cane and thrust the gleaming blade into the groin of the man who had grabbed her arm. She jerked her arm to deepen the damage and fell on her weak leg as she withdrew the blade and tried to turn. Bruno slammed the heel of his riding boot into Carlos's nose and then stood to meet Fernando's rush when with a guttural cry of '*Scheisse*' the third man in black jumped on Fernando from behind, slamming his gun onto Fernando's head with a loud metallic clang.

Fernando dropped, but his black cap was made of Kevlar armour and with the speed of a striking snake he pulled a long combat knife from his boot and sliced it into the belly of his attacker. He followed it with another slash at the face. The victim's balaclava ripped apart and through the line of blood that welled from eye to mouth Bruno recognised the face of Jan the blacksmith. Wounded as he was, Jan wrapped his burly arms around his attacker and clung on, trapping Fernando's arms and roaring German oaths.

'Bruno,' came Isabelle's cry and he turned to see her

limping forward, her swordstick pointed at Carlos, whose face was a mask of blood as he reached for Bruno's gun, his hand almost on it but for Gigi hanging grimly on to his outstretched arm.

Bruno dived at him, but his riding boots slipped on the polished floor and he sprawled, his hand managing to clutch Carlos's leg below the knee. He tightened his grip and rolled to try to break the ankle, scrabbling his feet on the floor for some purchase. Carlos's shoe came off in his hand and the Spaniard was on his feet. He grabbed the back of a chair with one hand and hurled it at the advancing Isabelle as Gigi leaped in again to fasten his jaws around his ankle. Then he picked up another chair and threw it at Bruno's legs as he tried to stand.

Bruno sprawled again, but in a moment of clarity took in the entire tableau in the salon: Jan still squeezing the life out of a squirming Fernando; the man Isabelle had stabbed mewing in foetal position as he clutched his groin, a pool of blood spreading around him: Isabelle herself using the table and swordstick to stagger to her feet; Carlos with bloodied face and the dog savaging his stockinged foot. Carlos staggered as he glanced wildly around, his shoulders sagging as if realising it was over. But he had Bruno's gun in his hand.

Suddenly Carlos made a decision, lowered the gun and fired into Gigi's back. The dog jerked but hung on, still snarling. Carlos fired again, the gun pressed against Gigi's skull. It exploded in a red mist and Bruno felt his heart break through the shock, everything civilised within him swept away in a raw, barbaric rage. Somehow Bruno staggered to his feet. He knew he would kill this man. Carlos kicked the dog aside and half-ran, half-limped to the door leading to the stable yard and his parked Range Rover.

Knowing that the sight would be seared on his brain for as long as he lived, Bruno threw a despairing glance at the sprawled body of his dog and darted past Isabelle to pick up her gun from the floor where it had fallen. He released the safety catch as he turned and fired three fast shots at Carlos as he leaped down the steps. The gun was unfamiliar and he knew he had missed.

He ran after Carlos, pausing at the top of the steps to shoot again, aware of the two *Mobiles* in the yard, standing with their mouths agape and their weapons still slung over the shoulders.

'Stop him, he's the ETA leader,' Bruno shouted and fired again, but the gun jammed. Now Carlos was in the driver's seat, the engine kicking into life. Bruno threw the useless gun at him and then ran down the steps to grab a weapon from one of the *Mobiles*, but the Range Rover was coming straight at him.

The only thing to hand was the pitchfork in the pile of manure. In desperation he forked up a heap and hurled the stinking mass at the vehicle. It skidded from the bonnet and onto the windscreen, blocking Carlos's view. The big car veered as if to roar up the steps of the Domaine. Carlos put his head out of the window to see ahead and wrenched the wheel. He skidded, mounting just one step and toppling a small stone pineapple from the balustrade before accelerating past and out of the stable yard.

'Give me a gun,' Bruno shouted at the *Mobiles*, but they just stared at him as if he were mad, each of them trying to key his radio to find out what their orders were. Shouting curses at them, his pitchfork still in his hand, Bruno ran to the stable and mounted Hector. A cold rage in his heart for the killing of his dog, Bruno kicked his startled horse into life and rode out into the courtyard, knocking one of the *Mobiles* aside. Now he was in the lane behind the Range Rover.

As Hector accelerated into a fast canter Bruno summoned up his mental map of the Domaine and the lane that Carlos was taking. It led to the main vineyard, where a military jeep would block the path. He'd have to turn aside, but if he found the track the tractors used to collect the grapes, he might be able to get back towards the avenue and take the side route to the road.

The Range Rover was nearly two hundred metres ahead, but it was slowing and skidding. Carlos must have seen the jeep ahead. He tried to turn, but as Bruno galloped forward, closing the distance, he saw one wheel of the vehicle leave the ground, jolted by sturdy vine stumps that blocked its way. The Range Rover heaved back as Carlos threw the four-wheel drive into reverse. He came roaring back down the track towards Bruno, who could just see the Spaniard's head through the rear windscreen, trying to keep a straight line as he reversed at speed. Bruno could see the front wipers swinging back and forth, still trying to clear the smeared windscreen of the manure he had thrown.

Brake lights flared. Carlos had seen the entry to the tractor track. Wheels spinning, the Range Rover surged forward again and turned onto the track. Bruno reined in his horse and Hector found a gap between the wine stumps and began to race his way along a row of vines that ran parallel to the track, matching the vehicle's speed as Carlos fought the wheel through the bumps and deep ruts the tractors had left.

Carlos suddenly slowed and Bruno saw the gun aiming at him through a side window. He ducked as Carlos fired, and pulled on the reins to slow Hector. Now he was on the rear quarter of the vehicle, out of the line of fire. Carlos braked and fired again, his vehicle veering to one side and bouncing back from a gnarled row of vine stumps as he almost lost control. Bruno was just one row from him now, and the valiant Hector was still speeding between the vines. In the distance Bruno saw one of the jeeps racing to block the end of the track.

Carlos must have seen it, too. He tried to accelerate to force his way through the vine stumps but bounced back hard, two wheels in the air, the car almost turning onto its side. The engine stalled and the Range Rover was now stuck sideways on the track as Carlos tried to start it again.

Bruno saw Carlos's bloodied face staring grimly at his through the open side window. The gun, Bruno's reliable gun that did not jam, was rising in his hand when Bruno rose high in the stirrups and with all the force in his body and a great roar from deep in his throat unleashed the pitchfork.

It flew like a javelin through the side window and with

a rush of satisfaction and vengeance Bruno watched as one shit-smeared tine went through the spokes of the steering wheel while the other speared deep into Carlos's arm.

Bruno heard a shriek of pain and frustration from inside the car. The pitchfork's wooden haft poked from the window.

Then the engine caught. Carlos must have jammed his foot onto the accelerator and the Range Rover surged suddenly forward, bouncing off the row of vines with its engine screaming in bottom gear. But ahead was a parked military jeep, a machine gun mounted on its rear and pointing down the track towards Carlos. He must have spun the wheel, for the vehicle swerved and careered into the vine stumps. For a moment it seemed Carlos had forced his way through, but then it reared up on two wheels and fell hard onto its side with a crash of glass and metal that overwhelmed and then silenced a human scream.

Steam jetted from the battered radiator. There was no other sound.

Hector had slowed but Bruno leaped off before the horse stopped and advanced at a careful crouch towards the stricken Range Rover, his elation at Carlos's defeat damped by the uncomfortable knowledge that he was now unarmed. He reached the wreck just before the military jeep arrived.

'I need a weapon,' Bruno shouted. The soldiers looked at him blankly. He glanced behind to see Hector raise his head at the familiar sound of racing hoofs. Major Sauvagnac was coming up fast on his exhausted mare.

'Give me a bloody gun,' Bruno shouted again, and this

time one of the paras in the jeep handed him a FAMAS submachine gun, a weapon he knew so well he could have stripped and reassembled it in his sleep. He released and reseated the magazine, cocked it and advanced on the Range Rover, its two free wheels still spinning, and tried in vain to peer in through the smeared windscreen. The rear was jammed against vine stumps and the glass cracked and smeared with earth. He had no idea what he might find inside, if he could ever get in to see.

'Corporal, all of you here on the double,' shouted Sauvagnac. 'Get to the side of this damn truck and push it back onto its wheels.'

He and the Major helping, they rocked it back and forth until with a final heave it toppled in a slow, dignified fall. It bounced hard and then settled, and Bruno looked inside.

Carlos was pinned into his seat by the splintered haft of the pitchfork, his head hanging limply. Its tines were stuck into the instrument panel, one tine pinning his arm and the other through the spokes of the steering wheel. The broken haft had penetrated his chest. One airbag had been punctured and drooped over Carlos's waist, slick with his blood. The passenger airbag and the side one held him upright. He was either unconscious or dead. Bruno poked him hard in the cheek with the muzzle of the gun. There was no reaction. The place stank of petrol. He backed away.

'Get him out, fast as you can,' said Bruno, forcing himself to think above the raw delight in victory that still flooded him. 'Before the fuel tank goes up.'

Another jeep appeared, bringing a soldier wearing a Red Cross armband. The wheels had at last stopped spinning. Then Carlos was on the ground, his head lolling, the medical orderly working on him. Bruno restrained himself from going over to stamp his foot into the face of the man who had killed his dog.

The orderly looked up and shook his head. 'He's had it, sir,' he addressed the Major. 'This stick went through his ribs and into his heart.'

Somewhere behind him, Bruno heard the clatter of an approaching helicopter. He shivered, delayed shock finally hitting him. He closed his eyes and breathed deeply. He'd never take Gigi hunting again, never watch him search the woods for truffles, never feel that familiar warm tongue lick his face when it was time to wake up. He felt a nudge at his shoulder, turned to see Hector gazing at him, and buried his face in Hector's warm neck, feeling guilty that he'd forgotten this morning to put any apples in the pockets of his best uniform.

'Here,' said Sauvagnac, handing Bruno a carrot. He spoke loudly, above the sound of the choppers. 'I think your horse deserves this. But you can stand down now, it's over.'

'No, it isn't,' said Bruno, moving along Hector's side to mount him again as the two helicopters passed overhead. 'There's a missing Professor to be found, a friend of mine. They kidnapped him to make his brother help them.'

'Want a hand?'

'Probably. I'll let you know over the radio net.'

'Where's that dog of yours?'

'That bastard shot him,' said Bruno, jerking his head back to the wrecked Range Rover. 'He's paid for it now.'

He turned Hector's head back up the lane and settled into a steady trot that ate up the distance. He could see the helicopters flaring in for their landing and he felt rather than heard his phone ringing. He answered it, wanting to put a hand to his other ear but needing to hold the reins.

'Bruno, is that you?' he heard Pamela say.

'It's me,' he said. 'But it's also helicopters. Hold on, they've landed and the noise will stop.'

'How's Hector?' he heard her ask, after a pause.

'Magnificent, a hero horse, I'm riding him now,' he said, as the rotor blades slowed and halted. The noise died away and men scurried out while others saluted. He was about to tell her of Gigi's death, but with a great effort that Pamela would never know he forced himself to hold his tongue and to think of Pamela. She had enough to cope with. 'How's your mother?'

'No change – well, there is some change for the worse. She's still in a coma but she's had a brain scan and there's some damage. It looks as though there's not much hope of a recovery.'

'I'm sorry,' he said. 'Do you want me to come?'

'No, I want you to stay and look after the horses and take care of things for me there. Are you busy?'

'A bit,' he said. 'But it's all right. You must be tired, you've probably sat up with her all night.'

'There was no point,' she said. 'But it's not easy, sleeping. And I miss you.' She paused. 'I presume those helicopters involve something you have to attend to. I'll call again, take care.'

As she rang off, his phone buzzed again and he heard the familiar voice of the retired veteran from the military archives, saying he'd faxed a copy of Captain Carlos Gambara's file from his time at Eurocorps.

'It's an interesting file, more for what it doesn't say than for what it does,' he went on. 'No names of parents, which is unusual even for orphans. His education is listed as a Church-run orphanage in Tarragona and he joined the military as a boy soldier at the age of fifteen, just like you.'

'Thank you,' Bruno said, remembering that Tarragona had been the orphanage where Teddy's father had been raised. 'We're just clearing up a terrorist incident here in which Gambara has died. You may or may not read about this, that's not my decision. But would you have any contacts with your opposite number in the Spanish archives?'

'I'm afraid not. But I've a contact in the NATO registry who deals with them all the time.'

After asking for any more information that could be obtained from NATO, Bruno rang off and rode into the stable yard with the ambulance following him, Carlos's body inside. At the top of the steps, the double doors to the salon were closed, and Isabelle sat on the balustrade outside, holding the small stone pineapple that Carlos's Range Rover had knocked from its pedestal. She put it to one side and rose to her feet as he dismounted and climbed up the steps towards her.

She looked weary beyond exhaustion, her hair tousled and her face frighteningly pale. He dragged his eyes away to look through the doors to the salon where Gigi had died. It seemed to be full of security men and medics bending over prone figures, blood smeared on the floor. Men were shouting, radios crackled and from a distance he heard ambulance sirens. He had steeled himself to see the body of his dog but it wasn't there. Then he climbed the final step and she was there.

'If it wasn't for Gigi he could have shot us both,' she said.

He saw the tears in her eyes as he took her in his arms. She seemed to slump against him and from deep inside himself came a spasm of grief that turned into a sob so convulsive it almost choked him. It felt like a release, that at last he could acknowledge the sense of loss. And his own tears spilled down his cheeks at the memory of Gigi, shot in the back but refusing to relax the grip of his jaws on the man who had attacked his master. He took a deep breath, and caught the familiar scent of her.

'Are you all right?' he asked her. 'I never thought that swordstick was so real.'

'Nor did I,' she said into the hollow of his neck, 'until it worked. The bomb was in the flower urn.' She paused. 'I had Gigi's body taken away to be wrapped. You don't want to see him.'

'We can bury him at home, just behind the chicken coop where he used to go into the woods. It's a good place,' he said. The rage he had felt at Gigi's death had become something sadder and more forlorn, a hollowness in his chest.

'I'll get you a new hound,' she said.

'You'd better talk to the Mayor about a puppy from his next litter. That's where Gigi came from.' He paused, still holding her close, remembering Gigi clambering onto their bed and squirming to try to make a place for himself between them. 'Where's Jan the blacksmith?'

'Dying, but he's told us where to find his brother. And he told us about the dynamite theft and the bomb at the foie gras factory. That was apparently Carlos's idea, to distract us. Like the bomb in his car. He set it himself, and sent one of our own people to start his car and get blown up.'

She let him go and sat again on the balustrade, wincing as she straightened her bad leg. She leaned her cane against the spot where Carlos had eaten his foie gras on the day they had met. Bruno asked where they would find Horst.

'In an empty manor house they were using in St Chamassy where Jan had worked, installing a wrought-iron circular staircase. He knew the owners were still in Holland. He told us that the kid, Galder, who's watching him, is armed, so we're bringing in the hostage specialists.'

'The thing about Jan is to figure out who he was working for.' Bruno spoke as if thinking aloud, but he was watching carefully for her reaction. 'I don't just mean this time, when the ETA gang coerced him by kidnapping his brother. I mean who was he working for when he was able to bury the gun that shot Teddy's father all those years ago?'

Isabelle returned his gaze, but her eyes became guarded as though the conversation had shifted from the personal to the professional. She waited for him to continue.

'If Jan was helping ETA, why did he have the gun that

was supposed to have been used by a death squad of under-cover Spanish cops?' Bruno went on. 'And I couldn't see Jan working for the Spaniards. But what if Jan was truly working for ETA and the reason that Teddy's father was shot was that ETA had condemned his as a traitor? But then I thought about that vast amount of information that you had about Todor in your secret database, the one I wasn't allowed to see.'

'I don't think you should play this game much further,' Isabelle said, a faint smile on her lips. But she didn't turn away.

'Indulge me. I'm trying to work out just what it was that Gigi died for,' he said. 'As I kept trying to put the pieces together, I thought how vulnerable Todor would have been, a foreigner living in France with a pregnant girlfriend. And he seemed to get a work permit and a residency permit very easily. Knowing the way that people like the Brigadier like to work, I wondered if we had somehow used that vulnerability to turn Todor so that he became a French informant inside ETA.'

'Idle speculation,' she said, casting a glance to the door.

'But it all fits. If Todor was our man inside ETA it explains why they knew where he was buried and why Jan had the gun that killed him. It also explains why we got so little help from Madrid. They had nothing in their files about Todor being a victim of their dirty war.'

'You forget about the map that came from the Spanish files, the one you found in Teddy's rucksack, the one Fernando gave him that showed Teddy the way to his father's grave.'

'But it was you who told me how it could have come from our own French files. I think Todor worked for us and that's why ETA had him killed by Jan, their German comrade from Baader-Meinhof. Why was Jan allowed to live here quietly for so long? Did we really not know about his past? I think our intelligence services are better than that.'

'I'm not going to fall into that trap,' she said forcing a laugh.

'Not for the first time, Isabelle, I'm feeling like a pawn in one of the Brigadier's complicated games. I think all this was a great charade and its real purpose was to smoke out the ETA mole inside Spanish intelligence. The whole idea of the summit was to force Carlos into the open.'

She looked at him solemnly. 'And you think the Brigadier is the one with the devious mind? No wonder he thinks you should be working for us.'

He shook his head. 'Not me,' he said. 'It took me a long time to work it all out.'

'And even now you aren't sure and you never will be,' she said. 'All that will die with Jan.'

'Whatever he did with Baader-Meinhof all those years ago, Jan saved us both,' said Bruno. 'And with luck he'll help us save his brother too.'

'I have orders to keep you here and not tell you where Horst is,' she said. 'And if you try to go and find him anyway, I'll stab you with my swordstick.'

'I agree,' he said, thinking that the first thing he should do was rub down Hector and find him the finest bucket of oats in St Denis. Then they could go home and bury Gigi together.

'And the Brigadier says thanks. I think he's planning to get you a six-gun and a Stetson.'

'What about my sheriff's star?' he said, trying to match her banter. What he really needed was a glass of water.

'I'll take care of that,' she said, and then looked away. 'Just as soon as I get back to Paris tonight.'

'Tonight?' It came as a thud in his stomach. They had shared just one night together. It didn't seem fair. 'So soon?'

'The Minister wants me and the Brigadier to return on the helicopter with him. Then I have to go to Madrid to debrief the Spaniards. They'll need to work out just how Carlos managed to get away with it for so long. Then it's back to the hospital for the plastic surgery.'

'You shouldn't be back on that kind of duty yet,' he said. 'You aren't fully recovered.'

'I'll have some leave when I get out of hospital. I want to be there to give you the new dog.' She turned to look at him, some life in her eyes at last. 'Maybe you can take some time off from St Denis.'

He smiled at her, thinking how little she knew of life in the country. It was springtime. There was his vegetable garden to be planted, ducks and geese to be fed and horses to care for. But no Gigi. And then the tourist season would start again. There'd be no leave for Bruno until the autumn. He tried to imagine the hunting season without Gigi.

'Can we slip away for lunch?'

She shook her head. 'Right now I have to draft a joint statement with the Spaniards on how Carlos Gambara died bravely
while helping to frustrate an ETA terrorist plot. But I'll get
Gigi's name in there as a hero if it's the last thing I do.'

ACKNOWLEDGEMENTS

Sometimes I get twinges of guilt when I think of the fictional murders and mayhem my tales of Bruno bring to the tranquil valleys of France's Vézère and Dordogne rivers, where life is sweet and crime is rare. It must be stressed that, like all the Bruno novels, this is a work of invention. The town of St Denis does not exist. A few of the characters may have originally been inspired by some of my friends and neighbours in the Périgord, but the people in my books and the plots are all dreamed up in my head.

The archaeological details in *The Crowded Grave* are as correct as I can make them, in view of our still limited knowledge of the transition from the Neanderthal to the Cro-Magnon type of human beings some 30,000 years ago. And while the genetic evidence seems clear that there was some inter-breeding, I have invented my archaeologists and the discovery of such a family. The details in the text of the dirty war waged by some elements of the Spanish state against the Basque ETA terrorists are also historically correct. This book was completed before the latest ETA cease fire brought the promise of a peaceful resolution of this conflict that has been under way for some forty years and more. Long may the cease fire endure.

As always, I am grateful to my friends in the various arms of the French police, to the people of the Périgord and to the various tennis, rugby and hunting clubs that have brought much pleasure and bonhomie and magnificent food and drink to my life. The St Exupéry family and their staff at the great vineyard of Chateau de Tiregand have my special gratitude for the splendid wines they make and for their welcome to me and an appreciative crew of international journalists exploring Bruno country. Special thanks, as always, to Jane and Caroline Wood, who are probably getting tired of my saying they whip these books into shape when their touch is far more delicate; along with my US editor Jonathan Segal they sculpt them into shape. Many friends and meals and restaurants inspire the cooking in the Bruno books, but each recipe must pass the expert eye of my wife Julia Watson, whose captivating blog, www.eatwashington.com, testifies to her skills with food. I am also very grateful to our daughter Kate, who writes on motor sports for girlracer.com. She has taken over, invigorated and transformed the www.brunochiefofpolice.com website, which is becoming an ever more useful resource for the attractions, the food, the wine and the history of the Périgord, and for the life and activities of Bruno and his friends. I recommend it to all Bruno fans.